Ryskamp

Fernsby's War Book 1
Book 1

J.C. Jarvis

WHERRY ROAD PRESS

Get a FREE Book!

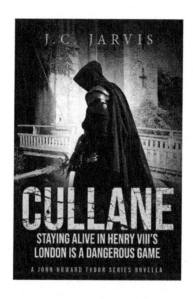

Before John Howard found sanctuary on the streets of Henry VIII's London, Andrew Cullane formed a small band of outlawed survivors called the Underlings. Discover their fight for life for free when you join J.C. Jarvis's newsletter at jcjarvis.com/cullane

To my wife, Glenda, who is my biggest supporter and my bedrock. Without her support and encouragement none of this would ever have happened.

My editor, Melanie Underwood, who patiently and expertly wove her magic through the pages of the manuscript and turned it into the thrilling book you see today. The deft touch and the care she poured into each page has made the book far better than it could have ever been on its own.

My cover designer, Jane Dixon-Smith, who far exceeds my expectations with the masterpieces she creates every time we work together. Jane is a true master of her art, and I am extremely grateful to be able to work with her.

To our beloved daughter, Tiffany Lattimore, whose memory inspires us every day. Though she is no longer with us, her spirit and love continue to guide and uplift us. Tiffany's bright light and boundless joy remain in our hearts, providing the strength to carry on and find hope in every moment. This book is a testament to her enduring presence in our lives, and we dedicate it to her memory with all our love.

WHERRY ROAD PRESS

Ryskamp

Print ISBN: 979-8-9883912-0-3

Fernsby's War Series Book 1

© 2023 by J.C Jarvis

Edited by https://melanieunderwood.co.uk/

Cover Design by http://www.jdsmith-design.com/

Foreword

Welcome to the first novel in a brand new historical adventure series set in the dark days of WW2.

Early on in my research, I made the decision to write my books in modern (British) English. All my novels are UK centric, so it made sense to write the story using the correct spelling from that region.

Ryskamp introduces a young man who has no experience of life outside his comfortable surroundings, and I tried showing that through the first-hand descriptions he gives us as he progresses through the adventure. Because of his limited understanding of the world, some of the things he witnesses are intentionally vague because he couldn't possibly have know otherwise.

For instance, one of the vehicles he comes across frequently is described *as he sees it*, so I have explained what it is here so the reader will know what he is talking about. As you will discover in the pages of the novel, the unusually described vehicle was in reality a VW Kübelwagen, and a basic search of the internet will reveal why

Michael would describe the vehicle in the manner that he does.

The one thing I didn't change was history itself. Any authentic events I describe are as historically accurate as possible, and when using real characters from history, I didn't have them doing anything they would have found impossible to do.

I hope you enjoy the epic adventures of Michael Fernsby and Ryskamp . . .

J.C.Jarvis

Ryskamp

By J.C. Jarvis

Chapter One

Freising, Germany, November 9, 1938
Frank Fernsby glanced at the grandfather clock in the corner of the room, the ticking filling the silence of his plush third-floor office in the once-thriving department store he owned with his grandfather, Herbert Guttmann.

It was 7.50 pm.

Suppressing a yawn, Frank massaged his weary eyes and permitted his lean, muscular build to slouch in the chair. Having been at the store since dawn, the toll of lengthy days at the office weighed heavily on his forty-three-year-old frame. Inhaling deeply, he mustered the resolve to concentrate on the array of reports scattered across his desk.

He raked his fingers through his short brown hair, which was swept back over his head, and muttered to himself in his native English. "I can't even keep up with my grandfather. He's eighty-nine and has more energy than anyone I've ever seen."

Herbert Guttmann was always the first person at the store in the morning and the last to leave in the evening. Eighteen-hour days were nothing to Herbert, and although separated by two generations, Frank struggled to keep up with his grandfather's energy and enthusiasm for his beloved department store.

The steady, rhythmic thudding of boots hitting the ground in perfect unison echoed up from the streets below, pulling Frank from his thoughts. He ran to the window that overlooked the main street running through Freising, but he couldn't see anything through the misty darkness of early evening.

Frank's breath quickened, and goosebumps rose on his arms. He shivered, trying to keep his unease in check.

The familiar sound of hatred filled the air, but this time it felt different. It was more intense and somehow more threatening. Adolf Hitler had been stripping Jews of their birthrights for years, but recently the violence towards them had increased, and the Reich did nothing to prevent it.

Frank sighed as he realised the police would do nothing to protect them. His stomach tensed as he ran down the stairs, turning off every light switch along the way.

He turned off the lights that illuminated the glass archways over the display windows and entrance. The last thing he did before opening the large wooden door that had borne witness to over a century of activity in this beautiful old Bavarian town, was to turn off the light over the fourth archway on the side of the building at the entrance to Brennergasse.

His hand shook on the door handle, and he paused to listen before pulling the door shut. The precise, synchronised beat gave way to a growing cacophony of voices that filled the air with a deafening chorus of hate that permeated the surroundings with menacing chants of aggression and intimidation.

Juden Aus!

Keine Juden mehr!

Frank's heart sank because he knew exactly what the words meant:

Jews Out!

No More Jews!

A chill ran down his spine as he looked down the street towards the approaching stormtroopers, or brownshirts as they had become known throughout Europe. Several hundred marched in step, carrying their antisemitic and terrifying message to the German people: Jewish people would no longer be tolerated in Germany.

The stormtroopers specifically targeted Jewish business owners, frequently harassing them by painting the Star of David on the front of their establishments along with the word "Juden". They would then stand guard outside, preventing anyone from entering, and encouraging everyday Germans to shop in Aryan stores instead.

Frank watched in horror as the crowd of brownshirts marched up Adolf Hitler Strasse, shouting hate slogans and giving the Nazi salute to the regular cries of Heil Hitler from their leaders at the front.

Frank wished the Guttmann Department store was located anywhere but its current location, which was near the intersection of Hindenburgstrasse and Adolf Hitler Strasse. Even though he had heard on the radio that other towns and cities within the Third Reich were experiencing similar treatment this night, the hopelessness he felt at this exact moment made it even more distressing.

The stormtroopers marched and chanted, brandishing large flags emblazoned with swastikas: a black symbol inside a white circle surrounded by a blood-red border that symbolised their supposed pure Aryan heritage.

The thought of innocent Jewish people, who were every

bit as German as the SA - or Sturmabteilung to give their full title - thugs causing chaos on the streets, being killed in the streets filled Frank with fear. He trembled at the possibility that unless the police did what they hadn't done previously and intervene to stop the Nazi thugs, his vision of bloodshed would soon become a reality.

They stopped outside a tobacco store, the shouts and threats getting louder and louder. Frank's heart quivered as the tension in the air rose to a fever pitch. He knew the owner of the tobacco store very well, and he wished there was something he could do to help as he watched the terrible scenes unfold before him.

The store owner was Jacob Honlee, and like Frank and Herbert Guttmann, Jacob and his family were Jewish, or at least they were according to the German Reich, after the passing of the Nuremberg Race Laws in 1935. Frank hadn't been raised in the Jewish faith but had converted in the 1920s to appease his grandfather after he moved to Germany to help him run the store after Herbert's son perished in the Great War.

Frank flinched as the sound of shattering glass filled his ears. He squinted, trying to see through the crowd as he inched closer. The mob was wild, their faces twisted in fury as they hurled stones and clubs at the tobacco store. Frank watched in horror as the windows caved in, one by one, until the entire front of the store was nothing but rubble and shards of glass.

The rioters surged inside, tearing everything apart with manic energy. Frank could hear the crash of shelves and displays as they destroyed everything in their path, leaving nothing but destruction in their wake. The store owner, Jacob, would never be able to sell anything again.

When the stormtroopers dragged Jacob and his wife

into the street and began beating them, Frank had seen enough. Whatever misfortune had gone before, this night was different, and Frank had to get his grandfather as far from the store as he could. He knew that after this night, there would be no going back to how things used to be. Germany was no longer safe for Jewish people, and they had to get out.

After locking the heavy front door behind him, Frank bounded up the stairs to Herbert Guttmann's office in the replica medieval tower on the third floor that overlooked Hindenburgstrasse on the corner of the street with Brennergasse.

As Frank climbed the stairs, his mind filled with thoughts of anger towards his grandfather. His fists clenched and unclenched, and his footsteps grew louder and more forceful. He couldn't understand why Herbert refused to listen to him. Hadn't he warned him repeatedly that their lives were in danger if they remained in Germany?

Frank had seen the danger signs as early as 1933 when Hitler became Chancellor of Germany on the thirtieth of January that year. Like many others, he had read *Mein Kampf* and had watched closely as anti-Jewish rhetoric ramped up month by month and year by year. After the passing of the Nuremberg Race Laws in 1935, Frank had urged Herbert to sell the store and leave Germany while they still had a chance.

He begged his grandfather to go to England with him, where they would both be safe. Frank's family had connections going back to Queen Victoria herself, and they were well-placed to help them prosper once they were safely out of Germany.

But Herbert wouldn't listen. Every time Frank tried to

reason with him, Herbert would get angry and yell at him, reminding him of the blood his family had spilt for Germany. By 1936, Frank had all but given up trying to convince his stubborn grandfather that they were in danger.

Now, Frank's fears had come home to roost, and if they survived this night, he would drag his grandfather over the border. Even if he had to beat him half to death to get him there.

Herbert was pacing up and down the plush carpet in his office as Frank burst through the door. With his tall, slender frame standing as straight as an arrow, Herbert walked as if he was marching in a military parade. His deep grey hair was cut short, and Frank noticed how taut his jaw was beneath his gritted teeth. His deep brown eyes hid behind round glasses, and, as always, they gave away little of what was going on behind them.

"The SA are rioting, and this time they're coming for us. They have already destroyed Honlee's tobacco store. Grandfather, they dragged poor Jacob and his wife from the store and beat them to a pulp in the street. The crowd bayed for their blood while the police stood idly by and did nothing. I saw it with my own eyes. We've got to get out of here or it'll be our turn next."

Herbert twirled his full moustache with one hand and pointed at a radio set hidden behind his desk by the large windows that overlooked the carnage farther down the street with the other. "It's happening all over Germany. The Nazis are burning our synagogues, and the fire department is doing nothing about it. They're pouring water on the Aryan houses that burn close to our synagogues, but they do nothing to help us. Jewish businesses are being attacked, and the police do nothing. It's as if they have been ordered to stand aside and allow it to happen."

"They probably have," Frank sneered. "Have you listened to Josef Goebbels recently? All he does is rant about the Jews and how we have no place in the future of Germany. Grandfather, we have to get out of here now. We can talk about it later."

"Do they not respect the blood my family has shed for this country?" Herbert stood his ground and ignored Frank's pleas. "Do they not understand that my only son gave his life for Germany in the Great War? I, myself, have given so much to this town, and we have helped so many families and charities over the years. I'm well respected in Freising, and they shall not damage my department store."

Herbert slammed his foot into the radio, knocking it to the floor so the voices sounded distant, like they were speaking underwater. Frank felt sorry for him, but he knew they only had a few more minutes before it was their turn.

"The Nazis don't care what you've done for Germany. They don't care what any of us have done. We're Jews, and in their eyes, we are nothing but vermin that need to be eradicated. And they'll eradicate *us* if we don't get out of here now!"

Frank grabbed his elderly grandfather's skinny arm more roughly than at any time in his life, but the time to be gentle was long gone. The baying, marching crowd was closer now, and their jeering could be heard clearly on the third floor of Guttmann's Department Store. The torches they carried over their heads lit up the dark, misty streets, and the lights they carried seemed to Frank as though they were illuminating the night sky to show the citizens of Germany what happened to Jewish men and women if they refused to heed the warnings of their violent ideologies.

Frank dragged his reluctant grandfather towards the door. It surprised him at how strong and agile Herbert was for an eighty-nine-year-old man. He wasn't frail in the slightest, but that didn't deter Frank.

"For once in your stubborn life, you're going to do as I tell you!" Frank yelled at him. "We're getting as far away from here as we can tonight, and then tomorrow we're getting out of Germany. You can thank me later for saving your life."

Herbert pushed Frank away. "I've lived here all my life, as did generations before me. My grandfather built this store from nothing, and we have given everything to this country. I am as German as they are, and I'm not leaving. They'll have to drag me out of here. You go, Frank. Leave now while you still can."

"They'll do just that, you stubborn old fool. They'll drag us both out and beat us senseless on the streets if we don't move. I'm not leaving without you, so we're going. Now."

Shattering glass below told Frank he was too late. The baying horde was here, and there was no escaping them now. Frank let go of his grandfather and instead clasped his hands as they joined together in prayer.

Chapter Two

"Jewish pigs!"
    "Jews out."
    "No Jews in Germany."

The shouts and insults could be heard clearly above the smashing glass from the floors below. Several hundred brown-shirted stormtroopers screamed at the top of their lungs, and Frank could feel their hatred. He could almost touch it; such was the deep intensity of their loathing towards them.

Herbert stood still, frozen in place. The wrinkles on his face deepened and his mouth hung open in a look of disbelief. His posture deflated, and Frank could see the pain etched all over him as the realisation of the situation finally hit home.

He, the great Herbert Guttmann, was not immune from the violence and antisemitism being unleashed on the German Jews. If their lives weren't in such danger, Frank might have felt sorry for him. Instead, he resisted the urge to shake him for refusing to listen to his grandson for over three years, and now it was too late to do anything about it.

The crescendo of noise continued unabated. Frank closed his eyes as he heard their precious family store, the store that had been in the Guttmann family for five generations, being systematically ransacked and destroyed. Footsteps thumping up the stairs told him that their time was almost up.

The door to Herbert's office burst open, and several men in the brown uniforms of the SA burst in. The red and black swastika stood out on their left sleeves, and Frank forced back the angry tears that welled in his eyes.

Something told him that this was just the beginning, and while today the Jewish synagogues and businesses were burning, one day the rest of Europe would burn alongside them.

The baying mob roughly shoved Frank and Herbert down the stairs and forced them outside to the streets that were alight with their torches. Several buildings were on fire, and the flames lit up the night sky as Frank surveyed the carnage and violence all around him.

Freising, this beautiful small town tucked away in the picturesque region of Bavaria, and yet only a short distance from Munich, joined other towns and cities all across the country as they burned synagogues, looted and destroyed Jewish businesses, and committed some of the worst crimes in German history to date. Frank knew this night would be remembered long into the future.

Feet and fists crashed into the two men. Frank watched as his elderly grandfather fell under the onslaught before he too, fell to the ground. Close to unconsciousness, Frank watched from the corner of his eye as they threw lighted torches through the shattered glass of his beloved store. He closed his eyes and wept as darkness descended.

He opened his eyes with a gasp as water was thrown

over him. A boy no older than fifteen or sixteen stared down at him with hate etched all over his face. The boy screamed at him as hands roughly picked him up and dragged him towards the rear of a truck that had appeared from nowhere.

The next thing he knew, he was being forced into the back of the truck, and when he sat down, he looked across at the battered and bloodied face of his grandfather. Tears stained Herbert's face, and Frank wept as he watched his grandfather mouth the word 'sorry' across the space between them. Herbert's glasses were missing, and for some reason, this bothered Frank much more than it should have, given their current situation.

"They're all going to Dachau," one stormtrooper glee-fully told one of his comrades. "They're going to love it there."

Dachau. Frank had heard of that place. It was the first of its kind. A concentration camp built by the Nazis back in 1933 when they first took power. From what Frank remembered, it was built for political prisoners of the Third Reich, so why were they being taken there? He knew every single man in the back of the truck, and every one of them was Jewish. Were they now political prisoners?

Frank knew that whatever type of prisoners they were classified as being, this was the beginning of the end for them. From now on, being Jewish in Germany was tanta-mount to receiving a death sentence, and he felt very sorry for his fellow occupants of the truck. Especially the battered old man that sat opposite him.

Frank's thoughts turned to Gerda Jung, the woman who started out as his secretary before he'd fallen head over heels in love with her. He wondered where she was at this moment, hoping fervently that she had got as far away from Freising as she could. Gerda wasn't Jewish, but she could be in trouble for working for, and loving, Frank Fernsby, who was Jewish as far as the authorities were concerned.

The truck lurched forward, and as it drove down the street, Frank watched as flames lapped up the whitewashed old walls of Guttmann's Department Store. He hung his head and hoped his grandfather couldn't see what he was seeing.

Many thoughts and emotions ran through Frank's mind as the familiar streets of Freising disappeared from view. He thought of his family in England and hoped that the last letters he'd sent had reached them safely. He thought of how much he missed his homeland at this moment and wished he were there right now. Tears of grief ran down his face as he realised he would probably never see England's green and pleasant hills again, and he forced his thoughts to the back of his mind.

Right now was the time to be strong, not weak. A new resolve coursed through Frank's veins. Whatever the Nazis threw at him, he would get through it, if only for his grandfather, who, at his ripe old age, needed Frank's help more than any time in his life before. Together, they would survive whatever the Nazis threw at them.

As the truck trundled towards Dachau, it stopped at some other towns along the way. Each stop was the same: Jewish men, battered and beaten, were shoved into the back of the crowded truck, their suffering and confusion and cries for help drowned out by the noise of a baying mob.

November 9, 1938, would become known as Kristallnacht, or the Night of Broken Glass, and its repercussions would reverberate throughout history as a day of infamy. It is a night that will never be forgotten.

Chapter Three

Cambridge, England. November 1938

Eighteen-year-old Michael Fernsby was in a hurry. He walked as fast as he could through the hallowed corridors of Trinity Hall at the famed Cambridge University and avoided eye contact with anyone so he wouldn't be stopped on the way out.

Normally he would take his time to admire the surroundings and pinch himself that he'd finally made it to Cambridge as a first-year student to join his brother, David, who was two years older and a lot smarter than he was. Michael was slim and athletic and was a promising runner.

David, however, was smart, and he always knew the right thing to do. He was the heir to their family brewing empire, but more than that, he was Michael's best friend and hero.

David had always been the sensible one of the two, unlike Michael, who acted on hot-headed impulses that had got him into trouble on more than a few occasions. Every time, David had been there to help and support him, and many a time he'd taken the blame, and the beatings, for Michael's stupidity.

He clutched the telegram in his hand and ran as fast as he could. Although addressed to David, the body of the telegram had mentioned Michael as well, and it was on this basis that the secretary had given it to him rather than seeking his brother. As it was almost eight in the evening, and the students could be anywhere in the city, the secretary did what anyone else would have done in her situation and passed it off as fast as she could before scurrying off home for the night.

Michael knew where David was. It was a Wednesday night, and he'd become close to one of the female students at the nearby Newnham College. In fact, according to Michael at least, David was becoming too close to Patricia Salter. If they got any closer, they'd be in a serious relationship.

Not that Michael wasn't happy for his brother. If anything, he was a little jealous because their relationship took David's attention away from him.

Michael hissed. *Grow up and don't be stupid.*

Patricia was a pretty girl, with bright green eyes and wavy dark hair that flowed down to her collar line. This seemed to be the popular style for girls these days, and Michael had to admit that he liked the look of it.

But what stood out the most about what he knew of Patricia, and to be honest, it wasn't very much, was that she was a serious and extremely smart student. In that regard, he could see why they were attracted to each other, because David had the same traits.

Whatever Patricia ended up doing after she left college, Michael knew she would be a raging success. She might even be his sister-in-law someday.

He ran, and the freezing drizzle soaked him to the skin as he splashed through the puddles in the darkness. Occasional gas lamps lit the dreary night sky, highlighting the constant rain as it soaked everything in its path. He cursed himself for not grabbing his thick coat, but the urgency of the telegram had spurred him to seek David as fast as he could, and he'd spared no thoughts to the elements outside the famous old hallway.

He did now. He ran down Sidgwick Avenue and burst through the doors of Newnham College. Freezing cold and dripping wet, he felt, as much as saw, the disapproving looks of the female students as they stared at the bedraggled mess in front of them. Michael ignored the icy glares and entered one of the reading rooms off to his left. He knew they would be in there because this was where they always met.

If they wanted somewhere more private, David took her by bus to the Fernsby home in the middle of Cambridge. As the university had been a family tradition going back generations, the family had bought a small home in the city many years earlier, and that is where they met for important occasions, or for when they got together over weekends.

"Michael! What on earth? You're soaked to the skin." David jumped up from his place at the side of Patricia and took off his jacket. He held Michael's gaze as he handed it over.

"What are you doing here?" David asked, raising his eyebrows at the state of his younger brother, dripping and freezing in front of him.

Michael shivered while he stripped down to his bare chest and put on the dry jacket. Then he rubbed himself with his hands to get the circulation going in his frozen limbs. Finally, he slumped onto a chair opposite the love-struck couple, who stared at him with furrowed eyebrows as they waited for his explanation.

Michael held David's stare and watched as he ran his fingers through his thick, curly black hair. He always did this when he was troubled by something. David was twenty years old and had the same athletic, some would say skinny, build that Michael himself had.

David was the taller of the two by a couple of inches, and where David had curly hair, Michael had thick black hair that was uncurled and lay flat on his head. Or it would have if he didn't plaster it with Brylcreem to make it look spiky and uncombed. Even soaked with rain, his hair held fast.

Both brothers had dark brown eyes, but David's face was thinner than Michael's, so his eyes looked more sunken, making his nose stand out more prominently than it otherwise would have.

Michael, on the contrary, had no such issues. His cheeks were full, and his eyes were bright and prominent. Everywhere he went, the girls had always noticed him before David, so he was glad that his brother had found someone that loved him for who he was - an intelligent and polite young man who was as loyal as they come.

"Stop staring and tell us why you're here." Patricia spoke up, breaking the connection between the two brothers.

"Sorry. My mouth was frozen, and I couldn't speak," Michael said, shifting his gaze to Patricia.

"That's a first," David interjected.

They all laughed, and Michael noticed, perhaps for the first time, what David saw in Patricia. Other than their obvious connection through their studious personalities, it was clear why David was smitten with her.

Patricia was a pretty young lady. She had curves in the right places, and Michael couldn't help but notice how her eyes lit up when she smiled. He berated himself for looking at her that way and pulled his gaze away from her.

"I'm sorry to barge in on you like this. I'm sure you were arguing the finer points of Einstein's theory of relativity or some other fascinating scientific fact, but I bring urgent news from Mother." Michael loved to poke fun at their nerdiness.

David ignored Michael's teasing and looked serious. "Is everything alright at home?"

"I'm not sure. One of the secretaries handed me this telegram before she went home. It's addressed to you, but as she couldn't find you, she gave it to me instead."

Michael handed the telegram to David so he could read it for himself. "At least you kept this dry," David commented.

Patricia and David put their heads together and bent forward to read the telegram. David read it out loud so they could all hear it together.

My dearest boys, your father and I hope you are studying well and enjoying your time in Cambridge Stop We received a troublesome letter from your Uncle Frank this morning and we need a family meeting to discuss it Stop Please take the train home to Sandwich on Friday night and stay here for the weekend Stop This is very urgent and you must come here Stop Love Mum Stop

David lowered the telegram and raised his head. He opened his mouth to speak and then paused as if to collect his thoughts before he spoke.

"Uncle Frank was good to us when we were young. Do you remember the time he saved us from Dad's wrath when we skipped school that time to watch the Oxford-Cambridge boat race on the Thames?"

Michael's mouth broke into a wide smile. "How can I ever forget? Father was on the warpath, and if it wasn't for Uncle Frank pleading our case and reminding him they had done the same thing when they were young, he would have beaten us until we were senseless."

They laughed as they reminisced about the good times they had enjoyed with their uncle.

"What about the time you smacked that pompous fool in Hyde Park for refusing to give our football back to us?" David smiled. "His uncle was a colonel something or other, and he was spluttering all over his champagne."

Both boys laughed as the memories flooded back. "He knocked it all over his picnic," Michael roared. "Uncle Frank promised him a month's supply to calm him down."

Both boys fell silent and bowed their heads, lost in their memories.

"He saved us many times." David became serious again as he looked at the telegram in his hands. "Now it looks as if he's in trouble. It must be something serious for our mother to send us a telegram asking us to go home. I wonder what's happened to him. I do hope he and our great-grandfather are okay over there. Hitler has turned Germany into a terrifying place for Jewish people, and it's just getting worse."

"The newspapers were full of stories just the other day of what those brownshirts were doing to Jewish synagogues and businesses," Patricia spoke up. "They're calling it the Night of Broken Glass, and it's frightening beyond belief. I tell you, we shall soon be at war again if something isn't done about that horrible man."

"Kristallnacht," Michael said. "That's what they're calling it over there. I fear something must have happened.

Don't you think it's unusual that she asked us to go to Sandwich? Normally, they would have come here for the weekend and stayed at our house in the city. Something must be seriously wrong, so we have to go, David. We have to see what he wrote to Mother and Father in his letter."

David said nothing. He just nodded his head in agreement and stared into space. They all knew the storm clouds were gathering over Europe, and there was nothing any of them could do about it.

Chapter Four

Michael walked back to his room alone. David stayed behind to spend more time with Patricia and say his goodbyes in private. He would join Michael later where they could talk about it in more depth.

The rain had abated, but the night was cold and damp. Michael had given David his jacket back and put his sodden woollen jumper back on, so he was already shivering before he left Newnham College.

He took a right turn down West Road so he could walk past the Victorian mansions that lined the street. He was especially interested in number three, as that was where Lucy Davenport lived.

Michael was both intrigued and fascinated with Lucy. She was stunning to look at, with wavy dark hair and the prettiest blue eyes he had ever seen. Neither overweight nor skinny, Lucy looked nigh-on perfect to Michael, and the more he saw her, the more he wanted to know. But she was mysterious, and never spoke of her past or where she came from. All Michael knew about her was that she was a lodger in the Bragg household at number three, West Road and that she sent electric sparks down his spine when she kissed him.

They had met for drinks a few times, and they made each other laugh every time they got together, which wasn't anywhere near as often as Michael would have liked.

Are we dating? I don't think so, at least not yet anyway.

Michael held a conversation with himself as he approached the big house. He smiled as he remembered the look on Lucy's face when he told her about the murder that had occurred there in 1930. A crazy student had got hold of a gun and shot the previous occupants of the house during a meeting. He knew little else, but it had been a great ice-breaker when he first met Lucy.

A whining sound from inside the gates of number five West Road caught his attention. It sounded like a dog, but it was so soft that he couldn't be sure. He stopped and listened, the cold and clammy jumper no longer an issue. All his attention was on whatever had made that pitiful sound a few moments ago.

There it is. It's behind the gate, out of sight of the road.

Michael peered over the gate but couldn't see anything. The whining got louder as whatever it was heard him approach. Then it barked.

It's a dog! What's a dog doing out here alone on a night like this?

Michael opened the gate and stepped into the darkness behind the high wall. The stone wall blocked any streetlight from the gas lamps, and Michael couldn't make out anything except the shape of a few trees.

There it is again.

Close to where he stood, he heard and then felt the dog brush against his leg. The dog whined and then barked loudly. So loudly, that two heads appeared at one of the upstairs windows.

He crouched down and stroked the dog, comforting it, and waited until it stopped barking. The poor thing was shivering uncontrollably and was obviously frozen to the bone.

Michael looked hard at the window and froze at the sight of a male and a female staring into the front garden. He knew that face. He'd recognise it anywhere. It was Robert Stourcliffe, the conceited aristocratic arsehole who hated the Fernsbys.

The feeling was mutual.

There were few people on earth that Michael disliked, and even fewer that he didn't get along with. But Robert Stourcliffe topped the list on both counts as a grade one prat of the highest order.

The dog pushed its head into Michael's knees, almost knocking him over. It was a big dog, but the light wasn't good enough to make out its breed. It was friendly, and that was enough for Michael right now.

"How long have you been out here?" he asked. "You're shivering, and you must be frozen. Who left you here? Is it that blabbermouth up there in the window?"

Michael reached down to pet the dog and was rewarded with a big wet tongue on his exposed hand. He felt the blood quicken in his veins as anger swelled inside him.

Michael had a deep-rooted sense of justice, and he couldn't stand to see an innocent animal being mistreated. He knew he had to act, even if it meant going up against someone as powerful as Stourcliffe.

"You're a friendly one, aren't you?" he said, rubbing the dog's body, trying to create some warmth for the poor thing.

"Well, you're not staying here, that's for sure. You'll freeze to death if you stay out here much longer."

As he reached around the tree, trying to see where the leash was tied, a voice behind him made him jump.

"What are you doing with my dog?"

Michael recognised the voice immediately, and his blood boiled as he turned to face him.

"Your dog?" Michael replied, trying to keep his voice steady. "More like your victim. Look at it, it's freezing out here."

Stourcliffe laughed, although sneered would be more apt. "Fernsby, is that you? Of course it is. You're always sticking your nose in where it's not welcome."

Stourcliffe's accent came from a distant century. His family might be titled and privileged, and his father might be Sir Robert Stourcliffe, the great British shipping magnate, but Robert Junior made sure everyone knew it by the way he spoke. The silver spoon was stuck firmly down his throat, and Michael had to fight the urge not to knock it down even further so he could choke on it. Even his glasses were gold-rimmed, and Michael had to restrain himself from grabbing them and smashing them under his shoes.

At over six feet tall, Robert Stourcliffe was trim and athletic, and he excelled at running. Until this year, he had been considered the star athlete at Trinity College, but his records, and his pride, had been bruised when Michael beat him badly in a race a few weeks earlier in October.

"How long has it been here?" Michael asked, ignoring Stourcliffe's jibes.

"That's none of your business, old chap. It's perfectly fine out here. You are spoiling my fun, Fernsby, so do run along and mind your own business."

Michael knew Stourcliffe chose those aristocratic words

just to rub him up the wrong way. The problem was that it worked, and Michael could feel his neck and face getting redder and hotter. It took all he could muster to stop himself from giving Stourcliffe a smack in his pompous mouth.

"The dog's coming with me. You're a cruel man, Stourcliffe, and about as unfeeling as they come. If you leave it out here much longer, you'll kill it, not that I expect you to care about that."

Stourcliffe laughed. "You want to take my dog? Why? So you can run it into the ground like your father did to his shipping business? You'd probably come crawling back to me in a few days begging me to take the stupid mutt back because you can't look after it, and I'd be forced to rescue it, just as my father did with your business. Let's be honest, Fernsby, you can't even be trusted to look after a dog."

Stourcliffe stepped around Michael and kicked the dog in its ribs, making it yelp in pain and fear. Michael watched as the dog curled up into a tiny ball, whimpering pitifully in the cold, wet night. It was one of the saddest things he had ever seen.

"That's for barking and making a racket," Stourcliffe hissed at the terrified animal.

Spittle formed in the corners of Michael's mouth. He stared at Stourcliffe, who even in the darkness looked smug and superior. He couldn't help himself. Without forethought, Michael lashed out with his fists, catching Stourcliffe flush on the nose. Stourcliffe fell backwards and crashed onto the wet ground.

"You're squealing like a pig, Stourcliffe. You're not so tough now, are you? How does it feel when the boot's on the other foot?"

Michael grabbed Stourcliffe by the lapels of his jacket and dragged him to his feet. Even in the dim light, he could see the shock and fear etched all over the spoiled brat's face. He took extra delight when he noticed his glasses lay broken in the grass.

"Your family are nothing but vultures that prey on other people when they need help. You stole my father's shipping business for a pittance during the Depression because we were struggling like everyone else was. Well, most of us were. Seemingly, leeches like your lot did alright out of it because you stole businesses like ours for next to nothing and then expected us to thank you for it."

He shoved Stourcliffe backwards. "I'm taking the dog because you are a cruel human being who doesn't deserve to have such a loyal and faithful companion. When did you last feed him?"

Stourcliffe stared at Michael but said nothing. Blood streamed down his face, and his handkerchief turned dark as he held it over his bloody nose.

"It's broken," he said finally. "You've broken my nose."

"I'll break your neck if you ever speak to me like that again. You're no better than me, Stourcliffe, and you're no better than anyone else here. You hide behind your father's money and his titles, but underneath you are a shallow boy who doesn't deserve what you've got. Respect is earned, not demanded. Now, what's the dog's name?"

"It doesn't have one."

"You're mumbling. Speak louder. What's the dog's name?"

"I never gave it one. I just called it dog."

"You never even gave it a name?" Michael snorted. "What kind of person are you? How long have you had it?"

"I never wanted it in the first place. It was a gift from my aunt. It's about a year old, I suppose, by now."

"You've had it a year and still haven't given it a name? You're a disgrace, Stourcliffe."

He'd found where it was tied to the tree, and he grabbed the leash as he released it. The dog ran to him as though it had known him its entire life.

"Look at the poor thing. It's standing here shaking. Did you kick it all the time, or was tonight a special occasion?"

Stourcliffe looked at the ground and said nothing.

Michael shook his head and held the dog's leash in his hand. "Come on, Fido, let's give you a proper home where you will be loved and cared for."

Stourcliffe gained courage as Michael backed out of the front garden and onto the street. "You won't get away with this, Fernsby. My family means something here, and I'll make sure you're expelled for assaulting me and stealing my dog."

Michael ignored him. He knew he would be in trouble for striking the golden boy of Trinity College. Stourcliffe's father *was* a big deal here. He donated lots of money to Trinity, and a long line of Stourcliffe portraits adorned the walls of the college.

He knew he'd probably lose his place at Cambridge, but at this moment he was too angry to consider the consequences. All he wanted to do was save the poor dog from further mistreatment. Whatever punishment he received would be worth it.

But would it? His father would be disappointed with him, even if he understood why he'd done it. Michael shrugged his shoulders. *It's done now. No use crying over spilt milk.*

He ran and played with the dog all the way back to his room, where he smuggled the animal inside as quickly as he could. Pets were banned from the accommodations, and he knew he'd be in even more trouble if they caught him with it.

He didn't have any dog food, and as there were no shops close by that would be open at this time of night, Michael raided his stash of snacks and fed the starving dog a mixture of biscuits, Rowntree's confectionary, and cornflakes. As sure as he was that it wasn't a good healthy diet for a dog, it gulped the snacks down without them even touching the sides.

"What are we going to do with you?" Michael asked, checking underneath to see if it was a boy or a girl.

It was a girl.

In the light of his room, he got a good look at what he'd just brought home. The dog was a jet-black Labrador, and it looked young. Stourcliffe had said it was about a year old, and from what Michael could tell, he was about right. She was terribly thin and undernourished, which told Michael that Stourcliffe had abused the poor thing something rotten.

It looked as if it hadn't had a good meal for weeks, and by the way she muzzled up to him, he wondered how much affection it had received from its previous owner. Knowing Stourcliffe, probably very little.

"Whatever happens next, we're in this together," Michael murmured to the dog lying on the bed next to him.

~

"What the...?" David stopped dead in his tracks when he opened the door to Michael's room.

"Sit down and close the door. Hurry." Michael's hand gestures beckoned his brother into the room in haste.

The big black dog jumped down from the bed and eyed David for a few moments before strolling up to him. David absent-mindedly petted the dog while he stared at his brother.

"Are you stark raving mad?" he asked. "We've just got an urgent telegram from Mother to return home with haste, and our uncle is probably either dead or in grave danger from the Nazis. You know we aren't allowed pets in the rooms. Where did you get it from? Whose dog is it, anyhow?"

David slumped on the bed next to his brother while the dog nuzzled the two of them affectionately.

"It's a friendly young thing, I'll say that. Please tell me it's not yours."

Michael closed his eyes and turned his lips downwards. "Well, it is now. I sort of inherited it on the way home from Newnham College."

"How? It was dark, and it was raining. We'd just received that telegram. Did you find it? Is it a stray?"

"Not exactly." Michael spent the next ten minutes telling David what had happened, and how he'd ended up with the big black dog in his room.

When he'd finished, David jumped to his feet. "You punched that arrogant prat in the nose? Wow, brother, you certainly know how to get us into trouble. You do realise that we will probably be kicked out of Cambridge now, don't you? The Stourcliffes are all over this place, and they'll take their side over us any day of the week."

"I know that, but you will be fine. I was the one who hit him, not you. You weren't even there. So don't worry, brother, I'll take whatever punishment they dish out. I couldn't just stand there and witness this poor dog being ill-treated like that. I had to do something about it, and when Stourcliffe taunted me about the shipping business, I'm afraid I saw red and lost it, and I'd smacked him before I had time to think about it."

"What do we do now?" David asked.

"You stay until Friday as we agreed, and then take the train to Kent after classes are over. I'll skip the rest of the week, as I'm likely to be suspended anyway, and I'll go first thing tomorrow. It's only a day early."

"What about the dog?"

"She's coming with me. Whatever else happens, I'm not allowing the poor thing to take any more abuse at Stourcliffe's hands. I'll pay him for her if that's what he wants, but she's going home with me."

"What do you think Mum and Dad will say about this?" David stroked the dog while he spoke.

"They will be furious. You know that as well as I do, but what's done is done. The dog is staying with us, even if I have to get a place of my own to look after it. Dad will read me the riot act when he finds out what happened, but I also think he'll be quite happy that I smacked the pompous fool after he calms down."

"You know Judith has been wanting a dog for a long time now." David looked at his brother. "She would love a Lab like this one. It's a pretty dog and well behaved, too."

"You want to give it to our sister? She's fourteen and growing up way too fast. She might not want one now she's older."

"She'll love it, just wait and see. In any case, you'll be off to college somewhere, even if it's far up north where the Stourcliffes can't reach you. We'll sort it out with Mum and Dad over the weekend. I'm going with you tomorrow."

Michael shook his head. "You don't need to do this, David. I'm the one who got us into trouble, and I'm the one who will face the music."

"Oh, believe me, Michael, I know. You *are* the one who will pay for this, but I'm not letting you do it alone. Who do you think I am? We're in this together, whatever happens. Now, what are we going to call it?"

"Well, she's a girl, so I'm going to call her Lucy."

"Lucy? Like Lucy Davenport?"

"Maybe."

"Fair enough. Lucy it is then. I can't wait to see the look on Dad's face when we show up tomorrow with a dog."

Chapter Five

The walk from the railway station to the Fernsbys' home in Sandwich, Kent, took about twenty minutes. The boys were quiet as they walked, and Michael was sure that David was as deep in thought as he was.

They were concerned about the repercussions from Michael's impetuous actions the previous evening, and worried about how their parents would react when they saw them walk in with a strange dog. But most of all, they were worried about the telegram they had received from their mother ordering them to return home for the weekend.

The newspapers were full of stories about how the Nazis were treating the Jewish population in Germany, and you had to live under a rock to not understand the seriousness of the situation over there. Especially when you had close family members who were directly in the firing line.

The boys had left word with the secretary who'd given them the telegram that they were leaving, but because they'd caught the early train to London, the Stourcliffe situation had not yet blown up. They knew that as soon as the administrators took to their desks that morning, Stourcliffe's father would be all over them, demanding retribution for Michael's actions.

Michael would have rather stayed and got it all over with that day, but family business always took precedence, and if his Uncle Frank was in trouble, then his future at Cambridge paled into insignificance.

The large stone house on New Street came into view. With its manicured front lawn and ivy-covered stones, the house cut an impressive sight compared to other homes that were close by.

It would have been impressive anywhere if Michael didn't always compare it to the house he'd spent most of his younger days growing up in. That home was at least four times the size of this one, and it was central to everything in the heart of London's swish Chelsea neighbourhood.

Like almost everyone else, the Fernsby family had seen hard times during the Great Depression. Financial misfortune had hit them hard, and to make ends meet they had been forced to sell their shipping business to the Stourcliffes for pennies on the pound. They still owned a large percentage of the southern breweries, but the shipping side of the business had been the Fernsbys' crowning glory, and it cost them a lot more than money when they sold it to Lord Stourcliffe.

What hurt the most, though, was the sale of their beloved London home. The house had been in the family for centuries, and it was rumoured that Queen Victoria herself went there when she visited her cousin, the shipping and brewery magnate Horatio Fernsby, a hundred years earlier. Whether or not it was true didn't matter to the current generations of the Fernsby family. The fact that it *might* have happened was good enough for them.

After the sale of their beloved home, Michael's father

and current head of the family, Gerald Fernsby, bought their current home in Sandwich, Kent. Although it was much smaller in comparison, the New Street property was big enough for a growing family. More importantly, it was affordable enough for them to weather the economic storm of the Depression.

Michael took a moment to compose himself before ringing the front doorbell. Normally he would just barrel in unannounced, but on this occasion he thought better of it. He looked up and saw Judith smiling and waving at them from the second-floor window on the far left. The other three sets of curtains remained drawn.

The large oak door creaked open, and Warhurst, the trusty butler who'd been with the family forever, appeared in the doorway. When Michael thought about it, Warhurst had been with the family ever since he was a boy. He had followed his father into service for the Fernsbys, and his father before him. Now in his late sixties, Warhurst was as much a part of the family as Michael himself was.

Warhurst's ageing features stiffened when he saw the two boys standing before him. Michael watched as his eyes wandered down to the black Lab straining at the leash, but he didn't say anything. Reliable old Warhurst had always been the epitome of see everything and say nothing. Whatever family secrets he knew, they were safe with Warhurst.

"Good morning, Masters David and Michael. Please pardon my surprise at seeing you here. I was informed that you wouldn't be here until tomorrow evening." His eyes never left Lucy, who barked and yapped as she tried to get close to the butler.

"We're early," David said casually. "A change of plans, shall we say?"

Michael pulled Lucy back and tried making her sit

down. He could have sworn he saw Warhurst smile faintly as he failed dismally in his efforts to control the dog.

"Please, allow me to show you to the sitting room, and I'll inform your parents that you are here." Warhurst turned and walked into the dark hallway.

Michael watched as the butler walked straight as an arrow in front of him. Tall, at over six feet in height, and as lean as any man Michael had ever seen, Warhurst still looked as fit and sprightly as ever.

And he should be, because even though he was ageing, Warhurst had always taken good care of himself. During his downtime, he had always been a keen runner, and the boys had frequently gone with him on long runs through the Kent countryside. Or they'd tried to, but more often than not they couldn't keep up with the super-fit older man.

A few minutes later, a furious-looking Gerald Fernsby crashed into the sitting room with his wife, Dorothy Fernsby, close behind. Then came Judith, their fourteen-year-old sister who looked just like a younger version of her mother.

"What on earth were you thinking?" Gerald stared at Michael. "And what is that doing here?" he asked, pointing at Lucy, whose tail was wagging furiously at all these new people to jump on and play with.

Michael looked at his father. Everyone stared at him. He took a deep breath and chose his words carefully.

His father was forty-one years old but looked much older. Overweight and greying, his plump body strained against the seams of his tweed jacket. His hair, once a vibrant chestnut, had dulled to a dreary grey, and a bald patch was starting to form on the top of his head. He reminded Michael of a stuffy old earl he'd known when he was a young boy in London.

Except that Gerald was anything but a stuffy old earl. For one thing, he carried no titles, and even though the Fernsbys were distant relatives of the royal family, his father was as down-to-earth as any aristocratic man could be. He loved his father. He loved all his family and would do anything for them.

"Lucy was left outside in the most frightful weather, and when I found her, she was shivering and in a terrible state. I didn't know she was Stourcliffe's dog until he came out and started taunting me about the shipping company."

"How did it go from finding his dog shivering to punching him in the nose?" Gerald's blue eyes flashed with anger. "We've got enough problems right now without you adding to them."

"I'm sorry, Father. Stourcliffe kicked poor Lucy and made her yelp, and I couldn't help myself, especially after his taunts. I gave him a quick smack before I thought about the consequences."

"You gave him a quick smack before you thought about the consequences? You broke the poor fellow's nose, Michael. That's a bit more than a quick smack in my estimation."

"He deserved it, Father," David said, but Gerald waved him silent.

"Whether he deserved it or not, and I must admit there's been plenty of times I would have loved to have given his father a quick smack myself, you have to consider the consequences before you act."

"I'm sorry, Father. I guess the college called you this morning?"

"The dean himself called. Stourcliffe's father is demanding you be arrested and charged with assaulting his son and stealing his dog. He also demanded your removal from Cambridge, or they would cease any future funding until you were gone."

"I figured as much." Michael slumped into a chair, still gripping Lucy as tightly as he could. She jumped onto the chair next to him, which caused his father's face to turn purple. "I'm sorry, Father."

"Get that dog off my furniture!" he thundered.

Michael heard Judith sniggering as he pushed Lucy to the ground. "Stay there, old girl, before the old man has a heart attack."

"So, for now, you are suspended from Cambridge until they complete an enquiry into your actions. Trust me, Stourcliffe will make sure you never set foot in there again. He is also demanding compensation for the dog. I have agreed to pay it, and it is coming out of your stipend. At least that should keep the police out of it."

"Gladly, Father. Lucy deserves a good home, not a cruel one like she had with Stourcliffe."

"Yes, quite, but she can't stay here."

"Why not?" Michael retorted. "It's not like we don't have the room, is it? In any case, I thought she'd make a great present for Judith. She's been wanting a dog for some time, as we all know."

"The dog is not—" Gerald didn't get a chance to finish.

Lucy broke away from Michael and ran between Gerald's legs. She ran straight to Judith and jumped on her, knocking her over. Then she stood over her, licking her face and neck. Judith's wavy brown hair fell away from her ears, and Lucy obliged with a big wet tongue. Judith laughed and screamed with joy.

"Get that dog under control," Gerald fumed at Michael. He tried to be angry, but everyone was laughing so hard that even he couldn't keep a straight face for long.

"Can I keep her, Father? Please? I promise to take good care of her." Judith pleaded with her father.

Gerald glanced at Dorothy, who smiled and nodded. "I suppose so. But you *are* taking care of her. And keep her off the furniture."

"Thank you, Father." Judith ran up and hugged him and then her mother before giving both her brothers a big hug. "Thank you," she said and then ran outside with Lucy, who followed with the kind of playfulness that only a dog can.

"I'll ask Warhurst to order some dog food this morning," Michael nodded towards his sister. "The poor thing's starving."

"We have more serious matters to attend to." Gerald looked sombre again. "I'll pay Stourcliffe for the dog, and it looks like you're going to have to find a different college. There will be repercussions, Michael, because even though you were provoked and did the right thing in rescuing the dog, you can't go around thumping people if they upset you."

"Yes, Father. I understand, and I'll take whatever punishment you decide upon. Thank you for allowing Judith to keep Lucy."

"What's happened to Uncle Frank?" David got down to the real reason they were there.

Michael watched his mother close her eyes tightly and clench her fists together. Her hair, which was always perfect with the latest wavy patterns, flowed straight and unbrushed. At forty-four years old, Dorothy's complexion was young and wrinkle free, in stark contrast to her husband, who looked so much older than his true age.

Dorothy's brown eyes looked heavy and clouded, and

she had slept little in recent nights. Whatever was going on, it had hit his mother hard.

"I'm sure you have read the news of what happened in Germany?" A female voice, speaking in broken English spoke up. "My son sent a troubling letter, and since Kristall-nacht, we haven't heard from him since. We are very worried about both him and my father."

Chapter Six

Giselle Fernsby, Gerald's mother, and grandmother to the boys, had walked into the room unseen. At sixty-four years old, she could have been mistaken for Dorothy's sister rather than her mother-in-law. Her long brown hair flowed with not a hint of the wavy fashion that most women preferred these days. Pictures of her younger self were hung all over the house, and with her high cheekbones and electrifying smile, Giselle had always been an extremely attractive and popular woman.

"Gigi, I didn't see you enter the room. Please forgive me." Michael said in flawless German. All the family spoke fluent German, which was something Giselle had insisted upon from the moment of their birth.

Gigi was the affectionate name her father had called her when she was a young girl, and she had insisted on her grandchildren using it once they were born. Even Gerald and Dorothy referred to her by that name.

"Everybody has heard what happened on Kristallnacht," David said, rising to his feet to greet his grandmother. "Gigi, it's so good to see you again. What did Uncle

Frank's letter say? It must be urgent for you to summon us here like this."

"What happened on Kristallnacht?" Judith had re-entered the room with Lucy, who was panting from racing around the extensive garden at the rear of the house.

Gerald shot a quick glance at Dorothy, who took a deep breath before speaking. "She needs to know, Gerald. Everyone in Britain should know what the Nazis are doing, especially as our weak Prime Minister stands there waving his piece of paper declaring peace in our time. He ignores the plight of the Jews as though it isn't happening. Well, we know first-hand that it is, and the violence and threats are getting greater every day."

Gerald looked over at his daughter. "We have tried to shield you from the worst, but the time has come for everyone to know the truth. A few nights ago, the Nazis burned synagogues and Jewish businesses all over Germany. The firemen and policemen stood there and did nothing to help, while groups of brownshirts smashed and looted Jewish shops and stores. Jewish men were rounded up and driven off in trucks, and we fear for their safety. Especially your great-grandfather and uncle Frank, who we haven't heard from since it happened. We are very worried about them."

Judith stared at her parents, her mouth open in disbelief. "Who can do such a thing?"

"The Nazis, that's who," Dorothy replied. "And since then, things have only got worse. The newspapers reported that after the Night of Broken Glass, all Jewish school-children were expelled from German schools, and all Jewish retail businesses like Herbert's were forcibly transferred to Aryan hands."

"So, Uncle Frank and Papa Herbert don't have the store

anymore?" Judith asked, rubbing her hands down her arms in disbelief.

Giselle gripped Dorothy's shoulders and turned to her young granddaughter. She shook her head as if to confirm Dorothy's words. "Mark my words, all of you. That madman is going to set the world on fire. He won't stop until every Jewish person in Germany is either dead or imprisoned, and he won't stop there. He will take his hate-filled rhetoric throughout Europe. None of us is safe from his evil, and if we don't stand up to him, he will march through the streets of Paris and London unopposed."

"There are voices warning against him, Gigi," Gerald said. "Winston Churchill for one. He's been saying for a long time that we have to stand up to Hitler before it's too late."

"I fear that moment has already passed us by." Giselle took a deep breath. "Kristallnacht is only a sign of worse to come for the Jews. There are millions of us spread throughout Europe, and I fear for us all. But right now, I fear for two of them in particular — my son and my father."

She stopped and closed her eyes, the pain behind them evident to all those around her. Even Judith, whose face crumpled as tears spilt down her cheeks. Up to this point, they had shielded her from the news as it came in from the radio, newspapers, and the weekly newsreels in the cinemas.

"Herbert and Frank are good men who have done a lot for Freising," Gigi continued. "And they don't deserve to be beaten and spat upon as they have been in recent years. My brother, Carl Guttmann, died for Germany in the Great War in that terrible battle in Ypres. My father had already lost me when I moved to England with your grandfather and your Uncle Frank, and then he lost his son and heir to a pointless war."

Giselle let go of Dorothy and sat on the couch facing the family, who stared back in stony silence. She had always been the type of person who kept her feelings to herself, and her grandchildren had never seen her open up like this before.

Gigi's shoulders shook, and she buried her face in her hands. Michael, David, and Judith all rushed to her side, but she waved them away with one hand while she held the other to her face.

"Sit down, all of you. There is much you don't know about what happened back then, but it is time you all knew the truth. Only then will you fully understand Frank's situation today."

Giselle took a deep breath and wiped her eyes. Dorothy struggled to hold back her grief, and even Gerald pawed at his eyes.

"You don't have to do this, Gigi," he said softly. "I can tell the children what they need to know."

"No. My actions caused this situation, and I am the one who should tell them."

"We already know what happened," David offered. "You have told us many times about how you met our grandfather in Germany and came over here to marry him. You made no secret of the fact that Papa Herbert wasn't happy that you married an Englishman, especially with the rising tension between the two countries right before the Great War broke out. We know all this already, Gigi."

"You think you know the truth, but you don't. I kept it from you because the shame I carry is my burden, not yours. But now their lives are in danger, I owe it to you to tell you what really happened."

Gerald looked at his mother, and when he spoke, his voice broke as he struggled to get the words out. "Let me tell them, Mother. They're my children, and I should have told them years ago."

Giselle waved her hand again. "Sit down, Gerald, and be quiet. They need to hear this from me."

Gerald did as he was told. Even though he was the head of the family and the owner of a multi-million-pound brewing empire, he still did as he was told when his mother spoke.

"You believe I came over here to marry your grandfather before the Great War. While there is some truth in that, there is much that has been left out."

Giselle switched from broken English to her native German.

"It's perhaps better I speak in my native tongue, so you understand completely what I am about to say. I first encountered your grandfather at Munich University, long before the war. He was on a sabbatical from his studies at Cambridge, immersing himself in the academic life of Munich. As for myself, I was a young woman captivated by Queen Victoria and the rich tapestry of everything that went with her."

"Frank swept me off my feet, and we were so happy. At least we were until I discovered I was pregnant in 1895. Both our families were disgusted with us, but my family were especially hurt because we were there in Munich, and it was them that had to deal with the disgrace we had caused."

"It was decided that I would remain in Germany until after the birth, and then we would move to England, and my father would disown me and never speak to me again. My mother, God bless her soul, was much more forgiving, and she helped us the whole way through it. She never stopped writing to me until the day she died of cancer in 1919."

Giselle squirmed on the couch, her hands twisting in her lap as she prepared to reveal her painful past.

"I'm sorry I have let you down. I know what shame this brings on a family, especially those as prominent as both ours are. Or were, in the case of mine."

She looked down at the floor and continued.

"Frank, that is my husband, wasn't Jewish. And that caused problems with my father because he wanted me to marry into the faith and continue our long family tradition. I failed him, and Frank understood my plight, so we agreed to allow our son, who we called Frank Junior after his father, to be circumcised in the Jewish tradition in case he chose to follow the faith when he got older. Your family in England were dead against it, but it was a condition of us staying in Freising until after the birth, and we both agreed to it."

"After Frank Junior was born, we moved to London. We married, and your grandfather quit college to take his place in the family business. As the only child, he was the heir to the family brewing and shipping companies, and he went to work for his father, who I might add was much more forgiving than my father had been."

Giselle looked long and hard at Gerald, who stared back with a sorrow that everyone in the room could see. Dorothy gripped his hand as they waited for Giselle to continue.

"My father didn't believe we would last, and he was adamant that I wouldn't be allowed to crawl back once our marriage ended. Carl, my brother, was just as adamant as my father, and together they cut me out of the family as if I'd never existed. Only my mother kept in touch, and it was through her letters that I knew what my family were going through."

She reached for a glass of water that Warhurst had delivered a few minutes earlier.

"Of course, we did last. Frank and I had a wonderful marriage. Gerald followed shortly after, and if it wasn't for the war, I'm sure we would have had more children."

"The situation got even worse after the war broke out. Suddenly, my brother and my husband were fighting on opposite sides. Then they called up both my sons, and you can imagine how I felt about that. On the other side, they enlisted Carl as an officer in the German army. I didn't know what to do. I love both countries and I cannot choose between them. All I wanted was for everyone to stay safe and for the fighting to stop."

Once again, tears fell from Giselle's eyes as she recounted the terrible days of the First World War.

"Of course, it didn't end as I hoped. Why should our family be spared when millions of others were not? Carl died at Ypres, and then a year later, in 1916, Frank died on the first day of the Somme. I was mortified, and I was frightened I would lose everyone I loved in that terrible conflict. Luckily, both my sons survived and came home to me. With Frank dead, I feared for my future, but Arnold Fernsby was good to me and allowed me to stay. Frank Junior, as the eldest, now took over as the heir to the family fortunes, and we tried to rebuild ourselves after everything we had lost."

David stood up and intervened. "We didn't know any of this, Gigi. Why didn't you tell us?"

"Because I shamed both our families, and it is a burden I alone must carry. None of this is your fault, and you would have never known if Frank and my father weren't in so much danger right now."

"Why did Uncle Frank go to Germany?" Michael asked. "You never really told us why he left."

"My father was distraught at the loss of Carl, who was his son and heir. The department store had been in our family for generations, and we did a lot of good for the local community in Freising. My father was ageing, and he had nobody to leave it to. Frank had witnessed terrible things in the trenches, and he felt guilty for being a part of the reason his grandfather had no heirs to pass his legacy down to. He knew Gerald was more than capable of taking over the reins in England, but Herbert had nobody in Germany, so he decided to make things right and move over there so my father would have someone to hand it down to when the time came."

"After much disagreement, especially with Arnold, Frank left for Germany. At first, my father refused to accept him, so Frank did everything he could to prove he was worthy. He even took up the faith and attended the synagogue with my father. In 1935, when the Nazis introduced those disgraceful Nuremberg Race Laws, Frank knew it was his last chance to save himself, but he remained loyal to the family. He's sacrificing himself to help my father, and that tells you what kind of man he is."

Giselle sobbed hard, and this time, Gerald ran to her side to comfort her.

"We had no idea," Michael said. "What were the letters Uncle Frank sent to you?"

"I'm coming to that," Giselle cried. "Just allow me a moment to compose myself first."

Chapter Seven

Giselle Fernsby, previously known as Giselle Guttmann, took several letters from under her cardigan and spread them out on the coffee table in front of her. After a long pause, she looked around the room at what remained of her family, who stared back at her.

Satisfied that she had their full attention, she sighed and continued with her story.

"As you can see, Frank sent a lot of letters during his time in Freising. It was because of him that my father's attitude towards me thawed, and we even began communicating again. You may remember that I visited them in Germany at the end of 1934, which was an emotional experience, let me tell you."

Gigi took a deep breath and closed her eyes as memories flooded into her mind. Her lips parted in a broad smile as she remembered the heavy emotions when she and her father embraced after so many years apart. It was a moment she would never forget.

"Frank warned me long ago of the dangers they would face should Hitler and his gang of Nazi criminals ever come to power. Few believed him, and I wish I had taken him more seriously. But he was right. He was dead right."

"At first his letters only warned of the dangers, but when Hitler became Chancellor of Germany in January 1933, his letters took on a darker tone. Even then, he wanted my father to sell the store and move to England, where he would be safe."

"Why didn't he?" David asked. "It seems to me as if he had plenty of chances to sell up and leave Germany before it got too bad."

Gigi threw David an icy stare. "Hindsight is a wonderful virtue, and even then, for many Jews, relocation wasn't, and still isn't, possible. Nobody in Europe or anywhere else wants them, and even those with money and privilege like my father would find it difficult if it wasn't for his family contacts."

"But if he had the chance to leave, why didn't he?" Michael asked.

Gigi sighed. "My father is a proud and stubborn man. You never had the chance to get to know him, but underneath his rough exterior, he has a heart of gold. He did so much good for Freising, and until the Nazis spread their poison, he was a much-loved and respected man in the community. He treated the people who worked for him with respect, and he gave them much more than just a job. If anyone needed help, both he and Frank were the first to offer both their time and their money. Nobody, or at least very few, had anything bad to say about either of them. Until Hitler came to power, that is. Then everything changed."

"It's wonderful that he did so much for the town he lived in," David said. "But it doesn't explain why he didn't leave when all the warning signs were there for him to see."

"As I said, my father is a proud and stubborn man. He saw the signs; he must have known. Frank begged him many times to open his eyes and see what was happening all around him. But instead of leaving, my father stayed and used his dwindling fortune to help other Jewish families with their groceries or their heating bills, or even their rent payments. He argued with Nazi officials who had once been his friends on behalf of Jews being thrown out of their apartments, but all was to no avail. They did it anyway. In quieter moments, those same officials warned my father to get out while he could, but he refused."

"I always thought our great-grandfather was a grumpy old man who hated us," Michael said. "I didn't know he was putting himself in such grave danger to help others. He's obviously a lot more of a man than I ever thought he was."

Gigi's eyes clouded over again as she looked at Michael. "Your great-grandfather is a complicated man who is too proud and generous for his own good. He knew the dangers. He must have seen what was coming, but he refused to believe they would ever come for him because of all the good he had done for the town. His only son died for Germany in the first war, and he believed that must count for something. Of course, it didn't, and he underestimated Hitler and the Nazis. Now I fear it may be too late."

"What did Uncle Frank's letters say?" David prompted gently.

"Frank sent many letters over the years, and each time the message became louder and clearer. Either they left or they faced ruin. I begged him to get out while he could, even if my father refused to go with him. I know what a stubborn old fool he could be, and as much as I love him, I didn't want my son to die for him. Frank refused to leave without his grandfather, even though he knew the danger he was putting himself in. I'm so proud and so worried about him. For both of them."

Gigi sank her face into her lap and took a deep breath. Everyone sat still and silent, allowing her to compose herself before continuing. Everyone knew how difficult this was for her because they felt the same way.

"Eventually, Frank's tone changed. He began asking us for help to get him and my father out of there. He said he would drag Herbert by the scruff of his neck if he had to, but they had to leave before it was too late."

"Every time either of them walked down the street, they faced danger. The brownshirts beat anyone suspected of being a Jew just for being outside, and both of them suffered many beatings. They painted the Star of David on the windows of the department store, and brown-shirted thugs stood outside and told the people to shop in Aryan stores. The business was failing, and they both knew it was only a matter of time before the Nazis took it away completely."

"They should have left." Michael spat the words out. "Why didn't you do anything about it, Dad? Why didn't you tell me and David about it? We could have gone over there and dragged the old fool back to England, whether he liked it or not."

"It's not that simple, son," Gerald replied. "Frank would have been fine, but we require permission from the government to get Herbert over here, and that takes time."

Gigi held up her hand. "You're getting ahead of yourself, Gerald. I haven't finished telling them what happened yet."

Gerald nodded his head and fell silent.

"My father might be old, but he's no fool, and he knew what he was doing. He told Frank to get out so many times, but Frank is as stubborn as he is, and that's why I think they get along so well. This isn't all my father's fault, no matter how it may seem to you."

Michael grimaced and shook his head. "I don't understand either of them. Why didn't they get out of there? They could see what was happening, and unlike most, they had the resources to do something about it. Now it seems they are in peril, whereas they could have left."

"That's all true, and Frank's letters to both myself and your father confirm what you just said. But the fact remained that my father refused to believe they would hurt him any more than they already had. Frank, although angry at him, refused to leave without him. So, they stayed."

"What are we going to do about it?" Michael asked. "We can't just sit here talking about it. We need to rescue them."

"Brave words, Michael," his father said. "But we're not welcome there and we're up against an entire population. How do you propose we get them out?"

"Frank sent a final letter before Kristallnacht," Gigi interrupted. "We received it the day after it happened. I want to read it to you, so you know what it's like for the Jews over there. Not just our family, but for hundreds of thousands of others in the same situation."

The room fell silent as Gigi picked up the letter and read it aloud.

"My dearest Mother,

I fear this may be the last letter I ever send to you, and I do not use those words lightly. The situation here is getting worse, and Joseph Goebbels has stepped up the antisemitic rhetoric to deafening levels in recent days.

Men and women who were once close friends now spit on us and refer to us as Jewish vermin. They refuse to shop in our store and our resources are dwindling rapidly.

I fear we are approaching the final window of opportunity if we are to get out of here alive. I have written not only to you and Gerald, but also to the British government for help. The last response I received was some time ago when they told me that as a British citizen, they advise me to leave at once. Unfortunately, they had no place for Herbert, as only children were being allowed into the country without their parents or other adult members of their family.

I am not leaving without Herbert, but I am prepared to drag him screaming and kicking if necessary. He still doesn't see the dangers he faces because he believes the Reich will recognise the losses his family has already taken for the nation. I hate to write this, but Herbert is an old fool whose pride will end up killing us both.

The brown shirts openly attack anyone they suspect is Jewish in the streets, and they beat us to the ground while they laugh and shout obscenities at us. Both Herbert and I have received beatings at their hands, and at his age, I don't know how much more he can take. I know it can't be much.

The department store is a ghost town. The stormtroopers stand outside and refuse entry to the few who try to buy their goods from us. They paint the Star of David on the windows and write slogans like Juden and Jews not welcome underneath it.

I fear the violence is only going to get worse. We are banned from public places such as parks, restaurants, and swimming pools, and we are no longer allowed to own anything electrical, such as radios. We're even banned from owning bicycles or motor vehicles. Our passports have been confiscated, and we are restricted from any foreign travel.

We are in serious trouble, and I am writing to plead for your help. Please, please, get together with Gerald and send *someone who can handle himself over here to help us escape over the border to France.*

From there, we can make our way back to the coast, and if necessary, Gerald can use the contacts he must still have in the shipping business to get us over there. We can hide Herbert until this all blows over, which is going to be easier said than done. I truly believe that Hitler will set Europe ablaze before he is finished, and it is past time that Britain and France stand up to him before it's too late.

Please do not take my words lightly, as we are in grave danger. Please help us, because if you fail, we will most likely die.

That is the seriousness of our situation, and I beg you to use our resources as best you can to get us out of here before it's too late.

Your loving son,

Frank Junior"

Giselle threw the letter on the table and looked around the room.

"We're going to help them get out of there."

Chapter Eight

Early the next morning, a nervous-looking Gerald Fernsby was ushered into a large, ornately decorated office overlooking the River Thames near Lambeth Bridge. The huge mahogany desk took up most of the space in front of the full-length window, and Gerald couldn't help but marvel at the intricate designs woven into the damask silk that decorated the desktop.

A repeating pattern of circular acanthus leaves woven in gold thread against a deep blue background was on full display, no doubt as a reminder to all who entered of the prominence of the owner's family name.

Large portraits of dour-faced men from long ago hung conspicuously on the wall, all staring down at anyone who entered. If Gerald needed a reminder of the power and importance of the man he faced, he was getting it right now, and if the intention was to make him feel insignificant, it was working. Gerald felt like a tadpole swimming towards the jaws of a large heron.

It helped to have friends in such high places, especially at times like this, when you really needed their help.

Except the man behind the desk wasn't Gerald's friend. In fact, he looked distinctly annoyed when Gerald entered the room. The temperature seemed to drop several degrees when the man looked up from his desk, and the disgust as he curled his lips towards the ground told Gerald that he viewed his visitor not as his equal, but as an inferior human being that had no right stepping into his domain.

Gerald swallowed hard, sat in the seat opposite the imposing figure and cleared his throat.

The man was his archenemy, and the one person in the world Gerald most wanted to avoid. He was facing Sir Robert Stourcliffe, the man who had driven down the price of their shipping business during the Great Depression so that Gerald had been forced to almost give it to him just to get it off his hands before it bankrupted the Fernsby family. Not to mention the little incident between their two sons in Cambridge two days prior.

"Sir Robert, it is good to see you again," Gerald lied.

"I presume you are here to apologise for your son's aggression and to make reparations?" Lord Stourcliffe sneered over his gold-rimmed glasses.

Although Gerald could be accused of having a cultured accent, it was nothing compared to the snotty tone of Lord Stourcliffe. Like his son, he sounded as though he spoke from a different century when the aristocracy ruled the country, and everyone else was there solely to serve them. Gerald, like both his sons, hated the Stourcliffes.

"I am here to apologise for Michael's actions, although from what I hear, he didn't know it was your son who owned the dog. He was merely trying to save it from freezing to death when your son appeared out of nowhere. The situation got out of hand, and for that I am sorry."

He wanted to tell Stourcliffe that his son was a heartless

bastard who kicked innocent animals for fun, but he knew that wouldn't help his cause this day. He had to eat humble pie and appear remorseful, which was hard to do when his blood was boiling inside his body.

"The situation got out of hand?" Stourcliffe's pock-marked face, which was pudgy from too many elaborate dinners, turned bright red. "Your delinquent son assaulted Robert and broke his nose. Not to mention that he stole his precious dog. How did you think I was going to react? With pity for your son's plight at the college? Robert can barely breathe, and his doctors are having to stay with him round the clock to make sure he doesn't suffer any seizures from the violent assault."

Gerald had heard enough. "Oh, come now, Robert. He got a thump on the nose. Surely even your family isn't too pompous to accept that this is what boys do when they get into altercations. Young Robert will be perfectly fine, and there is no need for all this drama to play out around him. He's been thumped in the nose, not shot in the head."

"How dare you?" Sir Robert rose to his feet. Tall like his son, Sir Robert had at one time been a star athlete but his once trim body now carried several pounds of excess weight that was no doubt caused by the unbridled privileges he enjoyed as Britain's wealthiest man.

And Britain's most arrogant man, Gerald mused as he watched him throw his juvenile tantrum.

"My son is a fine, upstanding young man who will one day inherit the greatest business empire in the realm. He stands for everything that puts the Great in Britain, and he is suffering at the hands of your no-good boy who will end up a common criminal if he doesn't learn to control himself."

"This isn't getting us anywhere." Gerald took a deep

breath. Although he was angry at Michael for striking the boy, he fully understood how he felt. Right now, at this exact moment, he too struggled to contain himself, and he was supposed to be responsible and restrained. There was nothing more he wanted right now than to smack this arrogant, aristocratic moron in the nose.

The Stourcliffes represented everything that was wrong with the aristocracy, and Gerald had long believed that if they were to survive the twentieth century, they had to adapt and accept that they were no longer untouchable rulers over the masses. Times were changing, and the ruling classes had to change with them, or they would end up going the same way as the dinosaurs.

"I came here to apologise and to offer reparations to your son for Michael's actions."

Robert Stourcliffe sat down and stared at Gerald. "Your son is to be expelled from Trinity. In fact, he is to be expelled from Cambridge in its entirety. I have spoken to the dean at length this morning, and I insisted those were to be his actions and that I would accept nothing less."

Gerald swallowed hard, and clenched his fists out of Stourcliffe's sight.

"That's not all," Stourcliffe continued. "I want a written apology in your son's handwriting, and I want one hundred pounds compensation for stealing the family dog. If I don't get this by next weekend, I shall have no alternative but to call the police and have your boy arrested. And believe me, Fernsby, if that happens, I shall insist on the full punishment the law has to offer."

"I see you are not open to compromise, Sir Robert." *Like there was ever a chance to begin with.* Gerald had expected this kind of attitude, so he shouldn't have been surprised.

He still found himself baring his teeth, and he fought his emotions to regain composure.

"I accept your terms, Sir Robert, although the compensation is a little high for a Labrador, don't you think?"

"If your son wanted one so badly, you could have got him one yourself. He didn't have to steal my son's pedigree dog, who came from the finest stock in Europe."

"Of that, I have no doubt. One hundred pounds it is, and I shall have it to you before next weekend, along with the letter of apology from Michael. As for the expulsion, even though I don't agree with it, and many students only get a warning for committing far more serious offences, I shall not argue with you over it. Naturally, we will appeal the decision when it comes, and I will take it to the highest levels of the university. Michael's future should not be destroyed over one thump on someone's nose, not even one so pampered as your son's."

He knew he shouldn't have said that, but he couldn't help himself. It felt good to see Stourcliffe turn beetroot red again and squirm in his chair.

"Is that all? If so, I shall look out for your correspondence. Good day, Fernsby."

Gerald didn't move. Instead, he looked at his feet and regretted his words of a few moments earlier.

"Well? If we're done, I have things to do."

"There is something else, Sir Robert, and I fear the incident between our sons might have scuppered what I am here to request."

Robert Stourcliffe leant forward over his desk and rested his arms in front of him. "You are here to ask a favour of me? So, you didn't even come here to apologise for your son's delinquent behaviour? You sink lower in my estimation every time I see you, Fernsby."

Gerald bit his tongue so he wouldn't say what he felt towards this pompous arsehole. "The timing is unfortunate, Sir Robert, but rest assured that I came here primarily to atone for Michael's actions. What I have to ask is of great importance to my family and has nothing to do with the incident in Cambridge."

"I'm all ears."

"You must know about the atrocities the Nazis are committing against the Jewish community in Germany." The words fell out of Gerald's mouth in a tumbled rush. He hated grovelling to Stourcliffe, but he knew of nobody else outside of the Royal Navy who had the resources he needed. The navy was out of the question, so Stourcliffe was his only option.

"Ah, now I understand why you are here grovelling to me, and agreed so readily to compensate my overinflated asking price for the dog. I do admit to being a trifle confused as to why you agreed to the hundred pounds so easily. Now I know why."

"Sir Robert, this is a matter of life and death, and believe me, if I had any other options, I would have used them. You know as well as I do that I would never have asked for your help if there was some other way."

"Go on. I'm enjoying this."

It was Gerald's turn to feel his hands and neck turn beetroot red, but he ignored his pride and continued. "My brother, Frank, and my grandfather are stuck in Germany, and after the events of the pogrom they held a few nights ago known as the Night of Broken Glass, I fear for their lives. If I don't help them escape soon, I believe they will perish under the cruelty of the Nazis."

Stourcliffe placed his hands behind his head and leant back in his chair. "Naturally, I know of what you speak, and

I agree it is a terrible thing they are doing. But what has that got to do with me? I run a shipping empire, not a search and rescue operation."

Stourcliffe looked up, realisation dawning over his features. "Wait a moment. Are you asking me to send one of my ships to Germany so your brother and grandfather can escape?"

"Not Germany," Gerald shook his head. "France. I'll get them to one of the channel ports, and from there they will need passage back to England."

"Why not just use the ferries? They travel daily without the need for a clandestine operation using my ships."

"You must have heard that the Jewish people had their passports confiscated by the Nazis? Neither of them possess the required paperwork to travel the conventional route. Believe me, I would have happily done what you suggested if it was possible."

"I see." Stourcliffe looked for a moment like he sympathised with Gerald and might even agree to help.

"However, what you ask of me is out of the question. It would put my ship and its crew at risk. It takes one of my ships away from their normal tasks, and you are asking me to smuggle men into the country illegally. Your brother might be alright doing that, but the other one might be a Nazi spy for all I know. After all, your family is full of Germans, isn't it? I shall play no part in possible espionage against my own country, because, unlike some of us, I am a true patriot. I'm sorry for your plight, Fernsby, but there's not a chance in hell I'm going to help you."

Gerald rose to his feet. "You know what will happen to them if I can't get them out, don't you?" He bit his lip hard and resisted the powerful urge to lean forward and swat Stourcliffe's smug face.

"Sadly, I do. It is the same for hundreds of thousands of other Jews as well, so do you suggest we bring them all over here? Why not save them all, Fernsby? Is that what you want?"

"It is, Sir Robert." Gerald took the high ground and didn't rise to the bait. "If we don't, I'm afraid history will remember us as the generation who stood by and did nothing while the Jews of Europe perished. That will be the legacy of our generation if we do nothing."

"Poppycock. That will not happen, Fernsby, and you know it. Herr Hitler will calm down once he's got what he wants. If you'd managed your family business better, you would still have ships of your own to do your dirty work. Now get out of here, as I have work to do."

Gerald walked towards the door, and when he got there, he turned around to face his nemesis one last time. "What is it that Hitler wants? Do you even care what he's doing over there? You're a disgrace to the upper classes, Stourcliffe. I warn you now, this country is going to war, whether you want it or not. And when it does, I hope you are the first in line to face losing everything."

The doorframe shook as Gerald slammed the door as hard as he could on the way out.

Chapter Nine

Lucy was having the time of her life. For the last hour or more, she'd been racing around the immaculate acre of rear garden chasing Michael, fetching a stick that was now soaked in saliva and felt disgusting.

But Michael didn't care. Running was his way of coping with the stresses of life, and the good Lord knew that the last few days had been the most stressful of his young life so far.

Although it was misty and hovering not much above freezing, Michael's body glistened with sweat. He must have run at least ten laps, and at almost one thousand feet per lap, he'd run almost two miles.

Lucy, on the other hand, must have run about five miles or more, and by the time David appeared outside the French doors above the patio steps, her tongue was hanging from the side of her mouth, and she was panting hard. But she wasn't stopping this game, not until Michael made her.

"Michael," David yelled and waved his arms. "Michael, get over here."

Michael jogged over the manicured lawn towards his

brother, with Lucy jumping around him with the dripping stick in her mouth trying to get his attention.

"Here, it's your turn." He took the stick from Lucy's mouth and threw it at his brother.

"You know where you can shove that." David pulled a face. "Anyway, we don't have time."

"What's going on?" Michael could see the seriousness in David's eyes, and he knew he wasn't just here to complain about Lucy's barking.

"Father has called a family meeting in the sitting room at ten. Everyone has to be there, so get yourself cleaned up and ready."

"What's it about?" Michael asked. "Has he said anything to you?"

David shook his head. "No. I'm just hoping they received word that Uncle Frank and Papa Herbert got out of Germany safely. Take a bath, Michael. I can smell you from here."

An hour later, Michael entered the sitting room. Except for Judith, who was tending to Lucy at the behest of her father, everyone was there waiting for him.

"Good of you to join us," Dorothy said as he sat in the armchair facing his mother and grandmother.

"Sorry, I had to clean up first."

"Now that we are all here, I have a very important announcement to make," said his father solemnly. It was time to get serious.

Gerald cleared his throat and looked around the room. "As you all know, I went to London yesterday for a series of business meetings. I also had two other very important discussions that I didn't tell you about, as they were hastily arranged."

"You met with Stourcliffe," Michael said.

"How did you know that?" his father asked.

"It stands to reason. I'm about to be expelled from Cambridge for a very minor infraction. Others have committed much more serious violations and received nothing more than a warning over their future conduct, but because I smacked the golden spoon, I'm getting the full treatment. It isn't fair."

"Your assessment is fairly accurate," his father concurred . "Lord Stourcliffe insists he wants nothing less than your expulsion, but I told him we would fight it all the way for the very reasons you just mentioned. He also wants a handwritten apology from you, which I told him he would receive. And you will write it, Michael. Today, after this meeting."

Michael scowled. "Fair enough, Father."

"He also wants one hundred pounds compensation for stealing the dog by next week."

"One hundred pounds?" Michael exploded. "I hope you told him where to shove it! That's extortion."

"It is, but I agreed because I had a far more serious request to make of him. One which, I am afraid, he declined rather rudely."

Nobody spoke. All eyes were on Gerald Fernsby as he rubbed his forehead and gazed at the floor.

"I asked him for one of his ships, as I have decided to go to Germany myself to rescue Frank and Herbert. We need one of his ships to transport us back from France, as they had their passports confiscated by the Nazis. I'm afraid he refused my request."

Michael stared at his father. From the corner of his eye, he saw his mother's jaw drop open, and even the emotionally restrained Gigi blinked rapidly.

"The prime minister generously allowed me five

minutes of his time yesterday afternoon. He was sympathetic to our cause, but he wasn't able to help. Any activity by the government, and especially our armed forces, could be deemed an act of aggression towards Germany, and the PM couldn't allow that. I understand his situation, and his answer was nothing less than I expected."

"Gerald," Dorothy said in a high-pitched tone. "You can't go running off to Germany. It's too dangerous, and we don't even know what has happened to Frank and Herbert. They might be on their way here right now for all we know."

Gerald was about to speak when Gigi stopped him. "It's a brave gesture, Gerald, but you know it isn't feasible. Listen to Dorothy for once, because she is right. Going there would be suicide, and then we'd lose you as well as them. Your health isn't that good, and you wouldn't be able to cope if it turned nasty, which it probably would. You have heart problems already, Gerald. It would kill you if you tried such a foolish thing."

Gerald looked at his two adult children. "What do you two think? I know it's folly and out of my league, but I cannot stand by and do nothing while they suffer over there. I have to do something."

"I think you are very brave," said David, the ever-wise voice of reason. "But Gigi and Mum are right. All you'll do is get yourself into who knows how much trouble for no reason. Have you written and asked them to meet you in France? That would be a more sensible option."

"Finally, someone is making sense," Gigi said.

"Of course I did. That was the first thing I did, but I have heard nothing back from them. I am worried they are stuck in Germany. They have no passports, as you know, and Britain, in fact, nowhere, will accept Jewish refugees.

At least we are accepting some children from the Kinder transport, but it's too little and perhaps too late. And none of this helps Herbert."

"You need to be patient, and give them time to respond," Dorothy said. "The mail is slow at the best of times, and God knows these are far from that."

"You all read the newspapers. You know what the stormtroopers did on Kristallnacht. Thousands of Jews were rounded up and carted off to who knows where. They need my help, and either with or without your blessing, I'm going to help them."

"It's a suicide mission," Michael said. "You'd never make it. With all due respect, Father, you aren't in any physical condition to do such a thing. You won't be able to help anyone when you're having a heart attack in a ditch somewhere in Germany, hiding from the Nazis. I don't mean to be rude, but that's the truth."

"I could tell them I'm on a business trip," Gerald said. "That happens all the time. People come and go, and I would have a genuine reason to be in Germany."

"What business would you have in a small town like Freising?" Gigi scoffed. "You have no reason to go there, and with Fernsby as a surname, it wouldn't take the Gestapo more than a moment to connect you to Frank. Then what do you think would happen?"

The atmosphere was tense as silence fell, each lost in their own thoughts. Finally, David broke the silence.

"Can't we pay someone, or even a team of people, to go over there and find them? That makes more sense. Hire someone with military experience who knows how to do these things."

"I thought long and hard about that, and I even put feelers out to see if anyone is interested, but so far, no one has taken up the offer. And before you ask, I am offering a tidy sum for the mission."

Silence fell again.

"All we can do is wait until someone comes forward who is willing and able to go there for us," Dorothy said. "Until then, we must be patient and wait. I will not have you running off on a suicide mission, Gerald."

"Unless I hear from someone in the next week, I am going to Germany. We don't have time to wait, and there are no other options."

Everyone spoke all at once, and Gerald waved his arms to quieten the room. "I am the senior member of this family, and it is my responsibility to make these decisions. Unless I hear from someone willing to do this in my stead, I am going, and that is final. Let's just pray that we either hear from Frank, or someone steps up in the meantime."

Gerald stood up. "This meeting is over."

Dorothy ran after her husband, protesting all the way down the hallway. Michael sat in silence, surveying the pale faces of David and Gigi.

"You two. Meet me in my bedroom in thirty minutes and don't be late." Gigi stood up and left the room without another word.

Chapter Ten

The boys shuffled into Gigi's bedroom and sat in two small chairs facing a four-poster bed in the middle of the room. The large window was open, allowing cool air to enter the room and fill it with a freshness that gave David a sense of hope that all was not yet lost.

The pink, floral wallpaper demonstrated Gigi's love of a well-kept garden, and the empty grey hot water bottle lay at the edge of her bed, waiting to be filled in the evening.

Gigi sat on the edge of her bed and faced her two grand-sons. "We can't allow your father to go to Germany. All he'll do is get all three of them killed."

"We agree, Gigi, but what can we do about it?" Michael asked. "He's already said he's going whether or not we like it."

"You two need to go. You're young, strong, and resourceful. And you will not be alone."

"You want *us* to go?" David leapt from his chair, the hair on the back of his neck standing up as Gigi's words registered in his brain. "That's impossible. We've never been there before, and we wouldn't even know where to look for them. Heck, we don't even know what they look like these days."

"Sit down, David," Gigi said.

Michael stared out of the window. "She's right," he said, his voice hoarse. "Dad will fail, and unless someone else steps up, we're the best bet to rescue them. We speak German, and we're young enough to handle it."

"This is folly," David snarled. "We'll die just as surely as Father would. None of us should even contemplate this. It's madness."

"It's your choice, of course," Gigi said. "But if you don't, you will never see your father again."

"How do we do it?" Michael asked. "We wouldn't know where to start."

"You start by taking a regular ferry to France and making your way to Strasbourg, which is a French town on the border with Germany by the side of the River Rhine."

"You're not seriously thinking about this, are you?" David stared at his brother. "It's suicide. I love my family as much as anyone else, but I have barely seen Uncle Frank in years, and I've never seen Herbert Guttmann. Tell me why I should risk my life for them when they never had the time for us?"

"You're not doing it for them," Gigi reminded him. "You're doing it for me and your father."

"That's not what you were saying in Cambridge," Michael reminded him. "You spoke of how he saved us when we were young and stupid. He needs our help now, David, and we have to stand up to be counted."

"It's madness. I can't do this."

"If you can't do it for them, then do it for me," Michael said. "I can't do this alone, and I need your help. If you refuse, then I'm going anyway. It's up to you, David."

David tensed, his body as rigid as Michael had ever seen. "This is madness."

"On that, we agree." Michael let out a deep breath.

"Does Mother know about this?" David asked, staring at Gigi.

"No, of course not. She would never agree to it. You know how upset she gets, so it's better she knows nothing."

"What about Dad?" David continued. "How do we stop him from going?"

"I've thought about that, and I have an idea," Gigi said.

"It seems you've thought this through, Gigi." David stared at his grandmother. "Have you considered the consequences if we die over there? How will you explain that to our mother and father?"

It was Gigi's turn to draw a deep breath. She got up from the bed and walked over to her eldest grandson. Grabbing his arms, she drew him towards her.

"Both of you mean as much to me as any person ever has. If I could find any other way, believe me, I would use it. Gerald isn't the only one who has been looking for someone to do this for us, but even hardened ex-soldiers won't attempt it. There is nobody out there willing to go, and if I do nothing, then Gerald will surely die. At least you two have a fighting chance. In any case, you haven't heard my plan yet."

"Former soldiers won't do it because they know it's suicide," David said. "Gigi, I love you, and I am sorry for Frank and Herbert, but I'm not risking my life and that of my brother for them. I won't do it."

"Hear me out," Gigi said. "My plan is to stop Gerald from going to Germany, not to have you two boys killed."

"What do you mean?" David calmed down a little and stepped back from Gigi's grip.

"As I said, I have a plan. Sit down and listen."

The boys did as they were told.

For the next thirty minutes, David and Michael listened as Gigi outlined her plan to save both Gerald's and their lives, while at the same time discovering what had happened to Frank and Herbert.

When she finished, she stood up and looked at the boys, who stared back at her with renewed respect. "Well, what do you think? Do you think it will work?"

"You've certainly thought this through, haven't you?" Michael said. "I think it will work as long as we're careful and don't deviate from your plan."

Gigi and Michael looked at David, who sat there staring into space.

"I can't do it without you." Michael gently prompted his brother.

"You left out some important details," David said, his fingers pinching his lower lip as he sat deep in thought.

"Like what?" Michael asked. "I thought she explained it very well. We get in and out rapidly without raising any suspicions. It's simple, and yet it's brilliant."

"Yes, except for the fact that we still have to stop our father from going to Germany. Then what happens if we find them? How do we get Frank and Herbert over the border into France? And then, how do we get them into England without a passport? Frank should be okay, seeing as he's English, but they won't allow Herbert into the country. They'll send him back to a very precarious future. And that isn't all. How do you propose we pay for all of this? It's going to cost a fortune. Not to mention the logistics of getting around a big country like Germany. It's a brilliant plan, Gigi, but it needs a lot more work if we're going to be successful."

"Good old David," Michael said. "Ever the wise old owl."

"I'm just being practical. If we're going to pull this off, we have to be fully prepared. Gigi's plans tell me we're not."

"We just need time to fill in the blanks," Michael offered.

"We don't have the time," Gigi said. "That's the problem. Your father will leave in a week, so whatever you decide to do, it has to be done within that timeframe. We have a week to finalise our plans."

"A week isn't long enough," David complained. "Not for something as complicated and delicate as this. At the end of the day, it's our lives that are on the line, so we can't skimp over the plans and leave it all to chance."

"I agree," Michael said. "So, we'd better get busy."

"I'm expected back at Trinity on Thursday morning," David said. "You're not, so you can stay here, but I have to leave tomorrow to get back in time."

"Leave that to me," Gigi said. "I'll send them a telegram stating that because of a family emergency, you are remaining in Kent for a few weeks. They'll accept that, I think. It will also stop Dorothy from asking where you are every ten minutes. If she thinks you are both in Cambridge, it will give us at least a week or more before she gets worried."

"And you're okay with that?" David responded. "You're okay with lying to our mother? What do we say to her when she finds out?"

"You'll be long gone by the time she finds out where you are, so don't worry about that. I'll deal with your mother when the time comes."

"I'm barred from Cambridge, so how do we explain my absence?" Michael asked.

"You are going back to collect your belongings and to say goodbye," Gigi answered.

"How are we paying for it?" Michael changed the subject. "This is going to cost hundreds of pounds. I mean, how much will it cost us to get the false papers? How do you even know this man?"

"It's a long story, but there are some things your father never told you about what he did in the Great War. Did you know he worked for British intelligence and specialised in working with the French to get captured soldiers out of enemy hands and back into Britain? He developed a lot of contacts in those days, contacts he still has. I know, because I found them and gave them to Frank a long time ago, in case he ever needed them. The man I told you about agreed to help, should we ever need it."

"You never fail to surprise me, Gigi," David said. "I suppose you've already resolved many of the questions I had?"

"I have," Gigi smiled at her grandson. "I have an envelope with more than enough to cover whatever you need. It has French francs, German marks, and of course English pounds. There are even Dutch guilders and Belgian francs if you need them. There is more than enough to cover any situation you might come across."

David sighed and cast a long look at Gigi. "I'm not happy at lying to Mother like this. And you still haven't told us how we stop our father from going next week."

Gigi smiled. "Leave that to me. Gerald is about to get a bad dose of food poisoning."

Chapter Eleven

E xactly one week later, the Fernsby family sat around the dinner table, deep in conversation about Gerald's plans for the following morning. David had secured an extra week's leave of absence from Cambridge because of an unforeseen family emergency, and these were his final moments before taking the evening train so he could attend class in the morning. Michael was going with him, but only for a few days while he collected his belongings and said his goodbyes.

Around the dinner table, David, Michael, and Gigi exchanged troubled glances as Gerald told them his final wishes. Dorothy just stared at her husband as though he was stark raving mad.

"I don't expect I'll be coming back from this, so please don't mourn me. All this is a bit morbid, but I've left the relevant documents with the solicitors to hand over control of the company to Dorothy, who will then hand it down to David once he's graduated from Cambridge."

"That's a bit dramatic, don't you think?" David asked. "Nothing is going to happen to you, Father. By the time you

74

get to France, this whole thing will be over. Uncle Frank and Papa Herbert will be at Calais waiting for you, just you see."

"I'd like that very much, but we all know it won't happen. No, I'm going to Germany whether I want to or not, Hitler be damned."

"There's still time to stop this nonsense," Dorothy cut in.

Gerald held up his hand to end the conversation. "I'm going and that's the end of it. Everything is arranged, and I have sent letters to my contacts in France. They'll be expecting me in the next couple of days, and from there I'll travel to Germany. Hopefully, I'll be in and out before the Nazis realise I've been there."

Gigi shook her head. "Don't underestimate the Gestapo or it will be your undoing. They are ruthless, and they don't miss a thing." She looked long and hard at David and Michael.

Michael's muscles tensed and a chill ran down his spine. The hairs on his arms rose, and a tingling sensation coursed through his body in waves of pulsating light. He took a deep breath to compose himself.

The clatter of cutlery on the plates was the only sound in the room, and the atmosphere was so heavy that Michael thought he could touch it. Each family member pushed their food around their plates, unable to eat, and he could see the tension in their shoulders and the lines on their faces.

Rumours were flying around that the government was about to introduce food rationing again, as they had during the Great War. Even King George and Queen Mary had a ration book in those days, and dinner tables all over Britain were full of stories about how they would cope should it happen again. Nobody wanted rationing to come back, but if the dark cloud hanging over Europe didn't lift, there was little doubt that it would return.

The same dark cloud seemed to take a chokehold over the Fernsbys' dining room that evening. Especially Gerald, who was sullen and not as enthusiastic about his dinner as he normally was. Michael smiled to himself as he remembered the jokes he and his siblings had made at their father's expense regarding his healthy eating habits.

But not tonight. Like everyone else, Gerald picked at his food and barely ate anything. Gigi and the boys exchanged worried glances, but as she had told the boys, if all else failed, she had hidden Gerald's passport so well that he'd never find it.

Gerald fiddled with his shirt and loosened his tie. He pulled at his collar, sweat beading on his forehead. Dorothy dropped her silverware and jumped to her feet. "Are you alright, Gerald?"

"I'm fine." Gerald's face turned a shade of grey. "It must be the stress of what I'm about to do."

Without warning, he leapt from his seat, knocking his glass of wine all over the table. He ran for the door but didn't make it. He stopped mid-stride and doubled over as if reaching for the floor.

He retched a couple of times, and then violently threw up all over the highly polished wood floor. He fell to his knees, clutching his stomach before hurling again.

Dorothy reached him first, with Judith not far behind. Gigi, still at the dinner table, closed her eyes tightly for a moment and then looked at her two grandsons, who hadn't moved from their seats. She nodded towards them and gave them a thumbs-up sign before turning to aid her stricken son.

Michael swallowed hard. *This is it. This is really happening. We must be stark raving mad.*

He glanced at David, who was rocking in his chair ever so slightly. He had a faraway look on his face, and Michael knew exactly how he was feeling because he was feeling it too.

He rose from his chair and nodded at his brother. Silently and unnoticed, they slid out of the room and ran up the stairs to Gigi's bedroom. They grabbed the two backpacks that were hidden at the rear of her oversized oak wardrobe and ran silently down the stairs and out of the front door.

Michael stopped and looked back at the grand old house one last time. Memories of his childhood flashed before his eyes, both here in Sandwich, and in the happy times they had spent in London.

He swallowed hard as he fought back the tears that dampened his cheeks. An overwhelming appreciation of his family and everything they stood for swamped his mind, and for a moment he stood rooted to the spot, unable to move. All at once everything became clear, and the reasons he and David were doing what they were doing stared back at him from the empty doorway of the grand house.

Filled with renewed purpose and with an energy he didn't know he possessed, Michael grabbed David's arm and steered him towards the open rear door of the taxicab that was waiting for them.

As the lights of their comfortable home on New Street faded, Michael sat back and closed his eyes. Whatever happened from now on, he knew their lives would never be the same. It was time to grow up and do his duty for his family.

Chapter Twelve

Arbeit Macht Frei.

Work sets you free.

The words would forever be etched into Frank Fernsby's mind, and the nightmares would live on long after the generation of prisoners that lived and worked in Dachau were gone. Of this, Frank was sure.

Those were the words over the iron gate at the entrance to the place Frank and Herbert now found themselves.

Although the stormtroopers hadn't told the truckload of prisoners they'd picked up along the way, Frank knew where they were because he'd overheard a stormtrooper telling his comrades where the truck was going.

Dachau. The first concentration camp built on the orders of SS Reichsführer Heinrich Himmler, the leader of the feared Schutzstaffel, or the SS, as they were better known.

He had been in this area with Gerda in happier times before the Nazis clamped their iron grip around what was once a picturesque paradise.

About forty kilometres from Freising, Dachau was an

old medieval town that was dominated by the ancient Dachau Palace which was first built around the year 1100. Sitting on top of a hill close to the River Amper, the palace had once been the home of Bavaria's rulers. Frank and Gerda had visited several times to enjoy picnics in the manicured gardens that overlooked the peaceful town at the bottom of the hill.

Gerda! Frank's thoughts turned momentarily to the beautiful, intelligent woman who had stolen his heart. *I hope she's somewhere far away from here, where she is safe from the evil that has taken hold of a once beautiful country.*

Images of them picnicking together in the shade of a tree by the River Amper during the previous summer not far from where he now stood brought calm to his raging heart. He had wanted to ask her to marry him that day, but the race laws known as the Nuremberg Laws had banned German citizens from marrying Jews, so they couldn't marry even if she'd said yes.

A screaming SS guard forced Frank from his thoughts as they opened the gates to the hell that was waiting for them inside.

He grabbed the arm of Herbert Guttmann and glanced at him as he stumbled and struggled to keep up. All remnants of the once-proud businessman were gone, beaten out of him by the hatred behind every kick and punch delivered by the SA stormtroopers outside the department store.

Frank knew he'd never forget the pained stare as Herbert watched his precious store being systematically destroyed by young men who had once been the sons of friends and loyal customers. Men, who at one time or another had come to Herbert for help, which he'd gladly given.

Frank gripped his arm and lowered his gaze. The look

on Herbert's face was too painful to witness. In truth, Herbert's face itself was too hard for him to look at. They had all taken a good beating before being thrown into the back of the truck, and Frank knew he must look just like every other one of the miserable souls he was marching alongside.

But Herbert was different. He loved this old man and would do anything for him. He should have saved him from this evil, and he berated himself for the millionth time for not forcing Herbert to leave Germany with him.

Now it was too late, and the sight of his battered face made his heart ache. Dried blood caked the side of his head, and large lumps had formed around his eyes from the stormtrooper's boots. At least he'd somehow recovered his glasses that now sat tightly over his bruised face.

As the truckload of men, all Jews as far as Frank could tell, marched through the gates, he wondered if he would ever taste freedom again. For some reason, the thought of his last letter reaching his mother and brother in England bothered him much more than it should have. There was nothing they could do about it now. It was too late for Frank and Herbert.

The iron gates swung shut behind them.

Chapter Thirteen

The newly arrived prisoners had already had their photographs taken and been assigned a number in a building just inside the main entrance to the concentration camp. Now, as the iron gates clanged shut behind them, Frank's body quivered as a sense of hopelessness gripped his soul. The atmosphere, already dark and heavy from the night's events, fell even darker.

"Welcome to hell," one of his fellow prisoners shouted out close by. He wasn't wrong.

The SS guards screamed and yelled as they herded them into a large room close to the iron gates. As the SS barked order after order at them, Frank watched as a group of forlorn-looking men dressed in shabby clothes stood behind a series of tables in front of them. Each man had a strange triangular patch sewn onto his uniform, and some had more than one. Every one of them had a number sewn onto the front of their uniform.

Frank quickly realised that these were not guards at all. They were prisoners, just like he was.

As they all gathered in front of the tables, the SS guards

yelled at them. "Take off all your clothes and hand over your possessions to the men at the table. Hurry, because we haven't got all night. And when we say that all your possessions are to be turned over, we mean everything. Anyone found hiding something will be severely punished. Now get a move on."

Frank had no doubt that severe punishment would follow if their orders were not carried out to the letter. He'd heard about the SS – everybody had – but this was the first time he'd had any interaction with them. Whatever else they were, Frank could sense a feeling of inhumanity the likes of which he'd never believed was possible.

"Hurry up, I said." The guard who seemed to be in charge struck one prisoner with his heavy stick, and the screams from the injured man sent Frank's body into involuntary convulsions. He looked over at Herbert, who was just staring back at him as though he was living in a nightmare.

He was.

The group of men stood naked in the room as one of the working prisoners collected their clothes. One by one, they handed over their meagre possessions to the men behind the desks who listed everything they had. Which wasn't much.

The SS ushered them into another room they called the prisoner baths. It was here that whatever dignity any of the men had left was stripped away, and Frank came to the realisation that at this moment, he'd stopped being a person. From now on, blind obedience was the only thing that mattered.

Blind obedience and survival.

Frank sat as they shaved his head. Then, with the SS guards screaming and haranguing them, they were disinfected and forced to take a shower.

All the while, Frank made sure he was close to Herbert, who swayed from side to side in the shower as though he was about to collapse. At eighty-nine years old, this was too much for him, and Frank knew it. The loss of dignity for this prideful, upstanding man must be crushing him, and Frank could taste the salt from the tears as they flowed down his face.

After the shower, he was given an ill-fitting jacket, a pair of pants, and a blue and white striped cap. The last piece of clothing was a pair of wooden shoes with a piece of linen on the uppers, which were several sizes too small.

The next thing he knew, the working prisoner handed over a piece of cloth with a five-figure number written on it, which Frank assumed was his prisoner number. Then he was handed two triangles, one yellow and the other one black.

"Get over there and sew the patches onto your uniforms. The triangles are to be sewn into opposites, so they form the star of David," the SS guard yelled. "Yellow on the bottom and the coloured one on top. Get a move on!"

The unfortunate men nearest the guard received several blows with his heavy stick, and everyone else was prodded and shoved in the direction the SS wanted them to go.

"The triangles classify what you are, which is vermin," the guard screamed. "The yellow is the Juden symbol, and the coloured one is the prisoner classification. Black means you're an antisocial Jew. If it's green, you're a criminal, and if it's pink, you're homosexual. Most of you here are antisocial, and every one of you is nothing. Nothing!" The guard repeated the word, screaming at the top of his lungs. "You are all worthless. Now get moving."

The men were ushered outside through what looked like some sort of parade ground.

"This is where you will gather every morning for roll call," the guard yelled. "Every one of you will be counted, and you'd better be here, or you'll regret it for the rest of your miserable lives."

Frank kept close to Herbert as they were roughly shoved into one of the blocks, which was to be their home from now on. The block Frank and Herbert were pushed into had two rows of bunks running the length of the building, or at least to the wall at the far end. Frank didn't know what was behind it. Each row of bunks had two rows, one on top of the other. Straw sacks were all they had for a bed.

The block was already crowded, with several men sharing a single bunk. Frank found an empty one at floor level and pushed Herbert onto it before someone else beat them to it. He joined Herbert, and together they sat and stared into space for a long moment, each contemplating what their lives had spiralled into.

Tears ran down Herbert's face as he looked up at Frank. "I'm sorry," he muttered. "I'm so sorry, Frank."

Frank placed his arm around his grandfather's shoulders. "There's nothing to be sorry for, Herbert. Nobody could have imagined the Nazis would ever do something like this to us. Whatever happens, we stay together, and together we will get through this. I'm sure it will be over before we know it and we can get back to what's left of our lives."

"There's nothing left," Herbert said. "I watched them destroy everything we had. It's over, Frank. Our lives are over."

"The store may be gone," Frank asserted. "But we're still here, and as long as we're drawing breath, we'll keep fighting. We'll survive this, and when it's over, we'll rebuild our lives and start again. We cannot allow the Nazis to win. Do you hear me?"

Herbert nodded, but Frank didn't think he was listening.

"Roll call is at first light," a voice Frank hadn't heard before yelled. "I suggest you get some sleep because you're going to need it."

Frank lay back on the bed and closed his eyes. His thoughts drifted back to London and the tranquil life he'd had after the Great War. He didn't regret moving to Germany to help his grandfather, but he felt pangs of jealousy as he thought of his brother, Gerald, tucked up safely tonight in his bed in England.

He hoped the last letter he'd sent had had some effect, and he wondered if pressure from the British government would help get them out of Germany.

Somehow, he doubted it.

Chapter Fourteen

The train pulled into London's Victoria Station with minutes to spare. Michael and David sprinted flat out towards platform two and their journey to France.

"Whoa, not so fast, young men." A man in his forties, wearing a smartly pressed uniform, held up his hand to block the boys from boarding the train. "This is the first-class section of the Night Ferry to Paris. Are you sure this is the train you want to take?"

With their chests heaving, the boys pulled out the tickets Gigi had bought for them and showed them to the guard. First-class tickets in a shared two-person sleeper on the Night Train from London Victoria, at a cost of eight pounds per person. Gigi had pulled out all the stops to make sure they reached their destination safely and well rested.

Michael's eyes had shot up in surprise when he'd first seen the price of the tickets on the packed train to London from Sandwich. He didn't dare say anything for fear of upsetting any of the other passengers, but it was clear that Gigi wanted to get the boys to France quickly.

David and Michael were well aware from the staff wages in their father's brewery business that the average wage in 1938 was around ten pounds per month. These tickets had cost almost a month's wages for most people, and the irony wasn't lost on either of them. Such was the power and the benefit of being part of the wealthy classes of peacetime Britain.

"All seems correct, young sirs. We will perform an onboard customs check momentarily, so make sure you have your passports handy. I wish you both a pleasant journey."

The boys retrieved their tickets and ran onto the train. They found the first-class sleeper cabin and had barely sat down when a knock on the door disturbed them.

"Customs check, please."

David opened the door and allowed the customs officer into the small, but well-appointed cabin. The boys handed over their documents and waited while the officer checked them against the train's manifest.

Eventually, the officer looked up and smiled at the two occupants. "Thank you, sirs, and have a pleasant journey to Paris." He backed out of the carriage and closed the door behind him.

As the train pulled out of the station, Michael sat back and took in the luxurious details of the cabin: thick, sumptuous curtains that blocked out the light, intricately carved wood panels that lined the walls, and plush pillows that would cradle his head when he lay down to sleep.

David slumped back into the comfortable seat and exhaled deeply. "Well brother, you got me into this and now we're here. I must admit it's all rather exciting, and now I'm here, I wouldn't miss it for the world."

"That's exactly how I feel too, and there is no one I'd rather be here with than you. I fear we will need each other before this journey ends, no matter if we find them or not."

The boys fell silent as the Night Ferry began steaming its way out of London towards Dover and the south coast. The first-class passengers would remain in their cabins as they loaded their carriages onto the ship that would take them over the English Channel to Dunkirk. From there, the train would travel nonstop to the Paris Gare du Nord station and its final destination.

It was exactly nine pm.

They would be in Paris at nine the following morning.

Chapter Fifteen

G erald Fernsby had a rough night. He'd vomited almost constantly for hours, and after that, he'd endured painful stomach cramps and dry heaving.

The following morning, Dorothy summoned the family doctor, Doctor Newsome, and as soon as he arrived, Gigi intercepted him at the doorway before anyone else knew he was there.

"Before you see him, there is something you need to know." Gigi spoke softly and scanned the foyer to make sure Dorothy wasn't within earshot.

Doctor Newsome raised his eyebrows and waited for her explanation.

"Gerald is suffering from a bout of food poisoning." Gigi looked up the stairs towards the floor where Gerald lay stricken. "I, erm, I might have given him something to save him from himself."

"What are you talking about, Giselle?" The doctor's eyebrows furrowed. "What did you give him? Why?"

"Gerald was about to leave on a foolhardy journey to Germany to try to rescue his brother and grandfather from the Nazis. It would have been suicide, and I couldn't allow him to throw his life away like that, so I, well, I stopped him from going."

"How? What did you give him?"

"I bought some Dover's powder from a local supplier." Gigi looked at the ground, refusing to make eye contact with Doctor Newsome. "I only used a small amount in his gravy. All I wanted to do was to make him ill enough so he wouldn't leave last night. I certainly didn't intend to kill my son, Doctor."

"You gave him Dover's powder?" Doctor Newsome's gaze pierced Gigi with the intensity of an eagle zeroing in on its quarry.

"I did," Gigi replied. "I thought a little stomach ache was better than being killed by the Nazis."

"Who else knows about this? Does Dorothy know what you did?"

Gigi snorted. "Of course not. You know how she overreacts to everything. She'd be hysterical if she knew I'd poisoned her husband, and she'd be even worse if she knew her sons were on their way to Bavaria in his place."

"Her sons are in Bavaria, and Dorothy doesn't know?" Doctor Newsome's mouth hung open after he spoke. "Words fail me, Giselle. This is outrageous and beyond my mandate, but if anything happens to either of them, you do realise that neither Dorothy nor Gerald will ever forgive you for not telling them?"

Gigi nodded. "I'm fully aware of the consequences, Doctor."

"My concern is Gerald, and if you gave him Dover's powder, then at the very least you would have certainly given him a nasty stomachache. As long as you didn't give him too much, he should be okay. Dover's powder is normally made into a syrup and given to induce vomiting after the patient has accidentally taken some kind of poison. It's pretty violent, and it appears as if it had the desired effect." Doctor Newsome stared at Gigi, making her feel even more guilty than she already did.

"I'm sorry, Doctor," she said. "I didn't think it would be as bad as it has been, or I'd have given him something else."

The doctor grimaced and stared at Gigi. "I won't tell Gerald what you've done. I'd be more worried about Dorothy's reaction when she finds out what you've done."

Gigi sighed. "Thank you, Doctor. I'll deal with Dorothy when the time comes. I'd rather face her wrath than have to stand beside her while they bury my son."

"That's all on you, Giselle, but now let me see my patient."

Gigi led the way to the bedroom where Gerald lay moaning and looking extremely green and sickly. Dorothy's hand trembled as she wiped his forehead with a damp cloth, her eyes glistening with unshed tears. Now and then, a soft sob escaped her lips, betraying the despair that gripped her heart.

Although she normally kept her feelings to herself, Gigi couldn't help but admire Dorothy for the love she so obviously had for Gerald. It was the same love she and Frank Senior had enjoyed, albeit only for a short time.

Gigi liked Dorothy more than she'd ever let on, and a better daughter-in-law she couldn't have wished for, but at times such as these, she was weak and unreliable. She wouldn't be able to make the hard choices that needed to be made, so although she pitied her, Giselle knew she had to take the lead and deal with the consequences later. She took a chair at the side of the bed and waited patiently for the doctor's verdict.

After a thorough examination, Doctor Newsome sat in a chair next to the bed and gave Gerald a concerned look.

"What's wrong with me, Doctor?" Gerald croaked.

Dorothy flinched when he spoke. Her face paled, and tears streamed down her cheeks. Gigi closed her eyes. Now wasn't the time to allow emotions to get in the way. Her family was in danger of being destroyed, and as the matriarch, she took it upon herself to act. Even if the guilt ate away at her like cancer.

"I'm afraid you've picked up a nasty stomach bug from somewhere. Tell me, Gerald, have you travelled anywhere outside your home during the last few days?"

Gerald looked at the doctor. Dorothy turned as well, and the anguish in her eyes broke Gigi's heart. It was all she could do to keep from blurting out what she'd done, such was the guilt she felt at hurting two of the people she loved most in the world.

When Dorothy looked at Gigi, she tried to hide how she was feeling. Over the years, she had become an expert at masking her emotions, so this was one act that she found easier than she perhaps should have done. Her face gave nothing away, or at least nothing that would indicate to Gerald or Dorothy that it was she who had inflicted this misery on them.

"I went to London for some business meetings." Gerald's throat must have been dry and sore because he sounded as though he'd been gargling with sand.

"Who did you meet with?" the doctor pressed.

"I met with that scoundrel Stourcliffe, that's who I met with." Gerald lurched forward, heaving violently into the bedpan beside him.

Dorothy's eyes closed each time her husband retched,

and Gigi stopped herself from reaching out to comfort her. Somehow, it didn't feel right.

Dorothy glanced at her, and she stared back as dispassionately as she could, as if her stern looks were trying to convey that it was better for Gerald to suffer from stomach cramps and sickness than it was to face the cold steel of a Nazi gun pointed at the back of his head.

"Was Stourcliffe the only person you saw that day?" the doctor asked, breaking the tension to Gigi's relief.

Gerald shook his head. "No, Doctor, I met with the prime minister. You must send word to make sure he is not suffering." He struggled to sit up, but Dorothy calmed him down.

"I'll get word to Neville," Dorothy said. "Don't worry, darling. I'm sure he's okay."

"We'll ask about the PM's health," the Doctor said. "Was there anyone else you met with?"

"No. That was it."

"There's nothing to worry about then, Gerald. You need to rest, and in a week or so, you'll be as fit as a fiddle."

"A week or so?" Gerald choked on his words. "You don't understand, Doctor. I have urgent business to attend to in Europe that cannot wait. I must leave immediately."

"That's out of the question, I'm afraid." The doctor was playing along skilfully. "You wouldn't get as far as the coast without being confined to a hospital. You're suffering from a nasty infection, and you are dehydrated. The only thing you can do is rest and wait for it to run its course, which, as I said, will be a week or more. If you try to go anywhere before that, you will be too weak and you will end up seriously ill and far away from home."

The doctor looked long and hard into Gerald's eyes. "I'm sorry, Gerald, but for the sake of your health, I must insist that you do as I ask and remain here until you're better."

Gerald groaned. "But you don't understand. My brother's life is in danger. I have to go."

The doctor looked at Dorothy and Gigi before turning his gaze back to his patient. "You won't be any good to your brother if you are stuck in a hospital somewhere in France. As dire as the situation must be, you must remain here until you are back to full strength, for I fear for both your lives if you try to leave sooner."

Gerald moaned and heaved into the bedpan. His eyes met with Dorothy's, and Giselle could see the anguish in his eyes. He must be feeling utterly miserable, and yet all he could think about was his brother and grandfather in Germany. She wanted to reach out and tell him that everything was going to be alright, but, of course, that would ruin everything. Instead, she remained still and appeared unmoved.

The love she felt for her son burned as brightly at that moment as it had the day she'd given birth to him, and she wiped the tears as they formed in her eyes.

The doctor made his exit with a promise to check on him the following day, and leaving Dorothy fussing over him, he gestured for Gigi to follow him out of the door.

"How much did you give him? And don't lie, for if you gave too much, his life could be in danger. He looks as sick as anyone I've seen in a long time, and if he doesn't improve by the morning, I shall have no choice other than to call for an ambulance and have him transported to the hospital. You don't need me to tell you the consequences should that happen, but my priority must be his health and well-being."

"I understand," Gigi said. "And if you feel he needs to go to the hospital, then, by all means, send him there. I'd rather deal with the consequences than with the undertaker."

"Harsh, but true. I'll be back tomorrow morning to check on him, and for all your sakes, I hope he's feeling a lot better."

Gigi felt the blood drain from her face as the doctor walked out of the house. "Please tell me I did the right thing," she pleaded, staring at the ceiling in the hope of receiving some divine intervention.

Chapter Sixteen

I t was just after noon when the boys stepped off the steam train that had taken them from Paris to Strasbourg. The closer they'd got to their destination, the more restless Michael's legs had become. By the time they'd pulled into Strasbourg railway station, his legs seemed to have a mind of their own, and Michael could not keep them still no matter how hard he tried.

He was glad to get off the train so he could walk and try to rid himself of this strange, irrational feeling that had taken control of his body. He knew he was anxious, but he'd never felt like this before. Michael felt physically sick, and his palms were slippery and wet.

Every instinct was telling him to get back on the train and go home, but the love of his family and his respect for his father and grandmother overrode any fears he was harbouring. He was going to see this through, no matter what his body was telling him.

His thoughts raced as he paced up and down the platform. *What if they were caught? What if they couldn't find the man they were looking for?* He felt like he was teetering on the edge of a precipice, and one wrong move could send him tumbling into the hands of the Gestapo.

"Well, we're here." David's voice sounded a little shaky. "There's no turning back now."

David pulled Gigi's handwritten note containing the contact details of the man they were supposed to seek out in the suburbs of Strasbourg from his backpack.

Following Gigi's directions, the boys took a tram to Hoenheim, and once they got there, they made their way on foot to their final destination: the home of a man they knew nothing about other than his name, and the fact that he'd worked alongside their father for the Allied Intelligence Services during the Great War.

Not much, Michael mused as they followed the rough, basic map Gigi had drawn for them. The mighty River Rhine stretched out as far as the eye could see to their right, and Michael felt the jitters as he realised how close he was to whatever awaited him on the other side.

"We're completely unprepared for something like this," he complained to David. "Mother is right, it's a suicide mission. We're never going to get over there without being stopped and searched. This is stupid, David, and we should turn back now while we still can."

"Don't think the same thought hasn't crossed my mind a thousand times," David replied. "We don't have to do this, Michael. I know we promised Gigi that we'd try our best, but we're woefully inadequate for this kind of job, and all we're going to do is get ourselves killed."

The boys stopped outside what appeared to be the town hall and sat on a wall. "Listen," David said. "I don't want to disappoint Gigi or our father, but we're going to get ourselves killed if we do this. I'm no coward, and I only agreed to come so you wouldn't do it alone. But let's get real,

Michael. We're not trained for this. Let's go home while we can and just tell them the truth, which is that we need trained men for this job, not two university students who are completely out of their depth."

Michael sat silently for a long moment. When he replied, he placed his hand on David's shoulder and looked at him beseechingly.

"It's our family out there that needs our help. Desperately, if what we read in the newspapers is to be believed. Nobody is going to help them, not even soldiers for hire or the British government."

He squeezed David's shoulder and took a deep breath.

"I know it's scary. I'm terrified, and I don't mind admitting it. But we're all Frank and Herbert have, even if we aren't worthy or even capable of pulling it off. We promised Gigi, and if we go back now, Father will be on the next Night Ferry over here. We have to do it for our family, both in England and in Germany."

"But you just said we should turn around and go home," David reminded him. "Make your mind up."

"I know I did, and I still think we're stupid for even trying, but it was a momentary lack of confidence. As much as I want to stop, we can't. We both know what would happen if we went home. We have to press on."

"You're right, brother." David hopped off the wall and stretched his limbs. "But that doesn't mean I want to do it. I'm terrified, Michael. I'm terrified that we will fail."

"Me too."

The two boys locked hands and took a deep breath. "In for a penny, in for a pound, as the saying goes," David muttered. "Let's do this."

The boys followed Gigi's map down the Rues des Vosges and turned left onto the Rue de Cheminots.

Michael's hands and legs trembled as they got nearer, and try as he may, he couldn't control the shaking and the light-headedness that accompanied it.

For God's sake, man. Snap out of it. He shook his body to regain control of himself, but after several attempts, he gave up. If this is what fear felt like, then he was gripped by it.

They turned right onto Rue de Fleurs, which was a short street that ended in a cul-de-sac. The house they were looking for sat at the end of the street on the right-hand side; the last house before the cul-de-sac.

The white-painted house with orange-coloured roof tiles took Michael by surprise. He didn't know why, but he was expecting to see a dilapidated old house in a poor state of repair. Instead, he was confronted with a freshly painted house that looked immaculate.

A white fence protected the small garden, standing about four feet high. Behind the fence, a neatly trimmed row of bushes hid the small yard from passers-by. The house itself was two storeys, with two windows downstairs and one upstairs that faced the street.

All in all, the house sat in a quiet suburb, in a well-maintained area that radiated peace and tranquillity. There was nothing to suggest that a former French intelligence officer lived there. Michael frowned, angry at himself for getting the entire vibe of the house wrong.

David stepped forward, and after hesitating for a moment, knocked loudly on the orange-painted front door.

Chapter Seventeen

The door creaked open, and a middle-aged man of average height and build stood before them. What wasn't average was the fact that his shirt was undone to his chest, and with his sleeves rolled up, the man looked in tremendous physical shape.

His muscular body was lean and hardened, and Michael immediately saw that he took great care of himself. Once again, he'd got his assumptions completely wrong. For reasons unknown, he'd assumed the man would be old and flabby and would wear clothes that were ill-fitting and well worn.

The reality was the complete opposite. This man was well dressed, and although ageing, his combed-back dark hair still lacked the grey streaks that most people his age possessed. His dark, narrow eyes scanned and surveyed the two boys standing in front of him in a way that Michael imagined a lion weighed up its prey before attacking.

Whatever he'd been expecting, this man and his surroundings were not it. He even wondered if they'd somehow come to the wrong place.

"We're looking for Edouard Abreo," David said in English, breaking the awkward silence. "We're sorry, but we don't speak French, although we do speak German if that helps?"

The man stared past the boys as if he hadn't heard them. "What are your names?" he asked in English with a distinct French accent.

"David and Michael Fernsby."

"I have been expecting you. Come in."

The man stepped aside and watched the street while David and Michael made their way inside the small but well-kept house.

The man ushered them into the first room on the left as they entered the small foyer. It looked to Michael like an office, with a tightly packed bookcase on the wall to the right of the door. A small desk with a chair sat opposite, and other than two chairs conveniently located on the other side of the desk, a pair of dark-coloured curtains were the only other things in the small room.

The man sat upright in his chair and beckoned the boys to sit down.

"Are you Eduard Abreo?" David asked once they were all seated.

"The one and only." He reached forward and shook both their hands.

An awkward silence filled the room. Michael didn't know what to say or where to look, so he stared at the ageing former wartime intelligence officer and waited for him to start the conversation.

"Your father and I were close friends during the Great War, and his actions saved many British and French lives. I was looking forward to seeing him again after all these years, so I admit to being a little surprised when I received a telegram from Giselle telling me to expect Gerald's two grown sons instead of him. Tell me, is your father keeping well?"

"Our father doesn't speak about the war." David took the lead. "And to be honest, we don't know anything about what he did. We'd never heard of you until a few days ago when Gigi told us about you. He suffers from heart issues these days, which is why we're here instead."

Abreo studied the faces in front of him, making Michael uncomfortable with his deep, intense stare that seemed to bore right through him. Eventually, he couldn't stand any more of it.

"Gigi told us you can provide false papers so we can get into Germany without arousing suspicions. She said you were the best in France at that sort of thing."

Edouard Abreo smiled, his perfect white teeth glistening in the dimly lit office. "Gigi flatters me, but yes, I do have a reputation for such things. But I am confused. Why do you need to enter Germany secretly? British and American tourists and businessmen are welcomed with open arms, but the French, not so much. Why don't you just enter as tourists? It would be much simpler and probably a lot safer."

The boys spent the next fifteen minutes explaining why they needed to get across the border into Germany without arousing any interest from the authorities. Once they'd finished, David addressed the question posed by Abreo.

"We asked the same question, but Gigi insisted that we'd be better off disguised as Germans," he explained. "The town where Frank and Herbert live is not a large place, and two English boys would stand out like a sore thumb, especially if we started asking questions about what happened to two Jewish men who owned a department store."

Abreo watched them both closely, listening intently to every word David said.

"From what Gigi told us, everyone in the town knows that Frank is English, so it wouldn't take a genius to connect us as soon as we started asking questions."

"What do you think would happen if the Germans connected you to Frank and his grandfather?" Abreo asked.

David threw his hands in the air. "I don't know. They'd probably arrest us and throw us out of the country."

"And what do you think would happen if they discovered two English spies pretending to be Germans?"

David sighed. "Again, I don't know. They'd arrest us for sure. After that, they would probably torture us to find out what we were doing there."

"They would." Abreo gritted his teeth. "And then the Nazis would kill you and bury you in a place where you would never be found. They would deny any involvement to the British government, and the entire matter would be quickly forgotten. Tell me, which exit scenario would you prefer?"

"We understand the dangers, Mr Abreo," David replied. "We've discussed them with Gigi, and we decided that we have a much better chance of discovering what happened to them if they think we're German. We wouldn't get close to the truth if they knew we were Frank's English family coming to find them."

"Fair point," Abreo said. "I just wanted you to know what could happen if you go ahead with this. However, before I decide if I am to help you or not, I need to know that you are serious about what awaits you on the other side of the Rhine. What do you know about life in Nazi Germany? What did Giselle tell you about it?"

"We know enough to get by," Michael lied. "The rest we'll work out as we go along. All we want to do is get in there, find them, and get out as fast as we can. If everything goes according to plan, we should be back in France in less than three days. Two if we hurry."

"It's a noble gesture, and I commend your loyalty to your family, especially to your father. The Gerald Fernsby I knew would have gone to rescue his brother without hesitation, and it is good to see he instilled the same bravery and sense of duty in his two sons."

Edouard Abreo leant forward and rested his arms on the desk. "Everything you said about what is happening over there is true. Worse, if you want to know the truth. You might not have heard, but since the November Pogrom known as Kristallnacht, the Nazis have acted further against the Jews. Amongst other things, they issued a decree a few days later ordering all Jewish retail businesses to be handed over to Aryan hands, and then after that, they expelled all Jewish pupils from German schools."

Abreo rubbed his temples and took a deep breath. "They rounded up thousands of Jewish males of all ages after Kristallnacht and took them to concentration camps. I fear your uncle and great-grandfather are already out of reach, probably in Dachau. And although I understand why you want to find them, I fear you will fail. All you are doing is risking your own lives for an outcome you cannot achieve."

He looked into their eyes. "I'm sorry my brave friends, but you are too late."

Michael and David looked at each other. They already knew most of this, but the hopelessness in Abreo's voice wasn't something that either had expected, and Michael could see the deflated look in David's eyes as much as he could feel his own despondency.

"We knew most of this," he finally spoke up. "We didn't know about the schools or the businesses, and we have no idea what's happened to Frank and Herbert, but until we know for sure, we have to try. Do you think our father would just turn around and go home if he was sitting here instead of us? He wouldn't, not as long as there is hope. And we won't either."

"You are as brave as your father, and as stubborn. He never listened to reason, and that is what made him so good at what he did. Tell me, what is your exit plan if something goes wrong?"

David threw Michael a blank stare.

"Please, tell me you have one?" Abreo pressed. "You must have an exit plan, or you will never get out of there alive. It's one thing entering Germany for genuine business or personal reasons, but for a search and rescue mission such as this, where you are trying to avoid the Gestapo, you will not make it back if you don't have a well-thought-out plan."

The blood drained from Michael's face as he realised once again how unprepared they were for such an undertaking. He raised his head and stared Abreo in the eyes with an act of bravado and defiance. "All we know is that we are trying to save our family from whatever the Nazis are doing to them. When we find them, and we will find them, we'll find a way out of Germany, even if we have to swim across the Rhine. That's our plan, and for better or worse, we're sticking to it."

Abreo smiled, although Michael could sense the anguish behind the facade. "You are just like your father.

Impetuous and impulsive, and yet brave and courageous. You will fail, but it is your lives you are throwing away. I will help you, but only if you do exactly as I tell you. Do we have an agreement?"

Michael's legs trembled as Abreo's words sank in. *He'll help us!* He turned to David. "We can't do it without him, and Gigi told us to do what he said, so we don't have a choice. I'm in agreement if you are."

"One more thing," Abreo added. "How good is your German? If it isn't perfect, then none of this will work. You must be able to speak it with no discernible accent whatsoever. If you don't sound like a native, then I cannot, and will not, help you."

"Our German is flawless," Michael said in perfect German. He sat up straight, relieved that for once, he could give a positive answer to the inquisitive Frenchman. "Gigi taught us from a very early age, and we were fluent by the time we were five years old. We may never have been there before, but we both speak the language as if we've lived there all our lives."

"Very good," Abreo said. "What about you?" he turned to David.

"I am just as fluent as Michael. Perhaps even better." He allowed a small smile to curl his lips upward for a moment. "We have many conversations in German, and we speak it as much as we do English when we're at home. We're both more than good enough to pass for native speakers."

Abreo nodded and pursed his lips. "Giselle taught you well. Your German is adequate enough for your needs."

"Will you help us then?" Michael asked.

"If you agree to do exactly as I say."

"I already said I would. What about you, David?"

David smiled weakly, and Michael watched his shoulders slump forward before he sighed loudly.

"Thank you, Mr Abreo," David said in a meek, shaky voice. "We agree to follow your lead. Now tell us, what do we need to do to get into Germany without arousing the interest of the Gestapo?"

Abreo scribbled something on a sheet of paper and handed it to the boys. "Stay there for a few days while I get everything organised. From now on, you are to only speak German outside this house. You are two German boys who are visiting France if anybody asks. There are spies everywhere, and as the tensions grow between our nations, more and more spies are appearing in border towns such as this, especially as the Maginot Line is close to here as well. Do not give any names or addresses to anyone, no matter how friendly they appear to be. Nobody is to be trusted. Come back here tomorrow morning and we will create new identities for you both."

Edouard Abreo stood up. The meeting was over.

Chapter Eighteen

Gerald sat up in bed when Doctor Newsome came to visit the next morning. Dorothy and Gigi sat by his bedside, and neither looked as though they had got much sleep the night before.

"How are you feeling today, Gerald? You look a lot better than you did when I came yesterday, that's for sure."

"Much better, thank you, Doctor," Gerald replied between quick breaths. "I don't know what you gave me, but whatever it was, it worked. I honestly thought I was dying yesterday, but today I feel like I might yet live."

Doctor Newsome smiled and patted Gerald's shoulders. "It was touch and go for a while, and I almost sent you to the hospital. In fact, I was going to do just that this morning if you hadn't recovered so well."

After a thorough examination, Doctor Newsome sat in the chair next to the bed and gave Gerald his assessment. "You've had a traumatic couple of days, and although the sickness and diarrhoea have abated, I'm afraid it's taken its toll on your body. Your feet are swollen, and you are short of breath. On top of that, your pulse rate is high. This tells me that your heart is struggling a little. I'm sorry to tell you this, Gerald, but with your history of heart problems, you need to go to hospital for a few days where they can monitor you and make sure you aren't heading for a heart attack."

Gerald's features clouded over as the doctor's words sank in. "I appreciate your advice, Doctor Newsome, but that is out of the question. I have to get to Germany as soon as I can, and I don't have time for any hospital visits."

"Let me put it to you like this," Doctor Newsome said firmly. "If you don't, you might die. You certainly won't make it to Germany in the state you're in, and even if you did, you wouldn't take one step towards helping your brother before you collapsed and died on a street corner somewhere. I'm not being dramatic, Gerald, but you've been through a very difficult twenty-four hours. I'm calling the ambulance right now, and I will leave it to your wife and mother to convince you to do as I say."

Doctor Newsome left the room to use the telephone, and as he did so, Dorothy grasped her husband's arm with trembling hands. Tears fell freely from her eyes, and Gerald's heart raced as he looked at his distraught wife.

Gigi stared, but she didn't seem to notice.

"I'll be fine," Gerald protested, suddenly feeling sick. "He's just being cautious, which is what he's supposed to do. I feel much better today, so whatever it was, it only lasted twenty-four hours. I wouldn't be surprised if Stourcliffe didn't poison me for what Michael did to his son."

Gigi looked up, her eyes suddenly brighter than they had been a moment earlier. "I bet that's it. You were perfectly fine when you left for London until you met with that awful man."

"I suppose it might have been Stourcliffe..." Dorothy started, but she stopped herself. "I can't live without you, Gerald. Please, for me if not for yourself, do as the doctor said. Go to the hospital for a few days and get thoroughly checked over. Please."

Tears rolled down her cheeks, and Gerald wiped them away with his hand. "Don't be so sad, Dorothy. I've never seen you like this before. Did the doctor say something to you that he hasn't told me?"

Dorothy shook her head, unable to speak. Her chin quivered, and she held his gaze only for a moment before looking away.

"No, the doctor has said nothing to us." Gigi took the lead. "You've been very ill, Gerald, and your heart is struggling. Please go to the hospital. Look at the state of your poor wife, and nothing has happened to you yet. The good Lord knows how she would act should something worse become of you."

"What about Frank and Herbert? They need my help."

"You won't be any help to anyone if you're dead," Gigi pressed him. "I'm trying to find out what happened to them, but in the meantime, you need to get better, so if you do need to go to Germany, you'll be in a better physical condition to go there."

Gerald clenched his jaw and took a deep breath. "Reach out to Edouard Abreo," he said to Gigi. "You know him. Tell him I'm delayed, but I'll be there as soon as I can. Tell him nothing else has changed."

"I know him," Gigi said, looking at Dorothy, who was shaking uncontrollably beside her. "I'll reach out to Abreo and inform him of our situation."

Gerald turned to his distraught wife. "Don't worry,

Dorothy, I'm fine. I'll go to the hospital and get myself right before I go. I'll be fine, I promise."

Dorothy wiped her eyes as Doctor Newsome came back into the room. "The ambulance is on the way. I assume you're getting in it?"

Gerald nodded, visibly upset at Dorothy's grief. "I'm getting in it."

Chapter Nineteen

Dorothy's throat tightened as she fought back a sob, but it was no use. Tears flooded from her eyes, their heat stinging her skin as they ran down her cheeks. She felt small and helpless, like a ship lost in a stormy sea, tossed and turned by waves of grief and fear.

Her husband was suffering from some mystery virus, and his heart was playing up. And even if he recovered quickly, which she doubted, he would leave for Germany as soon as he left the hospital. The entire situation was too much for her. All she wanted was a return to normality, whatever that meant for them in the coming storm.

Gerald, sitting up in his hospital bed in his pyjamas, stared at his wife's bloated face as if she'd gone mad.

Giselle's eyebrows furrowed as she impatiently turned away from Dorothy's tear-streaked face. She let out a sharp exhale before shaking her head in disbelief.

"For goodness' sake, woman. What is wrong with you? You're behaving like Gerald was killed by the death of a thousand plagues or something. Stop this at once. You're driving me crazy with your antics."

"Do you know something I don't?" Gerald asked. "Because if you do, tell me now so I can prepare myself."

Dorothy shook her head and looked down at the ground. "I'm worried, Gerald. I worry about your health, and I worry that you'll leave for Germany as soon as you get out of this hospital. And I worry that you'll die alone in a ditch somewhere before you even reach the border."

She closed her eyes, trying to gather herself together so she could carry on. "I can't help but worry about David and Michael, and what will happen to them if Hitler carries on the way he is. We've already lived through one war, and I don't want to face another."

A doctor wearing the familiar white coat entered the room, followed by Doctor Newsome and several others that Dorothy assumed were junior doctors learning their craft.

"Good morning, Mr Fernsby," the senior doctor said. "I'm Doctor Chattel, and these are my assistants. You already know Doctor Newsome, of course."

Dorothy watched Doctor Newsome throw Giselle a stern look, which took her by surprise. *Why would he do that?*

The next statement from the doctor in charge interrupted her thoughts.

"I'm in charge of the cardiology department at the hospital, and I'm afraid I have some rather bad news for you. You've had a rough couple of days from what I hear, and whatever ailed you took a toll on your body." The doctor looked at Gerald before glancing at Dorothy and Gigi.

"The infection seems to have cleared up, thankfully, but your heart didn't handle it too well. You've suffered a heart attack, and frankly, I'm surprised that you are looking as good as you are right now. We need to keep you in here for a while so we can keep an eye on you and make sure you receive complete bed rest. Whatever ailment you had, your body couldn't handle the stress it caused, and with your heart condition, I'm afraid it tipped it over the edge."

Dorothy squeezed Gerald's hand as the news sank in. She saw Gigi's face turn a shade of purple, which was most unlike her. Gerald just stared at the doctor.

"Am I going to be alright?" he asked. "You don't understand, Doctor. I have urgent business I have to attend to in Germany and I don't have time to stay here. I must go, because if I don't, my brother might die."

"And you might die if I allow you to leave. Doctor Newsome informed me of your situation, but my priority is you and your health. I am sorry about your family over there, I truly am, but I fear that if you leave this hospital today, you might not even survive the trip to Germany, let alone the adventures you'll encounter once you get there. I'm afraid I must insist that you remain here until you are well enough to leave."

The doctor's words hit Gerald like a ton of bricks, and Dorothy watched as his body seemed to crumple in on itself. He slumped back onto the pillow, his already pasty face even paler than it had been a moment earlier. His hand, which had been gripping Dorothy's tightly, went limp, and she could feel his body trembling with shock and fear.

"But what about Frank and Herbert?' He croaked weakly. Gerald looked at Dorothy and his mother, who avoided eye contact and stared at the floor.

"You won't be any good to anyone if you're dead," the doctor said.

"Please, Gerald, listen to the doctor," Dorothy pleaded.

"I'm sorry for Frank and Herbert. I truly am, but I cannot lose you, not for them, or anyone else."

"Do as the doctor orders." Giselle finally spoke up. "Frank and my father are no more important than you are, and you must remain here and get better."

Gerald sighed and slapped the bedsheets with his left hand. "Thank you, Doctor. I'll do as you ask, but as soon as I'm able, I'm leaving."

The doctor nodded his head. "I'm glad to hear it, Mr Fernsby. We'll have you in tip-top shape in no time." He turned and left the room, followed by the junior doctors.

Doctor Newsome remained behind, and Dorothy watched as he once again gave Gigi a stern look. *What's going on between those two?*

"I'm glad you decided to do the right thing," Doctor Newsome said. "Whatever is happening over there is out of your control, and for the foreseeable future you need rest and plenty of it."

He once again stared at Gigi, who refused eye contact. Dorothy made a mental note to ask her what was going on between them.

"How long did they say I was going to be here for?" Gerald asked, struggling to keep his eyes open.

"For a while, whatever that means," Dorothy replied. "I suppose it depends on how fast you recover."

Her husband didn't hear. He was fast asleep from the morphine the doctor administered for the chest pain.

Chapter Twenty

As the boys started what they hoped would be the final part of their mission – which is what they'd been calling it in recent days – Michael reflected on their adventure so far.

They had remained in Strasbourg for almost a week, most of it hidden inside a dingy room in a bedsit run by a stern woman who did nothing but shout and tut at them every time she saw them.

They discovered from Abreo that the woman had lost both her husband and son in the Great War, and as a result, she hated Germans. Abreo had sent them there on purpose for two reasons: One, their German had to be good enough to convince the woman they were natives, and second, she hated the Germans so much that she would never be a spy for them, which was vital if they were to get across the border safely.

Glad to be out of the cramped bedsit, they happily responded to Abreo's summons to his home where he gave them the papers he'd forged. They were now lifelong friends from Dortmund, and they were taking one last ski trip together before joining the Wehrmacht.

David was to become Ralf Fischer, an accounts clerk, and Michael was Willi Bauer, and he worked in a munitions factory on the outskirts of Dortmund.

The boys were delighted with them, and although they had cost a king's ransom, they knew they would be grateful for Abreo's expertise by the end of the mission.

The first part of the adventure, and the trickiest by far, was to get them over the border into Germany unseen. Then, and only then, would they be able to use the new identities that Abreo had forced them to study and learn back to front. He'd questioned them for hours to make sure they knew their cover stories, and it was only when he was satisfied that they knew their new life stories back to front and inside out, that he'd arranged transport over the border.

The two boys moved south in the dead of night to a small town called Boofzheim, which was close to the mighty river separating the two countries. Under the cover of darkness, Michael and David were taken by rowing boat across the Rhine, where they were met on the other side by a friend of Abreo's, who drove them thirty miles to Appenweier.

The boys were now in Germany.

The driver, who didn't speak a single word the entire trip, dropped them off by the railway station as dawn was breaking. They were finally alone in enemy territory.

"Remember," David said. "I'm Ralf from now on, and you're Willi. David and Michael were left behind in France."

I've never felt as alone in my entire life. Michael fought to control the tingling sensations all over his body, and he felt the hairs on his arms rising with the tension. He watched David scramble out of the car behind him, and at that moment, he realised just how much his brother meant to him.

His eyes welled up, and he struggled to contain the intensity of the moment. His heart raced, and he was relieved that David was with him. *I'd never do this on my own. I'm too much of a coward.* He shook himself and forced his mind to concentrate on what they were about to do.

The two-hour rail journey to Stuttgart was interesting enough. Their papers were thoroughly scrutinised, and a pleasant-looking middle-aged man sat in the seat in front of them the whole trip, even though there were several spare seats in more private areas available.

"What are two handsome young men doing travelling to Stuttgart at such an early hour?" the man asked in a friendly tone as he turned to face them.

Michael watched as David prepared their well-rehearsed answer. The man was tall and gangly and looked smart in his dark suit and tie that were visible underneath a long grey coat that had several large buttons fastened down the front.

What gave him away was the oval-shaped badge made of nickel silver that was pinned to the lapel on his suit jacket, and clearly visible from where Michael sat. It depicted a raised German eagle sitting on top of a circular reef. Inside the reef was the Nazi swastika.

Abreo had shown the boys several badges and items of German identification, and this was one of them. In fact, this was the one he'd warned them to be wary of above all others.

Michael knew the words that would be etched on the rear of the badge. They said "GEHEIME STAAT-SPOLIZEI" in capital letters, and they were two of the most feared words in Nazi Germany. Below the letters would be four numbers that were the personal identifier for this particular man.

Abreo had warned the boys of men such as this. They knew exactly who he was and what he was doing. He was a member of the Gestapo, and they were to be avoided at all costs. Now they were in Germany, and almost immediately they had run into one of them on a train close to the French border.

Michael's skin felt clammy underneath his heavy coat, and he bit hard on his bottom lip to stop it from quivering.

This was their first test, and they were determined to pass it. If they didn't, the mission would end before it even started.

"We're friends from Dortmund, sir," David spoke for them both. "We're about to join the Wehrmacht, so we're going on one last skiing holiday before we report for duty."

"Good for you," the man said, eyeing them both as a cat would watch a mouse. "Where are you going to ski?"

"We're going to try the slopes at Hanslmühle – Mauern because that's where we, or at least I, used to go with my parents when I was young."

"Where is that?" the man asked sharply. "I haven't heard of that place before."

It was obvious the Gestapo agent was testing them because the slopes at Hanslmühle – Mauern were well known in the area.

"It's near Freising, sir. About twenty kilometres away."

Michael's pulse was racing, and his chest was beating so hard that he was sure the Gestapo agent could hear it. *Thank God Abreo made us study our plans until we were sick of it!*

The man from the Gestapo studied them intently. "What were your names again?"

"I'm Ralf Fischer, and this is my friend, Willi Bauer, sir." He gestured to Michael to get their papers out, and his hands trembled as he handed them over.

Michael choked back the bile rising in his throat. He stared at the floor, waiting for the inevitable moment when the Gestapo agent saw through their false identities.

Five intense minutes later, the agent handed back their papers. "It's always a pleasure to see our young men join our glorious armed forces. The experience will do you good. I wish you a pleasant skiing trip."

The man stood and then did something that caught both Michael and David off guard. He stood and raised his right arm straight out in front of him.

"Heil Hitler!" he yelled out, loud and proud.

Michael felt his entire body tingling, and as he rose to his feet alongside his brother, the words stuck in his throat as he responded. In unison, both he and David raised their right arms and shouted back at the Gestapo man.

"Heil Hitler!"

The man smiled and sat down again. He never spoke another word for the rest of the journey to Stuttgart, which suited the boys down to the ground.

David held his hands in front of him as though in prayer, and he bent forward once they'd found a seat at the rear of their next train from Stuttgart to Munich. He sighed, and Michael could see the sweat on his brow. He placed his hand on his brother's shoulder and whispered in his ear.

"That was close, but we passed. If we'd sounded even a

little off with either our German or our story, we'd have been arrested by now."

In contrast to David, Michael felt a wave of excitement course through his veins. They'd met the enemy head-on and beaten them at their own game. *Now, if only the rest of the mission goes as smoothly!*

"It's not over yet," David reminded him. "He might be calling for backup right now for all we know. I'll be happy once we get to Munich and get off this train."

He was right, of course, and Michael grimaced at the thought of the train being stormed by armed German police searching for them.

He shuddered and put the bad thoughts from his mind.

Chapter Twenty-One

Soft snow fell while Michael marvelled at the picturesque scenery surrounding them. The moment they stepped off the train in Freising, both he and David found themselves captivated by the tranquillity and beauty of not only Freising but the entire Bavarian region.

He found it difficult to imagine that the Nazis could commit such heinous crimes amidst this breathtaking display of nature's finest beauty.

Gigi had given them a thorough explanation of the history of Freising, and she'd provided a rough map of the locations of both Guttmann's Department Store and the large house that Frank and Herbert shared on the outskirts of the small Bavarian town. It may have been close to Munich, but it might as well have been a million miles away, such was the poetic beauty of their surroundings.

Everywhere he looked in the medieval town, the colours and the serene beauty of the Bavarian mountains brought pleasure to his eyes and joy to his senses, and for a moment he almost forgot why they were there.

Pointed red brick roofs stood side by side with black

ones, and three-storey houses packed tightly on either side of the narrow, cobbled streets gave the town its character. White-painted houses blended with orange and green, and ancient domes standing atop centuries-old buildings made Michael's jaw drop.

He pulled the collar of his jacket around his neck and snuggled as deep into it as he could. The mountain air might have felt fresh in his lungs, but it was freezing cold, and his hands and feet were already like blocks of ice. His breath steamed from his mouth, and he covered its warmth with his hands to provide a modicum of feeling in them.

I need a pair of gloves and a hat.

Gigi's map showed the route to the department store starting at Freising Cathedral, which she'd confidently told them they couldn't miss. And she was right. The town skyline featured the cathedral's two tall white-painted towers, visible from any direction. The cathedral's immense presence was further accentuated by two green pointed roofs, while large crosses adorned the top, serving as a symbol for all who gazed upon it.

"A church has stood on that site since the eighth century, according to Gigi," Michael said as the boys made their way towards the impressive cathedral.

"I know. I was there when she told us," David reminded him. "This place is magnificent. I wish we could have been here in better times. I'd love to explore the area and really go skiing on the slopes. No wonder Uncle Frank wanted to move here. I would too if the Nazis hadn't ruined it."

"Shh," Michael put his finger to his lips. "You're going to get us noticed." He pointed to a store off to their right. "We need some winter hats and gloves. I don't know about you, but I'm freezing."

David agreed, and they entered the store to purchase

some warm protection for their heads and hands. Another benefit from wearing a woollen hat was they'd be harder to recognise, and at this stage of the mission after their run-in with the Gestapo, the boys would take any advantage they could.

"Remember," David whispered once they were back outside in the swirling snow. "All retail stores are now in Aryan hands, and I bet there's more than a few that were Jewish-owned only a few weeks ago. These people are not friendly, so let's not give them any opportunities to turn us in."

"You'll get no argument from me."

It took about twenty minutes to reach the cathedral, and when they got there, Michael stared in humbled awe at the sheer magnificence of the ancient architecture on display.

"This place is enormous." David nudged him in the ribs. "Look at it, Willi. I've never seen anything like it."

"I'd love to explore the cathedral," David, or Ralf, said. "But it's already mid-afternoon and we don't have long before it gets dark. I suggest we find the store and their house so we know where they are, and then we can search for Frank and Herbert tomorrow morning."

"I don't know about you, but I'm hoping they're home and will be glad and surprised to see us when we get there," Michael replied. "They'll invite us in and tell us what happened over a nice cup of hot tea. Then tomorrow we convince them to come with us back to France. That's what I'm hoping, anyway."

"That's wishful thinking, brother, but I agree."

Michael once again reminded David that they were no longer brothers, but best friends.

Within a few minutes, the boys reached Freising's main street. Renamed Adolf Hitler Strasse, the sea of red captivated Michael as he hastened towards the department store.

He nudged David gently and gestured with his head to direct his attention to the sight, but there was no need. The all-encompassing sea of red flags would have been impossible to overlook.

Swastikas flew from what looked like every building, sometimes even from each floor. The red background mixed with the fading light, made it difficult to see anything else over the outpouring of support for the Nazi regime. It left the boys in no doubt where the town's loyalties lay.

About five minutes later, they reached the junction of Adolf Hitler Strasse and Hindenburg Strasse. Michael felt that all too familiar feeling of tingles, as he'd come to call it, and the hairs on his arms once again stood to attention like a soldier in the presence of a superior officer.

They had reached Guttmann's Department Store. Or at least that's what it used to be. Michael's heart skipped a beat when he looked at what it was now. He remembered the many photographs Gigi had shown him, and their Uncle Frank had sent many pictures of the distinctly Bavarian white-painted department store that had served the Guttmann family for decades.

Three arched windows overlooked Hindenburg Strasse, while another faced the narrow Brennergasse side street. Boards covered each window, making them unrecognisable from the photos Michael remembered. Likely smashed during Kristallnacht, the large windows were a testament to the many instances of harassment the Jews had experienced, not just on that one night.

What truly disturbed Michael, as evidenced by the expression on David's face, was the crude attempt to cover the store's name with fresh white paint. Above the arched windows, someone had painted over the bright red lettering that read, "Guttmann's Department Store. Proudly Serving The People of Freising." The red colour had bled through, making the store's name clearly visible to the naked eye.

So, too, were other slogans painted in the same red colour. Jews Out! Dirty Jews!

Michael closed his eyes and tried to imagine how Frank and Herbert must have felt when they saw those words on the walls of their beloved store. As bad as it was for him, he knew it must have been a thousand times worse for them and all the other Jewish store owners who faced the hatred of the angry mob.

Three swastikas flew in the wind underneath the first-floor windows, and this bothered Michael more than the words so crudely scrawled on the walls. It was as though the flag was the ultimate insult to the people who had lived there in peace for generations. He wondered if it would ever be safe for the Jewish people to return and reclaim what was rightfully theirs.

Right now, that looked doubtful.

A shadow in an upstairs window caught his eye. As the sky darkened, the light from the windows illuminated the inside of the store more and more. On the corner of the building at the junction of the two streets, the department store had what Michael could only describe as a medieval turret. He'd seen this in every picture he'd ever looked at, and it always fascinated him. He knew that would have been Herbert's private office.

Today, a man looked down towards the cobbled road below him. Michael's gaze caught his eye, and for the longest moment, they made a connection through the glass. The man seemed small, but that could have resulted from the distance and the angle between them.

Whatever his height, the man appeared to be in his mid-forties and had his hair slicked back. He was portly. No, sod that. He was fat and overfed. Michael wasn't going to play nice with this man who'd stolen the store from its rightful owners.

What was most noticeable was the narrow moustache the man was stroking absentmindedly with his left hand. It looked exactly like the one worn by his famous Führer, and the sight of it made Michael sick. He wanted to shout at the top of his lungs, but he didn't. Instead, he just stared back at the aberration watching the town as though he owned the place.

He probably did. After all, the department store was a jewel in the town of Freising, and whoever had taken control of it after Frank and Herbert had been forcibly removed must be an important man. Perhaps the mayor, or a high-ranking officer in the Gestapo. To Michael and David, he was the enemy. Nothing more and nothing less.

The man threw his arm up in the now familiar Nazi salute, and Michael returned the gesture. The last thing they needed was an act of defiance that would no doubt lead to their arrest. He broke eye contact and headed away from the store with David (Ralf) not far behind. It was time to move on before they roused any suspicions.

Chapter Twenty-Two

It took thirty minutes and several wrong turns before the boys found Herbert Guttmann's home close to the River Isar. Along the way, they had walked past the headquarters of the *Hitlerjugend*, or the Hitler Youth movement.

A lone drummer in uniform stood outside beating his drums, and as they shuffled past, Michael couldn't shake the feeling of unease that settled in his stomach. The steady beat of the drums only added to the tension, and he quickened his pace, eager to leave the area.

One building they passed held a large mural with the words 'Ein Volk, Ein Führer, Ein Wille' underneath a large Nazi eagle. This translated as 'One People, One Leader, One Will.'

There was little doubt in Michael's mind that the people of Freising were right behind Hitler, and whatever he was doing to the Jewish people was either supported or ignored. Either way, he knew he wouldn't get much help from the German population if it came down to the wire.

The night had closed in by the time they reached the

large white-painted house close to the Isar River. The snow had stopped, and the sky cleared, allowing the stars to light the way for them as they looked around for any signs of life.

The weather was frigid, and Michael was freezing. He'd long since lost feeling in his hands and feet, and the winter clothing he'd brought from England was totally inadequate for the Bavarian winter. His breath poured from his mouth in streams of warm vapour, and he blew on his hands repeatedly to warm them up.

"If we don't get inside somewhere soon, we'll freeze to death," he whispered to David, who shivered beside him. He nodded in agreement.

The house was large for the area, but nowhere near as big as the Fernsby home in Sandwich. Michael was a little surprised to discover the modest abode the wealthy and esteemed Guttmann family called home. He'd been expecting a large, sprawling mansion with massive gardens. This was almost the complete opposite.

But still, it was pretty, and fit perfectly with the picturesque mountain town and its majestic views.

The bright, white-painted exterior glowed under the starlit sky, creating a mesmerising mosaic of nature and man-made structures. He couldn't imagine a more peaceful place to live, and yet here he was, surrounded by symbols and imagery of hatred everywhere he looked. The contrast was striking, and he struggled to get his head around it.

The house itself was three storeys, like many of the homes in the area. The third floor looked like it was an attic window, so he imagined the room to be cramped and probably used for storage.

One feature stood out, and it reminded him of the department store. A rounded turret structure stretched around the right-hand corner of the second floor. Two small windows, one on the front of the house and the other on the side, brought daylight to what looked like the most important room in the house. Michael imagined this to be Herbert's private quarters, just as they were in the medieval turret in the department store.

Other than that, there wasn't much else for the boys to take note of. Trees grew around the rear and the left side of the house, and the front garden wasn't large at all. A small open courtyard large enough for a single horse and carriage took most of the space, and there wasn't much room for visitors, who would have to leave their vehicles on the side of the quiet roads at the front and sides of the home.

As he looked around him, David prodded him in the ribs. A car was parked on the road to the right side of the Guttmann residence, close to the trees at the rear. Michael had missed it, but his eagle-eyed brother hadn't.

They crouched under the cover of trees to the left of the detached home and watched for several frozen minutes. The house was still and dark, and David waved his hand, indicating they move forward to check the downstairs windows for any signs of Frank or Herbert.

They assumed it was a futile task, but it had to be done before they could rule out the remote possibility of them hiding somewhere in their home.

As they approached the front door, it suddenly swung open in front of them. David jumped back, knocking Michael off his feet. They both tumbled down the three front steps and landed on their backs in the snow-covered grass below.

As they jumped up and prepared to run, a middle-aged woman struggled out of the door carrying a large wooden box that looked heavy. When she saw the boys stretched out in the garden below her, she dropped the box in surprise.

"Who are you, and what are you doing here?" she demanded. The woman mispronounced her words, and they came out so fast that Michael had a hard time understanding her. She sounded as frightened as he was.

The woman had short brown hair that reached the bottom of her ears, and her rounded features looked kind and caring in the light of the stars. Deep lines were etched into her face, and her eyes were red and puffy.

She was wearing a dress beneath her heavy coat; Michael could see her calves sticking out from the bottom. There wasn't much else to see in the dismal light, but he was wary of the unimposing figure standing before him after all he'd seen in the town already.

"I asked who you were and what you were doing here?" The woman stepped back and placed a hand on the front door handle. Her words sounded garbled, and Michael was having a hard time understanding her.

"Who are *you*? And what are *you* doing here?" David asked, rising to his feet and stepping forward.

"If you're Gestapo, please show me your identification." The woman's words were once again mispronounced and very hard to grasp, especially for non-native people like Michael and David.

It suddenly hit Michael what was going on. This woman had a hearing defect. This explained why her words sounded as they did. He knew who she was!

"What is your name?" he asked, stepping in front of his brother.

"My name is Gerda Yung, and I am here on legitimate business. Why are you here? And who are you?" The woman stepped inside the house, and Michael spoke quickly before she slammed the door on them and disappeared.

Recognition seemed to have dawned on David's face too, and he stepped away from Michael so they wouldn't look as threatening to her.

"I was going to ask if you were Gerda," Michael spoke in his native English. He knew he was taking a colossal risk, but he was sure he knew who this woman was. Their Uncle Frank had mentioned her in his letters.

The woman looked dazed, and she took a few steps backwards. "Who are you?" she asked, still in German.

David stepped forward and took the lead. "Do you speak English, Gerda?" he asked.

She nodded.

"My name is David Fernsby, and this is my brother, Michael. Our father is Gerald Fernsby, and Frank is our uncle. Herbert is our great-grandfather, and we are here to rescue them."

Michael looked around to make sure nobody else was around to hear their treachery.

Gerda's jaw hung open as she stepped aside. "Please, come inside. It isn't safe to talk so openly out here."

The boys helped her lift the heavy box and followed her inside. After she closed the door, she showed them into a humble sitting room that looked like it was from another era.

An antique rug lay on the dark wooden flooring, with traditional Bavarian furniture occupying the heart of the room. A deep blue, velvety sofa faced a pair of matching single chairs, their plush fabric inviting comfort. Black and white photographs adorned the walls, chronicling multiple generations of the Guttmann family in an array of poses harking back to the era of the German Empire.

Michael was intrigued and wanted to look at them, but they had important business to attend to.

Gerda closed the curtains and sat in an armchair. She left the lights turned off, obviously not wanting to arouse any unwanted attention from prying eyes.

"Uncle Frank mentioned you in his letters to our father and grandmother, Giselle Guttmann," David spoke softly. "He seemed to be very fond of you. He said you were his secretary, but we all suspected you were much more than that."

Gerda's lips formed a brief smile before reality once again took over. Even in the poor light, Michael could see the heavy lines underneath her eyes. "You are too late. Frank and Herbert are not here anymore. The Nazis took them on the night of the pogrom, and I haven't heard from them since."

"Where did they take them?" Michael's voice cracked and wavered.

"I don't know. I've asked repeatedly, but they won't tell me. All they said was that I am asking too many questions and that I needed to be careful, or I may end up joining them. The mayor, Johann Schreiber, assured me I wouldn't want to be where they are."

Michael bit his bottom lip, and his ribs seemed to tighten, restricting his breathing and making it hard for him to concentrate on what he'd just heard her say.

"You say they're gone? Gone where? We're here to rescue them, so we have to find them."

David tapped his arm and said, "Do you recall what Abreo told us? They've likely been taken to a concentration camp. Dachau, I believe he said."

"Dachau is a town not far from here," Gerda said. "I know of a concentration camp that was built there over an old munitions factory, but that was supposed to be for political prisoners, not Jewish business owners who have done nothing wrong."

Tears welled in Gerda's eyes, and Michael felt deep sorrow for her. Unlike them, she had lived through the evil, and she had genuine reasons to be upset and frightened.

"Frank had written to his brother to ask for help, but Herbert would never leave Freising. His whole life has been dedicated to serving the people of this town. Did you know that his only son gave his life for Germany in the last war? He loved this place, and he could never understand why they turned on him the way they did."

David spoke gently. "We know. We understand why Frank came over here when he did, and why Herbert wouldn't leave. Our presence here is because of our father's poor health. We had hoped to locate them quickly and get them out before anyone grew suspicious. Unfortunately, it seems that plan has fallen apart."

"I have worked for the Guttmann family for a long time, and they have always been kind to me. No doubt you can tell I have a hearing defect, and all my life people have made fun of me for it. Herbert and Frank were different and never seemed to notice. Frank and I were very close, and we had discussed marriage until the Nazis changed the citizenship laws a few years ago. I would have still married him, but as he always did, Frank looked out for me. He told me to wait until it was all over, which he said wouldn't take long. Now we know he was wrong."

Gerda leant forward, her cheeks dampened from the tears that fell freely. "I haven't been able to talk about this with anyone until tonight. You have no idea how grateful I am that you would risk your lives to come all the way from England to help them. I'm just sorry that you're too late."

"We're not giving up, Gerda," David said. "We've come too far to stop now. If you'll tell us how to get to this Dachau place, we'll go there and try to find them."

"We can't stay here, it's too dangerous." Gerda stood up. "Schreiber is moving in here tomorrow, and although I was ordered not to take anything, I had to get Frank's belongings before that horrible Nazi took everything and destroyed it. That's what is in the box."

"The mayor is moving into this house?" David asked, the tone of his voice several pitches higher than normal. "Why would he do that? They might not be here, but surely it still belongs to Herbert and Frank?"

Gerda shook her head. "There is much you don't understand. Not only are the Nazis taking over Jewish businesses, expelling all Jewish children from the schools, and banning Jewish doctors from seeing German patients, but they are also stealing their properties and possessions once they've been sent to Dachau, or wherever else they've gone. It's as though they're removing every trace of them ever being here, and they are profiting from every move they make. It's disgusting, but there is nothing I can do about it."

David looked at his brother with pursed lips. "We didn't know this. We're so sorry this is happening to you. To them. So, this Schreiber, the mayor, is moving in here tomorrow and claiming everything for himself?"

Gerda nodded, her face flushed.

"Where can we go for the night?" Michael changed the subject. "We need somewhere to stay before we leave tomorrow."

"You can stay with me. You'll be safe until we work out what to do next."

Gerda stood up and gave them a long hug. "You are brave and thoughtful to come all the way here to help your family. I will help you as much as I can because they are as much my family as they are yours."

Michael grabbed the heavy box from Gerda and followed her outside.

Chapter Twenty-Three

The sound of screaming and yelling pulled Frank Fernsby from his deep, exhausted sleep. Shadowy sounds and images emerged from the fog enveloping his weary mind, and he struggled to his feet as he had done a thousand times before.

He knew what was happening because the SS guards seemed to enjoy this particular game, which is what it seemed to be for them. Already exhausted from a long day's hard labour, the prisoners had been allowed to fall into a fatigued sleep for what felt like only a few minutes.

There was no way of truly knowing how long they'd been asleep because they banned clocks and watches. The only thing they had to go on was the sound of screaming SS guards, and the fact that daylight meant hour after hour of intense physical labour.

"Get up!" the SS guard screamed. "Get outside for roll call. Now!" The guard walked along the bunks, banging his heavy baton against the wooden frames. Everyone knew he would aim it at them if they didn't immediately jump up and gather outside for the dreaded roll call.

Frank reached over to help Herbert to his feet. At almost ninety years old, Frank didn't know how much longer the old man could hold on. Overworked and underfed, he wondered how much longer he could continue, let alone Herbert, who was twice his age.

Another prisoner named Jonathan had joined them in the bunk. The three of them shared the cramped space, and the only way to get some sleep was if they lay virtually on top of each other. In any other world, this would be an affront to human dignity, but here it was the accepted norm. Sleep came easily because of the terrible physical condition of the prisoners.

Once on their feet, the three men joined the melee as tired bodies hurried outside to form rank for the evening roll call. The SS guard was joined by two more, and together they screamed and beat the men as they made their way out into the cold, wet late November darkness.

In block order, they lined up and maintained silence. Guards, yelling like rabid dogs, circled around them. Any prisoner who spoke or moved suffered a brutal beating as an example to the rest.

The night was freezing, and the falling snow swirled in the glow of searchlights as they danced around the courtyard. It wasn't long before their inadequate, ill-fitting uniforms became drenched and heavy. Frank quivered in the sub-human conditions, and he forced back the strangled cries of frustration when he caught sight of Herbert rocking back and forth beside him as the searchlights caught him in one of their frequent sweeps.

How long have we been here? Frank tried as hard as he could to keep up with the days as they passed, but each one rolled into the next, with nothing to look forward to other than hour after hour of forced labour and little to no food.

All they got in the morning was a small, steaming cup that barely contained the foul-smelling liquid they called coffee. The prisoners huddled over their cups, greedily sipping at the meagre offering that only left them feeling emptier than before.

Lunch was even worse; a thin broth that barely passed for soup. The Nazis filled their bowls with a grey, watery mixture that reeked of rotting vegetables and tasted of nothing but salt. It did little to stave off the constant hunger gnawing at their stomachs, leaving them feeling weak and lightheaded.

New prisoners often refused to eat the soup, but as the days wore on, they tolerated it like everyone else did. It was either that or starve, which most of them were doing anyway.

Dinner was nothing more than a slice of bread, with either a small amount of sausage or cheese. The bread was supposed to be enough for both dinner and breakfast the following morning, but of course, the men were so hungry that most nights they consumed it all in one sitting.

Many of the prisoners stumbled as they went about their daily grind, their emaciated bodies barely able to support them. Sunken eyes and trembling hands betrayed the extent of their malnutrition and exhaustion, which was a testament to the daily struggles they endured. The brutality of the SS only added to their physical and emotional torment.

Frank's mind drifted back to his earlier question: *How long have we been here?* It had been weeks, maybe even as long as a month. He knew it must be somewhere around the end of November, but that was as close as he could get. Hot breath seared from his nostrils as he grunted out loud. *I wonder if they'll give us a break for Christmas?*

The grunt was because he already knew the answer.

The bedraggled, tired men stood to attention for at least two hours while the SS yelled and belittled them. Frozen, weary limbs struggled to remain upright, and now and then, someone would fall to the ground in sheer exhaustion.

This was exactly what the SS wanted, and they pounced like a pack of hungry wolves onto their victims to teach them a lesson they would never forget.

The badges they wore illustrated their supposed crimes, with most of the men in Frank's block being nothing more than Jewish. Even within the prisoners themselves, the badges had become a sort of group sorting order, with all the others sitting above the Jews, who sat at the bottom of the pecking order. Political prisoners, homosexuals and Gypsies; all got the SS treatment, but none worse than the lowly Jew.

Finally, the SS began calling out names from their ledgers. Frank was nearly delirious from fatigue, and his body shook from the sub-zero temperatures and falling snow that soaked him to his skin.

He looked over at Herbert, who was rocking back and forth in ever-increasing movements. Herbert was mumbling to himself, and Frank could see he was barely holding on. He reached out to steady the old man, but all it did was make him worse.

"I served my country with pride all my life. My son died for Germany in the trenches. Why are you doing this to me? To us? Why?"

The SS guards, who until now had been circling around the outside of the massed ranks of their sub-human captives, shifted their gaze towards the screaming old fool who wouldn't stand still.

"Herbert, please, for the love of God, stop," Frank pleaded quietly, hoping the guards wouldn't hear him.

They did.

Batons and boots rained down on the two men, knocking them to the ground in a frenzy of blood and violence.

After a beating that left Frank dazed and confused, they dragged him to his feet. A red-faced SS man hit him in the stomach with a baton, doubling him over in agony.

"Get up and shut your mouth. For your insolence, roll call has been extended, so all your friends can blame you after they've been out here all night. Now stand still and shut up!"

Herbert was delirious, and even when they dragged him to his feet, he fell right back down again. Frank's chest caved in at the sight of his beloved grandfather's struggles. He couldn't contain himself.

"Leave him alone," he yelled. "Don't you know he's nearly ninety years old? Would you do this to your own grandfather?"

Batons and feet crashed into him again, and this time everything went dark. A few minutes later, he felt himself being dragged along the ground. Someone threw liquid in his face, and he was jerked upright to his feet.

An SS officer wearing a long leather jacket appeared on the scene, and although Frank didn't know him, he knew it wasn't good. He gasped as he realised they had dragged Herbert out alongside him.

The two men were now standing in front of the massed prisoners, who stood in quiet shock at what was unfolding before them. They remained in separate groups in their block order, no one daring to move or speak a word.

Frank looked around in desperation. "Please, sir, do

whatever you want to me, but let my grandfather go. He's old and can't stand much more of this. Please, I beg you."

Frank reached out to grab the man in charge, but was roughly beaten back. "Get your filthy Jew hands off me," the officer screamed. "You dare to touch me?"

The officer walked behind Frank and Herbert. Frank closed his eyes as he heard the unmistakable sound of a pistol being cocked. His mind drifted to Gerda, and the hope that she was as far away from Bavaria as possible.

Images of his mother and brother flashed before his eyes. He thought of them, snug and warm in their beds back home in England, and although a part of him wished he was there, he was glad he was by Herbert's side as they faced the SS together.

He stiffened and took deep breaths, waiting for the short, sharp pain of death to enter his brain and put an end to the misery he saw no escape from.

Just shoot and put us both out of our misery.

"This is what happens when you disrespect my men and disregard their orders," the SS officer yelled.

Frank stood his ground and clenched his fists in anticipation of the momentary pain before everything went dark.

A loud noise pierced the silence as the gun went off. Frank froze in silent shock, swaying from side to side as Herbert fell to the ground with a cold, final thud. Blood oozed from his head, and the SS officer kicked him in a final insult as his body released its last vestiges of life.

Frank screamed and lunged at the officer, but another guard bludgeoned him over the head with his heavy stick. As he was being dragged back to his block, he heard the SS men screaming at the rest of the prisoners.

Frank's body trembled from head to toe, and hatred burned deep within his soul. Whatever happened, he would use the renewed energy Herbert's death had created within him to stay alive and survive this hellhole. What just happened would not go unpunished, and Frank would do all he could to make sure he lived long enough to bring this evil man to justice.

Even if he had to kill him in the process.

Chapter Twenty-Four

The aroma of hot steaming coffee wafted into Michael's nostrils, and when he opened his eyes, Gerda was holding a fresh cup in front of his nose. He stretched and sat up on the couch that had been his bed for the night.

David must have smelled it too, because his head appeared from behind the couch. "That smells good," he said, stretching his arms high into the air. "What time is it?"

"It's early," Gerda answered. "It isn't safe for you here. Someone will report your presence, and the Gestapo will come searching for you. Being English, you'll stand out like a sore thumb, and you'll be easy to find."

"We have papers and a good cover story," Michael said. "We've already had one run-in with the Gestapo, and we passed with flying colours. So we know our story is solid."

The hot coffee tasted wonderful, and it was even better when Gerda popped up with a boiled egg and some cold cut ham. When he thought about it, Michael realised they hadn't eaten anything since they'd grabbed a sandwich at the Munich railway station the previous day. No wonder they were starving.

"What is your cover story, and why am I with you?" Gerda asked. "I need to know in case I am asked."

"I am Ralf Fischer, and Michael is Willi Bauer," David said, smacking his lips and licking his fingers. "We're friends from Dortmund who are about to join the Wehrmacht. We're here for a skiing holiday before we're enlisted."

"Do you have papers to prove who you are?"

"We do."

"Why am I with you?"

The room fell silent for a moment while the boys worked out a believable reason why Gerda would be with them.

"A mutual friend in Dortmund put us in contact with you after you agreed to take us to Hanslmühle – Mauern. We can say you were a friend of the family from years back when you were young. How does that sound?" David sat back and looked at Gerda for direction.

She shrugged and pursed her lips. "It's weak and easily disproved, but it will work for now. I grew up in Bielefeld, which is not too far from Dortmund. I could have gone to school with your mother. What was her name?"

"Dorothy Fischer."

"Okay. Dorothy was born in 1898, and she helped me with my hearing problems when we were little girls. I haven't seen her for years, so I can't describe what she looks like if anyone asks me."

"That's very good," Michael said. "But what do we do now? If Frank and Herbert are in the concentration camp at this place called Dachau, how do we get there and how do we get them out?"

Gerda half laughed and half grunted. "From what I hear of that place, there is no getting them out. Once they're in, they're in for good."

"So, what do we do then?" Michael asked again. "Do we just go home and tell our father we were too late to rescue them?"

"I didn't say that," Gerda answered. "Whatever we do, we can't stay here. Freising is a small town, and your presence here will not go unnoticed, no matter how good your cover story might be. We have to get out before they find us together."

"What's this we business?" David asked. "Our mission has nothing to do with you, and the last thing we want is to put you in any danger. You've helped us enough already, but whatever we do next, we must do it alone."

Gerda's face broke into a smile. Michael noticed that when she did, she looked younger. The years of stress had taken its toll on this attractive lady, no matter how much she tried hiding it.

"You sound so much like Frank," she said. "You both do. Stubborn to the core, and always thinking of others before yourselves. That's what I think I loved most about him. He was so kind and generous, and he always had time for everyone he encountered."

Her eyes clouded over as she thought about Frank Fernsby. Even though they hadn't seen him for a long time, both boys loved their Uncle Frank. He'd always spent time with them whenever he visited his mother and brother in England when they were younger.

He'd spent hours kicking a football around with them in the pouring rain, and then taken them, covered in mud, to a local cafe for hot tea and scones. Michael smiled at the memories of the cafe owner as she threw a fit when they sat in her spotlessly clean cafe with mud dripping onto the floor.

Frank had paid far more than the price of the scones and tea for the inconvenience, and by the end of the day, they had all become good friends. These were the kind of memories Michael and David had of Frank Fernsby.

"Uncle Frank was so good to us when we were young, and we owe it to him to at least see where he is so we can describe it to his mother back home," David said. "If we don't do something for him, then we've wasted our time and put you in danger for nothing."

Gerda slapped her knees with her hands as she rose from the rocking chair opposite the couch in the cramped sitting room in her modest home somewhere in Freising. It was dark when they'd arrived the previous evening, and neither of the boys had any clue where they were in relation to the town.

"I'll tell you the same thing I told Frank. Your kindness means everything to me, and the Fernsby family is all I have left in this world. Whatever you do next, I'm doing it with you. It's the least I can do for Frank and Herbert after all they've done for me."

"Are you sure, Gerda?" David asked. "We don't want to get you in any trouble."

Before she could answer, Michael butted in. "I don't mean to be rude, but I have to ask. Are you Jewish, Gerda? Obviously, we don't care. Half our family are Jewish, but if you are, it wouldn't make sense to risk your life knowing how much the Nazis hate you."

"I'm not Jewish," Gerda shook her head. "And although I've not heard any reports of Jewish women or children being arrested yet, I'm sure it's only a matter of time. Frank wanted me to move far away from Freising and pretend that

I'm as antisemitic as the Nazis, but he knew I could never do that. Frank and Herbert are my world, and I will not abandon them now when they need me the most."

"Fair enough," Michael said. "So, what do we do then?"

"I have friends in Munich who will help us. It's less than fifty kilometres from here, and that's where I suggest we begin. Munich is a big city, but it is full of Nazis, so be careful who you speak to. Unless I tell you otherwise, assume they are all against you."

"Who are these friends of yours, and why would they help us?"

"I'll tell you on the way."

Gerda strode out of the room and grabbed a bag of clothes and supplies she'd prepared earlier. She had obviously planned this during the night. Whatever happened next, Gerda was fully committed to their cause, whether they wanted it or not.

The tension eased a bit once they cleared the boundary of Freising. Gerda's grip on the steering wheel of her shiny blue Volkswagen Type One gradually loosened, and she broke the uneasy silence that enveloped them.

"Not many of my friends have automobiles," she shared, affectionately tapping the dashboard. "Frank was clever. He foresaw the danger and bought this car for me before it was too late. After Kristallnacht, a decree forced all Jews to relinquish their driver's licenses. They were prohibited from owning or driving vehicles, but since this was registered under my name, they couldn't take it away from us."

"Smart move," Michael replied. "It gave you the freedom to roam and get away from the aggravation. It's a pity you didn't use it to get them out of Germany while you could."

"Don't think I didn't try. In some ways, owning this

Wagen only made matters worse, because we were constantly looking over our shoulders in fear of being reported to the Gestapo for circumventing their stupid laws. You have no idea how hard it's been not being able to trust anyone, not even people who were once our closest friends."

Silence returned, and although they didn't suspect anyone of turning them in to the local Gestapo, after Gerda's warning the boys now believed that everyone they met was a potential threat to their safety.

The journey to Munich was one of the most scenic trips either of them could ever remember taking. The small Bavarian towns looked so picturesque and inviting, and it was hard to believe the simmering undercurrent of hatred that was present in these sleepy towns and villages.

"Who are these friends of yours in Munich?" David asked once Freising was in the rear-view mirror.

"They are close friends my husband and I made when we first moved from Bielefeld many years ago. They were happy times that existed in a different life. Things have changed now, and people have to choose every word they say carefully. If they don't, they risk being turned over to the Gestapo, and we've all heard stories of how people disappear, never to be seen again over something they might or might not have said."

"You moved here with your husband?" Michael picked up on her words. "I thought you and Uncle Frank were together?"

"We were. I mean, we are. My husband died in an automobile accident back in twenty-five, and I moved to Freising to get away from the memories. Nobody wanted to hire me because of my hearing defect, but Frank and Herbert never even seemed to notice it. They hired me on the spot, and

I've been with them ever since. Or at least I was until the pogrom."

"We're very sorry to hear that," David said. He turned towards Michael in the rear seat. "We didn't know."

"It's okay. Not many in Freising know about it. I keep my business to myself, as it's a lot safer that way. Especially now."

"Can we trust these friends of yours?" Michael asked.

"They are close friends who helped me through the worst years of my life. I have no reason to think they've changed so much that they won't help me again now."

"What exactly are we asking them for?" David asked. "Why do we need their help?"

"If we're going to find Frank, we need all the help we can get. I know where the camp is in Dachau, and we'll go there perhaps tomorrow. But we need a place to stay, and I can't think of a safer place than with Sophie and her husband, Stefan Meyer."

The car fell silent as they approached Munich, Gerda keeping to the backstreets as much as she could to avoid any potential roadblocks. The bustling city looked just like London, albeit in a much prettier location, but on closer inspection, Michael noticed the people seemed to keep their heads down as if to avoid attracting any attention to themselves.

"The headquarters of the Gestapo in Munich is close to here," Gerda explained. "It's in an old palace that cannot be missed. Nobody wants to attract their attention, so everyone, whether it's here or in Freising, or anywhere else in Germany, we all keep our heads down and our mouths shut."

They went around a large cemetery and then turned right onto a street called the Schellingstrasse. Tall apartment buildings standing five stories tall towered high above the street on both sides, blocking the weak wintry sun from shining its light on the road below.

Gerda pulled up outside one of the buildings and turned off the engine. "We're here," she announced. "Let me do the talking."

Chapter Twenty-Five

Gerda led the way up the narrow stairs to the fourth-floor apartments. David followed close behind, panting as though he'd run a mile uphill through deep snow. Michael, on the other hand, barely broke into a sweat, and he was the one carrying Gerda's suitcase filled with clothes and goodness knows what else. Whatever it was, it weighed a ton.

Finally, Gerda stopped outside apartment 1412. She took a deep breath and knocked on the door. It was still fairly early in the morning, and although the streets were alive with people going about their daily lives, the hallways and stairways of the apartment block were dark and empty.

And yet Michael couldn't shake off the indescribable feeling that they were being watched. The tingles were back at that now familiar point between his shoulder blades, and try as he might, he couldn't stop his upper body from quivering. He turned around full circle, almost knocking David over with his backpack, but nobody was there. The dimly lit narrow corridor was empty and still, which was in total contrast to Michael's imagination.

Snap out of it. You're imagining things.

The knocking echoed in the still atmosphere of the old building, and Michael cringed as the sound of Gerda's knuckles on the wooden door seemed to amplify and announce their arrival in every corner of the building.

A few moments later, the door creaked open a few inches. Michael couldn't see anyone from where he was standing, but he heard the surprise in the female voice behind the door.

"Gerda? Is that you?"

"Hello, Sophie. It's good to see you again."

The two women embraced, and as they did, Michael got a good look at the woman as she emerged from the doorway. She was tall, so tall that she towered over Gerda. Long blonde hair fell over her shoulders, and even in the dim light of the hallway, Michael could see the shimmering blue eyes staring at him and David before they turned back to Gerda.

Sophie was around forty years old, and the thing that stood out most to Michael was the warmth in her smile. Her lips curled up in a big grin, and she looked genuinely happy to see her old friend.

"Don't stand out here in the cold. Come on inside." Sophie stood aside to allow Gerda to pass. She stared at the two boys without saying a word as they filed past her.

"Stefan is at work, but he will be happy to see you when he gets home." She threw her arms around Gerda once the door was closed and embraced her tightly.

"Who are your two friends?" she asked.

"This is Ralf and Willi. They are relatives of one of my old friends from Dortmund, and they wanted to see Munich before they join the Wehrmacht. Boys, this is my great friend, Sophie Meyer."

As they shook hands and introduced themselves,

Michael noticed Gerda spoke louder than she normally did. In fact, she was almost shouting, such was the volume of her voice. He also noticed that she stood close to the apartment door, which made him wonder what she was doing. He'd put it down to her hearing defect, but something about her demeanour told him there was more to it.

"I hope you are taking good care of my friend," Sophie said, indicating the boys sit on the couch against the wall underneath the window on the opposite side of the cramped apartment from the door. "It's so good to see you again, Gerda. We were only talking about you the other day."

"What's really going on?" Sophie continued in a quiet voice once they were away from the apartment door. Her hands made funny shapes that took Gerda's attention. Although he'd never seen it before, Michael immediately recognised it as the sign language deaf people used to communicate.

It was obvious these two women were close friends, and Michael wondered if Gerda had told the truth when she told them they hadn't seen each other for years. From their body language, if not their words, they looked as if they knew everything about each other's lives.

Gerda remained silent, but her hands were going at a rapid pace. Sophie responded in kind, and whatever conversation they were having, it appeared serious from the looks on their faces.

Michael felt uncomfortable and began to wonder if they were being set up, although, from everything they'd learned of Gerda, he couldn't understand why. He exchanged worried glances with David, who, from the look of him, felt the same.

Michael got to his feet. The silent, intense conversation

that was exclusive to the two women had his skin prickling and his heart racing.

Have we walked into a trap? Was Uncle Frank set up by the woman he loved and trusted? Has she set us up as well?

David joined him on his feet, and the two boys edged towards the door. All the way, Michael kept his eyes fixed on the two women locked in deep, silent conversation.

As they reached the door, Gerda looked at them, her eyebrows raised at the sudden realisation of what was happening. She made some furious hand gestures at Sophie, who turned towards the worried boys.

"Please, sit down. You are safe here, and we mean you no harm." Her voice was low and not much above a whispered pitch. "You must understand there are eyes and ears everywhere, and we have to be careful how and who we speak to. Please, sit down."

Michael looked at David, unsure of what to do. "I don't trust you," he said bluntly. "What were you talking about, and why did you use sign language, knowing we wouldn't be able to understand what you were saying to each other?"

"I understand your worries," Sophie said. "Believe me, we both do. We need to be careful with our words to make sure they don't fall into the wrong ears."

Gerda took David's hands in hers and guided him away from the door back to the couch. "Please get away from the door. You never know who is listening."

Once the boys were back in front of the couch, Gerda sat down in one of the two chairs facing them. "Please, sit down," she said.

Neither did so. "Not until you tell us what is going on," Michael said. "We trusted you, Gerda, so please don't let us find out that you've betrayed us."

Gerda's eyes filled, and she moved her head violently

from side to side. "I would never betray the Fernsby family, not after all they've done for me. I love Frank very much, and I'll do anything to help him."

"Please, you must trust us," Sophie hissed. "Gerda was telling me who you are and why you're here. We can speak freely as long as you stay away from the door. You are Michael and David Fernsby, and you are here to find your uncle and great-grandfather after they were taken during the pogrom. Gerda and I tell everyone we haven't seen each other for years, but that isn't the truth. We meet regularly to help each other and to keep up with what is going on in our lives."

"Why didn't you tell us the truth?" David demanded, staring at Gerda.

Gerda's hands worked swiftly. Sophie watched carefully and then turned to the boys. "She is worried that her voice will carry outside these doors. Because of her hearing loss, she doesn't know how loudly she speaks."

"Why didn't she tell us in the car?" Michael asked. "Nobody could overhear us then."

"She is sorry about that," Sophie explained. "She was worried you wouldn't trust her if she told you everything before you got here. Please, let me explain. You see, my husband and I are Jewish, and we have to be extremely careful who we associate with. Every day, we wake up knowing that it might be our last day of freedom. Every time my husband steps out of the door, I worry I might never see him again."

Sophie blinked back tears as she looked at Gerda before returning her gaze to Michael and David.

"Gerda has been a blessing not only to us, but to an entire group of Jews here in Munich. She goes to places and discovers things we could never find on our own. She gets medical supplies for us and meets with people who forge the papers we need to get out of Germany. Gerda risks her life for us all the time, just as she did for your uncle."

"Why did she bring us here?" David asked. "If this is true, the last thing we want to do is bring attention to you and your group. We came here to help, not make matters worse."

"Gerda tells me you are both brave and kind. We are trying to get Jewish families out of Germany before it's too late. Gerda is instrumental in helping us, and so far, we've managed to get eight families out of here."

Michael felt ashamed for doubting Gerda. He looked at her with renewed respect. "I'm sorry," he said. "We had no idea."

"Nobody does," Sophie said. "That's what makes her so important to us, and it's also what makes her a big target for the Nazis. Your uncle Frank knew that which is why he tried his best to send her away. He is the one person above all others that she wanted to save, but he wouldn't leave without Herbert. And *he* wouldn't leave because of his stupid pride."

Sophie closed her eyes and stared at the floor. Gerda was doing the same, and they embraced in the centre of the room.

"Why are we here?" Michael asked gently. "What can we do to help you?"

"You have a very important task ahead of you," Gerda said. "Perhaps the most important task in the world right now."

Chapter Twenty-Six

Michael slumped next to his brother on the couch. He paused for a moment while he tried to come to terms with Gerda's words.

"I'm confused," he said after a long pause.

"What do you want us to do?" David asked. "Unless you're wanting to break the Jews out of the Dachau concentration camp, there's nothing else we can do."

"You're not breaking anyone out of Dachau," Sophie said. "That's suicide, and we'll play no part in that. What we're going to do is get you out of Germany before the Nazis find out who you are. If they do, they'll torture you, and you will disappear, never to be seen again. It's happened before and it'll happen again. You are in great danger, and your mere presence here puts everyone else in danger too."

"How is that an important task?" David's brow furrowed. "I'm confused."

"Everything will be clear," Sophie said. "As Gerda said, you have a very important duty ahead of you. Perhaps the most important duty of all. Your job is to go back to England

and make everyone sit up and listen to what is going on here."

Sophie exchanged a troubled look with Gerda. "The plight of the German Jews must be brought to their attention. The Nazis must be stopped. Hitler must be stopped before he destroys all of Europe, England included. You must go back and make them listen."

"How do we do that?" Michael asked. "I can't even get a dog to listen, never mind an entire country. What you're asking is impossible."

"Perhaps it is, but you have to try. Your government must know what the Nazis are doing because if they are not stopped, it is coming to your country as well."

"How do we get out?" David asked.

"We're working on that," Gerda said. "In the meantime, we'll stay here where we should be safe. Tomorrow, I will take you to Dachau so you can see for yourself where they are keeping Frank and Herbert, as well as thousands more just like them, whose only crime is that they are Jewish."

Michael looked at his brother. "What do you think?"

David grimaced and shrugged his shoulders. "They're right," he said flatly. "There's nothing more we can do here. We might not be able to get Frank and Herbert out of Dachau, but we can make a difference if we tell the world what we've learned. At the very least, we have to warn them what's coming if Hitler isn't stopped."

"How?" Michael asked. "Who's going to listen to us?"

"Our father, for one. He can take our message to Chamberlain and Churchill. We have to make them listen, Michael. We have to, for the sake of the world. At least that way, should Frank and Herbert die in that concentration camp, they won't have died for nothing."

Michael nodded. "Let's do it."

In the corridor outside apartment 1412, Benno Vogel, a middle-aged veteran of the Great War, pulled his ear away from the door. He hadn't heard much of the conversation, but he'd heard enough.

He shuffled off, dragging his left leg behind him towards the painful journey down the long flight of stairs and the exit. He normally cursed the shrapnel wound from the final days in the trenches for the pain that followed his every waking moment, but today he forgot all about his injury.

Today he, Benno Vogel, would do a great service to his country. Herr Kreise would be pleased with him.

Chapter Twenty-Seven

L ater that afternoon, the boys hid in the bedroom when a knock on the door sent everyone inside into a panicked frenzy.

Gerda remained with Sophie and helped to remove any evidence of the boys being there. Once satisfied, Sophie cracked open the door to see who was there.

Michael and David stood next to a window that opened onto a fire escape, and if something was amiss, they were to get out that way. Michael's legs tightened and cramped as he stood ready to evacuate at a moment's notice.

The codeword was 'Stefan', and if they heard that word they were to get out and never come back. Michael realised with trepidation that if they heard that word, he and David would be alone in the middle of a large city that was a Nazi stronghold. He had no idea how they would ever get back to the safety of France.

What have we done? How stupid were we to believe we could just waltz in here, find Frank and Herbert, and then waltz right out again? All we're going to do is get ourselves, and probably a lot of other innocent people killed for our stupidity.

He kicked himself for not taking their mission as seriously as he should have. Now it was a matter of survival, and not just for himself and David. Neither had considered the possibility that other people would risk their lives for them, and the thought of it made Michael break into a cold sweat.

"We cannot allow these people to die for us," he whispered into David's ear. "As kind as they are, we have to leave here tonight and find our own way out of Germany. We can't have their deaths on our consciences." He gestured towards the fire escape with his left hand.

David nodded. "I was thinking the same thing. We leave tonight."

After several tense minutes, the door swung open, and Gerda gestured for them to come out. A tall, skinny man with short brown hair and thick eyelashes that would stand out in a crowd stood next to Sophie. They were about the same height, and Michael wondered if they were in the land of the giants. Normally he would have smiled at such a thought, but not today. Not here.

"You must be Stefan?" David asked.

The man nodded curtly. "My wife was just telling me all about you. I'm sorry about your uncle and great-grandfather, but rest assured that we will do all we can to get you out of Germany safely."

Michael's gaze dropped to the ground. His mind raced with thoughts of their failure and the dire situation they found themselves in. Why had he ever thought that he, a mere teenager, could make a difference? The weight on his shoulders felt heavier than any burden he had carried before, and he struggled to stand upright. His thoughts drifted back to his home in England, where he could be carefree once again. But here, in the heart of Nazi Germany, he knew he had to face the harsh reality of the situation and grow up faster than he'd ever imagined.

"We're grateful to you," his voice croaked. "But we insist you don't put yourself in danger on our behalf. You have enough to worry about without us making it worse."

Stefan strode over to Michael and grabbed his slumped shoulders. "Believe it or not, you are our best hope of salvation. Britain and France need to know what is happening before it's too late. War is coming, and soon all of Europe will be ablaze with Nazi hatred. Jews everywhere will be persecuted and killed. You are our one chance to get the word out so your governments can stop this before it gets any worse."

"That's a lot of responsibility for two young men to bear," David said. "We don't feel worthy of your support, and the last thing we need is for something to happen to you because of us."

"You are a well-connected family," Sophie said. "You alone may not get your government to listen, but your father and his peers can. Your task is to convince them of the seriousness of the situation. It's up to them to do the rest."

"It's a lot of ifs and maybes," David said. "If we're all you have, then it's not much of a plan. I'm sorry to say it, but we're not worthy of such an important task."

Gerda stepped forward and gathered David's hands in hers. "It may not be much, but what you have provided is hope, which is what we didn't have before. Please don't take that away from us."

The room fell silent in the intense atmosphere. Michael clenched and unclenched his fists, staring at the wall in front of him as if he could will away the feeling of inadequacy gnawing at him.

"Well, today is quite the day." Stefan broke the silence. "We have visitors from England, and I lost my job at the factory."

Michael watched Sophie's glassy-eyed stare of hopelessness. Never in his life had he experienced such a terrible feeling of inadequacy. It was as though he was watching a theatre play of a family disintegrating in front of him.

"What happened?" Sophie asked with a trembling voice.

"The boss had a meeting this morning with some Nazis, and when it was over, he fired all the Jews who worked for him. He told us we were preventing true Germans from having good jobs and that we should be ashamed of ourselves for thinking we deserved it."

"What will you do?" Gerda asked.

Sophie shrugged her shoulders. "What are any of us able to do? We'll starve to death before this is over."

"There's more," Stefan said. "I've heard the Nazis are moving Jewish families out of apartments and rehousing them somewhere else. Men and older boys are being sent away, probably to the camp in Dachau, and they house the women and children who knows where. They say they need the apartments for German families."

"Why do they do this to us?" Sophie wrung her hands and turned to Michael and David. "This is not unexpected. Do you see why you must get word to your government in England? Without your help, we are all going to die."

Michael swallowed and nodded slowly. He understood.

"You need to be careful while you're here." Stefan changed the subject. "I'm sure Sophie already warned you, but there are eyes and ears everywhere."

Michael's head was swirling with so many emotions attacking him from different angles. He marvelled at how casually Stefan and Sophie had accepted the news that they'd just lost their livelihood. He'd never given much thought to his own privileged situation, but right now, at this moment, it hit him hard how much he took simple things like bread and milk for granted, never mind the more serious matters of housing and stability.

Whatever happened, he would find a way to return to help these people. That was the silent vow he made to himself there and then.

"She told us." David nudged Michael to bring him back into the conversation.

"Each apartment block has a Blockleiter, and ours is no exception," Stefan continued.

"What's a Blockleiter?" Michael interrupted. He'd never heard the term before.

"I'm surprised you don't know," Stefan said. "You both speak such good German that I'm surprised you haven't heard the term before."

Both David and Michael shook their heads. "Never heard of it," David said. "Why would we?"

"It's small things like this that will get you killed," Stefan said. "Every German knows what a Blockleiter is, and by not knowing, you are giving yourselves away as foreign spies."

"Tell us what it means then." Michael wasn't in the mood for any lectures.

"A Blockleiter is nothing more than a snoop, or a spy." Sophie spat the words out. "Each street or apartment block has a block warden whose job it is to spread Nazi lies and propaganda. Their other job is to spy on the residents and report any anti-Nazi activities to the Gestapo. They are vile traitors who prey on the people they either don't like or the ones who stand against the Nazis."

"You have one of those here?" David asked. "Is this what a dictatorship looks like in Germany? We've only ever heard of it from afar, and it's much different in real life."

"We have a particularly nasty one," Stefan said. "Vogel is a rabid Nazi with a huge chip on his shoulder. He had plenty of enemies in the block, and one by one he made up lies so they would be punished and removed. He hates us because we're Jewish, and he's looking for any reason he can find to have us arrested."

"What does he get out of this?" David asked. "Surely he won't have any friends left if he behaves like that towards everyone he lives around?"

Stefan snorted. "Vogel doesn't have any friends. They deserted him years ago, along with his wife. He gets extra privileges and a larger apartment, along with better living conditions."

"What does he look like?" David asked. "Just in case we run into him."

"Oh, you can't miss him," Stefan replied. "He's a veteran of the last war and has a war wound that he loves telling everyone about. He was shelled in the trenches by the British, who he hates by the way, so be careful you don't speak any English around him. His left leg was badly damaged, and he drags it behind him wherever he walks."

"He won't be hard to miss then," Michael said.

"If he's standing still, you might not recognise him," Sophie said. "He's short, or he is to us, maybe not so much for you. He's about our age, and he has a small beard that is more grey than brown. Surprisingly, he doesn't have the moustache that most of Hitler's followers seem to have, but he has the most terrible teeth you've ever seen. He speaks with a high-pitched voice, and he sneers whenever he looks at you."

"That about sums him up," Stefan said. "He's a disgusting man, but one who has the ear of the Gestapo, so he is very dangerous to us."

"What was his name again?" Michael asked.

"Benno Vogel and he lives in the biggest apartment on the first floor because he doesn't like using the stairs," Sophie explained. "The lift is broken half the time, so that can't be relied on to work. He had the family evicted for some made-up charges so he could get the apartment. They had young children too, but he didn't care."

"He shouldn't be hard to miss," David said. "Hopefully we won't come into contact with him, so he won't have any reason to watch you any closer than he already does."

"What are our plans?" Gerda asked. She'd been quiet for most of the conversation. "I was going to take them for a drive around the camp tomorrow so they could see it for themselves. Then I thought we could take a picnic in the gardens of Dachau Palace and look down on the town as Frank and I used to do occasionally. You can't see much from there because it's three or four kilometres from the camp, but you get a good idea of what the town of Dachau looks like."

"That's a good idea," Stefan said. "It'll give us time to get everything arranged for their exit. I've already left word for the others to come here tonight for a meeting."

"What time are they coming?" Sophie asked.

"Seven. We have to be quick, so we're not seen, but this is the safest place to meet. Hopefully, we'll have you out of here tomorrow night."

Chapter Twenty-Eight

Tensions rose as the clock on the wall approached seven PM. Sophie continually glanced at the apartment door as she set the table for four dinner guests. The other four would have to make do with the chairs and couch in the living room. The cramped apartment would be filled to bursting point that evening.

"Isn't it dangerous to have everyone coming here?" David asked. "Especially if this chap Vogel is as bad as you say he is."

"We all live in this apartment block," Stefan replied. "We've been friends for years, and we always have dinner at each other's apartments. Vogel knows this, and although he hates it when we get together, he won't suspect anything untoward."

"Why does he hate you getting together with friends?" Michael asked. "It seems like a perfectly normal thing to do."

"Because we're all Jews," Sophie answered for her husband.

The apartment fell silent again as each of them became

lost in their own thoughts. Michael watched Gerda helping Sophie prepare the meagre meal that had to accommodate three extra people because she had shown up unannounced with the two Englishmen. How they would feed a further three was beyond him.

"Is there anything we can do to help?" he asked as Sophie shuffled by him. "We have plenty of money to buy food, and we're happy to pitch in."

Sophie smiled. "That's a kind gesture, but it's unnecessary. In recent times, everyone's been forced to bring their own food to these meetings because most of us are out of work and our resources are low. We get by, and that's all we can ask for in times such as these."

"Are you sure?" Michael prompted. "We're more than happy to help."

"It was different when our friends were allowed to own their own grocery stores." Sophie closed her eyes and gently swayed her head from side to side. "Then we could fill our baskets and buy whatever fresh goods we desired. Now, the Nazis make sure we struggle and starve. They harass us when we enter the shops, and we are only allowed to buy the food that non-Jews don't want because it's out of date."

She touched Michael's arm. "How do you think it would look if we suddenly filled our baskets to the brim with the best goods on offer? While it's tempting, such a gesture would quickly get back to the Gestapo, and the next thing you know, they'd be raiding our homes and arresting Stefan. It's better this way."

Sophie blinked and looked away.

Michael placed his hand on her shoulder and gave it a gentle squeeze. His heart hurt for her and the thousands of others who only wanted to live their lives like everyone else. He ground his teeth in anger at what the Nazis were doing to these kind, wonderful people. He might have only just met them, but they had already won him over with their generosity and bravery.

He watched Gerda going through the motions as she helped Sophie ready the apartment for the night's get-together. He wondered how she kept herself so grounded after all that had happened to her. If it were him, he'd have gone berserk by now.

He looked around for David and found him sitting in the room at the rear of the apartment by the window next to the fire escape. He was deep in conversation with Stefan, so Michael wandered over and sat on the floor next to them.

"I was just telling your brother what is going to happen tonight, so I'm glad you've joined us. Our friends are Jews, just like us. Also, like us, they don't want to just sit and wait for the Nazis to arrest them without doing something about it. Tonight, we'll work out a plan to get you out of here, and if we're lucky, we might get at least one other family out with you."

"What will happen to them once they get into France?" David asked. "I don't think we can get them into England without a passport and a good reason for them to be there."

"They won't be going to England with you," Stefan answered. "They will remain in France, or they may even head to Holland or Belgium, where they know people that will help them find their feet. We just need to get them out of Germany."

"Consider it done," Michael said. "We'll take care of them and help them across the border. That's the least we can do."

"Thank you."

The apartment fell silent when a loud knock sounded on the door. Stefan jumped to his feet and placed his finger over his lips, telling the boys to remain quiet. He closed the door to the room, leaving them in darkness as he left.

Michael opened the window in case they had to make a fast exit, and they waited with bated breath for the all-clear. Another series of knocks was followed by another, and their hearts beat louder with each bang on the door.

Whatever was going on out there, not knowing was killing Michael, and he paced around, unable to stay still. The voices were low and muffled, and although he couldn't hear what they were saying, they didn't sound like words of anger or fear.

After what seemed an age, the door swung open, and Stefan stood there with a big grin on his face. "Ralf, Willi, I would like you to meet our friends from the apartment block. Please, come join us."

Michael pressed his palm into his chest and sighed in immense relief. He followed his brother out into the crowded room and shook hands with the three guests who had just arrived carrying their own dinners.

"Gentlemen, these are Walter, Hans, and Walter's wife, Ella. My friends, please meet Ralf and Willi, who are friends of Gerda's."

Michael thought it surreal as they all shook hands in the middle of the apartment. It felt forced, and the smiles hid the anguish that their eyes could not. He went along with it and wondered when they would get down to the serious matters that couldn't wait.

Sophie turned her back on the greetings and turned up the radio until it was so loud the conversation could barely be heard. She gestured in sign language to Gerda, who was standing next to David.

"Vogel hates it when they have their get-togethers, and

he always listens outside the door. The radio should prevent him from hearing our conversations."

David relayed the message to Michael, who nodded in agreement.

The conversation was light as the group found places to sit and eat. Michael felt pangs of guilt with every mouthful, and he made a silent promise to repay Sophie and Stefan before he left.

He weighed up the visitors as best he could from what little he knew. Walter looked like a younger version of Hans, and although nobody had said anything, he knew they were father and son. Walter was around thirty years of age, and Hans was somewhere in his sixties. They were both of average height with broad, strong shoulders that told of heavy manual labour. Walter's short black hair sat in tight curls over his head, which was the same as Hans, except his hair was greying and thinner. They both had dull brown eyes as if the hard life they were being forced to endure was taking its toll on them.

Ella was around the same age as Walter, and like the others, she looked as if the heavy burdens of life were getting her down. Small, at around five feet tall, her slender frame looked fragile. Her blue eyes sat in an oval-shaped face that Michael imagined used to shine with life and happiness. Her brown hair was parted on the right-hand side, which flowed to her neckline.

David noticed his brother weighing up the new guests and kicked him under the table. "Stop staring," he said in English. "You're making everyone uncomfortable."

Stefan leant forward towards the two boys. "Please, German only." He pointed at the closed doorway. "Eyes and ears."

Once the dishes were cleared, the tone became more

serious, and Michael knew it was time to get down to business. His stomach knotted at the thought of what they were about to do. He felt a mix of excitement and fear, but whatever it was, he was ready to get out of this totalitarian dictatorship and get back to his own country, where freedom was taken for granted.

"These two young men are going to help us," Stefan started the conversation. "They are going to tell the world what Hitler is doing to the Jews in Germany."

Nods of agreement from all around the room followed a moment of silence.

"Suffice it to say, we have to get them out of Germany. We need to use the opportunity to get Walter, Ella, and their two children out at the same time."

More nods of approval.

"I don't know if this will help," David spoke up. "But we have perfectly good identification papers that got us into Germany with no problems. We had a run-in with the Gestapo in Stuttgart and we passed with flying colours, so there's no reason we can't use them to get back to the border with France. How we get across is a whole other matter, of course, but we shouldn't have any issues getting there."

The conversation stopped, and everyone stared at David. "Gerda knows," he added meekly.

"We also know this," Stefan said. "I do not doubt that you could reach the French border with no problems, but as you said, how would you get across? We only have one chance at this, and we can't afford for you to be stopped. We're also sending Walter, Ella, and the children, and you will have to be together until you reach France. After that, you will go your separate ways."

"So, our identification papers are no good?" David asked.

"They will work if you are stopped between here and the Rhine. You will need a cover story as to why you were with a Jewish family, but the papers will tell them who you are."

"So, they're no good then," David repeated.

The room fell quiet again.

"Gerda is taking them around the camp tomorrow in Dachau," Stefan explained. "This gives us time to make the arrangements. There will be a truck waiting for you at seven tomorrow night. It will take you via the back roads to a town called Breisach, which is on the Rhine, close to Freiburg. It's a long drive of around five hours, so be prepared, and may God help you."

"How do we get over the Rhine?" David asked.

"Once you arrive in Breisach, a small boat will be waiting for you. The codeword will be Luxembourg. If you don't hear that from the boat owner, then run for your lives and hope for the best. Hopefully, it won't come to that, but it's happened before and I'm sure it will happen again."

"How are you paying for all of this?" David, ever the pragmatist, asked.

"That is none of your concern," Stefan replied tersely. "We have sufficient resources for the operation. We have to get you out so you can spread the word, and this is the last chance Walter, Ella and the children might have, so we have to make it work."

"I ask because we have the resources to help," David said. "We want to help, and we can. Please allow us to contribute, at least to future operations, if not this one. It's the least we can do."

"I'll consider it. For now, this meeting is over. Unless you hear otherwise, meet at the abandoned warehouse at seven tomorrow night. And be prepared." Stefan turned to

Ella and Walter. "Take nothing more than you have to, because it's going to be a long and dangerous journey."

After a shared prayer, they all stood up and got ready to leave. Sophie turned down the radio and spoke loudly. "Thank you for a wonderful dinner. Until next time, may God bless us all with his grace and kindness."

Everyone answered in kind as they moved towards the door. David and Michael walked into the exit room and left the door open just enough so they could see everyone leave.

Benno Vogel hid in the doorway of an apartment farther down the corridor as Stefan opened the door and peered around. Walter, Ella and Hans went the opposite way, and once they'd gone, Vogel emerged from his hiding place and limped after them towards the lifts that he desperately hoped were working.

Chapter Twenty-Nine

He wasn't sure whether it was the loud bangs or the kick to the ribs that woke him up, but whatever it was, it got Michael's attention. His bleary eyes searched the darkness for clues, but his foggy mind wasn't ready to give up on sleep.

David kicked him again.

"Get up," he hissed. "There's someone here."

The fog cleared as he grasped what was happening, and he leapt to his feet to join David, who was peering through a small crack in the bedroom door.

Dawn was barely breaking, and dark clouds blocked whatever dim light was trying to squeeze through. Heavy rain slammed into the bedroom windows, and at first, Michael thought that was what they had heard.

"Is it the thunder that's woken everybody up?" he whispered, hoping to hear an affirmative response.

A second, even louder crash on the apartment door told them otherwise. Sophie ran to the room where the boys were and pushed the door open. Stefan waited by the apartment door until she was ready.

Gerda, who hadn't heard the commotion, was now on her feet after Sophie had shaken her awake on the couch where she'd slept, their hands exchanging messages in rapid succession.

"Open the door! Now, or we'll break it down."

"Get out of here, now. Go," Sophie hissed. "They must not find you in here. Get out. Go."

"What about the plans for tonight?" David asked as Sophie pushed him back towards the window.

"They're off. Someone reported us. Probably Vogel, but who knows? There are eyes and ears everywhere."

Michael got a glance at Gerda rubbing her eyes as she headed to the apartment door to join Stefan. It was too dark to see the expressions on their faces, but he knew they must be terrified.

He knew he was. His chest pounded as he threw open the window and allowed the winter storm to enter their sanctuary. Even though it was cold, he felt the sweat dripping down his forehead, and he fought to keep his knees from buckling beneath him.

Heavy wind and rain drowned out most of the noise from the apartment, but the last thing he'd seen before Sophie closed the door was the apartment door crashing open and four men running in with pistols raised. They were screaming something that Michael couldn't hear, but he knew what they were saying.

Stefan and Gerda held their hands above their heads and fell to their knees.

How brave are they? Michael closed his eyes for a moment, feeling inadequate and cowardly. "How can we run off when they're facing the Gestapo? We're the reason they're here, and we're the ones running away and leaving them in the lurch."

"It's not us," David replied. "It's Vogel, and if they find us, it'll make it worse."

David pushed himself through the window. Michael followed him and was immediately soaked to the skin from the driving rain penetrating every gap in his inadequate clothing. Howling winds shook the metal steps on the fire escape, and it felt anything but safe. He gripped the sides for dear life and climbed down as fast as the wavering frame safely allowed.

David ran down, two or three at a time, with Michael not far behind. When they reached the platform on the third floor, Michael stopped.

The light in the room they'd occupied moments ago had been turned on. Was it Gerda? He couldn't tell from the angle he was looking. Driving rain hurt his exposed face, and it forced him to squint as he looked up.

Whoever it was – *I'm sure it's Gerda* – she had her back to the open window. Another shadow told him someone else was in the room with her.

The boys huddled into a small recess against the wall, hoping it would be enough cover for them not to be seen. A small ledge above their heads protected them a little, but not much.

A scream pierced the early morning downpour, and the boys heard the distinct sound of a gunshot above their heads.

Michael stepped forward to look up just in time to see the shadowy figure fall forwards. She – Michael was convinced it was Gerda – was replaced at the window by the figure of a man wearing a brimmed hat leaning over, staring at the rain and wind-lashed fire escape below him.

Michael pushed himself back into David, hoping the Gestapo agent couldn't see them. The boys huddled together for several minutes and waited for the rattling and shaking as someone climbed onto the fire escape.

"He mustn't have seen us," David said. "Let's go."

"We can't leave like this." Michael didn't budge. "I'm pretty sure they shot Gerda. We can't run away when they need our help. We have to go back."

"It's suicide." David tried reasoning with his brother. "They knew the risks, and if they were shot, it's not because of us. We'll only make it worse if we go back."

"Worse or not, I'm going back to help them. I can't leave here knowing Gerda's bleeding to death up there because of us."

"It isn't because of us," David corrected him. "It's Vogel. I bet he turned them in and told them they were planning something. Having the radio so loud was probably enough to raise his suspicions."

Michael didn't wait another second. He would argue with David later. Right now, Gerda and the others needed their help, and he wasn't about to abandon them.

He took a deep breath to steady himself and clambered back up the steps of the fire escape.

Chapter Thirty

Soaking wet from the atrocious weather, Michael peered over the window ledge to see if the man was still in the room. All he saw was a woman's legs sticking out from under the windowsill.

He climbed back inside, being careful to make as little noise as possible. He stepped over the woman's body lying prone on the floor and knelt beside her. Adrenaline had kicked in, and although his heart beat like a hammer, the shaking had stopped, leaving him feeling surprisingly calm, given the enormity of the situation.

As expected, David was right behind him. He'd never abandoned his brother before, and Michael knew he wouldn't do it now in the moment of his greatest need.

An angry stare was all he got from David, but they both knelt beside the fallen woman, who was face down on the floor. Michael gently turned her over, and he choked when he saw her face.

It *was* Gerda! Her eyes were closed, and Michael gently raised her head and held her in his soaked arms.

"Gerda, I'm so sorry. Please don't die, not for us." He

gently shook her, and as he did, he saw a large pool of dark liquid on the floor beneath her. Her chest was oozing blood, and the two boys exchanged anxious looks as they realised her life was in the balance.

Shouts and yells from behind the closed door made him flinch as he rocked Gerda back and forth like a parent would rock a newborn child. Her eyes flickered open, and she grabbed Michael's arm with a blood-soaked hand.

"I'm so sorry." Tears fell freely, joining the rainwater that fell onto Gerda's damaged body. A wave of relief washed over him as he whispered into her ear. "You're going to be okay, Gerda. We'll get you out of here and find a doctor."

"Go back to England and tell the world what they are doing to us," Gerda struggled to speak. "Don't die here with us today. That's how you can help us. That's how you can help Frank."

She opened her hand and showed Michael a crumpled piece of paper she was gripping. "Find Father Eise."

Gerda's eyes flickered and closed. Michael held her tightly, trying his best to control the heaving in his chest. David placed his hand over Michael's mouth and whispered in his ear.

"Quiet, Michael. They're still here." He pointed to the closed door of the bedroom.

Michael's insides were quivering and burning, and a red mist descended on him with an intensity he'd never experienced before. He gently laid Gerda's head back down and made sure she looked comfortable.

With fire raging through his veins, he joined David at the door. "It's awful, but now isn't the time to grieve," David said.

Michael nodded, glad of David's ever-wise presence.

Screams and yells told the boys the Gestapo were working on Sophie and Stefan, so Michael cracked the door open gently so they could see what was happening.

Sophie was on her knees with her hands behind her head. She was trying to speak through loud sobs because of what the men were doing to Stefan.

The four men were all dressed the same in long trench coats covering shirts and ties underneath. They looked like respectable businessmen, but their cruelty said otherwise. All wore the same type of brimmed hat, and Michael remembered the Gestapo agent on the train had dressed exactly the same.

This must be their uniform. It's good because they're easy to spot in a crowd.

One of them barked questions at Sophie, and each time she refused to answer, or didn't give the answer they wanted to hear, another of them hit Stefan with the butt of a pistol. Blood poured from several wounds on his head, but he knelt in resolute defiance against the onslaught.

Two of them stood over Stefan, and another stood next to the apartment door. The remaining agent, the one who seemed in charge, stood over Sophie and was barking questions at her.

"Where are the men who were here last night?" he yelled at her. "We know you had a meeting, and we know you are planning something against the Reich. Your friend is already dead in the bedroom, but it doesn't have to be that way for you. Just tell us who those men were and why they were here, and you'll be shown mercy."

"We already told you. We had dinner with some friends, as we always do," Sophie sobbed. "Ask Vogel. I'm sure he tells you everything that goes on here."

Another smack to Stefan's head.

"Why don't you ask Walter or Hans?" Sophie pleaded. "They'll tell you the same thing."

"Oh, we will. We are right now, in fact. And they'll tell us what you were up to. It's such a shame their children have to suffer, don't you think?"

A tense silence filled the room, and Michael struggled to control the heavy feelings of guilt and rage coursing through his body.

Another heavy blow to Stefan's head made Sophie scream. "Enough, stop. I'll tell you everything you want to know, but please leave the children alone."

"Finally," the man in charge said. "I'm waiting."

"We had dinner with our friends like we always do. That's all."

"I'm losing my patience with you." The man leant forward over Sophie and grabbed her jaw in his hand. "I'm telling you, you filthy Jew, I'm running out of patience. I know you're plotting something, so why don't you spare us both the time and the suffering by revealing your plans?"

"Perhaps we should take them to Wittelsbacher Palace, sir," one of the other Gestapo men said. "They'll talk there."

"Yes, they will," the senior officer agreed. "Perhaps that's what we'll do. Your friends are already on the way there and believe me, they won't enjoy it."

Another heavy blow to the head sent Stefan spinning to the ground. Michael watched through the crack in the door and didn't know what to do. He couldn't just stay there and watch the people who'd risked everything to help them get dragged away to almost certain death and do nothing.

Then again, the Gestapo agents had weapons, and they did not. It wasn't a fair fight, and Michael knew it. Vogel must have told the Gestapo about him and David, but if they remained hidden and out of sight, at least it gave

Stefan and Sophie a chance of surviving, which is more than poor Gerda had had. He knew nothing about the palace they'd mentioned, but whatever it was, it wasn't good.

"What about the woman in there?" a Gestapo agent asked his boss.

"She's dead. She attacked me and tried pushing me out of the window, so I shot her. I'll get someone over here to remove her body. Let's get these two back to the palace."

Michael felt a tug on his leg behind him. Assuming it was David wanting to get a better look, he shifted his position to make way. He was stunned when he saw Gerda, drenched in blood, push past him.

He and David stayed hidden behind the wall while Gerda opened the door. Without skipping a beat, she raised her hands and fired the gun she was holding at the chief Gestapo officer, striking him in the chest.

The man fell, and all hell broke loose. The three remaining Gestapo agents all opened fire at the same time.

Gerda fell under a hail of bullets, and with her went Sophie, who'd been caught in the crossfire. Stefan let out a guttural roar from his throat, and in one movement, rose to his feet and grabbed the gun from the man closest to him.

Before anyone could react, he turned it around and shot the Gestapo agent point blank in the neck. The remaining two agents fired back, and Stefan fell to the floor beside his wife.

Chapter Thirty-One

The acrid smell of gunpowder and smoke hung in the air, mixed with the metallic smell of spent casings, and the blood that spattered the walls and floor of the tiny apartment.

Michael's ears were ringing from the deafening gunshots, and he felt disoriented and confused. He glanced around the room, and his stomach churned at the carnage left behind.

Bullet holes had smashed through the walls and the shattered furniture, leaving broken glass mixed with blood as it spread across the floor.

Not knowing where to look, his gaze settled on Gerda's bullet-ridden body. She had been on her knees when she'd fired at the Gestapo chief, and when his comrades shot her, she fell backwards and off to the side before finally settling close to Michael's feet behind the door.

Everything seemed to have happened in slow motion. Each movement or vision had registered, and every sound had appeared to be octaves below normal. Before he knew it, Michael was acting on impulse rather than rational thought. He took Gerda's gun, still hot from where it had fallen beside her body, and rolled to the open doorway.

Although he'd fired a rifle at his father's firing range, this was the first time he'd ever seen a pistol, never mind fired one.

Neither of the two remaining men knew the boys were there, so they hadn't expected to see anyone else in the apartment. The one closest had his back to Michael and was on his knees beside his fallen chief. The other was facing the open doorway, giving all his attention to his injured and dying fellow secret police officer lying on the floor.

Blood was everywhere, and Michael blinked rapidly while trying to ignore the chaotic scene facing him. For some strange reason, an image of Al Capone, the infamous American gangster, entered his mind. He imagined the scene before him looked similar to some of the crime sprees Capone had been involved in during his heyday in Chicago a few years earlier.

He held his breath, aimed, and fired. His hand recoiled, but it wasn't as bad as he'd expected, at least not compared to his father's rifle.

A split second after he fired, the Gestapo officer yelped and fell on top of his fallen superior. As he was falling, the last agent standing spun around to see who was firing at them. His training must have kicked in because he threw himself to the ground as he spun and aimed his pistol at his enemy.

Michael was already aiming by the time the man had turned around, and he fired two or three shots – he didn't keep count – into the head and body of the man who'd killed Stefan.

With both men fallen, Michael dropped the weapon and stared at what he'd just done. He tried getting to his feet, but froze when he got to his knees. When he tried to speak, his words dried up mid-sentence. Whatever he'd just done, his mind was shutting it out as though trying to erase it from his consciousness.

His stomach churned, and he retched at the sight of the carnage spread out on full display before him. His hands shook, and he stared at them as if they had a life of their own.

He looked across at David, who sat against the wall staring at him with a face so pale he looked like all the blood in his body had drained away. He nodded his head towards his brother as if to say he'd done the right thing, but it didn't help. Michael wondered if anything would ever help.

As if by some divine intervention, reality seemed to return, and the groans and moans of the wounded suddenly got loud and clear. Michael could now hear nothing but his heartbeat and wounded men crying in agony. He wondered if this was what it had been like for his father and Uncle Frank in the trenches of WW1.

Don't be stupid. That was much worse.

Regaining some of his composure, Michael knew he had to act. David seemed paralysed by the gruesome events, and he just sat looking pale and out of it. Knowing he had only a brief time before reinforcements arrived, he shook his head and forced himself to act.

He knew there would be time to think about it afterwards, but right now he had to act, or they would both be dead within minutes. He forced himself to his feet.

He ran to the men and grabbed their weapons. He didn't know why he did that, but now wasn't the time for questions. After he'd collected them all, he forced himself to look one last time at the shattered bodies of Gerda, Sophie, and Stefan.

"You will not be forgotten," he whispered.

Michael locked the apartment door and ran to the bedroom where David still sat staring into space. He was about to say something when another thought entered his mind. He turned around and ran back into the killing zone behind him.

He ran to the front door and found Gerda's coat hanging on the hanger beside the door. He sighed and whispered one more time in Gerda's general direction. "Please forgive me."

He rummaged in her coat pockets until he found the keys to her vehicle, which he hoped was still parked outside. Then he ran back and found the crumpled piece of paper that was now covered in blood that Gerda had tried giving him earlier.

"Find Father Eise," she'd told him. He had no idea who Father Eise was or where he was located, but that was the least of his worries right now. He looked at his brother, who still sat frozen against the wall.

"Come on, David," he kicked his legs. "We have to go. They'll be here any minute, and they'll kill us if they find us."

David didn't seem to hear him, so he repeated it louder while shaking his shoulders. This seemed to stir him, and he mumbled something that Michael couldn't understand.

He pulled David to his feet, and although he struggled to get moving, he followed Michael out of the window and onto the fire escape.

Chapter Thirty-Two

The heavy rain had slowed to a drizzle, and the visibility was a lot better than it had been earlier. Daylight had forced back the darkness, and Michael could see the alleyway below.

It was clear, but he could already hear the sirens in the distance, and he had no doubt they were heading their way.

He bounced down the steps as fast as he dared, and when he hit the bottom, he looked up to see David taking his time as though he didn't have a care in the world. He ran back up the steps and grabbed him by the arm.

"Come on, David. Clear your head and take charge. I need you to guide me, so snap out of it and start moving." He knew his tone seemed harsh, but time was scarce for anything else. They had only minutes to leave the area before their escape route became impassable.

He dragged David to the blue Volkswagen Type One and stuffed him in the passenger seat, then ran around to the driver's side, jumped behind the wheel, and let out a loud sigh. Not in relief, because they were far from safe, but because he now faced a new dilemma.

It had only been a few months since he'd taken the recently introduced driving test, and although he'd passed, he'd barely driven at all since. He'd certainly never envisaged driving a vehicle with the steering wheel on the opposite side of the car, on roads where they drove on the right-hand side.

If the Gestapo had failed to kill them in the apartment, he might succeed on the roads out of Munich.

If they aren't blocked before we get out.

The car lurched forward, and Michael did his best to control both himself and the vehicle as he drove away from the carnage.

"The car's got kangaroo petrol." David spoke for the first time since they'd left the apartment, referring to the jerking of the car as Michael struggled to control the gear stick and the steering wheel at the same time.

Michael glanced at his brother, who still looked pale and weary. "Welcome back, brother. I thought I'd lost you for a moment back there."

David grunted something and slumped forward. Something wasn't right, but Michael didn't have the time to investigate it now. They had to get out of there as fast as they could without arousing any suspicions, which would be difficult with Michael's terrible driving skills.

He gripped the steering wheel tightly, sweat beading on his forehead. His foot clumsily worked the pedals as he tried to control the vehicle on Munich's unfamiliar roads.

After a few minutes of jerking all over the road, he got the hang of it enough to change gears smoothly. Now all he had to do was find his way out of the danger area. He relaxed his grip on the steering wheel and allowed himself to breathe.

Michael tried to remember the roads Gerda had taken on the way into the city, but he couldn't and soon got lost. He drove anywhere he could, trying to take the side streets rather than the main roads that he was sure were blocked by now.

Dark, heavy clouds hung overhead as he made his way out of Munich. Heavy rain soon followed, and Michael had to give all his attention to the waterlogged roads that were barely visible in the pouring rain.

Eventually, he saw a sign for Freising, and as it was the only place he knew in Germany, he headed towards it. He drove by a lake and stopped on the side of a country lane near a town called Erding.

Something was wrong with David. His head was slumped forward, and he wasn't responding to Michael's words. He turned onto the narrow lane and drove far enough down it so as not to be seen from the main road and pulled over by a clump of three small trees.

He opened the passenger door and David fell sideways towards the road.

"Whoa," Michael said as he caught him before he hit the ground, noticing immediately that his body was soaked in blood. They both were, but when he looked closer, the blood on himself was dark red and dry. The blood on David was bright red and fresh.

"Oh, no. David, are you alright? What happened to you?" His chest tightened again, and the all-too-familiar feeling of desperation returned.

He helped his brother to the wet grass on the side of the road and propped him up against a tree. The rain had stopped, leaving dark, heavy clouds to hang over the boys like the Sword of Damocles.

Michael quickly checked for any injuries and took a sharp breath when he pulled David's jacket back to expose a gunshot wound in his abdomen.

Blood oozed from the wound, and when he looked closer, Michael could see the bullet had gone deep into his body.

"The wall," David whispered hoarsely. "A bullet came through the wall."

Michael's thoughts flashed back to the bullet-ridden apartment. Bullet holes were everywhere, and he could easily see how a stray bullet could have gone through the thin wall and hit David.

With his eyes closed, he rested David's head on his lap. He rocked back and forth, tears pouring down his cheeks. He looked at his hands, which were still stained with Gerda's blood, and watched them tremble and shake as he cradled his brother.

Suddenly, everything became too much for him, and he let out a loud, piercing scream.

"It's my fault. It's all my fault. I'm so sorry. You didn't want to go back up the fire escape, but I made you. Hell, you didn't even want to come here in the first place. It was me who persuaded you, well, me and Gigi."

David reached up with a bloodied hand and touched Michael's shoulder. "It's not your fault," he said in a hoarse voice. "I wanted to come just as much as you did. I'm alright, Michael. You can't get rid of me that easily."

He laughed. They both did. Then David coughed, and fresh blood rolled out of his mouth. Michael stared, wide-eyed in horror as his brother, the man he loved more than anyone else in this world, convulsed and shook. The whites of his eyes shone up at Michael, and with one final effort, he reached up and grabbed his neck.

As Michael watched in horror and disbelief, David's eyes fluttered and closed. He emitted one last sigh and then fell limp and silent.

David Fernsby was dead.

Chapter Thirty-Three

Dorothy Fernsby paced up and down the oversized hallway in her home in Kent from one end to the next. The look on her face told anyone who saw her to keep their distance, and even the ever-reliable Warhurst stayed out of the way.

"What are you doing, Dorothy?" Gigi appeared on the stairs. "It's barely daylight outside and you're down here pacing around like a scalded cat."

"I'm waiting for the college to return my call. The woman I spoke to was locating the dean, and she promised to call me back."

"You called Trinity College?" The blood drained from Gigi's face.

"Of course I did. It's been over a week since David and Michael left without saying goodbye. I've tried calling, but they never called back, which is most unlike them. Nobody can give me a good explanation for their disappearance, and I'm worried they've done something stupid. Those boys would do anything for their father. And Frank, for that matter. I'm worried sick, Gigi."

Dorothy paced up and down the hallway, her steps quickening each time she walked past the table where the telephone sat silently waiting to ring.

"Everyone keeps telling me not to worry, and that they're just being boys, but I can't help it. This is so unlike them, and you know it. They call me at least once a week, and they would never just leave without checking on their father. So don't tell me not to worry."

Gigi hurried down the stairs and stood in front of Dorothy, barring her from pacing any further. "Come sit with me."

"Why? I'm waiting for the telephone to ring. I swear, if they haven't called me by lunchtime, I'm going to Cambridge myself to find them."

Giselle grabbed her arm. "Please. Dorothy. Sit down. The boys aren't in Cambridge."

Dorothy's footsteps slowed until she came to a sudden stop, her breath coming in quick gasps. She turned to face her mother-in-law, her eyes narrowed, and her mouth set in a tight line.

"Where are they? Do you know where they are? Please tell me they aren't in Germany trying to find Frank and Herbert."

Gigi could see the tension in her jaw as she clenched her teeth and folded her arms across her chest in a defensive posture. Dorothy's gaze bore into Gigi like a laser, conveying her anger and frustration.

"I know where they are, and if you'll sit down, I'll tell you."

Gigi steered Dorothy towards the sitting room, but as they got there, a shrill ringing stopped them in their tracks. Dorothy ran back to the hallway.

"Yes, hello? This is Dorothy Fernsby. To whom am I speaking?"

Silence.

Gigi watched Dorothy's face turn a shade of deep purple before she hung up the telephone with a curt thank you. She turned to face Gigi, the fire in her eyes so hot that Gigi could almost reach out and touch it.

"They aren't there. They never returned after the trouble Michael got into with Stourcliffe's boy. The secretary just told me that you sent a telegram informing them that David would be taking some time away because of a family emergency. Is that right, Giselle? Did you send the college a telegram?"

Her eyes pierced Gigi like a knife, but Gigi steadied herself. She had been expecting this.

"Perhaps I should have told you sooner, but with Gerald being so poorly, I didn't want to upset you any more than you already are."

"Are you behind all of this?" Dorothy's voice rose in pitch and her cheeks turned as red as beetroots. "This has your fingerprints all over it. Tell me where they are right now."

Gigi bowed her head. "I may have overstepped the mark a little, but I was trying to stop Gerald from running off to Germany and killing himself."

"What have you done?" Gigi had never seen her like this before, but she didn't blame her.

"Please, sit down, Dorothy."

Dorothy perched on the edge of a chair and leant forwards towards Gigi. "I'm listening."

"We all read Frank's letters. He and my father needed help, and Gerald was determined to help them. You and I both know that he would never have made it if he'd tried to go."

Dorothy's stare fixed on Gigi, making her uncomfortable. Avoiding eye contact, she continued.

"I merely told the boys my concerns, and they agreed to go instead of Gerald."

"You sent my boys to Germany? How dare you?" Dorothy jumped up and approached Gigi with her arms raised. For a moment, she thought her daughter-in-law was going to strike her.

"You never thought to discuss this with either Gerald or myself? These are my children, Gigi, not yours, and they are not pawns you can use for your own benefit. Where are they now? Have you heard from them?"

Gigi shook her head. "They were supposed to just go to Freising and look for Frank and my father. If they weren't there, they were to come straight back without delay. They had two weeks maximum to get into Germany and get home. That's all. They are in no danger because they aren't doing anything wrong."

Dorothy glared at Gigi as though she were the devil himself. "How did they get into Germany? Gerald was supposed to visit that friend of his from the war who made fake passports. Is that where you sent my boys?"

Gigi nodded. "I thought it safer if they acted as Germans rather than Englishmen searching for their Jewish relatives. They're in no danger, Dorothy. All they were told to do was to see if they were there and then come home. That's it."

"We all saw the news in the cinema about that dreadful night when they smashed the Jewish shops and burned the synagogues. It's chaos over there, and you sent my boys right into it without telling their parents. Who do you think you are, Gigi?"

"I'm a concerned parent and daughter, just like you are. I was trying to help Frank and my father, that's what I was thinking, and I didn't tell you because I knew how you'd react, which is over dramatic as you always are."

"How dare you?" Dorothy thundered. She stood over Gigi like a hungry wolf. "You put the lives of two old men who could have left Germany years ago above the lives of my two boys, who had nothing to do with any of this. Who do you think you are, putting their lives above the lives of David and Michael? How dare you?" Dorothy screamed the last sentence.

Judith peered around the doorway. "Are you alright, Mum? I could hear you yelling upstairs."

Dorothy stared at Gigi, seemingly oblivious to Judith's appearance. Gigi waved her into the room and beckoned for her to sit down near her mother.

"Please, Judith, come join us. You might as well hear this."

"I heard. You sent David and Michael to Germany to find Uncle Frank and Papa Herbert without telling Mum and Dad first."

Gigi shrugged. "It's not like that, but yes, I suppose you're right."

Judith gripped her mother's arm. "Are they alright? Has anything happened to them?"

"If they don't come back safely, I shall never forgive you." Dorothy glowered at Gigi. "You've always acted as if you are in charge of this family, but if anything happens to my boys, I swear I shall kill you myself."

Gigi didn't respond. How could she? There was

nothing she could say that would make Dorothy understand.

A thorny silence filled the spaces in the room. Judith held onto her mother, and both of them stared at Gigi.

"I was acting in the best interests of our family," Gigi said eventually.

"You were acting in the best interests of yourself, as you always do," Dorothy corrected her.

"Do not speak to me that way." It was Gigi's turn to get angry and raise her voice. "I'm still the matriarch of this family, and I will be treated with the respect I deserve."

"You are a bitter old woman who feels guilty for abandoning your father years ago in Germany." Dorothy stood up and glared at Gigi. "You've never been anything other than a self-centred bully, always wanting your own way with everything. Well, if anything happens to either of my two boys, you'll see who the matriarch is, and I assure you, it won't be you. This is our house, not yours, and from now on you won't do anything without asking me first. Do you understand?"

Gigi scowled and looked away. "I didn't mean to upset you, and that is why I didn't tell you. I thought they would be back by now."

"Well, they're not. You've seen how upset I've been this last week. You lied to all of us, and yet you sit here looking all sanctimonious and expecting us to accept it. I won't, and I assure you that Gerald won't either when I tell him what you've done."

"Surely you won't burden Gerald with this? He's in hospital recovering from a heart attack."

"He needs to know what you've done to his sons, and if his heart gives way, then that's your fault as well. I'm finished with you, Giselle. You have gone too far this time."

Dorothy took Judith's arm and guided her out of the room. At the doorway, she stopped and turned back to a visibly stunned Giselle Fernsby.

"I don't know why you look so surprised. You should have known I'd react this way. You've always put your precious family in Germany above mine, but I swear that if anything happens to either David or Michael, I shall never forgive you."

She turned to walk away, but at the last moment, she paused and turned around.

"You didn't have anything to do with Gerald getting sick that night, did you? I've thought about it a lot since it happened, and it's terribly convenient that he got sick the very night before he was supposed to leave. Especially as that was the night the boys left as well. It seems a bit planned, don't you think?"

Gigi looked at the floor. "I'm sorry," she said. "It wasn't supposed to be like this. They should have been back by now."

"I thought so. Pack your bags and get out of here. I want you gone as soon as Gerald gets home from the hospital. You are no longer welcome here."

Gigi stared at the floor, wishing it would open up and swallow her.

Chapter Thirty-Four

Michael sat in the wet grass, holding David's head in his lap until it was dark. The rain came in waves all day long, but he didn't seem to notice.

He didn't feel the familiar pangs of hunger or thirst, and his mind never drifted far from the abject guilt and sorrow he felt for killing his brother.

Yes, I killed him. I might not have pulled the trigger, but I might as well have. He warned me not to go back up the fire escape, but as usual, I didn't listen. I ran in like a bull in a china shop without thinking of the consequences. David was right. He was always right. We should never have come here.

Tears fell freely one minute, then the next he was filled with rage at the Gestapo for killing David and all the others.

What for? Why did they kill them? What had they done that was so bad they had to be executed for it?

They were Jewish, and in Hitler's world, that was enough. Gerda and David weren't Jews, of course, but they loved and helped them. Was that enough reason for them to die?

Of course it wasn't, but it didn't matter. They were

dead, and that was it. Nothing could bring them back, nor the four Gestapo agents who died alongside them.

Michael sighed. His hands were shaking so hard he could barely hold David's head. *What have I done? Why did I talk him into coming here? He had his life planned out ahead of him. He would finish his studies at Cambridge, marry a beautiful girl, and one day take over the family business. That was the life meant for David, my ever-wise, placid brother.*

He wasn't supposed to die. Not here. Not like this.

And this is how it went the entire night. Endless circles of rhetorical questions that led back to the same thing.

I killed David. How do I explain that to our parents when I get home?

He laughed out loud. *When I get home! Who am I kidding? I'm not getting out of here alive. The entire Gestapo, and probably the German army, will be out searching for me by now. I'm a dead man walking.*

Heavy clouds promised another miserable day as dawn broke over the horizon. Michael opened the back of the car to see if there was a blanket or sheet to wrap around David. He knew he couldn't drive around with him in the car, but what was he supposed to do? Just leave him at the side of the road?

He could never do that to his brother. No, he'd have to find a suitable place to bury him where he could lie undisturbed until he returned to take him home. That was the least he could do, not only for David, but for himself, and their mother and father back home, who would be distraught when they found out. Their mother would be hysterical, and Michael dreaded having to tell them what had happened.

During the night, he'd seriously considered using one of

the guns he'd taken from the Nazis on himself. Everything had gone so wrong, and he couldn't face the dawn without David.

He chased away the dark thoughts. *It's bad enough that our parents have lost one son, but to lose them both would destroy them.*

He put the gun away and turned his thoughts to his current situation. It was hopeless, and he knew it. By now, the entire German apparatus would be out searching for him, and it was only a matter of time before they caught and executed him for what he'd done. All he could do was head for the Rhine and hope to get across before they caught up to him.

He rated his chances as slim to none.

During his search of the car, he discovered a spade that was presumably there to dig it out of snowdrifts during the Bavarian winters. Michael took the shovel and a flowery blue cloth that looked more like an old curtain than any blanket he'd ever seen.

But it would have to do.

As soon as it was light enough to see, Michael wrapped David carefully in the curtain/blanket and dragged him to the farthest tree on the left-hand side as he looked at it from the road.

He reluctantly removed the papers that identified him as Ralf Fischer and put them in his pocket. For now, it was better for David to be unidentified, should he be discovered by the locals.

It would be a travesty if he was removed and reburied somewhere as a fictitious man that had never existed. He was David Fernsby, and when he lay in consecrated ground, that would be the name that was written on his gravestone.

Michael gripped the handle of the shovel, feeling the

rough edges of the wood digging into his skin. He pushed it down into the soft, muddy earth, feeling the resistance give way under the force of the blade. The muscles in his arms and back strained as he lifted the dirt out of the hole, tossing it aside with a determined grunt. The damp earth clung to his clothes, leaving his shirt and trousers heavy and clinging to his skin.

His breath came in ragged gasps, and he wiped the sweat from his brow with the back of his hand. He dug deeper, his movements becoming more frantic as he fought against the rising panic inside him. The image of his brother's lifeless body flashed before his eyes, and he worked faster, desperate to get the task done and give his brother a decent, if temporary, burial.

He lost track of time as he dug, his mind consumed by the physical effort and the weight of his grief. By the time he finished, his hands were raw and blistered, his clothes caked in mud and sweat.

Michael's lips were dry and cracked, and he felt incredibly thirsty. He knew he'd have to find water soon, or he'd be in serious trouble.

During the night, when he was at his lowest ebb and contemplating suicide, he'd pulled himself back with a firm promise that he'd do all he could to survive and get home to tell his parents what had happened.

David deserved a proper funeral in England, and they would have to kill him to prevent that from happening.

Eventually, he had a hole big enough and deep enough to protect David from any animals that might be scavenging in the area, and he pulled his corpse to the edge, where he stopped and looked around to make sure nobody was watching.

Luckily, he seemed to be in the middle of nowhere, and there wasn't a house or person to be seen for miles.

David's body was as stiff as a board, and Michael could barely stand to look at him with dry eyes. His face had taken on a pale complexion that didn't look natural, and he was cold to the touch. Michael knew he'd have to bury him now before it got any worse.

He didn't want to see his brother like this. He wanted to remember him as he was, full of the joys of life and excited about what the future held for him.

Then he fell to his knees and prayed.

He rolled David into the grave as gently as he could and winced as he fell into the five-foot-deep hole. Then he shovelled the dirt back into the grave, his heart breaking with each shovel full of dirt that hit David's body.

With the grave filled, Michael replaced the grass he'd carefully removed so it wouldn't look too obvious unless someone walked right up to it, which he doubted would happen, as he was far enough away from civilisation for David to rest in peace until he could come back for him.

He broke a branch from the tree and stuck it in the ground above David's head below. He didn't want to make a cross for obvious reasons, but he had to mark the grave with something.

Then he fell to his knees again and recited David's favourite prayer. It was the one they said every Sunday morning at church, and he hoped the words would allow his brother safe passage to the other side, where peace and tranquillity awaited him.

As he recited the Lord's Prayer, his voice cracked, and he had to stop several times to regain composure.

Our Father, who art in heaven,
hallowed be thy name;

thy kingdom come;
thy will be done;
on earth as it is in heaven.
Give us this day our daily bread.
And forgive us our trespasses,
as we forgive those who trespass against us.
And lead us not into temptation;
but deliver us from evil.
For thine is the kingdom,
the power and the glory,
for ever and ever.
Amen.

Mindful of the fact that he may never find this place again, Michael spent a few minutes in the car sketching a rough map of where he was. He noted all the landmarks he could see, which weren't many, and tried to be as accurate as he could to describe how far it was from both Munich and Erding.

He drove down the narrow lane as far as it went, which wasn't much more than about five hundred yards. At the end, he found a small river, and although it was freezing cold, he stripped to his underwear and waded in.

The frigid water attacked and numbed his senses, and the shock made him feel something. Anything other than pain and guilt would do, and if freezing half to death in a river worked, then so be it.

As the mud and blood washed away, his hands and arms turned a strange shade of blue. Goosebumps rose all over his body, and he shivered and shook in the water.

But he felt something other than deep regret, and that was all he wanted. Even if it would only be a momentary relief.

He thought about rinsing his filthy clothes as well, but it

was too cold, and the risk of dying from hypothermia was too great. He knew the risks of looking so shabby, but until he could find new ones, he was stuck with the ones he had.

Once dressed, he jumped up and down and performed squats at the side of the motor vehicle to get his circulation going. Satisfied he was as warm as he was going to get, he searched the glove box for the map he'd seen Gerda refer to when she drove them to Munich.

At first, he plotted a route to the River Rhine and France, but he stopped when an image of Gerda entered his mind, holding out her hand with a crumpled note.

"Find Father Eise." Those were her words.

Who is Father Eise, and how can he help me?

He searched his pockets and pulled out the crumpled, blood-stained note. His eyes welled up at the sight of Gerda's final message. He imagined her scribbling it down as the Gestapo beat down the door at Sophie's apartment.

Even to her last breath, she had put their well-being above her own. No wonder Frank had loved her so much.

He smoothed out the piece of paper and read it aloud to himself. "Father Albert Eise, Pallottine Church. Tell him who you are, and he will know what to do."

Underneath her words was a rough map of Freising with an X marking the spot where he was located.

Michael pondered for too long. Did he head straight for the Rhine and France, or was it better to do what Gerda suggested and try to find this Father Eise?

In the end, he decided it was safer to follow Gerda's advice and seek the priest. It wouldn't hurt, and if he couldn't help him, then he'd run for the border.

He gunned the engine, turned the car around, and drove off, slowing as he passed David's makeshift grave.

"I'll be back for you, brother. I promise."

Chapter Thirty-Five

The forty-minute drive to Freising would have been the most nerve-wracking minutes of Michael's life if it hadn't been for the events preceding it.

At every junction, he expected to see a roadblock manned by angry men hellbent on making him pay for the deaths of their comrades.

His hands gripped the steering wheel tighter with each bend in the road, and his heart thumped in his chest as he imagined the sound of boots clomping towards his car.

Munich would probably be in total lockdown by now, and as soon as they identified Gerda, which they'd probably already done, Freising would follow suit. He might be driving into a trap, but he'd made his decision, and he was sticking to it. He doubted the route to the river was any less dangerous, so no matter where he went, he was living on borrowed time.

The only saving grace was that the Gestapo wouldn't know who they were searching for, at least not yet. There was little doubt that Vogel had told them about the men in the apartment, but they couldn't yet know who they were.

Any roadblocks would be for the Jewish associates of the Meyers, or at least that's what he told himself as he got nearer to Freising.

A road sign told him he was five kilometres away. He looked down for a fuel gauge, but there wasn't one. He had no idea how much farther the car would take him before it ran out of petrol, but whatever it was, he'd take it. Each mile was one mile closer to freedom, and as he was measuring his life in hours and minutes rather than months and years, that would have to do.

He rounded a corner, and his heart almost bounced out of his chest. A line of cars was stopped ahead of him and were being searched one by one by armed, uniformed men. They were too far ahead for him to see who they were, but he was under no illusions as to who they were searching for.

Has word got out already? Are they searching for me and David? He forced the pain of David's memory to the back of his mind and slammed the car into reverse.

Michael turned around with his heart thumping so loud he was sure they could hear him at the roadblock, and raced away as fast as he reasonably dared. He took one left turn and then another. He didn't know where he was, but he didn't care as long as he got away from the roadblock.

Suddenly, the realisation hit him like a hammer, and he slapped himself on the forehead. *How stupid am I?*

It wasn't him and David they were searching for – *it was Gerda's vehicle!* They'd identified Gerda from her identification papers, and they knew exactly what vehicle she owned. Michael was a sitting duck, and he'd never have made it through the roadblock.

He turned the car into a side street and jumped out. He'd walk the rest of the way.

Chapter Thirty-Six

A small path wound its way between the houses at the end of the cul-de-sac where Michael had dumped Gerda's vehicle. He had no clue where he was going, but all he cared about was putting distance between himself and the vehicle. And water.

His tongue stuck to the roof of his mouth, and all he could think about was water. In some ways, he was happy, because the intense thirst distracted his mind from David and the two men he'd killed in cold blood.

He was also mindful that his appearance would give him away the moment anyone saw him. His initial plan had been to find the Pallottine Church, and hope Father Eise would give him what he needed, but he knew he couldn't walk the streets covered in mud and blood. The local Gestapo would be all over him in a flash.

Two houses sat on either side of the winding path, close to where it ended on another road. Michael noticed the house to his left had a small shed in the back garden. Hoping against all the odds that the shed might have a pair of overalls or something that could conceal his soiled clothes, he crept around the sides and peered into the window.

The shed was full of wooden boxes, and his hopes plummeted when he saw the heavy padlock and chain that secured the doors. He tried the window, but that, too, was firmly closed. Unless he was prepared to smash the glass, he wasn't getting into this shed.

He was about to leave when he had a crazy idea to try the house doors. The need for water was driving him crazy, and he was at the point where he would do just about anything for a glass of the life-giving liquid.

He crept around the house, staying low when he crawled under the windows. Just like the shed, the house was locked and there was no way inside unless he smashed his way in.

Desperate for liquid, he made sure nobody was watching as he crossed the path to the house on the opposite side. Unlike its neighbour, this house didn't have a shed, but it did have a couple of trees near the rear of the house that provided some cover while he tried to find a way in.

He crept around to look for any signs of life, but it looked empty.

The rear door was locked, but as luck would have it, the downstairs window closest to the path was slightly ajar. Michael broke off a small branch from one of the trees and slid it into the gap between the window and the frame.

A narrow bar about a foot long held the window open. Using the stick as leverage, he pushed the window lever up and over the prong until it fell loose. Then he pulled the window wide open and jumped inside, pulling the window closed behind him.

After pouring himself several glassfuls of the best-tasting tap water he'd ever savoured, he helped himself to several slices of bread and German sausage. Then he ventured up the stairs, hoping to find something that would pass for clothing.

Whoever lived here obviously had children, because two of the three bedrooms were full of kids' clothes, along with a few toys. The first room he tried was set up for a young girl, so that was no use to him.

The next one was more like it. A teenage boy had this room by the look of it. Trousers and shirts were thrown over the back of a chair, and dirty socks were scattered over the floor. It reminded him of what his room would have looked like when he was a younger teen if it weren't for the house-keeper his parents employed.

Michael stepped back in shock when he opened the wardrobe door. Hanging in full view was a light brown shirt with a swastika wrapped around the left sleeve. A black tie hung over a pair of black shorts, and a light brown cap sat on top of the hanger.

Michael was staring at the uniform of the Hitler Youth!

He fell to his knees, his body trembling and gasping for breath. The sight of the uniform with its hateful swastika symbol brought back everything that had happened since he and David set foot in Nazi Germany, and he felt as though his soul was being torn apart. Try as he might, Michael couldn't stop the tears from flowing down his face, and he knelt there for what felt like an eternity, his world consumed by grief and rage.

Several minutes later, he got to his feet. He was shocked at his response to the sight of the uniform and felt sorry for the people of Germany who were following this evil maniac towards another global war.

He backed out of the room, no longer wanting to be in the house. The swastika seemed to suck the life out of it, and he struggled to breathe. In a hurry, he went into the third and final bedroom.

This was the parent's room. A double bed stood in the middle of the floor underneath the window, and unlike the young Nazi's room, this one was tidy. He bit his lip as he opened the wardrobe door.

Please don't let it be full of Nazi uniforms, or even worse, be a Gestapo man's house.

He was relieved when he saw what looked like normal clothes hung up tidily. One side was for the lady of the house, and the other for the male.

The man's clothes were a bit bigger than Michael was, but at least they'd fit. He took a pair of trousers and a white shirt. He put his old clothes in a bag and threw them in the rubbish bin on the way out.

He grabbed a thick jacket from the hanger at the side of the rear door and left a handful of German reichsmarks that should more than cover the cost of replacing what he'd taken.

He left the house the same way he'd entered.

Feeling much better about his chances, Michael made his way around the outside of the house and walked down the street like any other law-abiding citizen.

Or at least that was how he hoped he appeared.

Chapter Thirty-Seven

Several wrong turns later, Michael found himself standing outside the Pallotti Church on the corner of Vimystrasse and Pallottinerstrasse.

His heart raced, and he took a deep breath while he wiped his sweaty palms on his trousers, trying to calm his nerves. The weight of the situation hit him like a ton of bricks, and he felt dizzy and disoriented. He tried to focus on his surroundings, but everything seemed to blur together, and his mind raced with thoughts of escape and survival.

What am I doing here? I should have gone to the border and left this place behind.

But it was too late now. The only thing he could do was hope that Father Eise could help him. Whatever transpired in the next few minutes would determine whether he lived or died.

He hoped Father Eise was the man Gerda believed him to be. He gulped another lungful of air and stepped inside the church.

It took a few moments for his eyes to adjust to the dim light, and by the time he could focus, a middle-aged man in a priest's frock was approaching him down the aisle from the front of the church.

"How can I help you?" the man asked in a kindly, but questioning voice. Like everyone else in Nazi Germany, even the priests had to be careful with their choice of words.

Michael took a long moment to weigh up the priest standing before him. What he said next could determine the outcome of his life, and the consequences of his choices weighed heavily on him. Sweat beaded on his forehead, and he wiped it clear before it became too noticeable.

The small but pretty church was laid out like every other church he'd ever been in: Two rows of pews on either side of a narrow aisle that led to the altar at the front.

The priest stood, patiently waiting for Michael to respond. He was in his forties and had thinning black hair that was cut short above his ears. His forehead was prominent, but that was probably because he didn't have much hair on the top of his head. A pair of round glasses sat tightly on the bridge of his nose, and his eyes peered from behind them in a kindly, but no-nonsense way.

How ridiculous. How can I judge this man by the look he's giving me? Michael stared at the priest standing in front of him.

"Can I help you with anything, young man?" the priest asked again.

"I'm looking for Father Eise," Michael finally answered. "Is he here?"

"I am Father Eise." The priest looked Michael up and down.

"Gerda Jung sent me." Michael waited to see if there would be any reaction to the mention of Gerda's name.

"Gerda Jung? Ah, lovely lady. How is she doing? I

haven't seen her in a while. Is she with you?" Eise looked past Michael towards the door of the church.

"No, she isn't here. She sent me because she seemed to think you could help me. Perhaps she made a mistake. I'm sorry to waste your time, Father."

Michael backed away slowly and turned to leave. He had been stupid to come here. His stomach felt heavy, and for a fleeting moment, he thought he might throw up on the floor of the church.

He was dizzy and lightheaded, and at that moment all he wanted to do was get out of there and put distance between himself and Freising. He could have been close to the border by now if he'd gone there instead of following Gerda's last message.

"Stop." Father Eise grabbed Michael's arm and pulled him towards the front of the church. "Not here. There are too many eyes and ears."

The priest never stopped looking at the entrance to the church as he dragged the reluctant young man to a small, sparsely appointed room off to the side of the altar. Once inside, Father Eise closed the door.

"Where is Gerda? What has she been up to? And who are you?"

Michael pulled away from the priest's grip. "Gerda is dead. And so is my brother." His voice broke as he continued. "Two of Gerda's friends are dead as well, and probably several more by now."

"You look pale and in shock. Please, sit down." Father Eise vanished for a moment and returned with a large glass of water, which Michael gladly gulped down.

"She gave me this note right before she died." Michael handed the bloodied note to the priest so he could see for himself that he wasn't bluffing.

Father Eise studied the note for several minutes before returning his gaze to Michael. He winced as he spoke. "What happened?"

Michael told him everything except the whereabouts of David's body. He was keeping that to himself. When he finished, the raw wounds opened the floodgates once again, and Michael found himself in Father Eise's arms sobbing for all he was worth.

"So, you are the Englishman the authorities are going crazy about?" It was more of a statement than a question, but it piqued Michael's interest and he sat up, pulling away from the priest.

"What do you mean?" he asked.

"Haven't you been listening to the radio? The police, and even the army from the barracks close to here, are setting up roadblocks all over the town. The public has been told that two English spies are in the area, and they must be apprehended at all costs. Radio broadcasts state that they have already killed four members of the Gestapo in Munich, and they are possibly heading to Freising because they have ties to the area."

Father Eise's words hit Michael like a hammer blow. The manhunt was real, and they were looking for him and David. Panic rose inside, threatening to choke him. He took a step back, feeling as though the walls of the church were closing in on him.

Michael stared at Father Eise. "No, that can't be true. How could they possibly know that? They never saw us. Father, they never knew David and I were even there, so how could they suddenly know everything about us just a few hours later?"

Father Eise placed a comforting hand on Michael's shoulder. "You don't know the Gestapo very well, obviously.

If they arrested Sophie and Stefan's friends, they would have tortured them into telling them everything. You told me they had children, so that makes it even more likely they told the Gestapo all about you. Parents will do anything for their children, as you well know."

Michael felt sick to his stomach. He couldn't believe that his actions had put so many innocent people in danger. He closed his eyes and took a deep breath, trying to calm himself down.

"Okay, but how would they know we would come back here?"

"They don't, but they are taking no chances. We are to look out for a blue Volkswagen Type One, which they believe you are using. I happen to know that Gerda had such a vehicle, so I know it's her vehicle they are looking for. What did you do with it? Did you bring it here to this church?"

"No," Michael shook his head. "I ditched it outside of town after I ran into a roadblock. I realised they were looking for it, so I left it in a cul-de-sac somewhere in Freising."

"So, they know you are here. The Nazis are on the warpath, and they won't stop until they apprehend you. It's such a shame for poor Gerda and her friends. I knew as soon as I heard the broadcast that it was probably about them. She did so much good for the Jews of Freising and Munich, but her life was always in danger. I told her it was only a matter of time before they caught up to her, but after the pogrom and the arrest of Frank and Herbert, she gave up caring for herself. If her ultimate gesture was to help you escape, then she would have died content. That I can assure you."

"What am I going to do?" Michael asked, his voice barely above a whisper.

Father Eise looked at him with pity in his eyes. "Leave Freising. It's not safe for you here."

Michael nodded, feeling a sense of resignation wash over him. He had no choice but to trust Father Eise and hope that he could help him escape.

"I don't want any more deaths on my conscience. I will never be able to come to terms with those who have already died, especially my brother, so please, Father Eise, I can't allow anyone else to die for me."

"You sound just like your Uncle Frank. He was also a proud, upstanding man of high morals, and I see you are just like him."

"Can you help me?" Michael asked bluntly. "I mean, without getting yourself killed?"

"Perhaps."

"How? If they have blocked all the roads in and out of here, how can I escape?"

"You must understand that I am not involved in helping people get out of Germany. I support those that do, and I am no friend of the Nazis, but I have no first-hand knowledge of helping people escape."

"How can you help me then?"

"I can help you out of Freising, and I know people who will take you across the Rhine to France as long as you have enough money to pay them. Other than that, I'm afraid I will be of no use to you."

"Why did Gerda send me here if you can't help me escape?"

"Because she trusted me, and she knew I would do all I can to help you."

Father Eise paused before continuing. "And she knew

that I have contacts at the border that can get you across. Gerda knew you needed a friend because you'd never get out on your own, especially after she knew the Gestapo were onto you. They will never sleep until you are arrested and publicly punished to show their power to both Germany and the outside world. She knew that I'd be the only friend you'd have in the entire country."

"Fair enough, but please don't do anything if it puts you in any danger. I couldn't stand another death on my hands."

Father Eise grunted. "I'm already a public enemy and well known to the authorities, so I am in no more danger whether I help you or I don't. So, you will stay here for a few days where you should hopefully be safe. Come, I'll show you."

As they stood, Father Eise took Michael's arm and closed his eyes. Michael followed suit when he realised what he was doing. He was saying a prayer for Gerda and the others who'd perished in Munich. He saved David until last, and when he prayed for his soul, Michael once again felt the warm splash of tears fall down his cheeks.

"Thank you, Father, that helped. It will take a lifetime to come to terms with what happened, but this helped."

The priest nodded as he led Michael to a small store-room at the back of the church. With Michael's help, he moved a large metal box that felt like it was full of rocks out of the way, revealing a wooden trapdoor underneath.

"What is this?" Michael asked. "And what's in the box? It's really heavy."

"The box is necessary for some of the work I do. This is a place that will keep you safe until I can get you out of here. I need time to make the necessary arrangements, and that time will allow the roadblocks to be cleared, or at least relaxed a little. By nightfall, not even a mouse will get in or out of Freising. You have to be patient, Michael, and wait for the temperature to drop a little before making your move."

"How long do I need to stay here?"

"I don't know"—Father Eise shrugged his shoulders—"Perhaps a few days, perhaps a few weeks. I don't know."

"A few weeks? I can't stay here that long, Father. I have to get home."

"It's better to be late than not to arrive at all. Be patient, and I will get you out of Freising. Now go, before someone comes."

"What about food and water? And toilets?"

"Everything you need will be provided. As for toilets, there is a large pot down there that will be emptied every few days. It's the best I can do, so please do not complain."

Michael did complain, but nobody was listening. He climbed down a rough ladder and held the lantern the priest had given him next to his face so he could look around.

The tiny room was about eight feet deep, so he had plenty of room to stand up. He could just about lie down in either direction, but his feet and head touched the damp walls no matter which way he lay. The cold concrete floor was covered with straw, and there was a large pile in a corner that he assumed was for bedding.

Two blankets lay on the straw, and there were two empty bowls that were probably for food and water. A large pot stood alone in the opposite corner, and Michael needed no explanation for what it was.

Cold condensation covered the walls, and the room felt damp and intimidating. What it did offer, though, was protection. And in his current situation as Bavaria's, if not Germany's, most wanted man, that alone was worth the discomfort.

He just hoped Father Eise would be true to his word and that he would get him out of there. In less than a few weeks, preferably.

Michael sighed and fell to the floor. He grabbed a blanket and curled up on the thick straw. He hadn't slept in days, and as he drifted off, he realised that the straw was a lot more comfortable than it appeared.

Chapter Thirty-Eight

Days turned into weeks, and Michael grew ever more impatient with each passing day. Being alone in the darkness twenty-four hours a day was destroying whatever resolve he had left because it gave him time to do the one thing he didn't want to do – dwell on what had happened in Munich, particularly David's death.

One good thing the time alone gave him was the opportunity to memorise in great detail the exact whereabouts of David's temporary grave. He memorised every tree and every turn, and he even counted the number of paces from the tree to where he'd buried him.

The map he'd drawn was dangerous to him, so it was a relief when he could finally destroy it and distance himself from any evidence of his true identity. Whoever he would be when he left Freising, it wouldn't be Michael Fernsby or Willi Bauer.

Day after day, it was the same: silence and solitude from being sealed off from the outside world. He might be safe, but the isolation was killing him. Alone with his thoughts, the nightmares were not restricted to his dreams. He would break out in cold sweats as images of that fateful day returned with wave after wave of memories, each one worse than before.

He tried focusing on his mum and dad back home with Judith, and he allowed himself a rare smile when he thought of how happy Judith looked when she played with Lucy.

How I wish I was there.

Thoughts of France and a route back to England consumed his thoughts, and it was here where he tried to focus when his mind drifted back to Munich.

I owe it to Gerda to get out of Germany and tell the world what's happening here, and I owe it to David to survive, so I can come back one day and give him a proper burial where he will be loved and remembered for the brilliant man he was, and for the years that were torn away from him so cruelly. I owe it to Sophie and Stefan, and I owe it to Uncle Frank and Papa Herbert, who will hopefully survive and one day reunite with the rest of the family. I have to get across the Rhine and live to tell the tale.

Sometimes he would hear Father Eise performing a service in the church above his head, and he looked forward to those moments when he could join in with the prayers offered from above.

Every day, usually in the evenings, Father Eise would move the box and open the trapdoor, allowing the remnants of the day to enter his safe space. The heavy box sounded like a tank rolling over his head, and it left no room for doubt that someone was coming.

Father Eise allowed Michael out once darkness fell for around thirty minutes each evening. This gave him time to stretch his legs and get some fresh air while he emptied his bowls and restocked with fresh water and food, which consisted of bread and German sausage. Fresh fruit and vegetables were always welcome, and sometimes the priest brought him warm potatoes, which Michael devoured instantly.

He looked forward to these moments each day like a child looked forward to Christmas, or, as he inwardly mocked himself, like Lucy probably was when she knew it was nearing time for her food. If it wasn't for these moments, Michael was sure he'd have gone completely mad by now.

Keeping track of time was difficult in the darkness below the ground, and the only thing he could do was to scratch rough lines on the wall with a stone after each nightly visit with Father Eise.

One night, as Michael devoured a warm dinner, Father Eise looked distant and sad. Michael picked up on his body language and sensed that something had gone wrong.

"What's happened? I know something has by the look on your face. Please be honest with me, Father. Can you not get me out of here? If I stay much longer, I fear I will be a danger to both of us. I'm going crazy down there, and I have to get out. I'm willing to go it alone if it's too dangerous for you. Believe me, Father, you've done more than enough for me already."

Father Eise shook his head slowly from side to side. "No, my English friend. It's not that. It is almost time for you to leave, and we must prepare you for what happens next."

"What is it then?" Michael sensed the tension rising, and he instinctively knew something bad had happened.

"The Nazis are furious that they haven't been able to find you, and they are going from door to door searching for you. I'm expecting them here any moment, so this must be the last time you emerge from the hiding place until I come for you. I'm sorry, but it's the only way we can all stay safe."

Michael touched the priest's arm. "It's okay, Father. I understand, and I'm very grateful for all you have done for me. I know what you're doing is a massive risk, so just let me leave so we can all get some peace."

"There's more." Father Eise locked eyes with Michael.

"The Gestapo arrested known friends of Frank and Gerda. Not all of them are Jewish, and stormtroopers beat them half to death in the streets when they were lined up outside. I witnessed this, and it grieves me to know I couldn't protect them."

"Why did they do that?" Michael asked as once again the terrible weight of guilt thrust itself to the fore. "Was it because of me?"

"They are doing all they can to find you, and to make sure that everyone knows the consequences of helping you. It's not just here either. From what I hear, they are searching everywhere between here and the borders of France and Switzerland. They aren't bothered with Austria because that's under their control, but the others aren't, and that is where they expect you to be heading."

"Which is true," Michael said. "What happened to those they arrested? Are they alright?"

"They threw the men into the back of a truck, probably destined for Dachau. They sent the women and children to some place they called a Jewish housing area. I have never heard that term before, so I don't know what they mean. It's not good, whatever it is."

Michael sat on a pew and threw his head in his hands. "This is all my fault. I, we, should never have come here. All I've done is get people killed and made it worse for everyone else. I'm so sorry, Father. I didn't mean for any of this to happen. All I wanted to do was to help Frank and Herbert get back to England."

Father Eise placed his hands on Michael's shoulders. "While you may be the catalyst for what is happening, you are not to blame for it. That is solely down to the Nazis and their antisemitic and hateful actions. If you want to blame anyone, blame the Führer. He's the one that could stop this any time he wanted. Instead, he stokes the fires of hatred and prepares Germany for war."

"What should I do?" Michael asked. "I can't just stay safe in that room while others are being beaten and arrested because of me. I will have to hand myself in to them. At least that way, nobody else will get hurt."

"And betray Gerda's and your brother's memories?" Father Eise thundered. His eyes took on a dark inflexion as he spat the words out. "These are the times we live in, and nothing will be done about it if you just hand yourself over to them. All they'll do is carry on beating and killing until the rest of the world wakes up to what's happening. They are the only ones who can stop Hitler now. You must honour the memories of those who gave their lives by telling the world what happened here."

Michael stood up. "You're right, Father. Please forgive me, but this burden is too heavy for me to carry."

"I know, my son, and I wish there was a way I could relieve you of it. But I can get you out of here. Be ready tomorrow night, because that's when you're leaving. If this goes as planned, you'll be home by Christmas."

"That's nice because it's less than a week away," Michael allowed himself a half smile.

"It's time," Father Eise gestured towards the hole in the ground.

Michael listened as Father Eise grunted over the heavy

box above his head. He closed his eyes and allowed his mind to drift back to the last time he was home with his family.

He remembered the sound of his mother's laughter as they played board games by the fire, the smell of his father's roast beef wafting from the kitchen, and the sight of Judith giggling as Lucy chased her around the living room.

He could almost feel the warmth of the fire and the softness of the rug beneath him. For a moment, it transported him back to that peaceful moment of tranquillity, and he felt a pang of longing for his family's company. But then the memory faded, replaced once again by the cold, stark reality of his hiding place.

Tranquillity? Who am I kidding? I'm safe down here while people up there are suffering. No matter how hard this is, I have to succeed and spread the word. That's the least I can do for them.

He tried to sleep, but the nightmares kept returning. Eventually, he gave up and lay awake with thoughts of the upcoming perilous journey foremost in his mind. The thought of evading Nazi bullets gave him cold chills, but then the memories of David and Gerda returned, strengthening his resolve.

I can do this.

Chapter Thirty-Nine

Early the next morning – or was it the middle of the night? – Michael heard footsteps crashing down the normally quiet aisle above his head. Loud shouts accompanied heavy boots, and he shot up from where he lay.

The Nazis! They're here!

Michael held his breath and tried calming his beating heart that sounded so loud in his cramped space. His body shook, and he sat there, silent and helpless.

Please don't find me now, not when I'm so close to getting out of here.

Father Eise's voice rose over the commotion, and Michael could clearly hear what was being said.

"What do you want at this ungodly hour?"

"You know why we are here," a stern voice that Michael sensed was used to being obeyed snapped back at the priest. "We're looking for the English spies who murdered four of our good men in Munich. We know they are here somewhere, and we know someone is hiding them. Is that person you, Father Eise? We know you have spoken words of treason before against the Reich, so it's in your best interests if you tell me the truth."

"What truth would that be, Kriminaldirektor Kreise?" Father Eise sounded incredibly calm given the situation. "The truth as it is, or the truth you want to hear? I know you are easily confused between the two."

Michael cringed in the room below. Eise was goading them! He knew the priest didn't like the Nazis, but he'd never realised the extent of his hatred until this moment.

"You need to be careful with your words, Priest," the commander snapped back. "You are not above being arrested for helping the Jews."

"I am doing no such thing, Kriminaldirektor Kreise. As you can see, there is no one here except me, so if you are done, I have work to do."

Heavy boots crashed all over the church floor above Michael's head. He didn't know what they were doing, but now and then he heard Father Eise scold someone for not handling something gently enough.

He stopped breathing when the heavy boots reached the metal box covering his hiding place. There was no other way in or out, so if they found the trapdoor, he was finished.

Michael could smell his own body odour as he started to sweat, and he held his breath as long as he could before exhaling silently in the darkness.

Get a grip! They can't hear you breathing.

Michael's mind raced with uncontrolled thoughts, and he struggled to quieten his mind so he could hear the Nazis over the commotion going on inside his head.

"What's this?" someone barked loudly.

Too loud. He's too close.

"It's a storage box for our more valuable items," Father Eise replied. "I'll show you if you like."

He sounds so calm!

"Open it," the man Eise had called Kriminaldirektor Kreise ordered.

"As you command."

Michael heard a strange rustling as he assumed Father Eise was opening the lock that secured the metal box.

"See? It's our more delicate and precious items we reserve for special occasions."

Heavy thuds above his head followed by sharp retorts from Father Eise painted a picture of what the Nazis were doing.

"Be careful, those are hundreds of years old, and they hold great meaning."

"There's nothing here, Kriminaldirektor Kreise," another voice said.

"What's underneath it?" Kreise asked.

Michael froze. *This is it. They've found me.* His body stiffened, and he waited for the tell-tale scraping sounds of the metal box sliding out of the way to reveal the trapdoor to his hiding place.

"The floor," Father Eise replied sarcastically. "We haven't moved it in years because it's too heavy. See, I'll show you."

Grunts rang out as more than one man pushed the heavy box, but it didn't budge!

"It won't move, Kriminaldirektor Kreise. It's too heavy."

After a long silence when Michael was sure his heartbeat and heavy breathing could be heard as far away as Munich, he heard the words he'd been praying for.

"That's enough. Leave it. I'll be watching you, Priest. I don't trust you, and I don't like you. If you hear anything, you must tell me at once. Do I make myself clear?"

"Perfectly, Herr Kreise. I bid you good morning."

"Heil Hitler!" Kreise shouted the words as proudly as Michael had ever heard a man shout anything, and the sound of boots clicking together in unison resounded like a church bell ringing out a warning of impending doom.

"Heil Hitler!" several voices responded, but Michael didn't hear Father Eise's amongst them.

"Be careful, Priest. Your time is coming."

Silence returned to the tiny hiding place, and Michael let out a deep sigh of relief. He was sweating profusely, even though it was freezing cold outside his warm blankets.

Hours later, strange sounds above his head alerted Michael that someone was handling the storage box. He stiffened and strained his neck to hear who it was. It couldn't be the Nazis, because they'd been so loud earlier. It must be Father Eise, but what was he doing?

Something made a loud bang as it hit the floor above his head. Then another, followed by several more. Eventually, it stopped, and the familiar sound of the box scraping over the top of the trapdoor carried down below.

Michael stood up and closed his eyes. Whoever it was, he was ready.

"Michael, come quickly." The friendly voice of Father Eise was music to his ears. "We don't have much time."

The priest led Michael through a door in the church into a small courtyard, where they were hidden from the road. From there, they entered another narrow passage that ended near a clump of trees that were squeezed together.

Father Eise stood in the early evening darkness in the courtyard's corner beside the doorway. He picked up a backpack and dropped it at Michael's feet.

"This is it, my brave young English friend. It is time for you to leave. Everything you need is in this backpack. There is enough food to get you to the border, and there is a map to guide you."

He reached into his pocket and pulled out a set of car keys. "There is a vehicle waiting for you once you get out of Freising. There are too many roadblocks around the town, so it is safer to get to it on foot. It is a black Opel Kadett, and it is hidden down a small lane out of sight of the Nazis."

"What happened earlier?" Michael asked.

"The Gestapo came to the church to look for you. Luckily, they didn't find you, but their commander didn't believe me when I told him I hadn't seen you. He'll be back with more men tomorrow morning, of that, I'm sure."

"Why couldn't they move the box over the trapdoor?"

"I loaded it with large stones yesterday after you went back down. Something told me they would come, and they proved me right. I removed the stones before I let you out this evening."

"Very clever." Michael smiled at the industrious priest. "But why didn't they find the stones? I heard them open the box and take some things out."

"My young friend, we don't have time for this. The metal box is of my own design, and I had a false bottom put in there for this very purpose. I hid the flat stones underneath what they thought was the bottom of the box."

Michael's admiration for the priest went up several more notches. "You are very smart, Father Eise. That's a brilliant idea."

"Keep to the trees and follow the paths between the houses until you reach a main road. Be careful when you cross, and from there you will enter the woods."

Father Eise handed a note to Michael and gripped his hands. "A narrow lane goes through the woods. Find it, but keep to the trees. The lane intersects with another, wider road, but make sure you follow the directions I gave you because there are other junctions before the one you need. Two hundred metres down the road to the right, you will find the vehicle behind the trees."

"You have gone to a lot of trouble for me, Father Eise. How can I ever repay you?"

"Expose the Nazis, as we have discussed. That is how you repay all of us. Make sure nobody is waiting for you with the vehicle, and if it is clear, then drive the way it faces. Follow the lane to the end of the woods where it intersects with another road and turn to your left. I drew the rest of the way on a map in the backpack."

"What about the Rhine? How do I get across? Where do I get across?"

"It's all in the backpack. Whatever you do, keep to the smaller roads, and if you come across a blockade, either find a way around it or abandon the vehicle. They are looking for you, Michael, and they will do terrible things to you if they find you."

Michael choked back the tears that threatened to fall. He gripped Father Eise's hands tightly as he struggled to speak the words he was trying to say.

"I feel unworthy of all the help you have given me. I promise I will do my best to show the world what has happened here. How will I know you are well? Can I write to you once I am back in England?"

Father Eise shook his head. "It is better that you don't. The Nazis monitor everything, and they will know I have helped you. What do you think they would do to me if they found you were writing letters to me? I'm sorry, Michael, but this is goodbye. Perhaps we can meet again once this is all over, but I fear it is going to get a lot worse before it gets better."

Michael hugged the priest one last time. "Thank you, Father. I shall never forget what you have done. I shall not give you away if I am caught."

"You are a brave young man. Now go, before Kriminaldirektor Kreise shows up and arrests us both."

Michael looked at the priest one last time before turning away and heading into the trees.

Chapter Forty

Warhurst opened the rear door of the gleaming black Riley Autovia that Gerald Fernsby was so proud of. Only forty-four of these luxurious limousines had ever been made, and Gerald had managed to get his hands on one of them.

The dashboard had more dials and gauges than an aircraft, and Gerald sat back, listening to the powerful one hundred horsepower, six-cylinder engine as it idled on the driveway outside his home.

He allowed his inner child a moment to enjoy the trappings of his privilege, and he sank back into the plush leather seats, enjoying the peacefulness he'd craved during his stay in the hospital.

The tear-stained face of his lovely wife ran towards him, pulling him from his daydreams.

Gerald looked towards the house and saw his mother standing at the doorway beside Judith. All three of them looked like they'd lost a pound and found a penny, and Gerald looked at each of them in wonderment.

"Why do you all look so sad?" he asked as Warhurst

helped him out of the rear door. "Is it that bad that I'm finally allowed to come home?"

His joke fell on deaf ears, and Gerald knew something else must be going on.

"What's wrong? I thought you would be glad to see me."

Dorothy almost pushed Warhurst over in her rush to get to her husband. "Gerald, you're home. I thought this day would never come. I'm so glad you are here."

She gave her husband an enormous hug and kissed him passionately. Almost sadly, Gerald mused.

"Come, husband. You need rest, and home is the best place for it."

His mother was unusually subdued, and even Judith wasn't her normal bubbly self. They moved out of the way while Gerald entered the house, and Dorothy guided him to the sitting room and helped him sit down in his favourite chair.

"Why all the gloom? Have I missed something while I've been in hospital?"

"Your mother has something to say to you."

Dorothy glared at Gigi, who looked at the floor. She looked as meek as Gerald had ever seen her.

"What's going on?"

"Tell him, or I will," Dorothy said sternly, staring at her mother-in-law.

"For God's sake, the man has just got out of the hospital," Gigi said. "Can't this wait until later, when he's had time to recover?"

"Tell him, or I will," Dorothy repeated. "This cannot wait, and he needs to know. This is your last chance, Giselle."

Gerald could tell from the tone of his wife's voice that

something was terribly wrong. "Well? What is it? I'm better now, and I can take whatever you have to tell me."

"I wouldn't be so sure about that," his wife replied. "We're waiting, Giselle."

Gigi cleared her throat and looked her son in the eyes. "Gerald, you must understand that what I did, I did in your best interests. It wasn't supposed to happen like this, and if I could take it back, I would."

"What have you done, Mother? Have you heard news from Frank in Germany? Is he alright?"

A deathly silence gripped the room, and Gerald looked at each of them. Deep lines etched under Dorothy's eyes told him she hadn't been sleeping, and even his mother's face had aged a decade since he'd last seen her.

"Well?" Gerald asked.

Giselle let out a deep breath and held her son's gaze. "Your hospitalisation was my fault," she began. "If you'd gone to Germany in your condition, you would have ended up dead at the side of the road somewhere. I couldn't allow it, so I put something in your food to make you ill. I didn't mean for it to be so bad, obviously."

"Even in remorse, your callousness is astounding," Dorothy said through gritted teeth. Gerald could feel the hatred his wife aimed at his mother.

"What did you do?" Gerald demanded. He could feel his blood pressure rising, and Doctor Newsome's words rang in his ears.

"You must remain calm and allow your heart to heal, so don't do anything to get yourself angry or excited," Gerald said. "Those were Doctor Newsome's last words to me as I left the hospital. Now I come home to hear my own mother poisoned me? What did you do, Mother?"

"I put Dover's powder in your gravy the night you fell

ill." Gigi sat ramrod straight and stared defiantly at her son and daughter-in-law. "It was for your own good to stop you gallivanting off to Germany as if you were a young man again. I didn't mean to cause you to have a heart attack. But that proved you were in no fit shape to be running off on a rescue mission."

Gerald gaped at his mother. He looked away and then did a double take and looked back at her. "You poisoned me?"

"I didn't do it to harm you. I did it to protect you from yourself. There is a difference, Gerald. I did the right thing."

"Mother, how could you do such a thing to me? You almost killed me, and yet here you are telling me you did the right thing?" Gerald felt his face burning, and he couldn't believe what he was hearing.

"That's not the worst of it." Dorothy's gaze never left Giselle's. "Why don't you tell him why we haven't heard from David and Michael?"

Gerald spluttered and bent forward in a coughing fit. Dorothy held his shoulders. "I know this is too much for you, but it can't wait," she said. "You have to know what she did. David's and Michael's lives depend on it."

Gerald's eyes narrowed as he pieced together in his mind what his mother had been involved in during his absence. "Where are my sons?" he asked calmly. "Did you send them to Germany?"

"I did. They were supposed to go to Freising and look for Frank and my father. They were to either get them out or come straight home. That was it, and they should have been back in a few days." Gigi lowered her gaze to the floor.

"Where are they?" Gerald demanded, feeling a rising discomfort in the pit of his stomach. "Are they here?"

"No," Dorothy interrupted. "They left the night you fell ill, and we haven't heard from them since."

"That's nearly a month!" Gerald thundered. He rose to his feet and stood over his mother, who avoided eye contact with her son. "What happened to them?"

"We don't know," Dorothy said. "Gigi sent them to your friend in Strasbourg, and nobody has heard from them since. We don't know where they are."

"You contacted Abreo?"

"I did because I thought it would be safer for them to enter as German citizens, rather than Englishmen searching for their missing Jewish family."

"And he agreed to help?"

"Abreo has his price, just like everyone else. He's the best in the business, Gerald. You know that as well as anybody."

"So, what happened to them? Where are they?"

"I've contacted the Foreign Office in London, but so far they haven't told us anything," Dorothy said. "I'm considering going to Germany myself and trying to find them."

"That's stupid," Gigi said bluntly. "The Foreign Office won't be any help either."

"Do you know something that we don't?" Dorothy asked, eyeing Gigi like she was the sworn enemy. "Are you holding something back from us?"

"If you know something, Mother, then please tell us," Gerald said. "If you don't, I'm taking the next ferry to France to see Abreo myself."

"I'm sure everything is fine," Gigi said. "There has been some..." She broke off and looked sheepishly at Gerald. "News. I spoke with Abreo a few days ago and he told me of some disturbing radio broadcasts and newspaper articles coming out of Germany."

The blood drained from Gerald's face, and from the look of his wife, she was feeling the same. Her face turned red, and her hands balled into fists as she glared at Gigi.

"You knew this and didn't tell me? What kind of monster are you? You knew I was beside myself with worry, and yet you still refused to tell me what you know. I despise you, Giselle."

"Easy now, darling," Gerald said. "We don't know what she found out yet." He turned to his mother. "Tell us everything and leave nothing out. You know I will be in contact with Abreo myself, so don't lie to me, Mother."

"Dorothy was already near hysteria, and I didn't want to make it any worse. I was hoping they would be home by the time you got out of the hospital, but it appears there has been some kind of altercation in Munich. There was no mention of David or Michael's names, but some German policemen were killed, and the authorities said it was the work of two British spies that are believed to be hiding in Freising. That's what the German newspapers and radios are saying, and Abreo thinks they are referring to our boys."

Stunned silence filled the air. Judith burst into tears and ran, slamming the door behind her. Gerald stared at his mother as if her words were toxic, and Dorothy looked as lost and angry as he'd ever seen her.

After a long pause, Dorothy reached forward and slapped Gigi hard across her face. Gigi threw herself back in shock and raised her arms in self-defence. Gerald grabbed Dorothy's arms to stop her from beating his mother any further.

"You bitch!" Dorothy screamed. "You did this to them. They had no reason to go there, but you sent them because you put the lives of your own family above ours. You talked them into it, and now they will die because of you."

She threw herself at Gigi, and it took all Gerald's strength to hold her back. "Dorothy, please stop," he panted. His chest was aching, and he grabbed at it, sending Dorothy into an even deeper rage.

"Dorothy, stop!" This time, his voice shook the ornaments in the room. He pushed her back roughly. "Sit down and stop this."

Dorothy complied, but he could tell that she was like a tiger waiting to pounce at any moment.

And he didn't blame her.

"I'm going to make a call to Abreo and then I'm going to make an appointment with the PM," he said calmly. "Mother, you have crossed the line, and you have put David and Michael in harm's way. You are to do nothing else without asking me first. Is that clear?"

Gigi nodded, holding her cheek that had red finger marks across it.

"Dorothy, my dear, I understand your anxiety because I feel it too, but slapping my mother isn't going to help any of us. Please remain calm and don't do anything stupid until I can sort this out. Can you do that for me?"

Dorothy scowled and glared at Gigi. "I want her out of our house. I don't want to see her ever again, and I want her out of our family's business. She isn't to contact us ever again, and most importantly, she is to stay away from our children."

"Dorothy, I..." Gerald began, but his wife waved him away.

"It's either that, or I'm leaving," Dorothy added. "I cannot live in the same house as this woman who purports to love her grandchildren and then uses them for her own ends on a dangerous mission without telling us. She almost killed you, her son, and she lied to me. It's either me or her, Gerald, so make up your mind."

Gerald sighed and closed his eyes. He was about to speak when Gigi broke the silence.

"Dorothy is right, Gerald. I admit to overstepping my boundaries, and I apologise for that. My intentions were solely to discover what happened to Frank and my father, and I never meant to cause harm to anyone else in our family, who I love dearly. Underestimating the situation in Germany is something I'll never forgive myself for, and I'll move out so you can be rid of me. Please understand, both of you, that I never intended any harm to come to any of you."

"I don't care what you meant. I just want you gone."

"What have you done, Mother?" Gerald asked. "If anything has happened to David or Michael, I shall hold you responsible for the rest of my life."

"I'm sorry," Gigi said, her voice cracking. "I'm so sorry."

Gerald walked towards the door. "This meeting is over. I'm going to call Abreo and make the appointment with Chamberlain. Mother, I want you out by nightfall."

Chapter Forty-One

The evening roll call was taking longer than normal, and all Frank Fernsby could think of was the cramped bunk he shared with two other prisoners.

He missed Herbert terribly, and the guilt he carried tore at his heart. He knew he had failed him and let him down in the worst possible way.

I should have fought harder and forced him to leave when we had the chance instead of giving in to the old fool's pride. And now Herbert's gone, just another victim of SS cruelty.

The night was clear, but it was freezing, and Frank stood with the other prisoners in their shared misery as the SS played their deadly games with them.

They'd been standing for around two hours when three new SS men appeared on the scene. They approached the other guards and had a whispered conversation. Frank thought this to be unusual, but he'd long past stopped caring about what they did. Whatever it was, it never ended well for the prisoners, so he turned his thoughts inwards towards the happier times when he and Gerda had made plans together for the future.

He wondered where she was at this very moment, and he hoped that wherever it was, she was far away from Dachau, safe from the clutches of the SS and their hatred of the Jews.

The three new SS men approached the area where Frank's block stood to attention. Two of the regular guards accompanied them, and as they walked amongst them, the prisoners all stared straight ahead, avoiding eye contact at all costs. They had learned the hard way not to look the SS in the eye.

"Step forward, 71257."

Frank's heart dropped like a stone. Others had been called before him, and not all of them had made it back to the blocks. Those who did return usually came back beaten to a bloody pulp, and more than a few had died from their injuries.

Frank sighed and stepped forward. Thoughts of Herbert ripped through his mind, and he took strength from the old man's resolve and fight for life.

I'm taking one of them down with me for Herbert. That's what I'll do.

Wild thoughts of killing the SS with his bare hands ran through his head, and as impossible as it may be, it comforted him as the men approached in their usual menacing manner.

One of the regular guards flashed his torch to check the number matched what had been called, and when he was satisfied, he hit Frank around the head with the torch, knocking him to the ground.

Stars and blood marred his vision, and he felt himself

being dragged towards the 'dreaded bunker' as the prisoners called it. Its official title was the 'Garrison Detention', and they'd all heard the nightmare stories of what happened there.

Frank closed his eyes and grimaced. He was ready for whatever they were about to do to him.

Chapter Forty-Two

Blood spurted from Frank's nose, but that didn't stop the SS guard. When blood splatter landed on his neatly pressed black uniform, the guard went berserk and laid into him even harder.

"Stop. That's enough."

Frank's head spun as he struggled to focus on the interrogator's words. The throbbing pain in his nose and abdomen made it difficult to concentrate, and his thoughts felt muddled and disjointed. He blinked rapidly, trying to clear his vision, but everything remained hazy.

He looked around the bunker to get his bearings. The interrogation room was dimly lit, with a single bulb flickering overhead. The air was thick with the smell of sweat and fear, and the sound of muffled screams echoed through the walls. Frank could feel the rough concrete floor beneath his feet and the cold metal of the chains biting into his wrists. In the distance, he could hear the harsh barks of SS guards patrolling the corridors outside.

He had every expectation that he was going to die in the bunker that night, so he'd prepared himself while they dragged him away from the roll call by filling his mind with thoughts of Herbert and Gerda. He thought of the good times he'd had with his brother when they were boys growing up in London, and of how strict and yet how loving his mother had been, especially after his father had died in the Great War.

Each crashing blow sent him further into the recesses of his mind, and he wilfully allowed his brain to block the outside world to shield himself from the abuse his physical body was receiving.

This was the reason he didn't hear the questions being barked at him by two men he had never seen before. His eyes were swollen to the point of being almost shut, but through the haze, he could see just enough to make out their shapes in front of him.

His interrogator stopped the onslaught and stepped back.

"I am Sturmbannführer Bachmeier, and this is Kriminaldirektor Kreise. You are Frank Fernsby, are you not?"

Hearing his name took Frank by surprise. Ever since he'd arrived at Dachau, the use of names had been forbidden. They were numbers, and nothing else. To the SS, they were sub-human vermin that needed to be eradicated.

The interrogator stepped forward and struck Frank violently once again. "Sturmbannführer Bachmeier asked you a question," he barked.

Frank wiggled his jaw to see if he could even speak after the beating he'd just received. A few teeth had come loose, but his jaw didn't feel broken.

At least not yet.

What does it matter? I'm not getting out of here alive anyway.

"Yes, sir. I am, or at least I was, Frank Fernsby."

"And you are an English Jew, are you not?" The other man who Bachmeier had introduced as Kriminaldirektor Kreise asked in perfect English. From the way he dressed in a trench coat and a brimmed hat, Frank knew he was a member of the Gestapo.

There was a time when he would have quaked in his boots at the sight of the Gestapo, but after what the SS had done to him, he couldn't feel anything.

"Yes, sir. I am originally from England, although I have lived in Germany for a long time."

"You have family in England?" Kreise asked, bending into Frank as he asked.

Frank's stomach tied in knots. He wasn't expecting these kinds of questions. "What has my family in England got to do with anything? They're not here, and if they have any sense, they will never set foot anywhere near Germany."

A wooden club crashed into Frank's abdomen, forcing all the air from his lungs. He lurched forward, coughing blood onto Kreise's polished shoes.

This brought another round of beatings, and for a moment, the relief of unconsciousness washed over him. It didn't last long, because the SS interrogator threw a bucket of water at him, bringing him back to his agonising reality.

"When was the last time you saw your family?" Bachmeier asked in German.

"A long time ago. Certainly not this year, that's for sure."

"You have two nephews, David and Michael, yes?" Kreise asked.

"Yes, sir, I do, but what has this got to do with anything?" Through all the pain and fog, Frank panicked. He'd always assumed Gerald and his family, including his mother Giselle, were safe from the clutches of the Nazis in England. *Why are the Gestapo interested in David and Michael? What have they done?*

"Your nephews are in Germany, and they have murdered four of my men in Munich. Why are they here? Are they spies for the British government, or are they here to rescue you?" Kreise barked the questions in such good English that Frank wouldn't have been able to tell he wasn't native if they had met in different circumstances.

"David and Michael are in Germany?" Frank shook his head from side to side. "I'm sorry, sir, this is the first I've heard of anything like this."

Another beating. Frank clutched his stomach and lurched forward, coughing up more blood onto the floor.

"Spies?" The words fell out of his mouth in a gurgled mess. "David and Michael? They're young university students who are interested in girls and football. They're about as far from being spies as I am from being treated fairly in here, and as for them killing four of your men, that can't be true. Neither of them has ever harmed a fly in their entire lives."

Another round of severe beatings with the wooden club followed while the two men stepped back and had a quiet conversation between themselves.

"Are you calling the Kriminaldirektor a liar, Jew?" the interrogator asked with spittle foaming out of the side of his mouth.

Frank didn't have time to reply because the club inflicted more pain and damage on his body. He closed his eyes and prayed for death to come quickly so he could end his misery.

As he drifted off, another bucket of water brought him around again. "You don't die that easily, Jew," the SS commander who Frank's frazzled brain couldn't remember the name of said. "We want answers."

"I know why they are here, and I know what they've done," Kreise continued, his tone harsher than it was a moment earlier. "Where are they, Frank? I need to find them before anyone else gets killed."

His tone softened. "I promise to give them a fair trial, and if you help us, I might even be able to secure a transfer to a better place for you, where conditions would be much more bearable. Who knows, I might even help you go home to England if that's what you want."

Frank knew he was lying. The SS had made no secret of their determination to remove all Jews from German life, and there was no way they would just allow him to walk out of Dachau.

"I haven't seen either of them for quite some time. As I said, they are students at university, and the last I knew, they were both at Cambridge. If they are in Germany, I know nothing about it."

"What friends and family do you have around Freising?"

Frank's thoughts turned to Gerda, and his stomach churned at the thought of the Gestapo getting their hands on her. "I have plenty of friends in Freising, but none I would consider close enough to hide anyone wanted for murder."

He knew the men were lying. Neither David nor Michael were in Germany. They were in Cambridge, and if he somehow survived this nightmare, that's where he'd find them when he went home to his brother in Kent.

What, or who, were they after? Gerda? He knew she was helping Jews get out of Germany with her friends in Munich, and he'd warned her against it several times. But she was determined to do all she could to help, and she had saved several Jewish families from suffering the same fate he now faced.

That's who they're really after. Gerda.

Frank would go to his grave before he gave up the woman he loved. The Gestapo had gone to a lot of trouble to find out about his past, so Gerda and her friends must have done something that seriously angered them.

Good for her. I just hope she stays safe and does nothing stupid.

"Your girlfriend, the one who's deaf. What's her name? Gerda, that's it, isn't it? Gerda Yung?"

Here it comes. I knew it. Frank remained silent.

"She's dead, unfortunately, killed in the crossfire between your nephews and my men. Your nephews killed Gerda, Frank. What do you think about that?"

Frank shook his head and shrugged.

Lies. All lies.

The wooden club went to work, and this time several teeth flew out of Frank's mouth, along with more blood. Still, he remained silent.

"You are a foolish man, Frank. We will find your nephews, and when we do, I guarantee them a painful death. But you can stop that by helping me. Do it for Gerda, if not for me, because they killed her before running away in her vehicle."

"I'm sorry." Frank struggled to speak as his mouth was now so swollen he could barely breathe, never mind speak. "I don't know anything about this. If they're here, I don't know where they are."

Kreise looked up at the SS Sturmbannführer and murmured something Frank couldn't hear. He didn't care in any case. They could do whatever they wanted to him, but he'd never betray Gerda. The Gestapo were well known for trying every dirty trick in the book to get people to talk, and this was no different.

Maybe Gerda and her friends got involved in a shootout with the Gestapo in Munich, and they were now using Frank's family to bait him into helping them find her. It would not work, and as far as Frank was concerned, Kriminaldirektor Kreise and his sidekick, SS Sturmbannführer Bachmeier, could go to hell.

"Very well, prisoner 71257." Kreise stared at the number sewn into the rags they called clothes. "Have it your way, but be warned. When I find them, and I will find them,– the British spies David and Michael Fernsby will regret the day they were born. And you will watch them die before I kill you myself."

Kreise turned to the SS Officer, who barked his orders at the junior interrogator. "He stays alive for now. Take him back to the block."

Chapter Forty-Three

Michael pulled the collar of his jacket over his ears and looked back at Father Eise one last time. A lump formed in his throat as the priest waved at him before going back inside the church. Michael felt a deep respect for Father Eise, and he hoped to return one day to convey his gratitude in much better circumstances.

He took a deep breath and headed into the trees, shining his torch on the piece of paper Eise had given him. It was a rough map of where to find the car that was supposedly waiting for him in the woods.

He checked his pockets for the last time, mentally checking off each item as he felt them. Car keys, check. Gun, check. Envelopes with reichsmarks and French francs, check. Identity papers, check. He wasn't sure how much good the papers would be now that they were onto him, but they were all he had.

He checked the other four guns he'd taken from Munich before putting them in the backpack, turned around a few times to get his bearings, and then stepped into the darkness, keeping between the houses as best he could. He was especially careful when crossing a road, as that was where he was most vulnerable.

Around fifteen freezing minutes later, he emerged from a copse of trees onto a narrow lane that joined the main road Eise had told him about. He could see the lane entering the woods on the other side, and he knew he had found what he was looking for.

He crouched down in yet another group of trees at the side of the road and listened. Happy that he was alone, he rose and crossed.

He hadn't gone three steps when he heard a motor vehicle approaching from his right. Michael leapt back into the cover of the trees and fell to his stomach.

Headlights approached, and the sound of the engine got louder as it came nearer. The vehicle drove slowly, and Michael's heart skipped a beat when he saw a bright light from the open-topped vehicle scanning one side of the road and then the other.

It's an army patrol!

He quickly removed the backpack and pushed himself as far into the ground as he could. The vehicle slowed as it approached the trees where Michael hid, and he held his breath when it got level with him.

Voices shouted at each other over the noise of the engine, and the light shone from side to side like a lighthouse in a rocky cove. He took a deep breath as the light shone on his position. He was sure they'd found him because a voice rang out and the vehicle ground to a stop.

Michael gulped in a lungful of air and held the gun steady in his hands. He didn't want to use it, but he wasn't going to allow himself to be captured either. He knew what they'd do to him if they caught him.

He listened as the men shone their light at something

close to his prone body, and was pleased to hear them laugh before the vehicle moved away from him.

He rose to his knees and got a better look at the silhouette of the vehicle in the moonlight as it drifted down the road and away from his position. He replaced the gun in his pocket and rubbed his arms to get the circulation going again.

The vehicle was the ugliest thing he'd ever seen, and the only way he could describe it was that it looked like a bathtub on wheels. The roof was folded back, and the long, rectangular doors along the side met in the middle, reminding him of the stable doors where Judith kept her horses. It might have been an efficient vehicle for the Wehrmacht's needs, but it certainly wouldn't win any awards for its looks.

Michael dropped to the ground again when the searchlight turned back in his direction, and he waited for several minutes until the sound of the engine could no longer be heard. Then he ran across the road as fast as he could to the safety of the woods on the other side.

Once he was happy that he hadn't been seen, he shone his torch on the map. From what he could see, there were two crossroads before the junction he should take, which looked easy enough to follow.

He put the directions away and followed the lane from behind the tree line. With his hands buried in his pockets, Michael took a deep breath that left his mouth in a steady flow of hot steam. His feet had long since given up complaining about how cold they were, and now they felt like two blocks of ice stomping the forest floor underneath him.

I hope the car isn't far because I'll freeze to death if I don't find it soon.

He reached one junction, but there was only a right fork, and it wasn't a crossroads, so he discounted it and continued. A minute later he stood at the first proper junction that had lanes going off to both his left and right.

One down, two to go.

The woods were dark and eerily quiet, and every footstep cracked and popped. It sounded like miniature gunshots going off each time a twig snapped or when he disturbed a low-lying branch. Not to mention the freezing water that dripped behind his collar and froze to his back.

Although Father Eise had warned him to stay off the lane, Michael decided it was safer if he ignored that advice and stuck to the sides of the lanes. The visibility was good because of the bright moonlight, which wasn't good, but at least now he could hear if anyone was ahead of him. An entire squad of soldiers could have marched past while he was in the forest, and he wouldn't have heard them over the sound of his own footsteps.

Even though he was freezing, Michael took his time to make sure he was careful and didn't walk into a patrol. He was making much better time on the lane, but he was more exposed, so he moved as close to the trees as he could while still walking on solid ground.

The second junction finally appeared, and he knew he was getting close. He was now in the thickest part of the woods, and the trees seemed to swallow him up as though he wasn't there. It gave him great cover, but it was the same for anyone watching out for him.

His senses tingled when he reached the next junction. *Not far now. Two hundred metres.* He moved back into the woods and slowed down to almost a crawl. Every few steps, he stopped and listened intently, checking for anything that sounded out of place.

Two hundred metres seemed like a mile, but he had to be careful. A minute later, he stopped once again to listen. Satisfied he was alone, he stepped forward and almost cried out when he saw the shape of a vehicle in front of him. Just as Father Eise had said, it was parked behind the trees just off the road.

Michael lay on the ground and watched for several minutes, his ears straining for any sound. The black Opel sat quietly in the darkness, waiting to sweep him away to safety, and he resisted the urge to jump in and drive away. If others knew it was there, it was the perfect place for a trap.

Nothing. I am alone.

The water-cooled engine sprang to life, and Michael cringed at how loud it sounded. *Nothing I can do about it. What did Eise say? Follow it to the end and turn left. That'll do.*

Still not fully comfortable behind the wheel, the car jerked and juddered as Michael fought to get control. The lights cast shadows on the sides of the lane, and he fought back images of soldiers jumping out in front of him with rifles raised. He was glad when he reached a junction at the end of the woods with a wider road.

He turned off the lights a few feet back from the junction and stopped the engine. He jumped out and ran to the main road to get a good idea of what he was facing.

Having only the light of the stars to guide him, Michael couldn't see too far ahead, but he knew the general layout. To his left were the forests and freedom, and to his right was Freising and certain death. In the distance to his right, he could see lights flashing in different directions, and although it was too far away to make out what they were saying, he could hear faint voices yelling in the darkness.

It was a roadblock! Father Eise had told him that

Freising was cut off from the outside world, and here was the evidence to prove it. The priest had been clever enough to lead Michael out of the woods to the other side of the known roadblocks. He prayed that Father Eise had been right, and there weren't any farther up the road.

He jumped back in the car and jerked it forward. He smiled to himself as he turned left, the words of his brother ringing out in his head.

The car's got kangaroo petrol.

Chapter Forty-Four

He drove for almost an hour before stopping outside a small town called Elsendorf by the side of a thick forest. He pulled over into a quiet country lane and stopped the engine.

Father Eise had thought of everything, and he'd even provided thick blankets for his legs so he wouldn't freeze while he was driving. He hoped he'd been as thorough with the directions as he'd been with the items of comfort.

He emptied the contents of the backpack onto the passenger seat and shone his torch carefully on each item. He found two bottles of water, and he gratefully guzzled several mouthfuls of the life-giving liquid down his throat.

The priest had also provided hard meats and cheese, as well as a loaf of bread, and Michael took about a quarter of what he'd been given and wolfed it down. He could have easily devoured it all, but he saved it for what lay ahead.

Then he got down to the serious business. He spread out the map and looked at where he was supposed to be going. A large circle around a town near the Rhine called

Schwanau got his attention, and the handwritten note that accompanied the map gave further details.

Werner Dalsing, 38 Südsstraße, Schwanau. Tell him Father Eise sent you and give the code name Offenburg. He will know what it means, and for a fee, he will take you over the river.

Michael checked the map, and after a few minutes, had his route planned out. It looked to be around four hundred kilometres from Elsendorf, which was about two hundred and fifty miles if his rough calculations were correct.

He didn't plan on driving during the daytime, so it would take a couple of days to reach Schwanau. Today was December twentieth, so with a bit of luck, he could be home by Christmas Day. What a surprise that would be for his mother and father.

He swallowed hard as he thought of the news he'd be taking home with him. *Perhaps it's best if I don't get home until after Christmas.*

A search of the car's boot revealed four petrol cans full of fuel. Father Eise certainly had thought of everything because if Michael had to stop to refuel, he ran the risk of being recognised if his description had already been circulated..

He checked the map one more time and said a prayer for David and Gerda. Then he gunned the engine and set off, hoping against hope the Nazis hadn't set up roadblocks anywhere along his route.

It was approaching midnight, so he had several hours of darkness before he had to pull over and find somewhere to hide for the day. He made good time, stopping only one time to fill the fuel tank to the brim so he wouldn't have to worry about running out of petrol at an inopportune time.

By four the next morning, his eyes were feeling heavy,

but he wanted to press on while the going was good. He had a few hours of darkness left, and he figured he'd look for somewhere to pull over sometime after five am to give him time to find a good hiding place. Somewhere in the trees would be great if he could work that in. Even better would be an abandoned barn, but that was asking too much.

He was now on the outskirts of Stuttgart, and he knew from his previous altercation that the Gestapo were active in the area. It was too big a risk to drive through the city, so he turned onto a smaller road and hoped for the best.

He drove through a few small towns and his optimism that he'd actually make it grew.

An hour later, those hopes were dashed.

He saw a sign for a town called Glatten, and as he approached a sharp right-hand bend in the town centre, his heart almost leapt out of his chest when he saw a series of lights ahead of him. It had to be a checkpoint, and even if they weren't specifically looking for him, he knew he couldn't take the risk.

He turned the car around and headed back the way he'd come. On the outskirts of the town, he took a left turn onto a country lane, and when he did, he slowed down and looked back at the road he'd just driven down.

To his horror, he saw the lights of another vehicle following him from where he'd seen the checkpoint. *Had they seen him turn around? Were they looking for him?*

Resisting the urge to speed up and go hell for leather, Michael drove off, smoothly for once, and hoped the road didn't dead end. He kept looking in the rear-view mirror to see if one of those bathtubs on wheels was following him, and he moaned when he saw the lights turn onto the lane he was on.

Now it was getting serious.

The lights of the vehicle behind him got closer each time he glanced over his shoulder. Although he hoped it wasn't a military vehicle from the checkpoint, he couldn't take the risk of it not being.

He turned off his lights and entered a small lane to his left. His heart was pumping wildly, and he couldn't see well enough for the speed he was travelling at.

He turned left again into an even narrower lane and put his foot to the floor. A few hundred yards later, he turned to look over his shoulder to see if the lights were still following him.

He never saw the T-junction ahead of him.

He raced the Opel into the junction, and his entire body tensed when he realised what he'd done. Everything seemed to slow down, just as it had in Munich in the apartment. And yet, everything happened so fast that he couldn't do anything to avoid it.

He threw his hands up to protect his face, while his right foot frantically pushed as hard as it could on the brake pedal. But he was too late. The car sped across the narrow junction and crashed into the trees on the opposite side.

The impact threw Michael forward, and he smashed his head on the dashboard in front of him. Before it went dark, he remembered a sharp pain as the steering wheel crushed his chest, knocking all the air out of his lungs.

For whatever reason, the driver's door flew open during the impact, and when he opened his eyes a few minutes later, he found himself hanging halfway out of the car. He rolled out and groaned when the movement hurt his chest.

He touched his head where it hurt and felt warm liquid running down his fingers. He felt groggy, and the sharp pain in his chest took his breath away when he staggered to his feet.

He tenderly checked for any broken bones, but his feet and arms seemed to be okay. Trying his best to ignore the fog in his head and the sharp, agonising pain in his chest, Michael struggled to get behind the trees and fell to the ground.

He looked and listened for signs of the vehicle that had been following him, and in the distance, he could see a set of lights moving slowly along the road he had been on just minutes ago.

Another set of lights joined the first, and for a moment they converged and stopped together, no doubt as the occupants conversed with each other.

Now there were two sets of lights circling around slowly, and Michael knew for sure they were from the checkpoint. *They must have seen me turn around and followed me. Now what do I do?*

His chest was on fire, and the intense pain made it hard to breathe. He was sure he'd broken one or more of his ribs, but right now wasn't the time for him to mope around and worry about his injuries. He leant back against a tree to take stock of his situation.

I've made a big mistake. I should have been looking where I was going and not behind me at the lights. He took a moment to berate himself for his stupidity, and then put it behind him.

I can't change what I've done, because if I could, David and I would be in a warm, comfortable bed in our rooms in Cambridge. Hell, I'd even apologise to Stourcliffe for smacking him and stealing Lucy.

Michael shone his torch to assess the damage, and his head dropped when he saw the left front wheel twisted out to the left, hanging almost parallel with the ground. There was no way this vehicle was going anywhere except on the back of a truck and sent for scrap metal.

The lights of the vehicles continued to drive up and down the roads, and it was only a matter of time before they found the damaged Opel Kadett. He had a brief window to get away from the scene of the accident, and he had to act quickly if he was going to put any kind of distance between himself and the Nazis.

He grabbed his backpack and the map, and searched the vehicle for anything else he could carry that might come in useful. He also searched for anything that would connect it to Father Eise, as he knew what the consequences would be.

The backpack straps caused sharp pains in his chest, but he thrust them aside and struggled off into the trees and headed for somewhere – anywhere – away from this mess of his own making.

Michael had no clue where he was going or what he was going to do. He had a rough plan to find somewhere to hide for the day, and then somehow steal a vehicle once it got dark. Then he'd continue his journey to the border.

If only it could be that easy.

Chapter Forty-Five

Dawn broke over the dark winter skies above Michael's head. He'd been stumbling along for over two hours. His chest felt like a red-hot poker was stabbing him with every step he made, and he stopped every few minutes to catch his breath and retch from the agony.

The deep gash in his head was bothering him as well. Blood ran into his left eye, and it stained his clothing crimson red. He was in trouble, and he knew it.

It was now broad daylight, and although he kept to the fields and the trees whenever he could, a few houses and lanes blocked his way. On a couple of occasions, he'd been forced to find cover and wait until he could proceed unnoticed.

His steps slowed, and he stumbled forward, his left-hand clutching at his chest. A sharp, stabbing pain radiated through his ribcage with every breath, and although he gritted his teeth and tried to ignore it, the pain was making it increasingly difficult.

He needed to find shelter where he could rest and take

stock of his injuries. He also needed to find some warmth because he was freezing.

Each step was a fresh hell, and he let out a string of curses under his breath. Michael had never felt more alone in his life, and he felt helpless in the biting winter conditions. Only the thought of David gave him the resolve he needed to carry on.

He entered a deep, thick forest, which he believed was the Black Forest. He was glad of the cover it provided, but he was travelling too slowly, and each step was more painful than the previous one.

He followed the rough path of a small lane, and to his right, he noticed the outline of a building in the distance. Desperate, he collapsed in agony to his knees and took stock of the situation.

To his left lay the Black Forest and his path to the border and freedom. It was a long and arduous walk through the Black Forest, and he had no idea how he'd navigate through the thick spruce trees.

Who am I kidding? I can barely walk, never mind navigate my way through a forest.

He sat on his knees and rocked back and forth for at least ten minutes, going over and over in his mind what his options were. In the end, he knew he had no choice. He had to find somewhere to hide for a few days while his chest healed. He knew he'd cracked at least one rib, and how painful that could be.

He cried out in pain as he struggled to his feet. He looked longingly at the forest and his path to salvation, and then staggered towards the building in the distance.

His mind filled with images of Nazis swarming all over the Opel that was smashed into a tree a few miles back, and he forced himself forward at the thought of German Shepherds on the end of long chains following his scent through the trees and hills of the Black Forest.

He found himself at a crossroads where four lanes converged, two into the forest, and two heading over the fields towards civilisation. Nestled at the edge of the forest, between the two lanes heading out of the trees, he saw the building that had caught his eye earlier.

It belonged to a farm at the end of the tree line. Fields stretched out before the farm for what looked like acres and acres, and he momentarily saw how serene and picturesque it must have looked in more peaceful times.

He didn't have the luxury of wonderment, so Michael drove himself forward towards the largest building on the right side of the farmhouse that sat back in the trees and was almost out of sight.

He passed by a sign that contained one word, which Michael assumed was the name of the farm. He stopped briefly so his eyes could focus on the letters.

Ryskamp.

Feeling exposed, he turned around and headed back into the trees.

Focus! You can't allow the pain to cloud your judgement, or they'll arrest you before lunchtime. Focus!

This time, he skirted around the rear of the farmhouse and emerged from the trees behind the barn. A large grey roof stood out, and Michael clung to the side of the building as he edged around it. He listened intently for signs of human activity, but there were none.

He held his breath as he tried the door, and was relieved when the handle turned and the door swung open before him.

He took a good look around the barn and saw a large

haystack in the loft. His only problem was how he was going to climb the ladder to reach it.

Closing the door behind him, Michael took a deep, painful breath and placed his foot on the ladder. He almost cried out as he hauled himself one step at a time up to the safety of the haystack above his head.

By the time he reached the top, he was sweating profusely from the effort, and he collapsed in a heap onto the soft hay. He covered himself with the blanket he'd brought from the wreck and buried himself as far down as he could.

Then he fell into a deep, exhausted sleep where the pain and the cares of the world melted away, if only for a short while.

He awoke with a start when voices echoed underneath him. A man was talking. No, two men. Three.

Who is down there? Is it the Nazis? Have they found me already?

He lay perfectly still, his heart pounding far too loud as the men spoke in low voices. The hay blocked most of the noise, so he could only make out the odd word here or there, but he made out the words Opel Kadett and crash, and then he heard a man say loudly that he hadn't seen anyone, but he'd report it if anything changed.

Michael lay silent long after the men had gone, and the voices had dissipated. Eventually, he looked at his watch; it was almost three in the afternoon. He'd slept most of the day, and he felt better for it.

Or at least he did until he tried moving. Every part of his body screamed in agony, and his chest felt as if it were being stabbed by a thousand sharp blades. He fell back helplessly, drowning in agony and doubt. He needed help, but he knew he was alone, and nobody was coming to help him.

Chapter Forty-Six

The train arrived at London Bridge exactly on time. Light snow scattered around in the wind as Gerald Fernsby stood outside waiting for a taxi to take him to Downing Street.

The streets were busier than normal, which was understandable given that Christmas was only a few days away. Gerald allowed his head to rest back on the rear seat as the taxi driver honked his horn at the crowds stepping into the road as they went about their last-minute shopping frenzy before the holidays began.

Holidays! Gerald scoffed to himself. They'll probably spend Christmas with their families and turn their radios off. They'll forget the growing threat of war with Germany, and instead enjoy the time they have together while they can. I'll wager their sons aren't hiding somewhere, hunted by Nazis intent on killing them for something they probably didn't do.

He pulled a small mirror from his pocket and looked at the haggard face staring back at him. His already thinning hair was receding faster than the tide at Brighton Pier, and the last vestiges of chestnut brown had given way to a dull grey. He looked terrible, and he had noticeably aged over the past few weeks.

Who wouldn't? Who else's mother would poison her son and then send her two grandsons off to enemy territory? No one's, that's who. No one's except mine.

Even though Doctor Newsome had ordered Gerald to rest and avoid stress, his life since he'd left the hospital had been nothing but stress and heartbreak. His chest ached, and it wasn't only from his recent heart attack. He'd barely slept, and even when he did, the nightmare visions of his sons being tortured and executed woke him up in a cold sweat.

There was no way either David or Michael could have killed those German policemen. David had never hurt anyone in his life, and although Michael had been involved in more than his fair share of fisticuffs, that was a far cry from shooting policemen in cold blood.

Gigi had always favoured Frank, and she had been both proud and heartbroken when he left England to live with his grandfather at the end of the last war. She clung to his letters, and although she wasn't welcome at her father's home, she always spoke of one day returning to live out the rest of her days in Germany.

That was all irrelevant now. She had gone too far by sending David and Michael into the enemy's lair, and although she was as repentant as he'd ever seen her, she was no longer welcome in his home. Dorothy had made it abundantly clear that she never wanted to see her again, and Gerald didn't blame her.

Giselle should be moving her things out today after checking herself into a London hotel the previous night.

From what she'd told him, she was going to rent a house in the upscale area of Chelsea later that afternoon.

Although Dorothy had told him not to, he planned on visiting her before he left London. He had to, for the sake of his sanity. He had to find out why she had done what she did. The mother he knew might have been strict and unemotional, but she'd never been heartless. There had to be more to it, and he had to find out what it was.

The taxi ground to a halt outside the famous black door of number ten, pulling Gerald from his thoughts. He paid the driver and climbed out, patting down his jacket and trousers as he did so. He had to look his best for the PM.

After several minutes of waiting to verify his hastily arranged meeting with the prime minister, Gerald was shown into an office and told to wait.

And he waited. And waited.

The meeting was supposed to have been at nine, but it was now quarter to eleven and there was still no sign of Neville Chamberlain. Gerald knew he was busy, but this was unusual even for a man as busy as the British prime minister.

Eventually, the door opened, and a tired-looking Neville Chamberlain walked into the room. Gerald jumped to his feet and thrust out his hand to greet his old friend. His hair had noticeably greyed since he'd last seen him, and the wrinkles on his forehead were deeper than before. Even his famous moustache looked grey and weary.

"Good morning, Prime Minister," Gerald said. "Thank you for seeing me at such short notice. I know you are busy, especially with Christmas just around the corner."

"Sorry I'm late, Gerald. I've been in meetings all morning. You know how it is, and I'm sorry to keep you waiting. I only have a few minutes, so what is so important that it couldn't wait?"

"I assume you have heard about my two sons, and what they stand accused of in Germany?"

"Of course I have, and I have to tell you it has caused my government severe headaches. We're not happy with your family, Gerald. Your sons have caused an international incident with Germany, just as we're trying to avert a confrontation with them. This is not helping, and the German authorities are rightly angry at what they've done."

"Allegedly done, Prime Minister. With all respect, we don't know if they've done anything at all."

"Are you telling me the Germans would go to all this trouble just to set up two young English boys? For what reason? I don't have time for this, Gerald. Please tell me why you're here so we can get this over with."

"My family needs help, Prime Minister. My sons need help. We need you to put pressure on the Germans to allow David and Michael to return home without delay, and if that isn't agreeable, then we need help in getting them back without their knowledge."

Neville Chamberlain sighed and sat back in his chair. "Gerald, you know that what you ask is impossible. If your sons have killed German policemen, they will have to stand trial for their crimes. It would be no different if the situation had been reversed and the same thing happened here. Under their law, under any law, they would have to stand trial for their crimes."

"Again, with respect, Prime Minister, you know as well as I do that the brown shirts are running around smashing Jewish synagogues and businesses. My brother and grandfather have gone missing, as have thousands of other Jewish men. There is no way my sons would get a fair trial, and you know it. I cannot believe they committed such a crime, and I need help to get them out of there."

Chamberlain's face turned red. "You march in here demanding that I send in troops to rescue your two sons, who may or may not have murdered four German police-men! Do you know where they are? Because we don't, and believe me, we have almost as much interest in this as you do. We're monitoring the situation as closely as we can, and we don't know where your sons are. So, if you know, then please tell me."

"I don't know where they are." Gerald let out a long breath. "This is killing me, Neville. They just released me from the hospital after a heart attack, and I swear this will put me into my grave. I'm worried sick about my boys, and I refuse to believe they could be capable of committing such a terrible crime. I'm pleading for your help, Neville, and I don't know what else to do."

The prime minister lowered his tone and leant forward on his desk. "As a parent, I understand your pain. Tell me what you know, and I'll see if there's anything we can do, but from where I sit, I cannot see any way the British government could get involved in this. It's an internal crim-inal matter between two boys who should never have been there in the first place, and the German authorities, who have every right to prosecute them in a criminal trial."

Gerald told the prime minister everything he knew. He'd spent the entire previous day on the telephone, making a rushed appointment with the prime minister and trying to connect with an operator in France who would connect him to Abreo.

He'd finally managed to reach his old friend, and although their conversations were guarded, Gerald had heard the latest news coming out of Germany.

"According to Abreo, David and Michael were on the run and believed to be heading towards the border with France. There had been several reported sightings of them, and the vehicle they had been driving had been found abandoned in Freising."

"Freising isn't a very big place," the PM said. "I know because I've been there myself. If they are indeed there, the Germans should find them fairly quickly."

"The Gestapo believe someone helped them escape and is even now smuggling them out of Germany," Gerald continued. "The German Minister for Foreign Affairs, Joachim von Ribbentrop, was in the press demanding the arrest of the boys just two days ago."

Gerald rubbed his temples and leant forward in his chair.

"There is an extensive ongoing search for them, and the Germans are confident they will be found and brought to justice. This is where I need your help. If Ribbentrop is involved, can't you speak to him and demand their safe return to England?"

Chamberlain frowned and stared at Gerald for a prolonged moment. "Do you think we haven't already contacted Ribbentrop? I have spoken to him more than once regarding this sorry matter. Their Führer is determined to put them on trial. I'm sorry, Gerald, but there is nothing I can do to intervene. You should have thought about the consequences before you sent them over there."

Gerald clenched his fists together behind the desk and struggled to keep his voice steady as he replied, "Do you honestly think my sons will get a fair trial? You know it will be a show trial, where the Nazis will make an example of them, and execute them in public to show how powerful they are. They will kill my sons, Neville. Do you understand that?"

Neville Chamberlain rose to his feet and headed for the door. "This meeting is over. I'm sorry, Gerald, but this is a crisis of your own making, and there's nothing I can do to help you."

Two uniformed policemen escorted Gerald out of the door and into the waiting taxi. His chest hurt, and he felt faint. He was angry at the prime minister, but if he was being honest with himself, he knew there was nothing the British Government could do. What had he been expecting? That they would send in a squad of soldiers to rescue them?

He told the taxi driver to take him back to the train station. He was furious with his mother, and although he'd told himself he would see her after meeting with the PM, he'd changed his mind. It would do her good to spend Christmas alone and reflect on what she'd done to his family.

Chapter Forty-Seven

The meagre rations Father Eise had provided didn't last long. Even though he'd stretched them out as far as he could, two days later they were all gone, and Michael was famished.

He'd barely moved since finding the farm two days earlier. His broken body needed rest, and it hurt to breathe. Strands of hay tickled his nose, and the sneezes that followed sent shards of broken glass through his chest. Taking shallow breaths helped, and Michael did everything he could to keep his movements to an absolute minimum.

He occupied himself by watching the family of farmers come in and out of the barn. There appeared to be a man and a woman, who Michael presumed were the mother and father, as well as two girls. One was in her mid-teens, and the other was around the same age as he was.

Every morning, Michael watched as the two girls came into the barn to collect eggs from the free-range chickens. He couldn't help but admire the older girl's grace and beauty as she moved among the clucking birds. Her long, blonde hair shone in the early morning light, and Michael found himself mesmerised by the way it cascaded down her back in gentle waves.

As she turned to reach for an egg, he caught a glimpse of her face; it was delicate and symmetrical, with a pert nose and full lips. He couldn't see the colour of her eyes from where he was hiding, but he imagined they were a clear blue, like the sky on a sunny day.

Michael felt a pang of guilt for admiring the girl's beauty. It seemed wrong to be thinking about such things when he was in dire straits. But he couldn't help himself; watching her work brought a small bit of joy to his otherwise bleak existence.

He lay back and daydreamed of a different time and place where they could have met, and how they could have been together. He used her image as a distraction from the pain and the growing hunger as his food ran out.

Another day passed, and by now, Michael's stomach was cramping and screaming in protest. He needed food, and he had reached the point where it dominated his thoughts above the pain of his injuries.

In the pre-dawn morning on the third day, Michael could hold off no longer. His chest had stopped hurting when he rested, but as soon as he moved, the sharp, dagger-like agonies returned with a vengeance. He cursed himself for getting injured the way he had and muttered to himself under his breath as he climbed down the ladder.

The chickens were making a racket on the barn floor, but he ignored the urge to grab one. As much as roast chicken sounded like food from the gods, he knew he wouldn't be able to cook it anywhere, so instead he grabbed two freshly laid eggs and immediately consumed them raw.

He walked over to where the girls milked the cows, and he drained the remnants from the bottom of one of the pails.

The milk was cold and thick, but Michael gulped it down eagerly, ignoring the taste of dirt and hay that lingered on his tongue.

The next thing he did was fill his water bottles from the trough outside the barn. It was below freezing, and he had to smash the top layer of ice so he could lower his bottles and gather the cold water.

Halfway back up the ladder, he stopped. Something felt wrong, and his senses went into overdrive. The hair on his arms stood to attention, and he had this uncanny feeling that he was being watched. He took a deep, painful breath and slowly turned around.

Dawn was breaking over the frosty landscape, and shadows jumped out at him as he spun around. Slowly, Michael focused his eyes and discerned the shadowy shapes that came into view.

Then he saw her. He stopped, his entire body frozen to the spot. His gaze locked onto the gaping eyes staring back at him from the barn's entrance.

It was the girl!

They stared at each other for a long, frozen moment. Her jaw dropped as she stared at the stranger hiding in her barn, and then the realisation must have hit her about who it was.

She opened her mouth as if to scream, and then stopped, her shoulders dropping. "Who are you?" she asked.

Michael climbed down the ladder and held his hands in the air. "Please, don't be frightened. I'm not going to hurt you. I'm just trying to stay warm for a few days before I go on my way."

"Who are you?" she asked again, stepping back, her eyes widening with each word she spoke.

"My name is Willi Bauer, and I'm from Dortmund.

"I'm hurt, and I needed shelter for a few days so I could recover. I'll be gone today, so please don't scream or make a fuss. I promise I'm not going to hurt you."

"You're him, aren't you?" the girl's voice rose a few notches. "You're one of those two Englishmen the army and the police are looking for." She stepped back and out of the barn.

Michael knew there was no point lying to the girl. He'd been stupid and lax, and he'd allowed his hunger to get the better of him. Now he had to face the consequences.

He nodded his head slowly. "Yes, I'm the one they are looking for. But please know that I'm not the killer they make me out to be. All I want to do is go home, and if you allow me to leave, I promise you will never see me again."

The girl stared at him, unmoving and unspeaking. Michael could almost see the cogs of her brain whirring around, wondering what to do.

"If you give me up, they will kill me. Please, let me go, and I'll get as far away from here as I can. I'll never tell them you saw me, and you won't have to worry about having my blood on your hands."

The girl shook her head, and she opened her mouth to yell out. But something stopped her once again.

"Are you Jewish?" she asked.

"No, I'm not Jewish."

"Then why is the Gestapo trying so hard to find you? Did you kill those policemen like they said?"

"I was with my brother and some friends in Munich when the Gestapo burst in. All we were trying to do was leave Germany, but they came in and started shooting. They killed our friends, and I fired back at them. That's the truth, whether you believe me or not."

"Why were you in Munich? Was it you who crashed

281

the car near here a few days ago?" The girl eyed him suspiciously.

"Yes, we were in Munich because we were trying to get out of Germany. And yes, it was me who crashed the car a few days ago."

"Were you rescuing Jews? Were you taking them out of Germany when you were caught?"

Michael knew this was the question on which his life hung. Was she a Nazi who wanted all the Jews rounded up and removed from society? Or was she opposed to the brutality the Nazis meted out to them?

He stood quietly while the girl weighed him up, waiting for the answer that would decide if he lived or died.

Chapter Forty-Eight

The standoff lasted for several tense moments. In the end, Michael sighed and decided to tell the truth. He hesitated for a moment, wondering if he could trust this girl with his secrets. But there was something in her eyes that made him believe she was different, that she might understand his situation.

In for a penny, in for a pound. He took a deep breath and spoke.

"If I am going to die, I will die knowing I stood up for my convictions and told the truth. We were with a group who were helping Jewish families escape Germany. My brother and I were leaving with them because we are not German. We are English, and we came here to find our missing uncle and great-grandfather, who are Jewish."

He paused, studying the girls face for any sign of betrayal. But all he saw was compassion and understanding.

The girl stared at him, her eyes never leaving his.

"My real name is Michael Fernsby, and my brother and I separated after what happened in Munich. We thought we'd have a better chance of at least one of us making it home if we split up. I don't know where my brother is, but I hope he's doing better than I am."

It was too painful to admit that David was dead, and he wasn't telling anyone where he was buried. That was a secret he'd take to his own grave if he had to, because the only thing keeping him going was the promise he'd made over David's body when he buried him.

He held his breath, waiting for her response. He knew he was taking a risk by revealing so much, but he had no other choice than to tell the truth and hope it was enough.

He stepped forward and held out his hands in front of him. "I understand if you are going to give me up. If I was in your situation, I'd probably do the same thing. Just know that I was only trying to do the right thing, and I only fired back at the Gestapo in self-defence."

"I used to be in the BDM," the girl finally said after another long pause.

"What's the BDM?"

"The Bund Deutscher Mädel."

"What's that? I'm English, remember."

"It's the female version of the Hitler Youth."

Well, that's it then. Michael sighed and looked her in the eye again, waiting for the inevitable to happen.

She remained silent, staring at Michael.

"Well, you'd better yell for help and turn me in then. If you don't, I'm going to leave, so now's your chance to be a hero and tell them you've found me."

"My best friend owned the general store in Glatten. We used to go to school together, and at weekends she would help on the farm, or I would work in her store after finishing my tasks here."

She clenched her fists at her sides; her knuckles turning white.

"We, that is my family, used to support Hitler. Anna and I were like sisters, and everything was fine until they changed the laws."

The girl's eyes filled with tears as she spoke, and she turned away from Michael to hide her face.

"I'm sorry," she said, her voice shaking with emotion. "It's just... it's hard to talk about."

Michael reached out a hand to comfort her but stopped himself just in time. He could feel the intensity of her emotions, and he knew he needed to tread carefully.

"My friend was Jewish, and the brownshirt thugs harassed them constantly. They painted terrible things on the windows of their store, and on Kristallnacht they smashed the windows and set fire to it, burning it down and taking everything away from Anna and her father. After that, we stopped supporting Hitler, although we keep our feelings to ourselves in fear of reprisals."

"Where are Anna and her father now?" Michael asked, hope rising inside him that he might yet get out of this alive.

It also brought home to him what life was like for everyday Germans who lived with this tyrannical madman as their leader. He was sure most Germans went along with him, but for those who had close ties to Jewish people, life must be terrible for them.

Michael closed his eyes and understood from the raw emotions on display some of the pain the girl must be feeling.

There was something about this girl that tugged on his heartstrings, and even though she may yet turn out to be the enemy, she pulled him towards her in a way he couldn't describe, not even to himself.

It wasn't her physical beauty, although to him she looked about as close to a fairy-tale princess as any girl could ever get. No, it was something else, something intangible that he couldn't put his finger on.

He frowned and shook himself. *Give over, you've only just met her. She might be about to hand you over to the Gestapo, so stop this at once.*

"They got out. They moved to Amsterdam, where they will be safe. Why are you staring at me like that?"

"I'm sorry," Michael blushed. "I didn't know I was. So, what are you going to do? I'm sorry about your friend, but I'm glad they escaped while they could."

"My name is Mina."

Chapter Forty-Nine

M ichael was stunned. This wasn't what he'd been expecting, and her words shocked him.

"Mina Postner. My sister is Senta, and we live here with our parents, Tim and Irma Postner. We are all sympathetic to the Jews, but we must keep our distance, or the Nazis will take everything from us."

"Hello, Mina. That's a beautiful name."

"Hello, Michael. That is also a beautiful name. For an Englishman, anyway."

They both laughed, and the tension between them broke in an instant.

"It is not safe for you here. You need to get as far away from Glatten as you can. Soldiers are searching everywhere for you, and there is no doubt they will be back here again with dogs and guns."

They stared at each other for another awkward moment before Mina broke eye contact. "My sister will be here at any minute, and I can't promise that she won't give you away. She is fascinated with the story of the British spies who crashed their vehicle near here. It's all she ever talks about."

"I'll get my things and be gone as soon as it's safe. Thank you for not handing me over." He backed away towards the hayloft and winced when he stumbled over a hen running under his feet.

"You're hurt."

"It's nothing," Michael lied. "I'm fine. I just need a minute to get my things and then I'll be out of your lives."

Mina gazed at the farmhouse to make sure Senta wasn't coming and approached Michael. "Let me look. We have to know how to take care of each other on the farm because we're a long way from the nearest hospital."

Her touch sent electric shocks through Michael's body, and he couldn't believe how he melted as her fingers made the slightest contact with his arm.

For God's sake, get a grip. Michael forced himself to ignore her touch. "I'm fine, honestly. I just banged my head and my ribs when the car crashed into a tree."

Mina ignored his protests and gently pressed around the wound on his head. Then she pulled his sweater up over his head, revealing the bruises that covered his chest. Electricity seared through Michael's veins when she touched his skin, and his heart pounded so loudly in his chest that he was sure she could hear it. He shuddered as a wave of shivers ran down his spine, and he struggled to catch his breath as her fingers traced the contours of his chest. The surrounding air seemed to crackle with energy, and Michael felt as if he was drowning in the intensity of his emotions.

What the hell is going on with me?

She made a garbled sound that was like an owl cooing in the trees before lowering his clothes back over his body.

"Your chest is black and blue all over. You might have

broken a couple of ribs, or they might just be bruised heavily, I can't tell. But you need rest so they can heal."

"You told me it wasn't safe for me here and that I had to leave."

"That is true. It isn't safe for you here. It's not safe if you leave either, because you won't get very far with bruising like that. You need more time to heal."

The sound of a girl singing close by drifted into the barnyard. "It's Senta," Mina said. "Quickly, go back up there and keep out of the way. You should be safe for another few days, at least."

"Thank you," Michael said. He started dragging himself painfully up the ladder.

"Hurry, she'll be here any second."

Michael had just about rolled into the hay when a younger version of Mina entered the barn. They looked so alike that if Senta was a couple of years older, they could have been mistaken for twins.

"Who were you talking to?" Senta asked her sister.

"Nobody. I was cursing the hens for getting under my feet. Like you, Senta, they never listen to me."

Laughter filled the air, and Michael lay back, enjoying the frivolity beneath him. Memories of when he and David joked around like that flooded back, and sadness mixed with fondness as the images of happier times replayed in his mind.

He thought of his father and wondered how he was feeling after his bout of food poisoning. Surely by now, he'd be chomping at the bit, wondering what was happening to his two sons. How was his mother coping, not knowing where they were or if they were safe? He cringed at the thought of telling them what had happened to David.

They're better off not knowing. Michael drifted off into a restless sleep.

The next morning, he watched as Mina and Senta went about their morning routines, laughing and playing. His heart ached as their interaction evoked memories of David, but he felt soothed when he stole an occasional glance with Mina while Senta had her back to the hayloft.

After they left, he fell asleep again.

He awoke with a jump. Someone was rattling the steps to the hayloft! Michael lay perfectly still, hoping that whoever it was wouldn't hear his heart crashing inside his bruised chest. Cold sweat ran down his neck, settling in the recesses of his collarbone, and panic rose in his throat.

He gripped the gun in his hand, for he had long ago decided that he would never allow himself to be captured and tortured. If the Gestapo found him, he was going down in a blaze of glory.

It wasn't unusual for one of Mina's family to climb the ladder for a bale of two of hay, but Michael was safe from that. He was at the rear of the loft, as close to the back wall as possible. They grabbed the bales from the front and tossed them down from there, so there was little likelihood he'd be discovered accidentally.

"Michael, it's me, Mina." The words drifted to his ears, sounding like the music he loved hearing over the radio from the famed BBC Symphony Orchestra.

He poked his head from under the hay and was shocked to see how bright it was in the barn. Dawn had barely broken when he'd closed his eyes, so he must have slept for a long time.

"Mina, is everything alright?"

"Yes, but help me with this before I drop it."

Michael rolled over the bales of hay towards the ladder.

His eyes widened when he saw what she was struggling to hoist up the steps.

"What's this?" he asked, hardly able to believe what he was seeing.

She was carrying a plate stacked high with food, and steam rose into Michael's nostrils, filling them with delightful aromas.

"I'm in heaven," he said with a grin stretching from ear to ear. "What is this, Mina?"

"Have you forgotten what day it is?" she asked as she handed the warm plate to him. "I thought you English celebrated Christmas Day just as much as we Germans do."

Christmas Day! Michael had lost all track of time and had completely forgotten that today was the big day itself.

"I lost track of time. Yes, of course we celebrate Christmas in England."

Mina joined him at the edge of the barn and sat with her legs dangling over the edge. "I can't stay long, and I need to take the plate back with me or Mama will miss it."

Michael didn't answer. The food he was holding in his hands captivated his senses. It had been so long since he'd sat down to a good meal, and he was beyond starving. He grabbed the fork and dove in.

"This is all from our farm," Mina explained proudly. "I brought you duck, potato dumplings, and, of course, the famous German red cabbage. I would have brought some apple and sausage stuffing, but my greedy sister ate it all."

"This is more than enough. I'm very grateful, Mina. I can't remember the last time I ate a good meal. This is fantastic!"

Michael handed her the plate back in less than two minutes. He'd licked it clean, and not even a single crumb remained.

"Was that quick enough for you?"

Mina laughed. "I hope you enjoyed it."

Their hands touched as they exchanged the plate, and Michael hoped she felt the same electric shock that he did. "It was wonderful, and I can't thank you enough for thinking of me, especially on such an important day as today."

"You looked like you needed a good meal," Mina said. "I'll try to bring you some more later, but for now, stay out of sight."

"I promise." He took her hand in his and shuddered as her touch caused the hair on his arms to rise once again. "Thank you again, Mina. You didn't have to do this for me."

Mina pulled a damp cloth from her coat pocket and gently washed the wound on Michael's forehead. "It's not too deep," she announced. "If we keep it clean, it will heal well."

"Thank you."

"You helped the Jews. That is enough for me. Anna would have liked you if she was still here."

Chapter Fifty

Dusk was about an hour away, and Michael whiled away the time watching Mina and Senta milking the cows in the barn. They moved together with ease and grace, and he smiled at the gentle gestures of affection they silently exchanged.

As he watched, he couldn't help but feel a twinge of sorrow at their closeness. It reminded him of the way he and David used to be before the dark clouds of a looming war had come crashing into their lives.

But as he continued to watch, a sense of warmth and affection spread through him. He saw the way Mina's eyes crinkled when she laughed, and the gentle curve of Senta's smile. They were a world away from the horrors of Kristall-nacht, and for a moment, Michael could forget everything else.

As the light faded, he felt a pang of sadness. He knew he would have to leave soon, to continue his journey towards the border. But for now, he savoured the peaceful moment, knowing it might be the last one he would experience for a long time.

The next morning, Mina surprised Michael again when she brought him two boiled eggs, an egg cup, and a spoon. She also brought a small loaf of bread and some German sausage wrapped in a handkerchief.

"This is for later," she explained. "The eggs are for now, but you must hurry."

"I know. You have to get the spoon and the egg cup back before your mother misses them."

Michael caught the glint in Mina's eyes, and not for the first time he saw her smouldering beauty, and the kindness and compassion in her heart stared back at him through the deepest blue eyes he'd ever seen. It reminded him of a time in Gibraltar when the early morning sun reflected across the deep blue serenity of the Mediterranean Sea.

"What are you staring at?" Mina's face turned crimson, and she looked down towards the floor.

"I'm sorry." Michael was surprised at how soft his voice had become. "I don't mean to stare, but I have to say that you have the prettiest eyes I've ever seen."

Mina gave a nervous laugh. "I bet you say that to all the girls in England."

"Actually, I've never said that to anyone before in my entire life."

Mina looked up and smiled at Michael, and he felt his legs quiver slightly.

Stop this at once. She's only helping me because her best friend is a Jew. As soon as I'm fit enough to travel, I'll be gone, and she'll never think of me again.

Michael chided himself all morning for the way he was acting around her. *I'm like a lovesick puppy. Hell, Lucy didn't even act like this when I saved her from Stourcliffe.*

❧

Mina brought food and bathed his wounds every day for the next week, and finally, on New Year's Eve, Michael knew he was well enough to make a move.

They sat together in silence as Michael wolfed down the soft-boiled eggs, and as he handed her the empty egg cup, their hands met, sending the now familiar lightning waves bolting through his body. Mina must have felt it too because he saw her judder just like he had done.

Instinctively, he placed his hands around her shoulders and pulled her towards him, and when she didn't resist, he kissed her long and hard on her lips. His eyes were closed, but his senses were as heightened as they'd ever been. His heart raced and his legs shook, and he momentarily lost track of where he was and why he was there.

For a fleeting moment, Michael was in an alternate reality where everything was different, safe, and happy. He knew what he was feeling, and he hoped Mina felt it too.

I'm in love!

Their heads remained close long after the kiss ended, and they stared at each other, unblinking and unmoving. Eventually, Michael broke away as reality returned.

"There is something about you I've never felt before," he whispered. "I know you feel it too, and if this is how love feels, then I want more of it."

Mina nodded. "I feel the same, but we both know you can't stay here. It's too dangerous for both of us, and my family too."

Michael nodded. "Thanks to you, I am feeling much better, and I will leave tonight after dark. I cannot thank you enough, Mina, and I will never forget you. I wish we could have met under different circumstances, and I hope we can meet again when this is all over."

Mina's eyes misted, and she held Michael's hand. "I

hope we can meet again someday. But you do not know the way to the border. It's about one hundred kilometres, so I can go with you and show you the way."

"That's very kind, Mina, but you've done more than enough already. That's about sixty miles, and there will be roadblocks everywhere searching for me. It's too dangerous, and I can't allow it. Just point me in the right direction and I'll find my way."

"I'd better go." Mina sniffed. "Mama and Senta will be looking for me."

Michael watched as she left the barn. She never turned around, but he could tell she was feeling the emotion. Whatever they had found together, it had been a perfect interlude to what had otherwise been a nightmare. He would never forget the beautiful girl who had done as much as anyone to save his life and make him feel again.

Chapter Fifty-One

The sound of an approaching vehicle jerked Michael from his thoughts, and he checked all around to make sure the hay covered him.

The doors to the barn were wide open, and the two sisters were milking the cows in the dreary afternoon's half-light.

He stiffened as he peered through the hole he'd made so he could see the barn below, and noted the anxious exchanges between the two girls. Mina shot a hurried glance in Michael's direction and strode to the barn doors.

The car door slammed, and boots crunched in the frozen farmyard. Michael's pulse raced, and he strained his ears trying to work out how many pairs of boots he could hear. His knuckles turned white as he gripped the Walther PPK tightly in his hands.

Was it one or many? Was it the army? The Gestapo? Has Mina turned me in, after all?

The boots approached the barn. Michael lay still, frozen in fear. He knew he'd been foolish to fall in love with Mina.

They were about to be on opposite sides of a great conflict, and as much as he wished otherwise, their loyalties clashed.

He thought about Gigi and his grandfather, Frank Fernsby Senior, and what it must have been like for them before the outbreak of the Great War in 1914.

He took a deep breath. *That was different. Frank and Gigi were lovers. They were already married and were living in England, so snap out of it. You've only just met Mina, and she's probably turned you in already.*

A young man, around his age, strode purposefully into the barn. Mina stood her ground and didn't move, but Senta moved behind her older sister and stood near the door as if she was ready to run.

Michael had seen a similar uniform to the one the boy was wearing before. It had been hung up in another boy's bedroom in Freising when he'd broken in to find sustenance and a change of clothing in what seemed a lifetime ago. This must be the winter version of what he'd seen.

The boy was a member of the Hitler Youth!

Mina positioned herself near the door, so she was facing the hayloft. The boy stood next to her, also in full view of the hayloft. Michael couldn't see his facial features very well, but he could make out a tuft of dark hair beneath a dark blue or black cap; he couldn't tell from his concealed position in the hayloft. The jacket and long trousers were the same colour, and he had a thick belt around his waist that had some insignia he couldn't make out.

What he could discern, though, was crystal clear. The boy was wearing the familiar swastika armband on his left arm that told Michael everything he needed to know.

There was a single pip in the centre of a collar patch, and Michael racked his brain to remember what Edouard Abreo had taught them regarding the ranking system the

Nazis used. He was a *Scharführer,* which meant he was a section leader in the Hitler Youth movement.

But what was he doing here, on New Year's Eve of all days?

"Fraulein Mina, you look as beautiful today as you always do." The boy kissed Mina's hand and bowed his head. "May we walk together?"

"Alwin, it's cold outside, so I'd rather stay here where it's warmer if that's alright with you."

The boy named Alwin gave Senta a dirty look, but he bowed his head towards Mina again. "Of course, Mina."

"I trust you and your family have had a good Christmas," Mina said. Michael could hear the tremble in her voice, and he knew she didn't feel comfortable around him.

"Very good, thank you. And I trust you have had a good Christmas too?"

"I had an excellent day, thank you, Alwin. What brings you out here on such a chilly afternoon?"

"Praise the Führer, I was worried about you and your family. I bring news from my father. I was hoping to tell you alone, but as you say, it's cold outside." He threw Senta another dirty look, but she ignored him and stood her ground.

Mina said nothing. Instead, she looked at Alwin expectantly, waiting for his next words.

"I'm sure you've already heard by now that two British spies crashed their vehicle a few miles from here a week or more ago after our heroic soldiers ran them off the road during a dangerous chase."

Michael silently snorted. Dangerous chase? The accident was caused by his own stupidity, not by any heroic Nazi chasing him.

"Of course we have," Mina answered. "How could we

not? It's all the radio and the newspapers talk about. Have you caught them yet?"

"Not yet, Fraulein Mina, but we're close. All the roads around Glatten are blocked, and we're searching every building around here for miles. Wherever they're hiding, we'll catch them soon enough, and when we do, they'll pay for murdering four members of our police force."

Michael took a deep breath. If what the boy was saying was true, neither he nor Mina's family were safe. He was glad he was leaving tonight before they found him and dragged him out of there.

"I'm glad you are working on it for us, even on New Year's Eve," Mina said. Michael could hear the sarcasm in her voice, but Alwin seemed oblivious to it.

"I assure you, they are not here. My father and I have searched everywhere for them, just in case they were hiding somewhere. I'm happy to report that they are not here."

"That's very good to hear, Fraulein, but the British spies are dangerous, and they could have crept in here during the night when you were asleep. My father believes at least one of them might be injured because of the amount of blood we found in the vehicle. They may hide while they recover."

"That's good to know," Mina said. "I'll let my father know about it."

"I thought I'd have a quick look while it's still daylight," Alwin said. "I need to know you are safe at night, Mina. My father even thought it might be a good idea if I stay here until we apprehend them."

Mina stared at Alwin as though he had developed some incurable plague.

What is he doing? Is he using my being here as an excuse to get near her?

Jealousy coursed through Michael's body, and he pinched himself for acting in such a ridiculous manner.

"Please thank your father for his kind gesture, but we are perfectly capable of looking after ourselves. It's New Year's Eve, Alwin, and you should be at home with your family."

"It's more important that I take care of you, and my father was right. I should stay here until we find them. After I search the farm, of course."

"Alwin," Mina's voice rose several levels louder. "You are not staying here. The British spies are not here, and my father would be insulted if you think him too weak to take care of his own family. Now please, it was good to see you, and we're grateful for your kind gesture, but we have work to do and it's getting dark. Please go home where you belong."

"But my father insists—"

"I don't care what your father insists!" Mina was shouting now. "He doesn't own this farm. We do, and we don't need your help. Now, if you'll excuse us, we have to finish milking the cows before it gets too dark."

Mina all but pushed Alwin out of the barn. The first tentacles of dusk were reaching into the farmyard, and Mina meant business.

"You have not heard the last of this, Fraulein Mina. The soldiers will be back to search the farm, and I hope for your sake the spies are not here."

"They are not here," Mina shot back at him. "And I hope for your sake that you can drive well enough in the dark to get home safely."

Alwin stomped off, and Michael heard him slam the car door before gunning the engine and ramming it into gear.

The tyres spun as he raced out of the farm with his ears still ringing from Mina's harsh words.

"Quickly," Mina said after he'd gone. "Go tell Papa what just happened. He needs to know what's coming. I'll finish here and I'll be right there."

Senta ran off, leaving Mina alone in the barn. As soon as she was out of sight, Mina dropped the pail and ran towards the hayloft.

Chapter Fifty-Two

"Who was that?" Michael asked once Mina had climbed the ladder.

"His name is Alwin Lutz. He's eighteen, the same age as me, and we used to be childhood sweethearts." She looked away as she spoke.

Michael's jaw clenched. Although he knew it was stupid, he couldn't help feeling the pangs of jealousy rise again.

"So, what happened?" he asked. "You didn't seem to be too close to him now, from what I saw."

"His father is the headmaster at the school we went to in Glatten. He's a fanatical Nazi, and it was he who threw Anna out of school. He's the leader of the Nazi Party around here, and he has a lot of influence. Alwin's entire family are Nazis. He has an older brother who is about to join the SS, and Alwin wants to follow in his footsteps."

"That's not good," Michael said.

"Alwin and his brother were with the stormtroopers when they smashed Anna's store. I've never forgiven them for what they did."

"Does Alwin know you don't like him anymore? Because he still seems smitten with you."

"Are you jealous?" Mina teased.

"I might be."

Michael felt his face turn bright red and burn. "Just a little."

Mina squeezed his arm. "I'm glad." Her face turned as red as he knew his was, and she turned away to avoid eye contact.

Michael reached out and touched her hand. The now familiar sparks flew through his body, and he hoped she was feeling it too. She turned around, and they kissed passionately for several minutes.

"What now?" Michael asked, his voice barely above a whisper. "I can hardly believe it myself, but every time I see you, I feel like my heart might stop. And when we kiss... well, let's just say it's like nothing else matters in the world. I don't know what the future holds, but I do know that I want to be with you, Mina. More than anything."

"I feel the same," Mina answered softly. "It's strange, because I've never felt this way before, and I hardly even know you. You are supposed to be this dangerous enemy that is going around murdering every German you come across, but I know you are not like that. I don't want you to die, Michael. I love you too."

They kissed one more time.

"I'm not going to die. I'm going to get out of here and tell the world what the Nazis are doing to the German people. The feeling at home is that war is once again coming between us, but I hope that isn't true."

"I do too. Papa fought in the last war, and he is worried it's going to happen all over again because of the Führer. We're all very worried, Michael."

"I need to leave," Michael said. "Alwin said the soldiers are coming, and I can't risk you getting caught hiding me. Enough people have died already, and I cannot allow that to happen to anyone else, especially you."

Mina nodded. "I know, but how will you find your way? How will you stay safe with your injuries?"

"I'm much better already, and I'm going to head for the border. It's better you don't know the details, so you won't have to lie to Alwin's father when he comes here tomorrow with the soldiers."

"Give me thirty minutes." Mina climbed down the ladder and headed for the barn door. "Don't you dare leave until I come back. I won't be long."

"You're bossy."

With one last longing look at each other, Mina disappeared into the early evening darkness. Michael settled down into the hay and checked his backpack to make sure he wasn't leaving anything behind. He checked his collection of Walther PPKs one more time and hoped fervently that he wouldn't have to use them before he reached the safety of France.

True to her word, Mina ran back to the barn around twenty minutes later. "I can't stay long. Papa is suspicious of why I'm spending so much time here, and why I'm suddenly eating a lot more than I normally do."

"I'm sure he is. How did you sneak that out with no one noticing?" Michael pointed at the bulging towel in her hand that no doubt contained enough food to last him several days.

"They think I'm feeding the chickens, so I can't stay long. This should tide you over for three or four days, which should be enough if you hurry."

Michael climbed down the ladder and opened his backpack. As he reached for the food, Mina grabbed him and pulled him to her. It was the first time their bodies had pressed tightly together, and Michael immediately lost any notion of where he was as the excitement washed over him.

Footsteps running towards them yanked him out of his euphoria, and he pulled away from Mina to face the danger. Instinctively, he stood in front of her and reached for his weapon.

He was too late. The onrushing Alwin Lutz crashed into Michael and grabbed Mina around the throat. He raised his own pistol and aimed it at Michael.

"I knew it," he panted. "I knew there was something wrong when I was here earlier. Mina couldn't get me away fast enough, so I knew you were here. Mina, do you know what you've done? You will hang for this."

Michael stepped forward and raised his hands in front of him. His gun was still in his pocket, and he knew by the wild look in Alwin's eyes that he'd shoot him if he reached for it.

"Alwin, don't do anything stupid. Let Mina go, and I'll come with you peacefully. Just think what a hero you'll be when you tell your father it was you who arrested the British spy."

"Where is the other one?" Alwin demanded. "I know there are two of you here."

"He's not here. We split up in Munich and went our separate ways. I don't know where he is."

"I don't believe you. Where is he? I won't ask again."

"He isn't here," Mina said, struggling to free herself from Alwin's grip around her neck. "It's just this one."

"You were kissing him, Mina. You never kissed me like that, yet you kiss the Englishman like he's your lover. Now I have no choice other than to tell my father what you've done, and he'll hang you for it."

"You don't have to do that, Alwin," Michael said. "I'll go with you if you leave her out of it. Nobody needs to know how you found us. Just tell them you found me hiding in the hayloft. I'll back up what you say, and you'll be the hero. Just let Mina go."

Alwin stared at Michael, confusion in his eyes. He was obviously contemplating his suggestion. He opened his mouth to speak when Mina pulled herself free and threw herself at Alwin.

"Run, Michael. Get out of here."

Michael wasn't doing any such thing. He wasn't leaving Mina to die at the hands of the Nazis while he ran like a coward.

He jumped towards Alwin, who had thrown Mina aside. Michael got there right as Alwin was raising his gun, and he batted his arm out of the way, knocking the gun out of his hand and away from him on the floor of the barn. With his other hand, he crashed his fist into Alwin's face, feeling a surge of satisfaction as blood splattered from his nose.

Alwin fell to his knees, and Michael kicked out as hard as he could, catching him under the chin. More blood splattered from his face, and Alwin toppled onto his back.

Michael ran to Mina, who was on her feet staring at the bloody brawl in front of her.

"Leave, now. I'll take care of Alwin." Her voice trembled.

"How? What are you going to do with him? You know he'll turn you in the moment he leaves here. I can't let him do that to you."

"What are you going to do? Kill him?" Mina's eyes were wide open.

"No." Michael shook his head. "I'm taking him with me. He's my insurance to get through the roadblocks without getting caught."

Alwin rose to his feet and snorted. His face was bloody and bruised, but he still had his wits about him. "I'm not going anywhere. You two are under arrest."

Michael put his gun away and grabbed Alwin by the collar. "Mina, tell your parents you found me here after Alwin came back to search for me. Until then, you didn't know I was here. Alwin, you're coming with me."

He turned to look at Mina one more time and was about to speak when a heavy blow to the side of his head knocked him spinning to the ground. Alwin stood over him with the barrel of another gun in his hand.

"Now it's my turn," he said triumphantly.

He raised his arm to shoot Michael, but Mina jumped between them. "Alwin, stop. How did you know? Tell me, I have to know."

"I knew you were hiding something, so I stopped the car down the lane and came back. I watched for a while until I saw you carrying something that I suspected was food for the spy. Then I saw you together, and I knew you'd been helping him. I saw you kissing him, Mina."

"Alwin, you won't understand, but I love him, and I can't let you hurt him."

Michael rose unsteadily to his knees, but before he could stand up, Alwin raised his hand in the air. "You have corrupted Mina and attacked a member of the Hitler Jugend. You are a dangerous man, and I have the right to kill you right here."

Alwin stepped to the side and aimed his weapon at Michael, who could see the fear in Alwin's eyes.

"You're not a killer, Alwin. Put the gun down, and I'll go with you if you agree to leave Mina out of it."

"Stop!" Alwin roared. "Get on your knees."

Michael closed his eyes and waited for the gun to go off. There was nothing he could do except hope he died instantly.

A loud shot rang out, and Michael waited for the inevitable thud followed by the pain of death.

It never came. Instead, he heard Alwin moan, and then slump to the floor with a crash. Michael opened his eyes to see Mina holding the smoking gun he'd knocked out of Alwin's hands moments earlier.

Mina had shot Alwin Lutz!

Chapter Fifty-Three

Mina's hands trembled uncontrollably as she stared blankly at the pool of blood spreading on the hay-covered floor. Her breathing came in short, ragged gasps, and her eyes were wide and unfocused. Michael rose to his feet and reached out to touch her arm, but she jerked away as if burned, her body wracked with sobs. It was clear that she was in a state of deep shock, barely aware of her surroundings.

Michael knelt by Alwin's prone body to check for signs of life.

There weren't any. He was dead.

Footsteps ran towards them, and Michael heard the shouts from Mina's father as he entered the barn. He skidded to a halt when he saw Alwin's dead body on the floor, and Mina stood close by with the gun still in her outstretched hand.

She stared straight ahead, unmoving and unspeaking, as if in a trance.

Her mother and Senta followed close behind, and Senta screamed when she saw what had happened.

"Mina, what have you done?" her father asked. "And who are you?"

Michael looked at the faces staring back at him. He took Mina's arm and gently removed the gun from her hands. Then he held her hand to comfort her as he addressed her family, who were all staring in shock at the intruder and the dead body in their barn.

Her father was a tall, wiry man with short grey hair. He was lean from years of hard labour, and his weather-beaten face showed he'd endured more than his fair share of hardship.

Michael felt sorry for what he'd done to this man's family, and his heart skipped a beat when he realised that everyone he cared for in the entire world was hurting because of his actions.

"Mr Postner, please do not blame Mina for what happened. This is all my fault, and the authorities will not blame you for Alwin's death."

Mina never moved. She seemed oblivious to her family's appearance, and instead just stared at Alwin's body on the floor.

"Who are you, and what happened here?" Tim Postner gently steered Mina away from Michael and towards the door, where the rest of his family stood watching in shock.

"You're one of them," Senta shouted. "You're one of the British spies that crashed the car near here." She turned to her father. "Mina's been helping him, Father. That's why she's been spending so much time in the barn. She's been feeding him and looking after him. Alwin must have found them together, so he killed him." She screamed again and clung to her father's side.

Mina's mother, Irma, said nothing. She just stared at Mina and then Michael in a repeating cycle.

Mina's father grabbed a pitchfork that was propped up by the door and stood in front of his family. "Get out of here, Irma, and take the girls with you."

He faced Michael. "You're not getting away with this."

"Please, let me explain," Michael said, stepping away from the approaching farmer and lowering his weapon. "We don't have long if this is going to work, but I can make this right for you. It is true that I am the Englishman they're searching for, but everything else they said about me is lies."

Irma didn't seem to listen, but Tim stared intently at Michael as he spoke. "We came here to find my uncle and great-grandfather, so we could take them home. They're Jewish, and we were concerned about their welfare. Some kind people tried to help us escape with another Jewish family, but the Gestapo found us in Munich."

Tim Postner stepped back towards the barn door. He tried dragging Mina with him, but she refused to budge.

"The Gestapo killed our friends. We fired back, and that's how they died. My brother and I ran for our lives, and we split up, so at least one of us would have a decent chance of making it across the border. I crashed the car I was driving, and I hid in your hayloft while I recovered."

"Where is your brother?" Tim Postner asked. "Is he here as well?" He looked around as if David might somehow appear out of nowhere and attack them.

Michael shook his head. "Please, listen to what I'm saying. We don't have time to argue if you want to save your family. I already told you we split up in Munich and headed for the border separately."

Michael stopped to see if his words had registered with the Postners. They seemed to have done, so he continued.

"Please don't blame Mina for any of this. She was just trying to help me recover enough so I could go home. Unfortunately, Alwin guessed I was here, and he came back and saw us together. Then he tried to kill me, and he would have if Mina hadn't intervened."

"I killed him, Papa." Mina suddenly spoke. Her voice was shaky and high-pitched. "I killed Alwin." She started shaking and burst into a hysterical sob. Her father grabbed her and held her tightly to him.

"I know you have a gun, so I cannot apprehend you, but I'll tell you now, Englander. I'm taking Mina back to the house, and I am going to telephone the authorities. You have caused my family untold harm, and I'm not allowing my daughter to take the fall for you."

Tim stood as tall as he could and faced his enemy head-on. "You are going to have to kill me if you want to stop me."

"Papa, it wasn't his fault!" Mina seemed to snap out of her trance. "Alwin was trying to kill him, and I shot him."

More tears.

"See what you've done?" Tim snarled. "I hope they hang you for this."

"Papa, no," Mina pleaded. "He was helping Jews escape Germany. You saw what they did to Anna and her father, so you know what they're doing. You said yourself that we should have done more to help Anna. We stood by and did nothing, and he's here all the way from England doing what we were too scared to do. Michael was here to help, and we should be ashamed of ourselves. Alwin and his family are all Nazis, you know that, Papa, and they will kill him if they find him."

"They'll kill us too," Irma finally spoke. "That's why we couldn't do anything to help Anna. It's too dangerous for us, Mina."

Michael looked at her and could see she was an older version of Mina and Senta. Even in her forties, Irma still had the poise and beauty that her daughters possessed, and Michael could see where Mina got her looks.

"We're done here." Tim stepped backwards, dragging Mina with him. When she realised what he was doing, Mina tore herself away from her father's grip and ran to Michael's side.

"You don't understand, none of you. This wasn't Michael's fault. None of it was, and if you telephone the Gestapo to turn him in, then I'm going with him, and you'll lose me too. I mean it, Papa. We did nothing when Anna needed our help, and I'm not doing that again."

"You're a silly girl." Tim Postner's voice was raised. "The Nazis will swarm all over this place when they realise Alwin is missing. What do you think they'll do to us when they find his dead body lying in our barn?"

"Mina, don't be stupid," her mother said. "They'll kill us all if we don't hand him over."

"Sir, if I may speak," Michael said, looking at Tim Postner. "I know how to make this right."

Chapter Fifty-Four

Everyone stared at Michael. Tim Postner pulled a face and grunted. "What can you possibly do to make this right? You'll do anything to escape and go back to England, leaving us here to face the consequences of Alwin's death."

"Not to mention we're harbouring a British spy," Irma added.

"It doesn't have to be that way," Michael said. "Please, let me explain."

"I'm listening." Tim Postner looked like he'd rather do just about anything else.

"Mr Postner, I have been here since I crashed the car over a week ago. Mina discovered I was here, and rather than turn me in, she bravely helped me recover until I was strong enough to leave."

Tim shot his daughter a stern look. "Stupidly, you mean. This is all your fault, Mina. Alwin's father will kill us all for what we've done to his son. I hope you think of that when they drag your sister off and shoot her."

Mina stared back defiantly at her father. "I refuse to be a coward anymore, Father. What the Nazis are doing is a crime and you know it. We have to stand up to them, and show them we won't accept their cruelty, not only towards the Jews, but against anyone, even us, who dares stand up to them."

"And how do you propose we do that?" Tim sneered.

"Stop!" Michael thundered. Nobody was more surprised at the anger in his voice than he was, especially given the situation. "We don't have time for this. I'm trying to give you a way out if you'll let me finish."

Tim shrugged his shoulders.

"Nobody knows Mina helped me except us, and if I'm caught, I'll tell them I killed Alwin after he found me when he searched the hayloft. You heard the gunshot and found Alwin dead in the barn, and that's all you know. It's obvious who killed him, and it will be me they go after. You are shocked and sorry that he died on your property, and you assure the Nazis that you searched the barn several times in case I was here."

"How can we trust you?" Tim asked. "What's to stop you from changing your story once they catch you, which they will? They'll bring in the entire Wehrmacht if they have to, but they'll hunt you down and find you. Then what happens to us? At least if we hand you over, we'll be showing that we tried to stop you rather than just allowing you to run off and escape."

"They'll kill me either way if they catch me, so what would I gain from telling them I didn't kill Alwin? I'm already accused of killing four members of the Gestapo, so one more Nazi won't make a difference to what they'll do to me."

Tim and Irma exchanged worried looks. Michael could see they were mulling it over, and he knew that when they thought about it, it was the only chance they had of getting out of this intact.

Mina stared at Michael with a distant, dull stare. Her look pulled on his heartstrings so hard it almost took him down to his knees.

"There's one more thing that might prove to you I won't change my story." Michael looked into Mina's eyes, trying to reassure her, but he could see that it wasn't working.

"What?" Tim asked.

"This might sound strange, and I know I've only been here a week. And before you say anything, I know the circumstances are against what I'm about to say, and we both know nothing can become of it, but I'm in love with Mina, Mr Postner, and I'll do anything to protect her and keep her and her family safe."

Michael's eyes filled up as he watched the tears tumble down Mina's cheeks. "I'll take my knowledge of what happened here to my grave if I have to, but I promise you, Mr Postner, I promise I will never do anything that will bring harm to Mina or you."

The whites of Tim Postner's eyes shone in the early evening dusk. He stared at Michael as if he'd just admitted to assassinating the Führer himself.

"What... what did you just say?"

"I knew it," Senta yelled. "I told you she's been acting differently this last week. She's been singing and dancing, and she's been way too happy. She spent far too much time in the barn, and we all saw how much more she suddenly started eating. I told you, Papa, but you wouldn't listen."

"Is this true?" Irma asked her daughter.

Mina bowed her head. "Mama, I know it sounds silly, but over this last week, I've got to know him. He's kind and thoughtful, and he's not frightened to help the people we abandoned. I feel strange, and my knees go wobbly when I'm with him, so if that is what love is, then yes, I'm in love with him."

"Young and foolish," Tim snapped. "But it doesn't change anything."

"It changes everything," Michael retorted. "Because it guarantees that I won't change the story we agree on, and it guarantees your safety, as long as you stick to it as well."

"He's right." Irma prodded her husband. "It's the only chance we've got."

"I don't like it, but you're right. It is the only chance we've got," Tim snarled. He looked down at Alwin's body. "What do we do with him?"

"Leave him where he is. Don't touch him and don't go near him," Michael said. "Allow me an hour to get a head start and then call the authorities. Tell them what we discussed, and that you heard a gun go off and found Alwin's body. You searched, but there was no sign of me anywhere."

Mina threw her arms around his neck. "Where will you go? They'll come after you with guns and dogs, and they'll kill you."

"They'll have to kill me if they find me because I'm not letting them take me alive. Hopefully, it won't come to that, and if I leave now, I might have a fighting chance of getting some distance between us before they come after me."

"How will you get to the border?" Tim asked. "There are roadblocks everywhere, and you won't get more than a few miles down the road before they stop you."

"I crashed my car, remember? I don't have a vehicle. It's better you don't know where I'm going because that way you won't have to lie when they ask you."

"We don't own a motor vehicle," Tim said. "But you can take Alwin's. He couldn't have hidden it far from here."

Michael shook his head. "They'll be on the lookout for Alwin's vehicle once they know I took it. No, I have to go on foot, at least until I get clear of the roadblocks."

"In that case, you need to go through the Black Forest," Tim answered. "It's dense, but at least it will give you some protection. Watch out for the dogs, because they'll follow your scent. It's cold, but stay in the streams as much as you can to throw them off."

"I will, thanks. Remember, keep to what we discussed, and tell them I killed Alwin."

Michael grabbed his backpack that was bulging with the food Mina had given him, and he addressed the Postner family one more time.

"I shall never forget the kindness you have shown me. I hope to return when this is all over, when I can thank you properly. In different circumstances, I think we could have been friends."

Tim Postner nodded his head slowly. "Wait here. I have something you might find useful." He ran towards the farmhouse, leaving the rest of them staring in silence at each other.

Michael turned to Mina and held her shoulders in his hands. "Mina, I shall never forget you, and I promise that should I live, I will return one day to find you. I will hold the love we found in my heart, and I hope you do the same. I owe you my life, so please say you'll wait for me."

Ignoring her mother and sister beside her, Mina pulled Michael into her and kissed him hard on the mouth. Senta looked away in disgust, but her mother looked on with sympathy in her eyes. Mina pressed a soft piece of cotton into his hands.

"I love you, Michael Fernsby, and I shall wait for you until the day you return. I will be here every day after the coming war, and I shall never give up hope you will return."

"What's this?" Michael raised the purple cotton garment in the air.

"My scarf. It's not much, but it might keep you warm." Mina held his gaze. "And it might help you remember me."

Michael put his mouth to her ear and whispered. "The Fernsby residence in Sandwich, Kent. Remember that, and if you somehow get to England, come find me. Remember that I love you, and I promise this will not be the last time we are together."

He kissed her one last time as Tim returned to the barn. He scowled when he saw his daughter intimately embracing the foreign spy.

"Here, you might need these." He handed Michael a small compass and a folded grey tarpaulin. "Do you know how to use a compass?"

Michael nodded.

"Keep going west and you'll find the Rhine. You can't miss it. Cross that, and you will be in France. I wish you a safe journey, Englishman, but you are not welcome here ever again, so please stay away from my daughter if you come back."

"Papa, no!" Mina shouted. "I'm going with him."

"No, you're not," Michael and Tim said in unison.

"I will be back," Michael added. "And when I do, Mina will be a grown woman who will make her own decisions. Until then, I hope our two nations avoid the coming war, but if we don't, I shall be back once it's over. Thank you, and stay safe."

He reached forward and kissed Mina one last time. "One hour, and then call Alwin's father."

Chapter Fifty-Five

Michael fastened his jacket and flipped the collar up. He moved as fast as his sore ribs allowed into the dark forest, moving roughly westward. The sub-freezing weather brought relief, as the rock-hard ground ensured his footsteps would be difficult to track by sight alone.

The moon was bright, but the conifer and beech trees blocked most of the light from getting through. He checked his watch and noted the time. It was seven o'clock, so he had around twelve hours of darkness before he had to hide somewhere for the day.

He estimated the journey would take around three nights if he hurried, probably longer if he played cat and mouse with the chasing Nazis. Mina had provided enough food for a week if he rationed it out carefully, and he was happy that he had everything he needed.

His heart yearned for Mina, and he couldn't get her out of his mind. Every time he tried, her soft smile, the look in her eyes, or her fragrance invaded his thoughts, and he drifted off into his own little world.

He didn't mind, because it stopped the repeating nightmares of burying David from stabbing at his heart, and he clung to them for as long as he could.

He took a deep breath and closed his eyes. He could picture Mina's smile and hear her voice in his mind. With a shake of his head, he forced himself to focus on the task at hand and pressed on through the forest. But every so often, he stopped to take a whiff of the purple scarf, which he had tucked away in his pocket.

He found a stream, and although his feet hurt from the freezing water, he waded through it for as long as he could stand it. He checked his watch, and about an hour after he'd left Mina, he knew Tim would make the call to Alwin's father. It wouldn't be long now before the entire world descended on Glatten and Mina's small farm.

Michael pushed all thoughts from his mind and pressed on as fast as his frozen legs would take him. His ribs hurt like the devil, and each brutal step reminded him of what a fool he'd been to crash the vehicle the way he had.

After three hours of bushwhacking through the Black Forest, Michael left the safety of the dense trees. Up ahead, he saw the lights of a nearby town and knew he needed to be careful. So far, he'd managed to avoid contact with either human or animal, but the intermittent sounds of dogs barking in the distance behind him had kept him moving at a rapid pace.

He could only imagine the anger aimed at him by the chasing Nazis, and he knew what they would do to him if he slowed down even for a minute.

By the time he reached the edge of the forest, Michael was frozen to the core and worn out. His feet were heavy and numb, and yet they hurt like crazy with each step his boots made on the frozen earth.

He was hungry as well, so he took a quick break to grab

something to eat while he took his bearings. Lights from the nearby town warned him of the impending dangers, so he walked a hundred yards or so back into the dense forest and sat behind the safety of a large tree.

Clouds had rolled in, and it was almost pitch black. Visibility was poor, and even with his eyes adjusted to the low light, he couldn't make out anything on his map.

He listened intently for the slightest noise that sounded out of place, and when he was happy he was alone, he pulled out the black metal flashlight Father Eise had given him in Freising. It was about the size of his hand, and he held it by the leather strap attached to the rear.

The battery was already inserted, and Michael hoped the cold weather hadn't sapped the life out of it before he'd had a chance to use it. He turned the switch on the flashlight's bottom casing, and a flood of bright light instantly illuminated his surroundings.

He turned the light towards the ground and played with the three sliders on the front casing. The first one turned the light red, and this was the one he used. It preserved his night vision and made it far more acceptable than the white floodlight he'd had it on a moment ago.

Satisfied with the light, he turned it towards his map so he could see where he was. He traced his fingers in the rough direction he'd been travelling and found what he thought was the source of the lights up ahead.

It was a small town called Baiersbronn, and from what he could work out on his map, this had to be where he was. After a refreshing meal of German sausage and some cold potatoes, Michael stood up and stretched his aching body. His feet hurt, but he ignored the discomfort and jumped up and down on the solid blocks that refused to allow warm blood to flow through them. Each movement sent daggers through his chest, and he winced at the sharp pain as it took his breath away.

Michael gathered his backpack with his frozen hands and stood at the edge of the forest. Most of the lights were to his right, which was north, so he headed south to avoid the town. He aimed to get across the valley unseen and back into the Black Forest on the other side.

He took a deep breath and said a silent prayer to the heavens, allowed one last thought of Mina to comfort his emotions, and as images of wet dirt covering David's body shrouded his brain, he shook himself and forced his tortured mind to concentrate on the dangers ahead.

Keeping to the trees, he edged his way down the valley and away from the lights in the distance. After a mile or so, the houses and lights had thinned out enough for him to risk crossing the road he was shadowing in the trees.

As soon as he stepped out into the clearing, the sound of approaching engines forced him back to the cover of the forest. He sank to his knees and hid behind a large tree.

A convoy of bathtubs got near, and as they did, search-lights pierced the darkness on both sides of the road. Michael lay on his stomach, trying to make himself as small as he could.

Dogs barked over the sound of the vehicles, and as they slowly passed him, Michael held his breath and hoped the spotlights didn't find him.

He didn't know how many bathtubs flowed past, but there must have been at least a dozen or more, and he had no doubt why they were there.

Once the coast was clear, he sprang to his feet and sprinted towards the other side. Thoughts of fatigue vanished from his mind as he raced toward the safety of the forest, with the promise of France and the River Rhine awaiting him.

As soon as he reached the forest, he threw himself to the ground and turned to face the road. He held one of his guns in his hands and aimed it in front of him. He'd long since come to terms with the fact that he'd die in a hail of bullets rather than allow himself to be captured, and he felt remarkably calm as he held that thought in his head.

Satisfied he hadn't been seen, Michael hurried away from the town before the army had time to park the bath-tubs and organise themselves into search teams.

He ran for at least thirty minutes until he tripped over a root and crashed to the ground in a heap. He lay there panting and sweating, his breath forming clouds of steam in the frigid air as he struggled to control the pain in his chest.

By five o'clock, Michael was exhausted. He'd trekked over valleys and hills, through streams and the forest, all the while listening to the incessant barking of dogs behind him in the distance.

He couldn't go any farther. His feet, although numb with cold, hurt as they'd never hurt before, and he knew they were bleeding and blistered to pieces. His chest was on fire, and each breath was like a dagger to the heart.

It wouldn't be too long before dawn broke, and he didn't want to be caught out in daylight, where he'd be an easy target, but he was worried that his pursuers wouldn't stop because it was light, and if he stopped, they would catch up and find him.

Reluctantly, Michael realised he had no choice other than to keep going, and hope he remained far enough ahead of his pursuers.

And the dogs. Especially the dogs.

He stopped for a quick rest and checked his map with

the red flashlight. While he ate more of the food Mina had provided, he tried to get his bearings and work out where he was.

The map was pretty much useless in the Black Forest. It was a large-scale road map, so he didn't have anything other than a rough estimate of his current location.

There was nothing he could use as a marker, so he made an educated guess by following his fingers west from the town where he'd seen the convoy getting ready to search for him.

He estimated he was somewhere near Oppenau, and that if he kept going west, he'd arrive close to the town soon. He almost cried when he realised it would take him at least another two days of hard walking to reach Ottenheim and the River Rhine from there.

Barking dogs in the distance brought him back to his senses, and he quickly stuffed everything back into his backpack. He took a deep breath and forced happy thoughts to enter his mind.

As his body protested with every step he made, Michael countered with thoughts of how he'd relax on the train to Paris, and how he'd sleep on the Night Ferry to London.

He thought of how he and Mina had found love even in the direst of circumstances, and of his mother and father at home in Sandwich who would be so happy to see him.

Then he was hit by how they'd react when he told them David was dead. What would they say? What would they do? How would Gigi ever come to terms with knowing that she'd sent her favourite grandson to his death? How would he even tell them?

All these thoughts kept his mind off his feet and chest, which hurt more and more with each painful step. *Only another two days to go. Just another two days, that's all.*

He kept repeating this mantra to himself over and over, saying and doing anything to keep the pain and fatigue from taking over and forcing him to stop.

That would be fatal. Got to keep going. Can't stop, no matter how you feel.

The next thing he knew, Michael had entered a clearing and was staring in the darkness at what looked like a ruined abbey or monastery.

What the...?

He threw his pack down and grabbed the map.

Chapter Fifty-Six

The red flashlight reflected off ancient, ruined walls, and an entrance archway reminded Michael of the magnificent monastic ruins he had seen all over England.

His jaw dropped as he stared around in amazement at the unexpected ruins in the middle of the mountains. This was the last thing he'd ever expected to find, and in different circumstances, he'd have loved to stop and spend some time exploring in daylight.

He had no idea why such majestic ruins were hidden so deep in the forest, but he couldn't help himself. He had to stop, if only for a few minutes, and stand in awe before them.

The incessant barking had been getting closer, and Michael knew his pursuers were closing in on him, but he was beyond caring. The fatigue and the cold had made him almost delusional, and as dawn approached, he was at the end of his tether.

He couldn't take much more, so he decided that, however unwise, he would take a thirty-minute break in these transcendent surroundings and deal with the consequences later, even if those consequences meant dying in a hail of bullets.

He shone the red light up towards the heavens at the stone entrance, and although the roof was long gone, he imagined what it would have looked like in its heyday, which was somewhere in the twelfth century, at a guess.

He could make out two distinct layers over the arched doorway, with each one having an open window to the world. The top layer had a more pronounced archway than the lower one, and Michael wondered if they had built it like that on purpose, or were they added at different times in the monastery's life.

Four more archways sat at a ninety-degree angle to the entryway, standing proudly side by side as they had done for hundreds of years.

It was still too dark to see properly, and Michael knew he didn't have the time to wait around, so he sat in a corner of the ruins beneath the first arch and ate more of the food Mina had provided.

Mina. I wish she was here to see this magnificent ruin. Does she know they are here? Has she seen them?

His mind drifted to an alternate reality where Mina gave him a tour of the ruins and explained in intricate detail the history and why they were located in such an unexpected place.

He snorted and laughed out loud. *She works on a farm all day and probably doesn't even know it's here, much less know its history.*

Still, it was a nice thought while it lasted.

He pulled off his boots so he could massage some life back into his feet, and when he shone the light at them, he wished he hadn't.

His feet and socks were soaked from wading through

streams, and his skin was red raw from chafing and blisters. They looked more like chunks of raw meat than feet with skin, and the pain intensified tenfold now he'd seen them.

He wrung out his socks and put them back over his damaged feet. He laced his boots and stood up, the pain making him yell out loud.

I'm done for. I can't carry on like this. The Nazis have won.

He looked around at the ruins towering over his head in the pre-dawn gloom and realised that they were as good a place as any to die.

He lowered his head to pray for forgiveness, and halfway through his silent prayer, he heard a sound that sent tremors through his heart. He was used to hearing dogs barking, but now he heard men shouting at each other just to the north, and he knew they were close.

Dogs barked incessantly, and at least three different voices shouted to each other. Then a fourth and a fifth joined in.

Michael's heart raced as he grabbed his backpack and ran. He knew he couldn't outrun them in his physical condition, but all the courageous notions of making a last stand in the ruins were gone, replaced by a fierce desire to survive and tell the story of what he'd seen and heard.

He owed it to David to fight, and not die with a whimper in the Black Forest just because he was cold and tired, and his feet hurt. No, he was better than that, and David, Gerda, Father Eise, Mina, and all the others who had either died for him or protected him deserved so much more.

He, Michael Fernsby, was made of sterner stuff than he'd ever thought possible, and he would give his all to escape and get back home to England.

He ran down the hill towards what he assumed and hoped was Oppenau below. He stumbled and fell, clattering to the ground and making way too much noise.

The dogs sounded even more excited, and Michael knew they must have picked up his scent. As he caught his breath, he heard running water, and realising it was his only chance against the dogs, he jumped to his feet and ran through the trees to his right.

A river wound its way down the steep hills, and the ice-covered rocks cast their white light to illuminate the imposing spectacle facing him.

The water was flowing too quickly, and the rocks made it impossible for Michael to jump into the water and head downstream. He wouldn't make it more than a few feet before he either slipped on the icy rocks and froze to death, was injured in the water, or the chasing pack caught up to him.

By the sounds of their voices and the excited barking, Michael knew they were close, so he made a snap decision, and with a silent prayer, jumped into the frigid river.

The water was freezing, and it took his breath away when he jumped off the riverbank. He immediately regretted his actions, but he knew it was his only chance of at least temporarily putting them off his scent.

He took a deep breath and grabbed onto the rocks as he forged his way across the ten-foot-wide river. It was waist-deep in parts, and the current was strong. Ice-cold rocks burned his hands when he grabbed hold of them for stability.

He reached the other side and dragged himself out of the freezing water. He jumped up and down to get some circulation going and then followed the river down a narrow path as fast as he could.

His body was numb with the cold, and his chest burned from his recent injuries. But Michael ignored the pain and instead concentrated on the danger closing in on him.

The chasing pack was about five or ten minutes behind, so he had no time to spare. Ignoring the biting cold that paralysed his frozen limbs, Michael moved as fast as his body allowed towards whatever waited for him at the bottom.

Probably a squad of armed and pissed-off Wehrmacht soldiers.

He could hear the confusion up the hill where he'd crossed the river. His scent had gone cold, and the soldiers shouted at each other over the sound of the running water.

Ten minutes later, Michael looked up beyond the trees and saw that dawn was slowly breaking above his head. Shadows were already forming in his peripheral vision, and it wouldn't be long before he was in full view of anyone close enough to see him.

Another fifteen minutes, and it was light enough for him to see what lay ahead. He heard it before he saw it, so it came as no surprise when the path he'd been following ended at the top of a large waterfall that dropped into a pool below.

He considered jumping and hoping that the pool was deep enough, but he'd heard horror stories of people doing that and dying on the rocks that lay unseen below the surface.

Movement on the opposite side of the river caught his eye, and he crouched down to see what it was. Two soldiers carrying rifles appeared out of the trees at the head of the waterfall and peered into the pool below. Michael couldn't make out what they were saying, but he didn't need to.

Another soldier appeared with a German Shepherd

that was barking loudly at the end of a tight chain. They stood at the top of the waterfall contemplating their next move, and as they did, Michael heard barking from his side of the river just above his position.

Another minute, and they would find him.

Michael looked around, wondering what to do. He held his weapon tightly just in case he had to use it, but just as he was readying himself for a fight, he noticed something.

Without hesitating, he jumped once again into the freezing river and took a deep breath as the shock of the cold water forced all the air out of his lungs.

He waded as close to the edge of the waterfall as he could, keeping himself out of sight of the soldiers on the opposite side by staying under the overhanging limbs of trees that drooped down with the weight of the ice that had formed on them.

He wedged himself between two rocks so the current wouldn't drag him over the edge, and pulled himself as deep as he could underneath the largest overhanging branch he could find. Then he clung on for dear life.

He couldn't hear the men's voices above the raging water, but he could hear the dogs barking like crazy as they picked up and then lost his scent at the river's edge.

Michael's entire body went numb. He couldn't feel anything, and the force of the water entered his mouth and nose, choking him, and forcing him to hold his head at an unnatural angle so he wouldn't drown.

At first, it hurt, but after a while, even the pain stopped. He felt nothing, not even cold, and he knew his body was shutting down. If he didn't get out of the water soon, he'd die of hypothermia, which was a better option than being tortured by the Nazis.

Michael drifted in and out of consciousness, but he

fought the burning desire to sleep, knowing he'd never wake up. Each time he closed his eyes, he risked death, and he fought the hardest battle he'd ever fought in his life.

After what seemed like a lifetime, the barking moved farther and farther away until he could no longer hear it. He forced himself to wait until he was sure he couldn't hear the dogs anymore, and then, second by agonising second, he dragged his ravaged body out of the frigid, raging water.

Chapter Fifty-Seven

The morning clouds brought fresh snow, and as Michael clambered out of the river, he was met with a blanket of wet powder that did little to alleviate his chilled and disoriented state.

The first thing he did was jump up and down on the spot and wave his arms around, but his limbs refused to respond. He wasn't even shivering, which alarmed his barely functioning mind.

He needed fire, but everything he had was soaked. His money and ID papers should be safe inside a rubber packet, but everything else would be useless.

He didn't have the means to start a fire, and even if he did, the smoke would give his position away in a heartbeat. He struggled with even the simplest of thoughts, and he shook himself violently in an attempt to get the blood flowing.

Oppenau was at least a two-hour hike, and he knew he'd never make it. He'd be dead long before he reached civilisation, and even if by some miracle he made it, he knew the reception waiting for him wouldn't involve rolling out the red carpet.

His only hope was that he'd find a farm on the outskirts of the forest where he could hide long enough to dry out and warm up, but that was wishful thinking. He was in serious trouble, and he knew it.

He looked up at the snow that was now easing off. The clouds were lifting, and it was going to be another cold winter's day. The wind whipped the fallen snow into Michael's face, but he barely even noticed. Normally, it would sting and hurt, but not now. He felt nothing, and even in his reduced mental state, he knew he couldn't just stand there waiting to die.

Happy New Year to me.

He found a steep path that followed the waterfall to the pool at the bottom, and he slipped and skidded his way down. At the bottom, he followed the path towards Oppenau.

He forced his mind to concentrate on the image of Mina's beautiful face smiling at him, and he could hear her encouraging him to put one foot in front of the other and to keep going.

Mina's face fizzled away, to be replaced by David's. He looked angry, and he shouted at Michael to man up and stop feeling sorry for himself.

"You think you've got it bad?" David yelled. "Try being where I am right now. You have a life, and I'm not letting you throw it away just because you're cold and wet."

David's voice echoed around in Michael's head, and he answered out loud as he shuffled down the slippery mountain path.

"I'm trying, so stop shouting at me. I can't feel anything,

David, and I'm frightened. This is all my fault, and I don't want to let you down. I'm sorry."

Michael stopped and fell to his knees. Looking up to the heavens, tears fell onto his frozen cheeks, and he sobbed loudly. "I've failed you. I've failed everybody, and I'm so sorry. I can't go any farther, David, and I'm going to die here. Which means our mother and father will never know what happened to you."

David's image flew from his mind as cold steel pressed into the side of his neck. Michael held his breath, not sure if what he felt was real or imagined.

"Hands in the air, Englander. Try anything and I'll shoot."

Is this real? Or am I still hallucinating?

Michael tried raising his arms, but they refused to move.

"I said, hands in the air." The rough voice spoke in broken English through the mists in Michael's mind. "I won't tell you again."

"I can't," Michael said hoarsely. "I'm frozen, and my arms won't work."

Whoever it was must have been real, because Michael felt a sharp pain in the side of his head from the rifle butt that struck him. His already dulled senses fell dark for a moment, and when he came to, he was sprawled out on the ground, staring at a pair of boots.

A single pair of boots.

His captor had taken his backpack and was opening it up to see what was inside. Michael saw he was a young man, not much older than himself.

The boy wore a long greenish-grey coat that almost reached the ground. He had a similar coloured hat that covered most of his head. Abreo had shown them pictures of coats like this while they waited for their German IDs in

Strasbourg, and Michael reached beyond the clouds in his brain to remember what he'd said they were.

That's it. I remember. It's a German army coat, and it looks warm.

With the fog in his brain lifting, Michael took stock of his situation. It was real, alright, and he was now a prisoner of a lone German soldier.

What now?

"We knew you were here somewhere, so I stayed behind to see if you came out." The soldier must have been reading Michael's mind. "Now you're my prisoner, and I will be famous throughout the Fatherland."

Michael watched the soldier pocket the small rubber bag containing his money and put everything else back into the backpack.

"On your feet, spy. If you try anything, I'll kill you."

Michael's limbs felt heavy and unresponsive as he tried to stand, his legs trembling beneath him. He willed his arms to move, but they hung limply at his sides, refusing to obey his commands. He gritted his teeth in frustration, clenching his fists and straining against his own body in a desperate attempt to regain control.

Warm blood dripped down his face, which in a sadistic way he enjoyed because it meant that he could feel something.

I can feel it!

Content that he wasn't about to die from hypothermia, Michael struggled to his feet. The soldier shoved him roughly, showing that he wanted him to get a move on, so he walked as fast as his frozen limbs would allow.

Whatever pace he was moving at, it wasn't fast enough for the soldier. "Get a move on. It's cold up here and I'm ready to be in front of a warm fire."

The barrel of the rifle poked into Michael's back, and he knew there was nothing he could do to save himself. He was now a prisoner, but the soldier had made the mistake of not searching his soaked clothes carefully for concealed weapons.

Although the soldier had taken the guns from his back-pack, Michael still had the one he'd taken from Gerda hidden under his trousers where he'd stored it before jumping into the river. Now all he needed was a chance to reach for it without the soldier noticing.

And hope it still worked after sitting in freezing water.

They walked for forty-five minutes in silence. Each step was slow and difficult, and the soldier showed his frustrations by constantly jabbing him in the back with the barrel of his rifle.

Pain shot through Michael's legs and arms as feeling slowly returned. His soaked clothing was useless, and he shook and shivered in his attempt to fight off the hypothermic cold that threatened to take his life.

The path was slippery from the snow and ice, and Michael grabbed onto the vegetation to keep from sliding down the path. A yelp from behind, followed by a thud, told him that the soldier had slipped, and moments later, Michael's legs spun in the air as the soldier crashed into him.

They slid side by side for a few seconds before coming to a stop at a tree. This was Michael's chance, and he reacted as fast as his mind and body allowed.

The soldier had bashed his head on a rock as he fell, and Michael saw fresh blood spill from the wound. Seizing the moment, and knowing he wouldn't stand much of a chance if they were to get into a physical fight, Michael grabbed a loose rock and smashed it as hard as he could on the soldier's nose.

A sickening, crunching sound made Michael shudder, and the soldier made a strange gurgling noise before falling still.

Michael moved quickly before he came around and removed the rifle from his hands. He grabbed his backpack and stood up to get away from the soldier. Then a thought hit him.

He unbuttoned the soldier's heavy winter jacket and rolled him over to remove it. Then he went about removing his grey uniform from underneath the jacket; it was dry, and a lot warmer than his clothes ever were.

The soldier moaned and opened his eyes, so Michael did the only thing he could think of and struck him on his temple with the butt of the rifle. More blood flowed down the soldier's face, this time from the opposite side, and he fell silent once again.

Michael removed his clothes, but he didn't touch his boots, which were the wrong size. The soldier opened his eyes again and shivered in the freezing air.

"You can't leave me like this," he said, his eyes wide with fear. "I'll die out here with no clothes."

"I didn't notice the compassion you had for me earlier."

The soldier spat blood from his mouth. "I saved your life, spy. I was taking you to the town where my superiors would take care of you."

"Take care of me?" Michael laughed as he tore off his wet clothes and replaced them with the soldier's uniform. The fit wasn't perfect, but at least they were dry and warm. "You were taking me to be tortured and executed."

"That's not my decision." The soldier shrugged. "I was

carrying out my orders, that's all. You can't leave me like this. I'll freeze to death."

Michael checked to make sure his money was still in the coat pocket, and it was. He wrapped his wet clothes and placed them at the top of his backpack for later.

As he was about to leave, he stopped and opened the backpack again. He reached down and pulled out the tarpaulin Mina's father had given him.

"Here, that will keep you alive until you reach the town." Michael tossed the wet tarp at the soldier.

"That won't keep me alive," the soldier complained.

"It's more than you would have given me, but if you don't want it, I'll take it back." Michael reached for the tarp, but the soldier stopped him.

"No, no. It'll do. I'll take it."

Michael looked around one more time and then headed down the path and away from the soldier.

"I'll find you, Englander, and when I do, I *will* kill you."

Michael ignored the soldier's threat and moved away. The coat warmed his body quickly, and sharp pins and needles attacked his arms and legs as the feeling returned. Although it hurt, Michael welcomed the pain because it meant he was alive and recovering. Now he was warmer, he could make better time.

Now I've got to get out of here before his mates come to his rescue.

Chapter Fifty-Eight

Rather than follow the path to Oppenau and certain capture, Michael headed west and back into the forest. He didn't know what lay ahead, but what he did know was that the River Rhine was in that direction, and that was the way he was going.

The path was slippery, and he fell several times. Fearing further injury and lacking a shoulder strap for the rifle he'd taken from the soldier, he tossed it into the trees, freeing both his hands to steady himself on the rough trail.

At lunchtime, a small town appeared seemingly out of nowhere. Michael stopped in the safety of the trees and ate while he checked the soaked map to see where he was.

According to his best judgement, he was on the outskirts of a small town called Lautenbach, which was a lot closer to the Rhine than he thought he'd be, but by his reckonings, he was still around twenty-five miles from the river, which filled him with both delight and dread.

Twenty-five miles! My feet can't make it twenty-five more yards, never mind twenty-five miles.

He scolded himself for being a wimp and skirted south

around the edge of the forest to avoid the town. A lone house caught his attention because it had a vehicle parked outside.

Another Volkswagen! At least I know how to drive them now.

Michael crept up to the car out of view of the house and crawled on his knees for the final hundred yards so he wouldn't be seen. He tried the driver's door, which he still had to remind himself was on the opposite side from what he was used to.

It opened! He slipped inside and pulled the door to without fully closing it so the noise wouldn't alert anyone that was in the house. He felt for the keys, but they weren't in the ignition, so he checked the dashboard and the glove compartment, but they weren't there.

He was about to give up and get out when he checked underneath the seat. His hand closed around cold steel, and he knew he'd found them.

Thanking his lucky stars, Michael gave a silent prayer of thanks for his good fortune and held his breath while he turned the keys in the ignition. It made way too much noise, and he expected a squad of soldiers to leap out of the house with their guns blazing at any moment.

Instead, it remained quiet, as if nobody was home. The car started, and Michael wasted no time in putting it into gear and moving. He spread the map on the passenger seat and checked where he was going. Ottenheim was southwest of his location, so he headed out in a westerly direction and hoped to pick up some road signs that would take him towards freedom.

A half-mile later, he pulled over and scraped the ice off the windshield with his sleeve. It wasn't great, but at least he could see what was in front of him.

His heart was in his mouth as he drove through the town of Lautenbach. While the military uniform afforded him some protection, he was worried that someone would recognise the stolen car, or even worse, that he would run into a roadblock. When neither happened, he allowed himself to breathe again, and he took a closer look at his surroundings.

As he drove, he couldn't help but notice the strange mix of familiarity and foreignness. The streets were narrow, and the buildings were old and picturesque, with timbered facades and colourful shutters. But there was something off about the place, something that made him feel like he was in a dream.

Something too normal.

He caught glimpses of people going about their everyday business as though nothing was wrong, and that it was just another ordinary day.

Even though it's New Year's Day.

A woman carrying a basket of laundry, a man pushing a wheelbarrow full of vegetables; they seemed so normal and out of place, as if time was passing differently here. The air was thick with the smell of wood smoke and cooking, and he could hear the distant sound of church bells ringing.

As he passed through the town square, he saw a group of soldiers gathered around a bonfire, their faces illuminated by the flickering flames. They were laughing and joking, but there was an edge to their merriment that made Michael uneasy. He wondered if they knew he was in the stolen car, if they were watching him even now.

He shook his head and tried to focus on the road ahead. He couldn't be distracted, not now. The Rhine was close, and he had to get there.

Remembering what had happened the last time he'd

driven a vehicle, Michael paid attention to what was ahead, and he kept his eyes on the road. He reckoned he'd be at the Rhine within an hour at the rate he was going.

I'll be across the river and in France by nightfall.

The sound of the engine and the gentle bouncing up and down on the roads made his eyes feel heavy and drowsy. He hadn't slept for two days, and he was exhausted. He fought off the desire to pull over, telling himself that there would be plenty of time to rest once he reached the safety of France.

He wound down the window, allowing the cold air to rush into the vehicle. Hoping it would refresh him, he leant to his side and hung his head out the window. It worked, because all the fatigue and thoughts of sleep fell away, leaving his face once again numb from the cold.

But at least he was awake.

He hadn't driven more than twenty minutes when he approached Offenburg. *Not long now and I'll be there.*

The cars in front of him slowed down and joined the rear of a queue up ahead. Sensing immediately what it was, Michael once again hyperventilated. He threw the car into a late right turn, angering the driver behind, who shook his fist at him through his open window.

The road wound through a section of dense trees that reminded him of the forest he'd just traversed. Suspecting the angry driver would tell whoever was manning the road-block what he'd done, he knew he had to abandon the vehicle and go the rest of the way on foot.

He turned onto a narrow side road, and then another and another. Each one was narrower than the last, and finally, he drove the Volkswagen into a gap between the trees.

He drove it as far as he could before the wheels got

stuck in the snow on the forest floor, and when he got out, he was happy that nobody would be finding his getaway vehicle anytime soon. By the time they did, he'd be long gone.

He kept to the trees for as long as he could, but eventually, they thinned out, leaving him exposed in the open fields that stretched out before him.

Two hours later, he checked the map as he approached the outskirts of yet another town. Dusk was not far away, and shadows were already forming. The temperatures were dropping sharply, but the German greatcoat was keeping him warm and cosy.

The town was the last one he'd encounter before reaching the Rhine, which was only a few more miles to the west.

I'm almost there!

Relief coursed through his veins, but Michael stopped himself from getting excited. He hadn't made it yet, and anything could happen before he reached freedom.

He found a row of hedges outside the town that followed a narrow road running north to south. One particular part of the hedge was thick enough for him to squeeze into and remain hidden until darkness fell.

The area was too exposed to travel during daylight as the fields were open and a man could be seen for miles if he tried crossing them. Michael wasn't going to allow impatience and carelessness to stop him now he'd got this far.

He ate, and then settled down to rest for a few hours before making his final push for freedom. With the German greatcoat wrapped around him, Michael drifted off into a fitful, much-needed sleep, and soon he was dreaming of Mina and the short time they'd had together.

His dreams turned to David, as they inevitably did

every time he fell asleep. He found himself once again throwing wet dirt over his brother's body, but this time David was struggling and fighting, yelling at Michael to stop, and that he was only sleeping.

He awoke with a start. It was dark, and when he checked his watch, he was stunned to find out he'd been asleep for hours. It was past eight o'clock, and it was dark enough for him to leave.

After making sure the coast was clear, Michael took his compass and made sure he was heading west. He followed lanes and fields for another hour and a half and knew he was close when he reached another area of dense woodland. The river couldn't be that far now.

Ottenheim was farther south than his current position, and he didn't want to risk staying in Germany for a moment longer than he had to. The contact Father Eise had given him might end up being his only option to get across, but after all he'd been through, he'd take anything he could.

He crossed another lane that ran from north to south, and as he reached the other side, he heard vehicles approaching from the south.

Searchlights pierced the forest, and he knew immediately what it was.

Shit. Why now, when I'm so close?

Chapter Fifty-Nine

Michael ran across the lane and into the forest as fast as he could. His boots pounded through the snow as he fled, his heart racing with fear. The icy air bit at his lungs and he gasped for breath, his chest searing with pain from his injured ribs.

He gritted his teeth against the agony and forced his way deeper into the woods, seeking cover. For a moment, his vision swam, making it hard to focus on his surroundings. Trees loomed up around him, the snow-laden branches reaching out like gnarly fingers.

He stumbled over a fallen log, his legs refusing to obey him, and he fell to the ground with a jolt. Sharp pain lanced through his chest, stealing his breath. He gasped for air, the cold snow seeping through his jacket and biting at his skin.

He scrambled underneath a nearby branch that was weighted down by snow and ice, and it fell over his head and down his neck, chilling him to the bone once again, but he didn't have time to worry about it.

No sooner had he gone to ground than the searchlights lit up the trees around him. Michael hoped he hadn't left tell-tale footprints behind, but when he looked at the ground outside his hiding place, he recoiled in horror when he saw what he'd done.

Footprints were clear in the snow, and they all led to his hiding place. An intense urge to flee washed over him, and he knew he had mere moments before they found him.

As he dragged himself to his feet, he heard voices shouting and vehicle doors slamming. Searchlights from at least three vehicles focused on the spot where he'd entered the trees.

The cruel irony of being so close and yet so far wasn't lost on Michael as he ran for the river. He knew he wouldn't make it, and he waited with bated breath for the sound of the gunshot that would end his life just a few yards from the French border.

He found a lane running through the trees, and he ran down it as fast as he could. He could hear the bathtubs driving off, and for a moment, he wondered if he was panicking for nothing.

Until the German soldiers shouted at each other in the trees close by. He didn't know where the vehicles had gone, but the soldiers were still there, and they were closing in.

The snow had turned to ice on the lane, so although the footing was treacherous, at least he wasn't leaving footprints behind that gave his pursuers an easy way to follow and find him.

The loud engine of a bathtub got closer, and Michael's stomach heaved when he realised what was happening. The driver had found a road that dissected the lane he was running down, and it would reach the junction before he did.

He hurried back into the forest and ran for his life. A shout behind him, followed by a gunshot, forced him to the ground, which once again sent his body into involuntary spasms of agony.

Mouthfuls of snow entered his mouth, which was probably a good thing because it prevented him from crying out in pain and fear.

The bullet missed, but he heard it thud into a tree to his left. He scurried to his right and stopped when he came across another road going north to south.

The bathtub's searchlights were close. He could see them less than a hundred yards away, and he could hear the soldiers closing from behind.

This is it. This is my last stand. Either I live or I die, but this is it.

Michael took a gulp of air and held his finger on the trigger of the Walther PPK in his hand. Even with his limited knowledge of firearms, he knew the pistol didn't have a great range, and that the soldiers held all the advantages with their rifles.

Why did I throw away that rifle? He kicked himself, but there was nothing he could do about it now.

He ran, but then stopped and fell to his knees to make a smaller target. Up to now, all he'd done was react like a deer in a set of headlights, and he would die if he didn't stop. He hadn't considered the cloud cover that made visibility more difficult, or the trees that provided even more protection.

All the soldiers had to go on were his footprints, and while they had all the advantages, he wasn't done for yet. He took a deep breath and stopped acting like a frightened schoolboy, which was a lot harder than it sounded when he told himself those very words.

The soldiers were close, and he could make out three people whispering to each other. Their voices echoed in the darkness, and he could hear them tramping through the snow. He knelt behind the biggest tree he could find and waited.

The sound of his heartbeat more than matched the volume of the pursuers' feet in the snow, but he swallowed hard and concentrated on the sounds of their movements.

The bathtub's lights swept the trees close to the road, and it drove up and down the lanes in and around the forest. He could hear the other vehicles farther away doing the same thing.

A soldier came into view a mere ten feet from his position behind the tree. The other two were close, but he couldn't see them.

He fired.

The noise filled his ears, drowning out everything else for a few seconds. By the time his ears had stopped ringing, the soldier had fallen, and he lay moaning on the forest floor.

Shouts and hurried footsteps ran from two different directions towards him. Michael moved to a different tree and waited. Now he had the advantage, and he wasn't losing it.

He held his breath and waited. He pushed all thoughts of his injured chest to the back of his mind and concentrated as if his life depended on it.

It did.

A second soldier crashed through the forest and knelt at his fallen comrade's side. Michael was off to his left, and he fired two more times, hitting the soldier in the head and chest.

He fell silent on top of his wounded friend.

There was at least one more, and the bathtubs were closing in as well. They must have heard the gunfire and were coming to help.

Silence. Whoever was left wasn't taking any chances and was waiting for Michael to make the first move. As the vehicles approached, Michael knew he would have to break cover, which could be fatal.

He made a snowball and threw it at a nearby tree, causing a cloud of snow to drop from the leaves. A faint sound close to where the soldier lay hidden caught Michael's eye, and he fired off one more round.

The soldier returned fire, and Michael threw himself to the ground as bullets smashed into the tree above his head. He rolled deeper into the woods, away from the soldier, and settled behind another tree a few yards to his left.

A foot crashed into his head, sending stars flying in his brain. At least one tooth flew out, and he felt warm blood running down his jaw. As he tried gathering his senses, a rain of blows flew down on him with a rage he'd never sensed before.

The soldier must have run at him as he moved, but the sound must have been masked by the other noises in the forest because he hadn't heard or seen a thing.

Michael curled into a ball to protect his chest while the soldier punched himself out. He felt the soldier rise to his knees, obviously reaching for either a pistol or a knife, and Michael took the opportunity while he could.

He lashed out with his fingers pointed straight out and caught the Nazi in both of his eyes. Michael hit him hard and fast, and the soldier screamed in agony. He dropped the knife he was holding and threw his hands to his face.

Michael didn't hesitate. He grabbed the knife and plunged it into the soldier's neck. The soldier hissed, and warm blood spattered over Michael before he pushed the limp body aside.

He rose to his knees and vomited over the forest floor.

What the hell am I?

He didn't have time to find out, because the bathtubs were close, and he heard more voices shouting nearby. He stood up and ran for the river.

Less than five minutes later, he reached the edge of the tree line and stretched out before him in all its glory was the mighty River Rhine.

I've made it. I've finally made it.

He didn't have time to dwell, so he chose a direction – south – and ran.

Chapter Sixty

The lights and sounds of the bathtubs faded into the distance as the Germans focused their search on the area where the fight had taken place.

Michael ran towards Ottenheim, not knowing how far it was to the south. All he wanted to do was get away from the soldiers and cross the river. Nothing more, nothing less.

He ran for nearly two hours, only stopping to catch his breath for a moment before going again. He didn't allow himself to think about what he'd done, or he would have lost his mind.

There'd be plenty of time for that later.

If I make it.

He was sure that by now more soldiers were joining the chase, and he knew he was living on borrowed time. He checked his watch, and it was almost 3 am, so he'd been running for a long time.

Adrenaline had carried him this far, but now he was shutting down. He couldn't remember the last time he'd had a proper night's sleep, and his emotional state wasn't even worth thinking about. Mina was a distant memory, and all he could focus on were dead bodies and blood.

And David.

Without realising it, he had reached Ottenheim. He briefly considered finding the man Father Eise had told him about, but with German soldiers swarming all over the town, he doubted he would want anything to do with the British spy.

Vehicles and lights were everywhere, and it wasn't safe to try crossing here, so he carried on running south.

Woodland grew thick by the river, and he found himself in a narrow lane between the river and the town. He ran for another thirty minutes until the sounds of the vehicles disappeared.

Several boats were docked along the riverbank, and he knew this was the best chance he'd get. He ran to the edge of the water and looked for a suitable vessel.

He didn't dare risk a motorised boat because the Germans would be all over it, so he searched for a humble rowing boat.

Sitting right in the middle of a row of motorboats, he found what he was looking for. A small rowboat big enough for only two people. The oars were inside, so Michael untied the boat from its moorings and began pushing it away from the bank.

He was about to jump in when a bathtub approached. Its searchlights pierced the darkness around the tiny harbour, and it would be a matter of moments before they saw him pushing the boat into the river.

Michael pulled on the rope to stop the boat from going out any farther and jumped into the river beside it. Like the one before, the river was freezing, and as soon as he hit the water, he felt a shock of cold that ran through his entire body. His skin prickled with goosebumps, and he gasped for breath as the icy water surrounded him. His muscles tightened involuntarily, making it hard to move, and he felt as though his limbs were encased in concrete. He fought against the urge to panic and forced himself to focus on the task at hand.

He swam to the front of the boat and pushed against it, so it wouldn't drift out into the stronger currents farther out in the massive river.

The vehicle slowed as it reached the boats, and the searchlight shone on the water at the edge. Michael ducked his head under the water as it passed over his position, and he held his breath for as long as he could.

The searchlight passed over him and continued down the road at a slow pace. Michael swam back to the rear of the boat and pushed it out towards the deeper water. He jumped in and lay there, freezing and shivering in the bottom of the boat.

When he was happy the soldiers hadn't seen him, he sat up and grabbed the oars. Although the current took him back the way he'd come, towards Holland to the north, Michael paddled for all he was worth to get out of range before the Nazis noticed him.

The current was strong, and he had to fight it all the way to get across and not be swept to where he didn't want to be. The effort soon warmed him up, and even though he was soaked to the skin, sweat poured off his brow as he put everything he had left into getting across the river.

Each time he rowed, sharp pain ripped through his body. He didn't know how much more he could take without passing out, but the thought of what waited for him on the German side of the river drove him through the pain barrier.

Finally, he broke free of the current, and from that point, it was a relatively straightforward task to reach the riverbank on the other side.

Eventually, with dawn not too far away, Michael stood on the bank of the River Rhine in France.

He had made it.

He raised his hands in victory and threw the oars back into the boat. He pushed it out into the river so it wouldn't give away his landing spot.

Although he was on the French side of the border, he knew he wasn't safe. The Nazis had spies all over Europe, and it would be easy for them to kill him before he got away.

He left the river and walked in the darkness towards the town of Plobsheim in France.

Chapter Sixty-One

Three days later, Michael limped up to the door of the impressive stone house on New Street in Sandwich, Kent. To any passer-by, he would have looked like a homeless vagabond begging for money, and that was the first reaction Michael saw from Warhurst when he opened the door and saw the bruised and battered young man stood before him, carrying nothing but a weather-beaten backpack that was falling apart.

"Master Michael!" the trusty butler shouted with a guttural, almost primaeval yell when he finally recognised him. "Is it really you?" He looked over Michael's shoulder and scanned the manicured lawn for signs of David, but there were none.

"Are you going to let me in?" Michael pushed past the stunned butler.

"Of course, please forgive me, Master Michael. Are you hurt? Do you need a doctor? Where is your brother?"

"I need a cup of tea in the sitting room, and please inform my mother and father that I'm home."

"Of course." Warhurst scurried off, leaving Michael to

his thoughts in the living room. He picked up a black-and-white photograph of the Fernsby family that had been taken the previous summer, and his eyes filled when he saw how happy they looked. How happy *he* looked standing next to David.

He'd rehearsed what he was going to say to his parents a thousand times on the Night Train from Paris to London, but now he was home, he felt a large lump in his throat as signs of David's presence were everywhere. This was the moment he'd been dreading ever since that fateful day in Munich, and as glad as he was to be home, right now he wished he was anywhere else.

Gerald and Dorothy Fernsby rushed into the sitting room, followed closely by Judith. They ran to Michael and grabbed him, all speaking and crying together at the same time.

Dorothy's eyes were bright red, and as soon as he saw her, Michael buried his head in her shoulders and sobbed. Tears streamed down his face, leaving damp patches on her blouse. His breath stuck in his chest, and he gasped for air between sobs. His body shook with the force of his grief, and he clung to his mother as if she were his only anchor in a sea of pain. Everything he'd been through, every loss, every painful moment, came flooding out in an explosion of grief.

Michael and his mother held each other for a long moment, and when they broke apart, Gerald helped his son to a chair, and they all sat together in silence, waiting for Michael to explain what had happened.

"Where's David?" Dorothy asked for the umpteenth time. "Where is he? Is he alright?"

"What happened, Michael?" Gerald shouted over his

wife. "Where's David? Did you find Frank and Herbert? Where are they?"

Michael breathed deeply as his composure slowly returned. He looked at Judith, who squeezed his hand and smiled weakly at him.

"I'll tell you everything, but where is Gigi? She needs to hear this, too."

"What happened, Michael?" his father pressed. "Where is David? Where is he?"

Michael's eyes filled up again, and his voice cracked when he spoke. He looked at each one of his family members in turn. "He's dead. David's dead. They killed him." He grabbed hold of his mother and broke down yet again.

Stunned silence.

"David's dead?" a female voice with a heavy German accent spoke from the doorway. Michael looked up and saw a gaunt, pale Gigi enter the room.

Dorothy scowled at her presence, and even Gerald cast her a hateful look, but Michael ignored them and held out his arms towards her.

"Gigi," was all he could say before emotion overcame him once again.

"What happened?" Gerald demanded, his face pallid and etched with anguish. "What happened to David?"

"The Gestapo killed him in Munich. They killed Gerda and her friends and shot David. We escaped and got out of Munich, but he didn't make it very far. I'm sorry. I failed him."

More tears fell. Gigi sat with Michael, tears flowing freely down her face, staring into emptiness as if her soul had left her body.

"What happened to him?" Gerald asked. "What did you do with him?"

Michael tapped his temple. "I buried him in a temporary grave, and I memorised where it was. I swear, as soon as I can, I'm going back to bring him home."

Silence. The family sat, each lost in their own thoughts and emotions.

"It's all your fault," Dorothy suddenly screamed and launched herself at Gigi. "You did this. You killed my son."

Gerald pulled Dorothy away and stood in front of her so she couldn't get near a visibly shaken Gigi. "It's her fault," Dorothy screamed. "She shouldn't even be here."

"She was here to see Doctor Newsome," Gerald said. "You know that Dorothy. She'll be gone by the morning."

"Gone where?" Michael asked. "This isn't her fault. David and I volunteered to go. She didn't make us. It's my fault because I didn't listen to David in Munich. If I had, he'd still be alive now, so blame me if you want to blame anybody."

"Please, tell us everything that happened." Gerald sat next to his grieving wife and stroked her hand. "And leave nothing out. We, I, have to know."

Michael nodded his head slowly and began telling them everything that had happened from the moment they arrived in Strasbourg. He left nothing out, and the only time he felt anything other than despair was when he talked about Mina, and even that fell away when he explained how he left her to face the consequences of Alwin Lutz's death.

"There are good people over there who are resisting the Nazis," he said after he'd told them everything up to the point of reaching the banks of the Rhine just a few short days ago.

"Father Eise, Mina and her family, Gerda, Stefan, and Sophie, and so many more brave men and women who will die if we do nothing. War is coming, and there is nothing we can do about it. We have to stop the Nazis, or they will spread their hate all over Europe."

"So, you never found Frank or my father?" Gigi's voice sounded strained.

"No, I said I didn't. They were taken to a camp in a town called Dachau, and that's all I ever knew."

"How did you get home from France?" Judith asked. "What happened after you crossed the Rhine?"

"I slept in a shed for a few hours and discarded the German uniform I'd been wearing. I put on the wet clothes I'd worn in the Black Forest and took a bus to Strasbourg, where I stayed with Abreo for the night. He supplied me with the clothes I'm wearing today. Then I took a train to Paris, and from there I caught the Night Ferry to London."

"What do we do now?" Dorothy asked, her face pale and blotchy. "We can't leave David over there all alone. We've got to get him back."

"I buried him in a place where he'll lie safe until we can get back there and bring him home," Michael said. "I drew a detailed map on the train to London, and I'll get copies made so we all have one. Until then, there's nothing we can do. I'm sorry, Mother. I'm so sorry I couldn't protect him."

"This changes nothing." Dorothy stared at Gigi. "I want you gone, and I never want to see you again."

"Why did you send them over there?" Judith suddenly asked her grandmother. "You must have known they had no chance of rescuing Uncle Frank and Papa Herbert?"

Gigi sat still, her face as pale as Dorothy's. "I will never forgive myself for what I did. All they were supposed to do was find them and lead them to safety, but I never meant for them to get hurt. I underestimated the hatred the Nazis have for my kind."

"Underestimated?" Dorothy raised her voice. "You sent them to their deaths. You ought to be ashamed of yourself."

Gigi bowed her head. "I am."

"Playing the blame game isn't going to help," Michael said, rising to his feet. "I have grown up a lot over the last few weeks, and I can tell you that family is everything. We are going to need each other in the coming conflict, and we need to find a way to get past this and heal our differences. It isn't Gigi's fault, and she didn't force us to go. We went of our own accord because if we hadn't, Father would have gone and got himself killed instead."

"Are you blaming me for this?" Gerald asked, his eyes wide.

"No. I'm just pointing out that any of us could be to blame. We're all to blame, at least all of us except Mother and Judith. We all had a hand in the decision one way or another, and we need to accept what we did and move on. David would not want his death to be the cause of our family's break up, and I don't either."

"He has a point," Gerald said.

Dorothy said nothing. "What now?" she finally asked. "What do we do now?"

"I'm calling Doctor Newsome, and that's not negotiable," Gerald said, rising to his feet. "Michael needs rest and medical attention. After that, I've no idea, although I suspect the government will be interested in hearing what happened."

"The type of help I need is beyond the remit of Doctor Newsome," Michael said. "I don't see how I can ever recover from this. I'm responsible for David's death, and probably Mina's as well. Not to mention Father Eise, who risked everything for me, and Gerda too. I killed people with my own bare hands. Don't you see? How do you ever recover from that? Nothing can ever be the same again."

"Oh, Michael," Dorothy cried, smothering him in her arms.

Gigi sat with her head bowed. "I'm so sorry to all of you. My selfishness brought all of this about, and I shouldn't have done it. I hope you can find it in your heart to forgive me."

"No," Dorothy said. "I cannot, not at this moment."

"I understand, and I will be gone tomorrow."

"I'm calling Doctor Newsome." Gerald strode out of the room, effectively ending the sad family gathering.

Michael lay on the bed in his room and stared at the ceiling while he waited for the doctor to arrive. His mind drifted to David and Mina, and he made a silent prayer for both of them.

I will return for you. For both of you. David, I promise I will bring you home where you can rest in peace, and Mina, I vow to return and fall to my knees so I can beg forgiveness for all the trouble I have caused you.

He paused.

Then I'll ask you to marry me.

Warhurst's head appeared around his open doorway. "Doctor Newsome is here, Master Michael."

Michael got to his feet and went down the stairs.

Chapter Sixty-Two

The evening roll call was taking longer than normal. Fresh snow fell on the prisoners, but no one seemed to notice. Frank Fernsby stood in his block's formation, heavy with fatigue and starvation, and waited for the drawn-out procedure to be over so he could return to his bunk and get underneath his blanket for the night.

A new figure emerged in the SS ranks, and Frank's body twitched when he saw his face in the searchlights. It was Sturmbannführer Bachmeier, and the last time he'd seen him was in the bunker.

When was that? He struggled to remember because time seemed to stand still in Dachau. Surely, he wasn't here for him again, was he?

"Prisoner 71257, step forward," an SS guard barked.

Frank did as he was told. His stomach churned, and he wondered what had happened. Had they found David and Michael? Had they been arrested? Surely, they wouldn't have killed them, because it would cause an international incident with Britain. And it might shine the spotlight on what was happening in places like Dachau, which he was sure the Nazis wanted to avoid.

A wooden staff slammed into his stomach, winding him and knocking him to the ground in a heap.

"Get up, Jew," an SS guard screamed.

"Take him to Garrison Detention," Sturmbannführer Bachmeier ordered. He turned on his heels and walked away from the rest of the prisoners.

Once inside the bunker, Frank steeled himself for another round of torture at the cruel hands of the SS guards. He didn't have to wait long as a wooden staff whipped into his midriff, sending him into convulsions on the cold floor.

A figure emerged from the darkness, and Frank instantly recognised the perfect English accent.

"I'm going to ask you one last time," Kriminaldirektor Kreise said. "Where are David and Michael Fernsby? They've killed many good German men, and it is time for them to pay for their crimes. Where are they? Where would they go to hide?"

"I-I-I don't know, sir," Frank stammered. He truly didn't know, but wherever they were, he hoped they were safe from evil men like those standing before him.

"I believe him." Sturmbannführer Bachmeier walked behind Frank, who closed his eyes and bowed his head.

"Your nephew, I believe the one called Michael, killed many good soldiers on his way to the French border." Kreise bent towards Frank's ear. "We know he escaped and is even now sipping tea back home in Kent. We know where he is, Frank, and believe me, he isn't as safe there as he thinks he is."

Frank stared at the floor and said nothing. What could he say?

"Where is David Fernsby, Frank? We know he is still in

Germany, hiding somewhere. And we think you know where he is hiding. We think your deaf girlfriend, Gerda Yung, helped him before she died in Munich. You do believe she is dead, don't you, Frank?"

Frank stared at the floor and remained silent. He said a silent prayer and turned his thoughts to Gerda, and how her warm smile and kind heart had made him so happy throughout the years. If she was dead, then he had nothing else to live for.

"Go to hell, you Nazi bastards. I hope Michael and David kill you all."

Cold steel pressed behind his right ear, and this time he knew Bachmeier meant it. For Frank Fernsby, the nightmare was over. He would suffer at the hands of the SS no more.

The End.

Get a FREE Book!

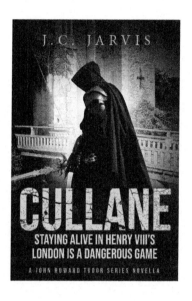

Before John Howard found sanctuary on the streets of London, Andrew Cullane formed a small band of outlawed survivors called the Underlings. Discover their fight for life for free when you join J.C. Jarvis's newsletter at jcjarvis.com/cullane

Please Leave A Review

If you loved the book and have a moment to spare, I would really appreciate a short review.

Your help in spreading the word is gratefully appreciated and reviews make a huge difference to helping new readers find the series.

Thank you!

More Books by JC Jarvis

Fernsby's War Series

Ryskamp

Alderauge

Ludsecke

Rotterdam

Evasion is available for Pre-Order NOW!

The John Howard Tudor Series

John Howard and the Underlings

John Howard and the Tudor Legacy

John Howard and the Tudor Deception

About the Author

J.C. Jarvis is the author of the breakout Fernsby's War series.

He makes his home at www.jcjarvis.com

Email: jc@jcjarvis.com

f

Printed in Great Britain
by Amazon

47190274R00215